On the Way to Pomona

On the way to POMONA

Charles Van Eman

CHARLES VAN EMAN

MUD PUDDLE DANCE

Copyright © 2012 Charles Van Eman
All rights reserved
No part of this publication can be reproduced or transmitted in any form or by any means, electronic or mechanical, without permission in writing from Charles Van Eman
First Edition, Second Printing: March 2013
Book design by Erika Q. Stokes

Cover design and illustration by Sandy Farrier
Cover illustration is, in part, reproduced from the Redlands Foothill Brand produce crate label. Courtesy of the Boston Public Library, Print Collection.

This is a work of fiction. While, as in all fiction, the literary perception and insights are based on experience, all names, characters, places, and incidences are either products of the author's imagination or are used fictitiously. No reference to any real person is intended or should be inferred.

ISBN 978-0-98556458-2-3
ISBN 978-0-9856458-1-6 (ePub)
ISBN 978-0-9856458-3-0 (Kindle)

mudpuddledance@gmail.com

For Sara

When one has weighed the sun in the balance, and measured the steps of the moon, and mapped the seven heavens star by star, there still remains oneself. Who can calculate the orbit of his own soul?

Oscar Wilde

1

BEEF STROGANOFF, THAT'S WHAT I smelled the minute I stepped through the front door. Down the hallway in the den Frank Sinatra was crooning "Strangers in the Night." In the kitchen my father was humming along with the music. From upstairs came my mother's muffled voice. I put my duffel bag down and quietly eased the door shut.

During the drive from New York City, winding my way along the Pennsylvania turnpike, I'd thought of a million different things to distract myself. I'd considered the Pirates' chances of winning their division. I'd calculated my gas mileage. I'd tried to estimate the time it would take to drive from one exit to the next. I'd thought about everything except what I was actually doing. I was like a junkie, but instead of heroin, I was shooting self-prescribed doses of denial into my veins.

In the kitchen something clattered on the floor. My father cursed under his breath. Like a heat-blasted layer of old paint, the cozy delusion I'd existed in since leaving New York City bubbled up and peeled away. There was no denying the truth. I was 35 years old, and I was moving back in with my parents.

Suddenly queasy with a desperate urge to flee, I quickly searched the familiar surroundings for reassurance. In the living room everything was in place, perfectly, immaculately in place. While growing up I had been forbidden to touch anything in there. It lost its status as a museum only when my parents were entertaining guests. On those occasions, much to my adolescent confusion, it was perfectly all right if people smoked, bumped into the furniture, and walked around in their shoes, muddling up the elegant symmetry of the vacuum tracks. "Don't go in the living room," my mother's voice from thirty years ago rang in my head. Immediately, a knot tightened in my solar plexus. Fifteen years of roaming the serpentine corridors of my consciousness searching for my truth, and still my mother's decades-old command was able to inspire fear and dread. I sadly shook my head. *I'm not a man*, I thought. *I'm just a kid in big pants.* With shoulders sagging, I walked to the kitchen.

My father was standing in front of the stove with his back to me. His thinning white hair stuck out on the side like some sort of turn signal.

"Dad."

He turned around. A dab of flour was on the front of his navy-blue sweater.

"Tommy! I'm making my famous Stroganoff for you."

"Great," I said, not having the heart to remind him, yet again, that I was a vegetarian. His normally ruddy complexion was pale, and his eyes were red-rimmed and tired-looking. He definitely looked older.

"How was the drive?"

"Fine."

I heard footsteps coming down the stairs. My mother swept into the kitchen wearing the white running-suit I'd sent her the year before for Christmas.

"I was talking on the phone to your Aunt Evelyn," she said. "She sends her love."

"Hi, Mom."

She looked at me and frowned. The creases in her face, carved by forty-five years of cigarettes and the trauma of raising me and my brother and sister, had somewhat toughened her beauty.

"Take off that silly hat," she said, reaching up and pulling off my battered Yankee baseball cap.

"Good to see you too, Mom."

"What happened to your face?"

I gingerly touched the bruise on the left side of my jaw.

"I ran into the bathroom door," I said, not wanting to tell them about what happened at my garden plot in New York. My father chuckled. I leaned down and gave Mom a kiss on the cheek. "I like the new centerpiece."

"American Wigeon," she said, admiring the carved wooden duck on the kitchen table. "Finished that one a few months ago."

"Merna," my father said. "Get the salad out of the fridge. Come on, come on, it's time to eat."

During dinner, as we discussed my brother's impending divorce, the new duck Mom was carving, the death of one of the pine trees in the backyard, and the skin disorder ravaging their terrier, Peanut, I could feel my parents cautiously sizing me up. They were obviously apprehensive about me moving back in with them.

"When does your new job start?" my father asked, attempting to sound casual.

"October."

He spread a glob of margarine onto a thick slice of French bread. I could almost hear him counting in his head, April, May, June, July, August, September . . . Six months? *Six months!*

He glanced up at me with a half-smile glued to his face. I'd seen that look before. It was his crisis face. He always slipped it on when things got bad. My older brother Rick crashed three cars by the time he was seventeen. When my kid sister Becky was ten, she spent three weeks in the hospital with rheumatic fever. Dad wore his mask of fatherly optimism a lot back then.

He winked at me, the corners of his mouth taut with uncertainty. "It's good to see you, buddy-boy."

My mother toasted me with her cup of coffee.

"Welcome home, honey."

From the basement I heard a low growl.

"Be quiet, Peanut!" Dad yelled.

"Leave him alone," Mom snapped.

I was struck again with the urge to flee. Living back at home with my parents? What the hell was I thinking?

2

In 1960, flush with money saved during the fabulous fifties, my parents built their dream house. The brick two-story with four bedrooms and a two-car garage was nestled on a quarter acre of land at the edge of a wooded hilltop called Davies Glen. The neighborhood at that time was middle-class, white, and predominately Protestant with a smattering of Catholics. My mother canned fruit, volunteered at the hospital, took care of my older brother Rick and me, and emulated Jackie Kennedy in dress and manner. My father was the newly appointed vice president of Grichor Advertising. As an ex-Marine and a staunch Republican, he regarded my mother's fascination with the First Lady as an overt act of insubordination. I think Mom just liked the hats.

When we moved into the house in June of 1960, Rick was permitted to choose which bedroom he wanted. Of course he picked the largest one. It was also the furthest from my parents' bedroom. I happily picked the room looking out over the garage roof. Even at the innocent age of four, I knew a good escape route when I saw one. While growing up, I crawled out on that roof many a night to stare at the stars. With the constant threat of Soviet nuclear missiles arcing in my head, and witnessing via the nightly news civil rights marchers getting hosed and beaten, rioters burning and looting, firefights in Vietnam, and student protests in cities all over the world, I was frequently in need of experiencing something that was solid and unchanging. The big dipper was my touchstone. With my old pal floating there, the dipper open and full of possibilities, I was reassured that there was some greater purpose at work in the world.

My old bedroom was now Dad's office. His roll-top desk next to the window was neatly arranged with bills, coupons, and magazine articles. Hanging on the wall in front of his desk were photographs and awards from his long career in advertising. Over the years he'd helped sell everything from Mercedes sedans to disposable diapers. "Life is a marketplace," he'd tell us kids. "A person needs to know what's out there." When one of the commercials he helped produce came on the television he would hush us into reverent silence. Then when it was over and "The Wonderful World of Disney" came back on the screen, Dad would settle back on the couch with a self-satisfied grin and say, "My effort toward a stronger economy."

I picked up the corners of the queen-sized futon that I'd brought from my apartment in New York City. As I wrestled it across the room into the corner of Dad's office, I nearly knocked over the oak and glass case containing his Japanese teacup. I leaned over to check it to make sure it was all right. Gray, with a pale blue chrysanthemum on the side, it didn't have a handle like American cups. When I was growing up, the cup was encased in a low wooden cabinet in the corner of my parent's bedroom. He wouldn't even allow my mother to clean it. It had something to do with the war, but all I knew for certain was that we were forbidden to touch it.

"Where's the frame?"

I turned toward the bedroom door. Dad was standing with his hands on his hips. It wasn't his most aggressive pose, but I could tell he wasn't happy. His eyes slipped off me and went to the case with the cup, then came back to me.

"I don't have a frame for it, Dad."

"The mattress just sits on the floor?"

"It'll be fine."

"I don't know if your mother will go for that."

"It's only for a short time."

"Your mother likes things a certain way."

"I know, Dad. I think it'll be okay."

He looked again at the teacup. "I'm not sure about that."

I was getting irritated. He was still a control freak.

"Come on, Dad."

He nudged the corner of the futon. "What kind of bed is this?"

"It's called a futon."

"Huh," he said frowning. "Looks like a damn hippie pad if you ask me." He turned and walked out of the room.

Hippie pad . . . I sat down on the futon. Hippie pad . . .

3

ON A CLOUDY SATURDAY morning in the spring of 1974, two months after the gas boycott was over and one month away from my high school graduation, my parents and little sister Becky left for a road trip to Geauga Lake, Ohio, to visit Sea World. Me? I was leaving on a different kind of trip. I was going to free myself from the shackles of third-dimensional reality. My brother Rick supplied the mushrooms. With the parting thumbs-up testimonial, "It's really cool, you'll like it," he climbed into his red Firebird and headed back to Clarion University where, as a sophomore, he played linebacker, threw the javelin, and sold some of the best pot in the tri-state area. Fifteen minutes after Rick drove away, my good friend Dee Dee Razinbach and her cousin Kim came over. They had enthusiastically agreed to join me on my maiden voyage into the psilocybin hinterlands.

It was eleven o'clock in the morning when we opened our cranial synapses to the wonder of magic mushrooms. Things went smoothly for the first hour. The warm, flickering glow of candles, the entrancing movement of my lava lamp, and the mellow scent of jasmine incense helped us relax and created the right mood. I'd read that mushrooms could be a pathway to higher awareness. They enabled you to see the big picture. Growing up as the three of us had during the chaos of the Vietnam War and disillusioned by the Watergate scandal and the sight of President Nixon scuttling about trying to avoid impeachment, Dee Dee, Kim, and I were looking for something to hang on to, something that made sense. We craved a deeper understanding of what life was all about.

As I lay sprawled on the hardwood floor listening to the girls making pleasant cooing sounds up on the couch, I silently asked to be shown the truth about myself: Who was I, really? What was my place in the world? What could I do to make a difference?

For the next ten minutes, I saw shiny, black circles floating in front of my eyes. I was concentrating on figuring out what the circles meant when Kim, believing that her hair had burst into flames, suddenly jumped to her feet and with bell bottoms flapping, rushed into the kitchen and began drenching her head with water from the sink. Dee Dee and I tried to wrestle her away, but Kim was a gymnast and quite strong. That, coupled with her absolute conviction that her head was ablaze, made subduing her nearly impossible. She kept throwing water and screaming for the fire department. Only after Dee Dee held up a lid from one of my mother's Revere Ware pans and Kim saw in the reflection that her hair wasn't ignited, did she finally calm down. Sobbing and clutching my arm, she pleaded with me to turn off the Uriah Heep album playing on the stereo. She was certain that it had somehow induced her hysteria. I was only too happy to oblige. I left her curled up on the couch in the den, contentedly examining the downy blond hairs on her left forearm and listening to the soundtrack from *Camelot*.

In the living room, much to my surprise and delight, I found Dee Dee naked and writhing on the carpeting. She was on her back grinding her hips into the air and softly moaning, "Oh, yes, oh yes." I had never seen Dee Dee naked before, and as I watched her undulating pelvis I realized that my feelings of friendship had suddenly become much, much more. As if reading my mind, she opened her eyes and looked at me. With an upward thrust of her narrow hips, she opened her arms and beckoned me closer. I walked to her and knelt down. Our fingers entwined. I leaned to kiss her but suddenly stopped. I was distracted by a buzzing sound followed by a loud pop. I turned to my right. A great blue heron was standing on the coffee table.

Five feet tall and a brilliant shade of turquoise blue, it looked at me and cocked its head. The right eye blinked. I squeezed my eyes shut then opened them. The blue heron was still there. *Oh wow*, I thought, *either this is a really vivid hallucination or I'm in serious trouble for letting this huge fucking bird in the house.*

Dee Dee fumbled with my belt. For a brief second I considered telling her about the blue heron but then decided not to spoil our romantic moment. I turned away from the winking heron and kissed Dee Dee on the lips. Her tongue swam into my mouth. I pressed myself against her. She pressed back. Immediately I forgot about the bird.

With Richard Harris in the den bellowing, "Camelot, Camelot," Dee Dee and I entered into a new phase of our relationship. Ass grabbing, hips bucking – we were going crazy. Obviously at this particular moment my sister's car sickness was not remotely on my mind. If it had been, I might have been better prepared, for at that exact moment the basement door swung open. Sporting a dried stain of vomit on the right shoulder of his suede jacket, my father stepped into the entryway. His reaction came at me like a bright orange wall of fire.

"Jesus, Mary, and Joseph! What the hell is going on here?"

Even in the face of that holy trinity, I couldn't stop. Dee Dee's arms clamped around me as she arched her back and thrust her hips up against me. My mother screamed, "Oh God! Not in the living room!" Everything let go and I poured myself into the pin-wheeling blackness. At the end of what seemed like a long velvet tunnel I heard my father shout, "This isn't a damn hippie pad!" My body shuddered. My weight pressed down onto Dee Dee's ample breasts. Becky giggled. My parents stormed into the kitchen. Then, from the corner of my right eye, came a blur of motion. I looked up. The blue heron was back on the coffee table.

This time it wasn't winking. It craned its neck forward, staring hard at me. Its feathers rhythmically pulsated and the pupils in its yellow eyes bored into me. Granted, I was an inexperienced traveler on the hallucinogenic highway, my frame of reference was nil, but I had no doubt that even Timothy Leary would have given this bird a second look.

Immediately, two distinct impressions formed in my mind: one, my large blue friend with the orange, pointy bill if provoked could disembowel me in a nanosecond, adding my bloody intestinal tract to whatever damage Dee Dee and I had already caused to Mom's white carpeting; and two: he, she, it, was trying to communicate with me.

Even though I was a novice at speaking with manifestations from my subconscious or other dimensions or wherever the hell big bird had flown in from, I felt that under the circumstances I should give it a try. I had just been caught by my parents desecrating the family home in a drug-induced state. If this giant blue bird had some sort of message or cosmic pearl of wisdom that would make sense of this unfortunate chain of events, then I wanted to know about it.

I bucked up my courage and looked into its eyes. They were dull and blank – no trace of emotion. It stepped toward me. I nearly jumped out of my skin but restrained myself for fear of pissing it off. Its pulsating feathers made a faint whirring sound. I stared into its eyes. They opened a little wider, and then slowly, not audibly but in my mind, words began to faintly come to me.

Don't let the rain hurt your head. Always wear a hat.

Hummm, I thought, *not exactly something that you'd want to carve onto stone tablets.* As if hearing my thought, the heron shifted its feet and ruffled its feathers. They crackled like static on a radio. Again it locked eyes with me. I felt myself drawn into the dark waters of those two round pools. It must have turned up the volume on its telepathy because this time when the words came they sounded like they were booming through a wall of speakers in my head:

SEEK YOUR TRUTH! IT'S ON THE WAY TO POMONA, CALIFORNIA!

Purple light ripped from the heron's chest, sizzling like a Fourth of July sparkler. I turned away from the glare. When I looked back, the bird was gone.

Becky was the first one to talk to me the next morning. She was twelve at the time and something of a pest. Bless her heart, that day she knew I was in big trouble and saw no need to throw more my way. My father and mother felt differently.

"Thomas, get down here right now!" My father shouted from the bottom of the stairs.

I looked at Becky standing at the foot of my bed. There was still a surreal, fuzzy edge to everything.

"Tommy," she said. "Dad wants you."

"Yeah."

I swung out of bed. Both of my knees had nasty carpet burns.

"Dee Dee has really big boobs," Becky said. She grinned and walked out of the room.

My father called me a fornicator. It was a strange word to hear coming from him. Never having broached the topic of sex with me in the past, the pained look on his face told me that he was less than enthusiastic about finally having to do it. He paced back and forth across the den humming, "Fly Me to the Moon," and nervously running his fingers through his salt-and-pepper hair.

Slumped on the couch in my faded blue terrycloth robe, I kept hoping he'd slip on his crisis face. I knew things would be okay if I saw that I'm-a-parent-I-can-make-this-better look pop into his eyes. It never happened. Instead, he abruptly stopped pacing. Apparently having come to the conclusion that he was heading through terrain that he had no hope of navigating in any reasonable manner, my father about-faced himself into a more familiar attitude.

"I never thought you kids would do drugs," he said, his eyes squinted in anger. "You know better than that. Look at Rick, he's an athlete. You don't see him whacking himself out on – whatever it was that you took. If you were younger, I'd smack your ass until you were black and blue."

He was deep into his accomplish-the-mission comfort zone. He had me in his sights and his finger was on the trigger. I began looking for cover.

My father was still very much a soldier. He was big and burly, as well as quiet and intense. As a kid, I never once saw him use a poker to stir a fire. He'd reach his hairy arms right into the fireplace and move the logs around with his bare hands. I'd be sitting on the couch, the stench of burned hair wafting through the room.

"Dad," I'd say. "You okay? Isn't that hot?"

"No, no. I'm fine."

He also possessed an incredible ability to see in the dark. I'd walk into the pitch-black kitchen, and there he'd be, cutting himself a piece of pie.

"Dad, you want me to turn on the light?"

"Nope, I can see."

It only made sense that a man with those kinds of supernatural gifts would be a tough taskmaster when it came to mere mortals. A fervent believer in the old adage, "spare the rod, spoil the child," discipline and control was the way he knew how to get things done.

"Honey," my mother said, "you have to realize—"

"I want to hear what he has to say for himself," my father snapped, cutting her off. "Come on, speak! You spend half your life on that roof staring up at God-knows-what, you must have a thought or two in that head of yours!"

"I'm sorry, Dad."

"Sorry doesn't cut it mister. This is your life we're talking about. And it's our lives too, because your behavior affects everyone in this family." He pointed at me. "It's that damn music you listen to, that Floyd stuff."

"Pink Floyd, Dad."

"Pink, blue, I don't care what color it is!" He threw his hands up in frustration. "I can't understand it. I really can't. What possible reason could you have had to take a drug that made you act like a depraved animal in our home?"

The clock on the mantle ticked five times while he glared down at me.

Would telling him how lost I felt help my cause? Could he understand my need to find something in our screwed-up world that made sense; that might be some sort of vessel for my faith? Assassinating smart people dedicated to change didn't do it. Corrupt leaders in our government didn't work either. Gunning down students protesting a war was far from inspiring. Would my father be able to see this? Could he?

No, I decided. We'd never seen eye to eye on anything. Why now would he all of a sudden be able to relate to me? I sunk deeper into the safe confines of the couch.

"You know," he said finally, "I always wondered what kind of a man you were. You never played sports like your brother."

There was a flash of macho cruelty in his eyes. He had meant to hurt me. Still, even with my manhood being challenged, I understood on a visceral level that attempting to shift the blame off of myself by shattering the myth my father had created about Rick would undoubtedly result in a kill-the-messenger scenario. Without that as a viable option, two other reactions welled up inside of me: *Screw yourself, Dad, I'm seventeen, I'm a fornicator, and I can do as I please.* And the second impulse was, *if I keep my mouth shut and don't lip off, I just might get out of this with my head still attached to my shoulders.* Self-preservation being high on my list of priorities, the latter option won out. I bowed my head and looked ashamed. My father grunted in disgust.

My mother, having recently read *The Feminine Mystique* and *Our Bodies, Ourselves*, was not shy about expressing her opinion. She plopped herself down on the couch next to me, clutched my hand in hers, and launched into a speech about birth control, venereal disease, the woes of drug addiction, and finally, my future.

"You don't want to end up like one of those spaced-out hippies we see on the news, do you honey?"

My father, having abruptly left the room for the birth control and disease portions of Mom's lecture, shouted from the kitchen, "Damn hippies."

In contrast to my father's deeply entrenched Methodist repression, my mother's southern Baptist upbringing enabled her to shout down sin vigorously and in explicit detail. Her comprehensive knowledge of the vilest of sexually transmitted diseases, although to some extent nauseating me at the time due to my magic-mushroom hangover, impressed me nonetheless. Mom had been taught early on by her mother that a woman's place was anywhere she wanted it to be. All she had to do was speak her mind and tell the truth. There were no limitations except self-created ones. Once when I was three years old, our washing machine broke down and Mom took Rick and me to a Laundromat. After she'd finished with the drying, I watched her carry a basket full of clean clothes toward the doors to go outside. Because of the pile of clothes, she couldn't see where she was going and veered ten feet to the right of the doors. She walked straight through a plate-glass window. The glass shattered and smashed to the ground. Rick started crying. I fled into the bathroom and hid under the sink. Other than a slight bump on her head, Mom didn't even get hurt. That was my mother, she made her own doors.

The message from the blue heron haunted me most of that summer. In between attempts at eclipsing the sexual frenzy Dee Dee and I experienced in my parents' living room, and in July cheering on the Judiciary Committee's approval of articles of impeachment against Nixon, and then in August celebrating Nixon's resignation, I spent long hours trying to figure out the meaning of the blue heron's message: *Don't let the rain hurt your head. Always wear a hat. Seek your truth. It's on the way to Pomona, California.*

Dee Dee thought I was nuts. But I was determined. I researched meteorological studies. I read about the history of hats. I bought different travel guides on Pomona, California. I learned that it had once been an agricultural community. Thirty-one miles from downtown Los Angeles, it now played host to the largest county fair in America. What all that meant to me, I didn't have a clue.

By the end of the summer, I'd had enough. I decided that Dee Dee was right; what I'd experienced was nothing more than a magic-mushroom hallucination. So, I quit searching for answers.

4

LOST IN AN APATHETIC daze initially ignited by President Ford's unconditional pardon of Richard Nixon's offenses against the country, and later fueled by the federal grand jury in Cleveland exonerating 27 National Guardsmen of any responsibility for the 1970 shootings at Kent State – my freshman, sophomore, and junior years at Penn State swirled by in a wash of beer, bongs, and bourbon. I made no attempt to gain further insight into myself or to understand how the world worked. If the president could get away with deceiving us, and unarmed American students could be gunned down, what was there to feel secure about? If the head is dead, the body will follow. So like everyone else I knew at the time, I chose to crawl inside and numb myself from the madness. My only accomplishment of any merit was constructing a smooth-drawing water pipe that my friends affectionately nicknamed Stony.

With an academic performance one notch below mediocre, I was a business major with no interest in business. My parents had come to believe that I was going to follow my father into advertising. I had no clue who gave them that idea. It certainly wasn't me.

It was a week after finals, and I was hitch-hiking home for the summer. The Donegal exit off the Pennsylvania Turnpike was swarming with cars. Rain fell in silver sheets across the gloomy, gray sky. It drummed against the bill of my Nittany Lions baseball cap, streaming down the front of my camouflage poncho, and soaking through the crepe-soled Hush Puppies I was wearing. For forty-five minutes I stood there with my thumb sticking out, countless cars inching past without a sideways glance from anyone. I was about to leap onto the hood of a red Pacer and force the driver to give me a ride when a jagged slash of lightning lit up the sky. The following boom of thunder resonated so deeply that my sternum seemed to vibrate from the force of it. It was time, I decided, to get in out of the rain.

Picking up my soggy duffel bag, I began trudging down the line of cars toward the truck stop across the highway. A horn blared. I looked up. A woman in a black Wagoneer two lanes over waved to me. I ran to the car. She rolled down the passenger-side window and pointed at my hat.

"Do you go to Penn State?" she shouted, her voice barely audible above the downpour. Another bolt of lightning lit up the sky. The rain started to fall even harder.

"Yes," I sputtered. "I just finished my junior year."

"Good for you," she said. She hit the electric lock button and waved me in.

Maggie was a Penn State grad. She was thirty-four and on the run from Jerry, her stockbroker husband. Three days earlier, she'd left their home, a quaint 1860s barn in Litchfield, Connecticut, which she had painstakingly restored and decorated with antiques from all over New England. After a stop in Philadelphia to cry with her sister, Maggie was on a mission to put as many states between herself and Jerry as she could.

"He broke my urn," she cried. "Last summer, after a badminton party at my cousin's, he pushed me and knocked me backward over my Amish butter urn. I broke my wrist and snapped the plunger on the urn. I loved that urn!" She hit the steering wheel. "It started four years ago," she went on. "He was passed over for a promotion. Oh God, why am I telling you this?"

Before I could say anything, she reached out and smacked the dashboard. "I couldn't take it anymore!" she cried. "My shrink told me to go, so I did. I mean, what else could I—" Tears flooded her eyes and spilled down through the remains of her makeup. She reached for a pack of tissues in her purse. With forced optimism and determination, she added, "I'm going out west to my younger brother's place; a new life. That's what I need, a new life."

All of this was blurted to me in our first six miles together. While she continued to sob, I sat frozen in my seat trying to determine if I was in the presence of a crazy person or someone who was truly heart-broken. And to think when I first climbed into the car I was worried about getting her seat wet.

She calmed down after a couple more miles and apologized for dumping her problems on me. We talked briefly about Penn State, the construction job I had lined up for the summer, and the movie *Star Wars* that just came out. She seemed to relax. The longer we talked, the more I began to realize that Maggie wasn't crazy. Her life had taken her down a rough trail. Her situation with Jerry made me think of my parents' marriage and the friction between them: My father's emotional absence and my mother's nit-picking attempts to bring him out. Once again, I pledged to not marry a woman with whom I would do battle for the rest of my days. Life was too short. I'd rather be alone than put myself through that.

"Oh I love this," Maggie said. She leaned over and turned up the volume and began to sing along with the radio. As she tapped her fingers on the steering wheel I noticed that she had already removed her wedding ring. Her fingers were long and the nails perfect; no chips in the polish, no chewed down stubs. She reminded me of an older version of a sorority girl. Her voice wasn't bad either. She turned and pointed one of those lovely fingers at me as she sang along with the radio:

> ". . . and when you're free, you're
> really free, like a bluebird,
> be the bluebird, such a bluebird,
> you're free . . ."

She winked, and that's when the flashback hit me: Dee Dee, the blue heron, and those words booming in my mind:

*DON'T LET THE RAIN HURT YOUR HEAD.
ALWAYS WEAR A HAT. SEEK YOUR TRUTH.
IT'S ON THE WAY TO POMONA, CALIFORNIA.*

I looked down. My fingers tightened on the rain-soaked baseball cap sitting in my lap. "Uh oh," I heard myself meekly mumble. It was the same hollow response a farmer in Nebraska might make when upon glancing up from the wheel of his red International Harvester he spots the black churning funnel of a tornado coming at him across his corn field. Not much you can do but hang on and hope for a soft landing.

My mouth went dry and pasty. My skin prickled. With a weird combination of exhilaration and dread, I watched the windshield wipers click back and forth, pushing the streaming water out of the way. The blue bird song on the radio ended. In a voice as normal as I could manage, I said, "Where out west does your brother live?" She turned to me with a big smile and said, "Pomona, California."

We were on Interstate 70, just west of Columbus, Ohio, when I finally called my parents to tell them that I wouldn't be coming home. I didn't have the nerve to tell them that I was following an omen that I'd received from a great blue heron on that fateful day three years earlier when they'd caught Dee Dee and me humping our brains out in the living room. Instead, I told them that a friend and I had decided to go to out west for the summer. I asked my mother if she would call the construction company and tell them that I wouldn't be working for them. On the upstairs telephone, my father let out a not-so-quiet groan of despair. Mom took the hint and quickly got off the line. With his voice pinched and edgy, my father told me that I was an irresponsible bum and that it would be a miracle if I amounted to anything. Then he hung up on me.

Two hours later, just east of Indianapolis, Maggie asked if I'd like to go to Florida. I told her, "Sure, why not." I was already committed to the journey. The blue bird song was one thing. That could easily be written off as a coincidence. And even though I was disappointed at the literal translation of the blue heron's message, I felt that the combination of events was way too much to deny. It wasn't exactly a burning bush, but it was a sign, and I wasn't about to ignore it.

After eating at a roadside diner on Interstate 65, I was standing by the car waiting for Maggie to come out of the ladies room. Looking up into the night sky over the roof of the restaurant, I could see the Big Dipper. What lay ahead for me, I wondered, gazing up at that familiar constellation? Would I find the truth of who I was? Would my purpose in life be revealed to me?

• • •

AFTER A PLATONIC FIVE-DAY whirlwind tour of Disney World, Sea World, and Busch Gardens, during which Maggie harangued me with quotes from the women's lib pamphlets her sister gave her, we ended up on a beach in Boca Raton. It was past midnight as we strolled along the edge of the water, carrying our shoes and enjoying the waves lapping luxuriously at our ankles.

"Jerry would have hated this trip," Maggie said. "He's not a fan of tourist attractions." She looked out at the tumbling surf. "I begged him for years to come down here."

"And he wouldn't do it?"

"No. Just another way he tried to control me." She leaned against my shoulder. "Thanks for making my dream come true."

"Hey, no problem, it was fun. Thank you."

Maggie stopped walking and turned to me. With a shy grin, she seductively unbuttoned her white cotton blouse and put my hand on her breast. She looked at me with a challenge in her eyes.

"Your breast is lovely," I said, focusing hard to look her in the eyes and not ogle her breasts. "But I don't want to – you know, you're going through a lot right now."

"Please," Maggie said. She leaned into me. Her lips brushed my ear. "Have you ever seen *From Here to Eternity?* It's my favorite movie."

I gave a silent thanks to Professor Neff and the film appreciation class she taught my freshman year. Apparently, doing it on the beach was another request Jerry had denied Maggie. So with the moon beaming down, the briny smell of the Atlantic awash in the air, and Maggie's shapely legs wrapped around my hips, I tried to help her forget about her husband's lack of imagination.

It must have been the tide surging around us or the amazing sounds coming from Maggie, because I felt extraordinarily wild and out of control. Slithering and groping and gasping on the beach, it suddenly felt, and I'm not kidding, as if we were amphibians emerging from the sea, breathing our first strangled gulps of oxygen and clinging to each other with the desperation of a species fighting for higher ground. As Maggie and I happily groaned and thrashed our way to a climax of such intensity that I was certain my right testicle had imploded, I knew that this night would be forever etched in my memory: The two of us cradled in the bountiful arms of the sea, the grit of the sand between our toes, the sublime urgency of some mysterious, ancient strand of DNA pulsing in my brain, arcing between us, triggering stimuli of a primeval nature and revealing to me the reptilian wonder of my glorious beginnings.

Two days later, she dumped me. We were in a Holiday Inn outside of Biloxi, Mississippi. I had gotten out of bed at 6:00 a.m. to take a shower. Our experience on the beach in Boca Raton had unsettled me. As I stood under the cascading water, carefully checking my neck for the emergence of gills, I thought I heard the door of the motel room open. I figured Maggie went to buy a newspaper or get something out of her car. When I came out of the bathroom, satisfied with the state of my anatomy, I found a note on the pillow.

Dear Tom,

It's dumb, I know, but I couldn't look you in the
face and say goodbye. You've been so sweet with me.
I've become too fond of you. But right now I don't
want to lean on another man for support. I need to

be there for me. I'm feeling pretty screwed up (no kidding) and I'm not sure who I am anymore. Don't be mad at me. Be a good man. Don't ever hit anyone.

Love,
Maggie

I looked around the room. Her things were gone. I opened the door. The car was gone too. I flopped onto the bed and stared up at the ceiling. Now what?

The signs had pointed me to Pomona, California. What was I supposed to do walk there? I should just go home, I told myself. I'd try and get my construction job back. I'd finish school and then – What? Go to work in an office like my father? Start the long climb up the corporate ladder? Integrate myself into the same lying, conniving system that got rich off of the guys fighting and getting blown apart in Vietnam? I began punching the pillow.

I wanted something different out of life. "Truth is what sells," my father had told me over and over, but I wanted a different truth. I didn't want to contribute to our already over-revved consumer culture by creating magazine ads or TV commercials that tried to tell people what to think, what to smell like, or what it meant to be a success. I wasn't going to be a good soldier of big business like my father and fall in line, wear blue suits, white shirts, and conservative striped ties. I wanted to be a part of something else, something that was deeper than a refrigerator commercial.

I stopped punching the pillow and sat up on the bed. What if the signs were false? What if the blue heron was a messenger of evil? What if I was being led to a dead end, or worse?

I clicked on the TV. As I mulled over what I should do, former Attorney General John Mitchell's basset hound face filled the screen. He was stepping out of a long blue Cadillac in front of a prison. The voice of a reporter announced that the institution in Montgomery, Alabama was where Mitchell was going to serve his time for the role he played in the Watergate scandal. As Mitchell was being ushered through the prison gates, a reporter called out to him, asking if he had any comment.

"It's nice to be back in Alabama," Mitchell said.

I stared at the screen, not believing what I'd just heard. The big porker had helped drag the country through a steaming shit pile of lies and corruption and all he had to say was, "It's nice to be back in Alabama." I packed my duffel bag, walked to the westbound ramp of the Interstate, and stuck out my thumb.

5

THE CHAINSAW TORE through the soft pine, sending a shower of sawdust to the ground. The bottom section of the dead tree swayed to the left, tightening the ropes I used to direct its fall. When I gave the white pine a final push, it fell into the yard exactly where I wanted. My father came out onto the back porch to survey my work.

"I planted that the day after we moved in here," he said, sadly looking at the tree.

"You don't know what killed it?"

"No. It just up and died."

"Do you want me to split it? You could burn it in the fireplace."

"Pine is crappy, too much sap. Throw it in the woods." He turned to go back in the house, then stopped and sniffed the air.

"Damn," he said. "Lud's got that smoker going again."

He walked to the corner of the porch and peered through the shrubbery at the neighbor's backyard. He sniffed the air again.

"Pork this time, I'll betcha." He grinned. "Smells good, doesn't it? I'm going to have to buy myself one of those."

My father and Lud Blakely had been one-upping each other with gadgets, lawn mowers, and appliances for the last thirty years. At sixty-seven, down on his haunches peeking through the bushes, Dad still hadn't lost his competitive edge.

"How is Lud doing?" I asked.

"Other than his triple-bypass he's been fine."

"When did that happen?"

"Six months ago. Guess I forgot to tell you. Yeah, he's got a big ole zipper scar down his chest."

"That's too bad."

My father nodded and walked to the door.

"I wonder how much those smokers go for," he said.

"I don't know, Dad. Why don't you call Lud and ask him?"

He looked at me to see if I was pulling his chain. I couldn't hold back the grin. Dad shook his head.

"I'll call Rick. He'll know."

He went inside the house. I yanked the cord on the chainsaw. The high-pitched whine stung my ears. I shoved the blade down onto the tree. Sawdust showered against my leg. I forced the blade deeper into the cut.

Rick and his wife Denise lived in the suburbs of Atlanta. They were upwardly mobile, favorite golf partners at the country club, but after ten years of marriage and two kids, Rick wanted out. He'd met Roxanne, a corporate headhunter, while he was shopping at the retail-clothing store where he bought Denise her Christmas present every year. Roxanne was twenty-six and quite a looker from what Rick said.

This bit of news had done nothing to change the exceptional relationship between Rick and my father. They continued to talk at least twice a week, badgering each other about sports, golf scores, and stock prices. They had been doing it ever since Rick accepted a job with TriMark Medical Supplies and moved to Atlanta after college.

I never figured out the password to get into their club. Rick seemed to know it from the beginning. When he was a senior in high school and I was a sophomore, we'd both go to the same parties. We'd drink beer together, get drunk, but when we'd come home, I'd scoot upstairs to hide my drunken stupor and he'd go into the den, sit down, and have a thirty minute conversation with the folks. While they were yukking it up watching Johnny Carson, I was in the bathroom chugging Listerine and shoving breath mints in my mouth. In the end, I was always busted. Rick was never even a suspect.

$147.95. That was how much the smoker cost. At least that's what they went for in Atlanta. Dad and Rick talked for an hour on the telephone going over various options and models available. Later, as we were finishing dinner, Becky called to say hello. She couldn't believe that I was actually going to live with Mom and Dad for an extended period of time.

"Aren't you going to go crazy?"

"Probably," I said.

"I want to come back for a visit so we can hang out."

"That would be great."

"You have to give me some scoop on this bimbo Rick is seeing."

"He said she's very bright."

"Sure she is. He's having a mid-life crisis, what intelligent woman would choose to get in the middle of that?"

Becky's education and career as a psychologist, coupled with five years of living in Manchester, New Hampshire, had deepened her perspective on human behavior. Having the ability to see through people's neuroses and better understand their motivations was a blessing and a curse, she'd once told me. It was not unlike making movies, she theorized. Once you understood the process, you could see through the glitter and flash to the inner workings of how it was all put together. With that insight came a certain loss of wonder and magic when you went to the movies. She felt the same way about human beings.

"When you're able to perceive the reeking pile of misery inside someone," she'd said, "what's the point in laughing at the funny mask they're hiding behind?"

I wondered what she thought of my return home. There was probably a womb theory she'd want to discuss with me.

"Have you gone to visit Aunt Helen yet?" she asked.

"Becky, I've only been here a little while."

"Last month when I stopped in to see her, she was shooing an old man off of her front porch. He walked away before I got out of the car. She tried to pretend that it was no big deal, but I could tell that she was upset."

"Who was he?"

"She wouldn't say. She told me that she caught him peeking in her window."

"I'll call the police."

"She said she didn't want me to do that. I think she knew him."

"Maybe Aunt Helen wants him to peep in at her. She's probably teasing the old guy."

"Tommy, that's gross."

My father, sitting at the kitchen table reading the sports section, grinned. Great Aunt Helen was definitely not one of his favorite people. At 94, and the younger sister of his deceased mother-in-law, he resented the fact that Aunt Helen considered it part of her duties as matriarch of the family to bust his chops whenever she had the chance. I, on the other hand, felt that she was performing a valuable family service. My father needed a good cage-rattling from time to time.

"Oh yeah," Becky said. "Tell Mom that I mentioned the skirt she sent me. Tell her I said it was lovely."

"Okay."

"I'll never wear it but . . . anyway, I'll see you soon, Tommy."

I looked forward to her visit. She would be a good buffer. Ever since my arrival, my parents and I had been tip-toeing around each other. It was strange being with them every day. My mother's crazy attempts to emotionally engage my father with her zinging comments about spending his retirement watching ESPN, and my father's relentless pursuit of the next TV show, seriously bugged me. In the past, we talked on the telephone every couple weeks, but our actual time together had been limited to brief and infrequent visits at Thanksgiving or Christmas. That's the way it had been ever since that summer when I took off with Maggie.

6

Texas was hot. The oppressive humidity had sucked every ounce of energy out of my body, leaving me weak-kneed and dreaming of banana popsicles. Three rides since leaving the Holiday Inn in Biloxi had taken me as far as Houston. After buying food and giving one guy five dollars for gas, I was down to $52 and change. I was standing on the side of the road watching the sunset paint the clouds burnt orange and pink, when a dark brown Monte Carlo pulled over. The driver was a white guy who looked to be in his thirties. He had Elvis sideburns and a cigarette dangling from chapped lips.

"I'm going to Austin," he said.

"Is that west?" I asked.

"Son, Austin is the west." He grinned, flashing a gold front tooth. "I ain't got all night. Do you want a ride or not?" He moved a six-pack of Miller long necks off the front seat, and I jumped in.

Every day when I was in 7th and 8th grade, I used to read about the Vietnam War in the newspaper. I'd pore over the details of body counts and B52 bombing runs. Even though I agreed with the protesters that the war wasn't good for our country, I secretly hoped that it would continue. I knew that I would make a great soldier. Not the snapping-to-attention-saluting, "Yes, sir, whatever you say sir," part of it. My father tried to instill that in me and it didn't work. What I was absolutely certain of was my ability to shoot and kill. For as long as I could remember, I'd had dreams about being in battle. It didn't matter if I was on horseback, running behind a tank, or on the wall of a castle, in my dreams I was always shooting or being shot at. So I wanted to go to over there and be in the fight. I wanted to prowl through the mountains and triple canopy jungle west of Chu Lai, slip through the fog with my face blackened, my M16 loose in my fingers, ready, alert. I wanted to set up Claymore mines and carry hand grenades on my belt. I wanted to feel every single beat of my heart as I crawled belly-flat on the ground at 2 a.m. with tracer bullets streaking overhead and mortar rounds throwing up great chunks of earth in all directions. I wanted to hunt down those skinny VC in their black pajamas that Walter Cronkite showed us on the evening news. They were evil communists and I knew I could kill them. I was positive that I could face the enemy, stare him down, and deliver him to his maker without a blink of worry.

With that in mind, after driving for an hour and drinking beer and bullshitting with my gold-toothed friend in the Monte Carlo, I was absolutely astounded by the abject terror that paralyzed my body when he pulled out a .45 automatic and stuck it against my head.

"Don't do nothin'," he said. "I wouldn't even blink if I was you."

My eyes immediately started twitching. Nerve endings all over my body crackled with adrenaline. I thought of the knife in my boot, but not before every bone in my body gelatinized into quivering mush. I was like Gumby in a toaster oven.

He moved the .45 from my temple and jammed it hard against my left cheek.

"Where's your money, kid?"

Gun metal has a smell to it. It's hard and cool and sticks to the roof of your mouth. I'd never realized the laxative effect that smell could induce in a human being.

"I'm gonna pull over, partner," he said. "Then you're gonna

make me a donation. It's Sunday, ain't it? Yeah, boy! Praise the Lord and gimme your money!"

He kept the gun pointed at me as I reached into my pocket for the wad of bills. Out of my peripheral vision, I could see his finger on the trigger. As he slowed down, preparing to pull off the road, I prayed that he wouldn't hit a bump.

He wasn't happy with the $52 I gave him. He searched through my bag, and when he made me take off my boots and socks and stick my hand down my pants to show him that I didn't have any more money hidden, I managed to palm the knife and put it on the seat next to my leg. He took my duffel bag of clothes to make up for my lack of cash.

"Welcome to Texas," he said, and shoved the .45 against my neck.

I waited for him to tell me what to do next. He didn't say a word. He just stared at me. A creepy stillness filled the car. I went clammy inside. *He's going to shoot me.* My fingers tightened around the handle of the knife. My brain told me to slash his throat and save myself. One stab and it would be over. But my body was filled with sand. I couldn't move. At the same time all of my senses were crisp and acutely aware: The pressure of the gun against my neck, the tightness in my lower back, the smell of beer and cigarettes on his breath. I could feel every beat of my heart; clear, distinct pulses of muscle and blood contracting and releasing. Capillaries, arteries, and valves working together in perfect balance and harmony inches from a high velocity fragment of lead. The bullet had one purpose only; to splatter my blood and bone, and keep going until it hit something solid enough to stop it. This wasn't one of my dreams and I wasn't a hero with medals pinned to my chest. I was a body waiting to die.

He made a noise. It was far back in his throat. It wasn't a laugh or a giggle, but there was a sense of fun in it.

"Makes you think, don't it?" He jammed the .45 harder against my neck. "Bang, bang, buckaroo." He laughed, snorting through his nose, then shoved me out of the car.

He took off in a rooster tail of dust and squealing tires. I watched, still shaking from the adrenaline rush, as the red glare of his taillights got swallowed up in the darkness. I looked around. I was in the middle of nowhere. The wind moved in whispers and muted rhythms through the sagebrush and pinion trees lining both sides of the road.

After a minute I took a breath. Something inside of me broke apart. Tears filled my eyes. I hung my head, letting the wetness run down my face. I don't know why, maybe it was embarrassment or shame, but I didn't make any noise. I sort of harrumphed and heaved my shoulders, silently letting the tears fall. Finally I stopped. I wiped my face with the sleeve of my T-shirt and glanced up into the night sky. I searched for the Big Dipper, but so many stars were visible that the constellations had blended together, leaving a huge mass of stars without structure or order. It made me shrink deeper into myself. I didn't want to be in the middle of chaos. I wanted to feel safe.

• • •

WATER, ICE-COLD WATER; that was the thought jabbing in my brain as the sun came up the next morning. I had walked all night. My feet ached and my eyes were scratchy and raw. Only a few cars went by after the Monte Carlo's taillights faded in the distance. None of them stopped. For half the night I'd been serenaded by a pack of coyotes. Their yipping and howling set my nerves twanging, every shadow had teeth and an empty stomach.

An hour after sunrise, a skinny guy in a battered El Camino stopped and gave me a ride. He was Mexican and his name was Louis. He was going to his new job at a machine shop in Austin. He had a jug of cherry Kool-Aid on the front seat that I proceeded to gulp down. He didn't seem to care. He was too busy laughing at my story. He thought it was hilarious that I'd been robbed. I'm sure he would have laughed even harder if he'd seen the soiled Jockey shorts I'd buried alongside the road.

"I'm looking for work," I said. "Do you know of any place I can get a job?"

Louis tugged at his straggly goatee and thought for a moment.

"My little brother, Ernesto, works at the Hyatt Hotel. Maybe they need another dishwasher, who knows."

Ernesto was half asleep when he answered his door. He had a round baby face and dark circles under his eyes. His pudgy belly hung over the waistband of his blue boxer shorts. Louis spoke to him rapidly in Spanish. When he finished, Ernesto stepped aside and gestured for me to come into his apartment. "Home sweet home," he said.

Two nights later, I was up to my armpits in dirty dishes. I had been hired as a bus boy in the room service department at the Hyatt Regency. It was my job to sort and stack the dirty dishes brought down from the rooms. After filling plastic tubs with the freshly scraped dishes, I would load them onto a cart and haul them back to the dishwashers.

My first night was a struggle. Alone in the bowels of the hotel, with creamed corn hanging from my wrist, I pondered the wisdom of my decision to come west. How was I going to discover anything meaningful about life mucking around in other people's dinner slop? After a few hours of self-loathing, I reminded myself that I had been given a sign. It was up to me to have the courage to follow where it led. I also reminded myself that the alternative to working at the hotel was to go home and face my parents. That did the trick. From that moment on I was committed to being the best bus boy I could be.

Ernesto and Louis Osorio became my benefactors. I learned that the reason Louis laughed at me the morning he picked me up was because he and Ernesto had been robbed when they first moved to Austin. A gang of Mexicans cornered them in a parking ramp and took their money and green cards. Louis had been cut in the fight, eighteen stitches in his right forearm.

Ernesto and his girlfriend Tereza Zedillo continued to let me sleep on their couch. They fed me and gave me rides to work. Tereza was a chubby eighteen-year-old with a warm laugh and silky black hair to her waist. She cooked spicy food I'd never eaten before: burritos with green salsa, chile rellenos, and fajitas. They'd laugh at me as the sweat beaded up on my forehead. Tereza's mother lived in a village south of Mexico City called San Rafael Ixtapalucan. She mailed Tereza red peppers from her gardens that were so hot even Ernesto would blink his eyes and begin to sweat.

Louis and Ernesto took me to parties and introduced me to their friends and families. Growing up in a lily-white middle class suburb of Pittsburgh, the only person of color that I knew was Nick Spinelli, a dark-skinned Italian. At Penn State, my circle of friends wasn't much different. The harsh judgments we'd dished out to "spics" and "greasers" whip-lashed back on me at Louis's family picnics. Now I was the minority, and his young cousins gave me hard stares and baited me with derogatory names in Spanish.

"Hey," Louis said to them, trying to smooth things over, "You should have seen him the morning I found him," he laughed and slapped me on the back. "He was scared man – white as a ghost." He waved his hands in the air. "Woooo, woooo, the ghost of the desert." Their tough-guy looks didn't change. Then his cousin, Rennie said, "Hey Casper." And they all thought that was hilarious. After that they were friendlier. And the nickname stuck.

Louis wanted to move closer to his new job so he suggested we get an apartment together.

"Hey man," I said. "I probably won't be staying in Austin too long. I want to make some cash, buy a car, and get back on the road."

"No more hitching, huh," Louis said with a grin.

"Nope," I said.

"I don't care how long you're here, Casper. It's cool."

We found a two-bedroom apartment down the street from his brother and Tereza. We decorated it in Early Salvation Army. In my bedroom I had a queen-sized mattress on the floor and an empty wine box for a nightstand. In the living room Louis had a paint-splattered Radio Shack boombox that served as our entertainment center. It was quite the bachelor pad.

During the several calls I'd made to my parents since leaving with Maggie, I'd told them that I was traveling around the west, taking in the sights. I hadn't told them that I stopped in Austin.

When I called them in August and my mother started reminding me about all the things I had to do to get ready for my senior year of college, it sort of plopped out of my mouth. I hadn't made a hard, fast decision about it yet. It just happened in the moment.

"Well, you know, Mom," I said. "I'm in Austin, Texas, now."

"Oh, that's nice. How long will it take you to get home?"

"I'm learning a lot here," I said, "about people and life. It's the kind of stuff not covered in a business school curriculum. The American dream is different for these people."

"Good for you," Mom said cheerfully. "Last week your father told me that he spoke with Craig Rall, a friend of his in New York, about setting up an interview for you in the spring."

"Mom—"

"I can't remember which ad agency he's with. It's one of the big ones."

"I've decided not to go back to school."

For a brief moment all I could hear was her breathing. Then the telephone erupted into a fiery barrage of profanity, the likes of which I'd never heard from my mother. She wanted me to come home immediately.

"Mom, I'm twenty-one years old and capable of making my own decisions."

She laughed, and put my father on the telephone. His expletive assault, though grittier and more rectally oriented, equaled my mother's in both its volume and duration.

"Get your ass on the next bus east!" he concluded forcefully.

"Goodbye, Dad," I said, and hung up the telephone.

I got a job as a bartender in the Longhorn Grill. It was the most popular restaurant in the hotel. I began making great tips and my lifestyle changed dramatically. Up to that point I had been taking the bus to work or bumming rides off of Ernesto and Louis. With my new prosperity, I purchased a used Honda 350 motorcycle. A month earlier, I'd begun having a recurring dream about a rough-looking, leather-clad guy wearing mirror sunglasses and driving a Harley Davidson Sportster. I figured the dream was a sign that I was supposed to get a motorcycle.

After buying the Honda, I decided to work two more months at the hotel. I would save as much money as I could, then hit the road for California. Six weeks later, after a late-night ride through the streets of Austin, I came home to find Louis in the kitchen eating out of a pint of chocolate ice cream.

"Casper," he said, "my cousin Rennie got killed tonight. Some fuckin' dickhead threw a brick off the overpass in Delwood. Smashed Rennie's windshield and split his head in two."

"Oh, man."

"Yeah."

"Did they get the guy?"

"Not yet. But someone saw him running away."

"Louis, man, I'm sorry."

Louis tossed the empty carton in the trash can next to the stove. He dropped the spoon in the sink and leaned back against the counter.

"Two seconds earlier or two seconds later, the brick fucks up the car but not Rennie's brains. That's some split-second shit there."

"Is your Aunt Sofia freaking out?"

"That's a stupid question. Of course she is. But tomorrow we're gonna go see Eldora. Auntie will feel better after she talks with Rennie."

"What do you mean?"

"Eldora is a bruja. Witch doctor. Healer. She talks with spirits."

"No shit? How does she do that?"

"With her kitchen table."

"Are you serious?"

"Yep. You want to check it out?"

"Absolutely."

Eldora Aguilar lived in a nondescript tract house north of town. Her assistant, a heavyset platinum blonde named Valerie, greeted us warmly in a breathy, lilting voice, resonating both her proclivity to the ethereal and a childhood spent in Brooklyn.

"Hello everyone. Welcome. Please come in."

In the living room, large doilies lined the back of an olive-green corduroy couch. On the mantle above the fireplace and on the coffee table, two clear plastic bowls overflowed with an assortment of hard candies.

"Eldora will be out shortly," Valerie said, before disappearing to the back of the house. Louis's mother Ireta and his Aunt Sofia sat on the couch. Ireta was a year older than her sister, but the two of them could have passed for identical twins. They wore their hair in the same bobbed cut and their broad noses and dark eyes mirrored each other exactly. Sofia's fuller figure was the defining difference between them.

Aunt Sofia began rocking back and forth on the couch. She moaned and dabbed an embroidered handkerchief to her tear-swollen eyes. Louis's cousins, Connie and Isabel, went back and forth from one dish of candy to the other. After five minutes or so, Valerie returned.

"Eldora will see you now," she said.

As she ushered us into the kitchen, I caught the faint smell of onions and bacon. Seated at a wooden drop-leaf table next to the window was Eldora. I did a double take. *This* was a native healer? Where were the blazing dark eyes I envisioned and the cascade of long white hair? Where were the crystals and mojo beads around her neck? She was as plump and pasty as the Pillsbury Doughboy. Crushing my preconceived image even further was the faint pink hue in her hair. She looked like someone's grandmother.

"Buenos dias. Sorry for making you wait," Eldora said in a husky voice. She stuck her left leg out from under the table. "Look at that. My ankles are so swollen today."

Connie and Isabel hurried to Eldora and hugged her. Connie immediately started crying. Eldora stroked her hair.

"Little sister, Eldora loves you," she said. She reached into her pocket and pulled out a piece of hard candy. Connie sniffled back her tears.

"Come and sit," Eldora said.

Louis nudged me forward. "Mrs. Aguilar, this is a friend of mine."

"Hello," I said. "I'm Tom."

"Welcome to my home," she said. She reached out her hand. I shook it, feeling the leathery dryness of her skin. She held my hand for a long moment looking in my eyes. Apparently satisfied with what she saw, she nodded somberly.

"Pull up a chair," she said. "Rennie is anxious to talk to his mother."

Aunt Sofia seated herself across the table from Eldora as the rest of us pulled up folding chairs Valerie had brought in.

Eldora closed her eyes and took a deep breath. She let it out in one long wheezing exhale. Without opening her eyes, she nodded to Aunt Sofia, who placed her hands palms-down on the table. Eldora then lifted her hands from her lap and placed them on the table.

"Jesus, please come into the table," she said.

The end of the table lifted up. My mouth fell open as I watched the forty-five-pound table rise up on two legs and nudge itself into Aunt Sofia's bulging midriff.

"He's hugging you," Eldora said.

A wracking sob burst from Aunt Sofia as the end of the table snuggled against her belly.

"That-a-girl. Don't hold it in," Eldora said, as Aunt Sofia began to wail. Ireta broke down and began crying. Connie and Isabel hugged each other. Louis lowered his head and stared into his lap. I started looking for wires.

This is not possible, I thought to myself. I leaned forward, elbows on my knees, trying as discreetly as I could to look under the table. I saw nothing. Above the table, a light hung from the ceiling. There didn't appear to be anything up there either. I was dumbfounded.

"He wants you to know that you are loved and appreciated for giving your son a beautiful life."

Aunt Sofia nodded. With one hand still on the table she wiped her eyes with the handkerchief. The table slid back and leveled itself.

"Thank you, dear one," Eldora said.

"Muchas gracias," Sofia said, lovingly caressing the table.

Louis nudged me in the ribs. His eyebrows bobbed up and down. "Crazy, huh?"

"Come on, my sweet one," Eldora said, "You can do it."

I turned back to the table. It creaked and shuddered. Eldora was intently staring at the center of the table. She gestured for me to come forward. She took my hand and held it three inches above the center of the table. The air was ice cold.

"Spirit exists in zero degrees," she said.

I nodded and walked back to my chair, more dazed than before. As soon as I sat down, the table rattled six inches across the floor, jamming itself against Aunt Sofia.

"Wait, wait dear one. You have to identify yourself."

The table obediently slid back to a neutral position between the two women.

"Give me the first letter of your first name," Eldora said. I looked at Louis to get a hint of what this meant. He motioned for me to watch.

The end of the table in front of Eldora rose up two inches and began tapping up and down on the floor.

". . . d,e,f,g,h,i,j . . ." Eldora was counting off letters for every tap on the floor that the table made. When it got to the letter r, it stopped. Sofia clutched her hand to her chest.

"Give us the second letter of your first name," Eldora said, with a serene smile. This time the table stopped tapping when it reached the letter e. This procedure was repeated until on the last e, Sofia cried out, "Rennie!"

Under their hands, the table clattered up and down, rocking from one leg to the next, and sliding around on the linoleum floor. Eldora chuckled. "He's glad to see you."

The table nestled against Aunt Sofia, gently rocking back and forth. When Connie and Isabel moved to the table and put their hands on it, the table tipped up to them, gently nudging against their stomachs. The table dropped to the floor and began tapping out another message.

C, I, love R. The two girls grinned.

"We love you too, Rennie," Isabel said. "Say hi to Grandma for us."

I was amazed. Eldora must have seen the look on my face.

"Jesus, come into the table with Rennie," she said. "Help him make it strong."

The table went still for a moment. Then the end that was under Aunt Sofia's hands rose up until the legs were six inches off the ground.

Eldora turned to me and said, "Push on it."

I hesitated. Louis shoved me out of my seat. "Do it," he said.

My rational mind was unhinged. Here was an inanimate object partially suspended in the air. The lords of gravity must have taken the afternoon off. I reached out and touched the table. It felt like a wooden table. I pushed against the raised end. It didn't move.

"Harder," Eldora said.

I leaned onto it this time and still it wouldn't budge.

"Lower, dear ones," Eldora said to the table.

"This is great," Louis said from behind me.

The table slowly lowered itself so that the two raised legs were only an inch off of the floor.

"Push on it again," Eldora said.

This time I put both hands on the end of the table and leaned all of my one hundred sixty-five pounds on it. It didn't give. I couldn't get it to touch the ground. I shook my head and stepped back. The table leaned toward me.

"He wants to touch you," Eldora said.

"Who does?" I asked, with a harder edge than I intended.

"Don't be such a chicken. Go closer," Louis said.

I reluctantly stepped forward. The table tilted, pressing against my thighs. I felt a tingling, fuzzy surge of energy. The table dropped to the floor and tapped out a message.

Casper, dead is not dead.

For the next week, my brain was like a blown fuse box. All of my intellectual theories and teenage musings about energy and other dimensions paled in comparison to what I'd experienced in Eldora's kitchen. Life beyond this reality was a reality. Of course, the skeptic in me had to have its say. It fought valiantly, pointing out that the thoughts of Aunt Sofia and the others had somehow been tapped into. Even if that were the case, I reasoned, something had moved the table. A powerful force had communicated clearly, intelligently, with humor and emotion. If it wasn't actually Rennie's spirit, it didn't matter. Something was out there. Someone was listening.

My lingering doubts about coming west with Maggie vanished. The blue heron had not steered me wrong after all. The big picture was being revealed.

7

I SPENT LONG HOURS riding my motorcycle around town, trying to assimilate what I witnessed in Eldora's kitchen. On the University of Texas campus, complicating my thoughts even further, I sat in the grass below the tower where years earlier Charles Whitman had gunned down twelve people and wounded thirty-three others. I wondered if, on that hot day in August, any of those students had a premonition of their fate. *Had their spirit guides or dead relatives tried to warn them? Was that sort of thing allowed? Were there cosmic, or whatever, spiritual laws about interceding in the lives of humans?*

To distract myself from the constant barrage of questions filling my head, I began frequenting the bars near the campus. I'd drink a few beers, remind myself that there was no real death, then pop wheelies and ride my motorcycle with no hands. It was on one of those crazy nights that I met Lilly. She was two years older, and a graduate student in Asian studies. She was petite, with curly brown hair to her shoulders and blue eyes the color of a swimming pool. There was a stillness about her that pulled me in. Even sweating on the dance floor with a bottle of Lone Star in her hand, she projected a peaceful, beatific serenity.

After leaving the bar, we talked all night in a corner booth at Denny's. Just before dawn, we went for a ride on the Honda. Watching the sun come up from a hilltop southeast of town, we held each other to stay warm. It was the first time in my life that I'd watched the sunrise with a woman in my arms. We dated furiously after that. Louis fell in love with her too. Every time she'd come to the apartment, he'd put on slow sexy music and try to dance with her.

After we'd been seeing each other for three weeks, Lilly and I got drunk one night on margaritas at Hector's Adobe, a Tex-Mex place. I ended up telling her about the blue heron and Maggie, and how I'd made my way to Austin. Much to my surprise, she didn't think I was a weirdo. Even when I explained to her about Eldora and the table, she didn't roll her eyes and laugh at me. Having read about the mystical traditions of the world's religions, she accepted what I'd experienced as a part of who I was.

Lilly introduced me to the literature of her master's curriculum in Asian studies. She taught me how to mediate. She encouraged me to become vegetarian. She showed me that discipline in my personal habits could result in spiritual growth.

On a Saturday morning at the beginning of December, I was watching the news on Lilly's TV. Pissed-off farmers from Virginia and Maryland had driven their tractors and trucks to Washington, DC, to protest the economic conditions threatening their way of life. Blocking intersections and snarling traffic, they moved toward the capital in columns stretching for miles. Signs strapped to the outside of their vehicles criticized president Carter for the job he was doing:

> Spring has sprung, fall has fell
> Carter went to Washington
> and farming went to HELL!

Another one read:

> Jimmy's a good ole boy. But there's

no place in Washington for boys. We
need men.

"If the farmers are going out of business," I called to Lilly, "who's going to feed us?"

She came out of her bedroom carrying a book. "Corporate America wants the farms. They want to control the food supply."

"That's not good," I said. "Maybe I should be a farmer."

She turned off the television.

"Hey," I said. "I was watching that."

"I have something to show you." She sat down next to me and handed me a book. "Turn to chapter six."

The title of the book was *Taoism*. I flipped the pages until I found the chapter. *Sexual Practices*. I looked at Lilly.

"Don't get weird on me," she said. "It's really interesting."

"How many positions do I need to know?"

"This isn't about positions. It's better than that."

"Tell me."

"Okay," she said. "The Chinese believe there are circuits of ch'i, life force, which circulate through the human body." She paused, looking at me for a long moment. "It's developing control of this ch'i which enables a man to make love without ejaculating."

I waited for her to break into a smile and tell me it was a joke. She didn't.

"In pursuit of health and longevity," she said, "which is highly revered by Taoists, men engage in the practice of retaining their seed."

"Retaining the – that's ridiculous," I said. "What's the point of having sex?"

"Taoists believe that a man's semen contains his vital essence. Throwing it away every time he has sex is self-destructive. It leads to degenerative disease, aging, and premature death."

"What?" I said, fighting hard to keep from laughing. "Guys can screw themselves to death? That sounds like a bunch of bullshit to me."

"Don't get defensive."

"Jesus, Lilly! You've already taken away my meat now you want my orgasms?"

"You still have them."

"What!"

"Yeah, partners channel their sexual energy throughout their bodies and then circulate it back and forth between each other. This leads to an orgasm without releasing precious life force energy."

For us it led to long, sweaty nights of practice, practice, practice. I was horrible at first. She'd be on top, slowly thrusting against me, whispering in my ear, "Breathe, baby. Pull all that energy up your spine. Bring it up to your crown chakra and then down. Let it flow into me." I'd nod like I was paying attention when actually all I was thinking about was how sexy she was, and how good her ass felt, and her lips and tongue and nipples and – oh baby, baby, please baby! The next thing I knew she'd be yelling, "No! Not yet! Save it! Save it!"

It took us a while, but I finally began to get the hang of it. I was a remedial student at best. I don't know about living longer or any of that, but it sure felt good. Who would've thought that kind of endurance could be sustained on a diet of vegetables, rice, bean sprouts, and miso soup. In the morning we'd drag ourselves down to the kitchen for a breakfast of granola and ginseng tea. Looking up from his bowl of Captain Crunch, Louis would give Lilly long lecherous smirks and ask her if she'd slept well.

It was clear to me that Lilly, like Eldora, was a teacher for me. I was both grateful and eager to know more. I wanted to forge a trust in something beyond our convoluted man-made world. I wanted to feel the truth, the absolute truth of something. The suburbs and TV culture that had been my generation's hollow inheritance wasn't enough for me. I needed a greater purpose than seeking profit for profit's sake.

I gave myself over to what Lilly had to share with me. Under her tutelage I began to study the religions of the world. I started with Zen Buddhism, Confucianism, and Hinduism. Then I moved to Judaism, Christianity, and Islam. I read about Jesus, Buddha, and Confucius; enlightened men who taught of the power to be found in kindness, compassion, and wisdom. From the Bhagavad-Gita I learned: "He who performs his task dictated by duty, caring nothing for the fruit of the action, he is a yogi." I began bowing to the man behind the counter at the laundry. I served cold sodas to the dishwashers at the hotel. I treated Lilly like a goddess: buying flowers, communicating my feelings, and doing my best to retain my seed. I was even able to watch Lilly and Louis dance a samba together without getting jealous. At the same time that I was doing all of this, and meditating every day, and eating highly energetic foods, and striving to attain an enlightened sense of who and what I was, I'd catch myself staring at some woman's breasts wondering what she looked like naked. I'd try to stop myself but I couldn't. That mutant Neanderthal, that old humping I-want-to-fuck-everything-in-sight-to-keep-the-species-alive beast was still ratcheted to my sensibilities. Where was the enlightenment and wisdom in that? What kind of compassion did that part of me possess? I wondered if I was alone in my schizophrenia, so I headed back to the library. Most religions spoke of a mystical origin of man. I didn't want any more of that hocus-pocus. I wanted the exact gritty truth of how I had become the way I was. I'd gotten a sense of my scaly beginnings that night on the beach with Maggie; the emergence from the sea, the first strangled breaths of oxygen, but what came after that? What else percolated along the twists and turns of my DNA? I turned to anthropology.

I discovered Australopithecus africanus, Homo habilis, Homo erectus, and Cro-Magnon. These guys were my brethren, my long lost marrow-sucking, cave-dwelling ancestors. I read about Louis, Mary, and Richard Leakey hunting down the past, unscrambling the riddle of our masterful evolution: the raising of the cranium to accommodate a bigger brain, the new brain, the neocortex, striving to exert control, going one on one with our deeply buried, quick to aggression survival instincts, the reduction in the size of the molar teeth, the decreased protrusion of the jaw, 100,000 years of cultural refinements, and bingo – Homo sapiens, the dominant species on the planet.

What did all this information mean to me? It was a confirmation of sorts. I finally understood why I was so confused. All of my life not only had I been wading through my parents emotional hand-me-downs, plus the trembling pull of God which filled my heart, took my breath away, and baffled the shit out of me, but there was also this hairy-footed, drag-down-a-deer-and-eat-it-raw, primal man within me who reared his festering, stinking head from time to time bellowing, sex, food, shelter, sex, food, shelter, sex, sex, sex! With all of those influences yanking at me, how was I to function in any kind of a reasonable manner? Depending on my parents or friends or, heaven forbid, the government, to show me the way, was insane. They didn't have the answers. Hell, they couldn't even recognize the questions.

I called Eldora. I needed to know the truth. I was Thomas Emery McInnes. I was born in Pittsburgh, Pennsylvania, son of Merna and Richard. I was descended from Scottish immigrants, and before that a long line of hairy, butt-scratching apes, and a slimy lizard or two. But who was I beyond the identity that my family and genetics had passed on to me?

When Valerie told me that I should come by Eldora's house at four o'clock the following day, I was ecstatic. I arrived an hour early, and drove around the block going over the questions I wanted to ask.

Eldora moved slowly as she came down the hallway from the back of the house. I helped her into her chair at the table.

"What I experienced here has really affected me," I said.

"Spirit has a way of doing that to people."

"There is so much I want to know."

"Put your hands on the table, and we'll get started."

My palms were sweating as I laid them on the white table top. This is it, I told myself. This is the moment I've been waiting for.

Eldora placed her hands on the table. Immediately her end of the table lifted. A gentle surge of energy flowed into my hands. Then the table legs began banging loudly on the floor.

"Slowly, dear one," Eldora said gently. The table eased back, but continued tapping out a message.

The first word was, *go*.

"Okay," I said. "Excellent. That's specific."

The second word was, *back*.
Go back.
The third word was, *to*.

Go back to. Go back to where? What? My mind hummed through a variety of options as the table continued to tap on the floor.

The fourth word was, *college*.

"Go back to college," Eldora said.

I looked over at her. "Huh?"

"That's your message. Go back to college."

The table immediately nudged up against my stomach. I stared down at it in disbelief.

"Go back to college? Did we get a wrong number? I was looking for something a bit more, I don't know, profound."

The table began tapping on the floor again. It gave two letters, GG, and then stopped. It slowly tipped up and gently touched me. Familiar warmth spread through my chest. I stretched my arms out on the table. It snuggled closer to me. My eyes got wet.

"Grandma is that you."

The table pressed harder against my belly.

"She's hugging you." Eldora said.

"I used to call her Gram Gram, when I was a kid."

"She's happy to see you," Eldora said.

I rubbed the table. "Gram, you look good in maple."

The table rocked back and forth.

"She liked that one," Eldora said, smiling.

"Wait until I tell Mom that I talked with you," I said to the table.

The table began tapping again. This time it moved gently.

My secret. Tell her when time is right.

"Okay," I said. "It would probably freak her out anyway. So Gram, give me some scoop. Tell me how it all works: God, angels, my soul, the whole thing."

The table began tapping. When it finally stopped, I couldn't help but laugh. Gram was never one to mince words.

I'm dead. I'm not god.

The table jiggled, nudged twice against my stomach, and then went still.

"She's gone." Eldora said. She took her hands off the table and started to get up.

"Hey," I said. "Wait a minute. There's more I want to know."

She turned away from me. "You got what you need." She shuffled across the kitchen. "It was a pleasure seeing you again, Tom." She rounded the corner and started down the back hallway. "Have some candy on your way out."

I was disappointed at not being able to ask more questions, but Eldora was right. The directness, warmth, and sense of humor were all so specifically Gram, I couldn't deny that it was her. Her spirit, or whatever, her energy, had somehow used that wooden table to communicate with me. But, *go back to college?* Was that really the next step on my journey?

That night, with Lilly sweetly asleep in my arms, I had a dream.

The unshaven man on the Harley Davidson, the one I'd been dreaming about off and on for the past several months, roared in through the doors of the hotel bar. Tables toppled over, glasses crashed to the floor, and a cloud of exhaust filled the room. He turned to me, his mirror sunglasses reflecting my startled expression.

"What are you some kind of weenie boy," he snarled. "Get your ass movin'!"

I woke up with a phrase from the Koran running over and over in my mind: "Those who believed left their homes and strove for the cause of Allah – those are the believers in truth."

I lay there, staring into the predawn gloom. It was time for me to leave. I looked at Lilly sleeping next to me. Her sweet face . . .

When she woke up I told her about the dream.

"Oh," she said.

"It's just a dream."

"The Koran thing . . ."

"I know, pretty specific."

She looked into my eyes. Neither of us spoke for a minute.

"I don't want to hold you back," she said. "I don't want to be that person in your life."

I pulled her into my arms. "You aren't holding me back. You're amazing. Without you I wouldn't be where I am. You teach me a lot."

She caressed my face. "The ghost of the desert is being called."

I shook my head. "No."

She held my face in both of her hands. "The path is the path. Your journey is your journey."

"You want me to go?"

"No, but come on, you've had some pretty remarkable experiences moving you along in your life."

"It's just a dream, Lilly."

"Casper, do you really believe that?"

She waited for my response. As much as I wanted to lie, I couldn't.

"No."

"Okay then."

So that was it.

After a raucous farewell dinner of enchiladas, grilled halibut, and chocolate ice cream, I said goodbye to Louis, Ernesto, and Tereza. I packed a few essentials into my duffel bag, and left the rest for Louis to give away or keep for his next roommate. I drove Lilly to her apartment on the back of my motorcycle.

Without spilling a drop of my vital essence, we made love all night. The energy flowed back and forth between us. It was gentle and tender, then hot and magnetic. The intimacy and vulnerability carried us into a steamy cocoon. It felt as if we were literally glued together. At four in the morning, when we finally stopped, I was tingling with energy but physically exhausted. Lilly spooned around me and held me.

"Casper, you've become a Taoist master."

We both laughed.

"Thanks for being a patient teacher, Lilly."

"My pleasure, really."

I rolled over and pulled her into my arms.

"I wish I didn't have to leave," I said.

"Oh, stop it. You can't wait to get on the road."

She kissed me, gently biting my lower lip. "It's going to be very exciting. Not as exciting as this, but . . ."

We held each other. Her breath was soft on the side of my neck.

"I'll miss you, Lilly," I said.

"I'll miss you too, Casper."

"I love you."

I think she was surprised. I never said that before.

"Wow," she finally said. And then we were quiet again.

The last thing I remembered before falling asleep was the feeling of her hand resting on my chest. It was warm and comforting. I felt safe.

8

AUNT HELEN'S HOUSE WAS on Alder Street in an artsy, upscale section of town called Shadyside. It was a brick three story in the middle of the block with a wide front porch wrapping around the left side. Aunt Helen had lived there for fifty-eight years. The first twenty-two were with her husband John Heinrich. After lung cancer took him in 1958, she'd shared the house for the next thirty-six years with her cats. First was Ripper, a monstrous Siamese who used to hiss and back me into corners when I was a kid. He lived for eighteen years despite my prayers for his quick demise. Tonka, a cuddly gray tabby, who loved everyone including the German shepherd across the street, only lasted a couple of years. One afternoon the shepherd got tired of playing and turned Tonka into lunch. Aunt Helen's current feline companion was Terry. Named after Terry Bradshaw, the great quarterback for the Pittsburgh Steelers, Terry the cat was all white, with one green eye and one brown one. At sixteen, he moved around fairly well. The only problem was he was completely deaf. At Aunt Helen's house it was important to keep your eyes open and watch where you were going. In his bubble of silence, Terry would walk right in front of you. If you accidentally kicked him or stepped on him, he'd get the most insulted look in his eyes. So would Aunt Helen.

"I'll take the one with the orange cap on it," she called from her sitting room.

In the refrigerator there were four plastic bottles of fresh juices. Every morning, she would stand in front of her industrial strength juicer, and grind up celery, apples, carrots, beets, and anything thing else she was in the mood for. I'd gotten her started on it back when I had my own juice company in Boulder, Colorado. Aunt Helen claimed that the juice helped keep her brain working. Who was I to argue? At ninety-four, she was more lucid than half the people I knew.

I found the bottle with the orange cap and poured its contents into a glass. It was thick and pulpy. I grabbed a bottle of Rolling Rock from the bottom shelf. The beer was there strictly for visitors. Aunt Helen never drank a beer in her life. She'd bang down one or two manhattans when she was in the mood, but never a beer. Drinking beer wasn't ladylike, she once told me.

When I returned with the drinks, Aunt Helen was in her easy chair next to the front window, cleaning her glasses with a tissue. Her white hair, short and wispy, was flat on the left side where she'd slept on it. She was wearing the Pittsburgh Steelers Super Bowl sweatshirt that Becky gave her in 1975. The logo on the front was completely faded except for one E and the bottom half of an L.

"Oh, this is good," she said, sipping the juice. "Makes my blood do a dance."

The sweatshirt hung loose over her arms and her cheeks seemed to have hollowed out. The stray hairs on her upper lip were an odd new addition. Maybe she hadn't had enough time to do her bathroom duties.

She put down her glass, and any concerns I had about her health quickly faded when she reached over and whacked me on the knee. She was still strong.

"So, what are you doing home at this time of year?" she asked.

"I missed you," I said, and gave her a big smile.

She pointed her index finger at me and shook it. "You weren't a good liar as a child, and you haven't improved."

"I'm on my way to Pomona."

"Back to that, huh?"

"Yep."

"You still didn't answer my question."

I fidgeted in my seat. "I'm broke. I decided to live at Mom and Dad's until I can put some money together."

"Oh, that should be interesting. How's your father handling it?"

"He's okay."

"It'll be good to have you two under the same roof."

"Yeah, right."

"It takes a lot of energy for me to irritate him and keep him on his toes. With you around, I won't have to work so hard."

"Glad to help out."

Aunt Helen laughed. She had a great laugh, deep from her belly. She pulled another tissue from the pocket of her corduroys. Pushing her glasses off the bridge of her nose, she dabbed at her eyes.

"It's good to have you home, Tommy."

Over lunch, I told her about buying my truck from the soap opera actor, and the drive from New York to Pittsburgh. I didn't mention the incident at my garden plot. That kind of thing would only upset her.

When she finished eating, she folded her hands in her lap and turned to the warm sun streaming in the window. The light shone across her face, highlighting her strong profile. As a tenured English professor at the University of Pittsburgh, she had undoubtedly turned the head of many a student and faculty member.

"So Thomas, what's the next adventure?"

I shook my head. "My life is a mystery to me."

"What fun would it be if you knew everything?"

Terry jumped into her lap. She rubbed him behind the ears. As I watched, something a friend of mine once said popped into my head. Duane was a chemistry major, and one of the brightest guys I knew during my years at Penn State. He used to get drunk on

Southern Comfort and pretend to be Confucius. During one of our out of control weekend drinking binges, he'd offered up this sage wisdom for the night: "The man who knows not where to go, knows not where he's going. But the man who always knows which way to go, is one boring motherfucker." To think that Duane was now working for Dow Chemical, helping to create products that affect our daily lives, was at best disconcerting.

"I'm happy to see that you're inspired to do *something*," Aunt Helen said. "You were stuck in a dark place for far too long."

"You're right," I said, thinking back on the bleakness of the last few years in New York. "Seeking truth can be a risky business."

Aunt Helen smiled and patted my knee. "I know you've been through a lot. But what an exciting life you've had."

"Yep," I said, pushing a smile at her. "And now I'm back. I'm on the road again."

"The world can rest easier," Aunt Helen said.

"Indeed," I said. "Thomas McInnes, truth-seeker extraordinaire, is once again on the job."

We laughed, and she reached over and took my hand.

"So what's your plan?"

"I don't have one. Planning isn't what I do best."

Aunt Helen sighed. "That's from your Scottish side, because the Germans on your mother's side were all planners. My grandfather used to say, 'Tomorrow is the future. What are you going to do about it?'"

"Didn't he die young of a heart attack?"

Aunt Helen wagged her finger at me. "It's time for you to settle down. Meet a nice girl."

"Don't worry about me."

"I can't help it," she said, with resigned smile. "It's what I do best."

I was halfway out the front door when I remembered the man Becky had seen on the front porch. "Aunt Helen," I said, "what about the guy who was peeking in your window? Do you want me to talk to the police?"

"Don't meddle in my business," she said, and shut the door.

• • •

IN THE SHORT TIME THAT I'd been back in Pittsburgh, I'd made little effort to look up any of my old friends. I did leave a message for Kirby Wynkowski at his office. He was my best friend growing up, and the only guy I'd kept in touch with over the years. I asked his secretary, Nancy, to let him know that I was spending time with my folks, and that I'd get together with him soon. I guess I felt a little strange. What was I going to say, "Hi, how are you? I'm broke and I'm living with my parents again."

I spent my time searching for a job, storing my things in their garage, and helping around the house. At night, my parents and I would hang out and watch television together. It wasn't that I was especially interested in sitting around all night staring at the glowing box, but that's what they did. Since they had been kind enough to allow me to live there, I felt I should spend time with them.

One night, my mother and father and I were lined up on the couch like a trio of those bobble-headed dogs you used to see in the rear windows of cars. At nine o'clock, they started arguing about which show they wanted to watch. Dad loved *The Streets of San Francisco*. Mom wanted to watch *Magnum P.I.* For five minutes, I listened to them debate the finer points of each series. What made it even more ridiculous was that they had cable. Ninety-nine channels to choose from, and all they ever watched, besides ESPN and a few cooking shows, were reruns of old television series. The VCR Rick gave them for Christmas had become a dust magnet.

In the middle of my father's dissertation on the finer points of Karl Mauldin's comedic timing, my mother gave up the fight. She rose quickly and silently, coffee cup in hand. As she walked out of the room, she shot Dad a look. It wasn't just any look. It was The Look. Regarded by many, or at least by me, as being the Germanic equivalent of the Vulcan death grip, The Look would have instantly killed any bachelor. Flesh would have been seared from the bones. My father, with forty-two years of marriage under his belt, didn't even flinch. He'd had decades to perfect his armor. For every chink and soft spot, he had two or three elaborate backup plans. On the anvil of marriage he had been tempered to such a fine edge that aimed at him, blistering looks were like shooting BBs at a tank.

As soon as my mother left the room to go upstairs and watch the TV in their bedroom, a look of satisfaction spread across my father's face. The thought entered my mind that we should staff our armed forces exclusively with men and women who had experienced 25 years of marriage or more. That policy, in my estimation, would result in the toughest, most resilient fighting unit on the planet. Whatever they'd lost in physical stamina would be more than made up for in cunning. Knowing only too well the psychological jigsaw puzzle of survival, they could easily withstand the trauma of battle, and keep on going. Then again, maybe it wasn't all married couples, maybe it was just my parents.

To the victor goes the prize. Dad reached over and grabbed the remote control. He flipped through the channels until he spotted Michael Douglas and Karl Mauldin in a car racing down a steep hill. He put his feet up on the coffee table.

"Your mother likes that fancy red car Magnum drives."

"It's a Ferrari, I think."

"He's not a bad actor. But he wears those silly shorts all the time. They ought to put him in some different clothes."

Michael Douglas jumped out of the car and drew his pistol. Karl Mauldin ran, or more accurately hobbled across the street.

"I'm sure the women love seeing him like that."

My father folded his arms across his broad barrel-chest. "That might be, but it doesn't mean I want to listen to your mother go on and on about him."

I realized then that my father didn't dislike *Magnum P.I.*, he just couldn't bear to hear my mother fawning over Tom Selleck.

Later that night, after watching the news, I took them out to get frozen yogurt. There was a shop over in Pine Creek Plaza that was open until midnight.

"Pitching for the Astros this afternoon is Rick McInnes." Dad chuckled at his bad impression of a sports announcer. He pointed at the little league field across the highway from the Yoo Yoo Frozen Yogurt stand. "Remember going to that place?"

"Yeah," I said.

"I was there for the last game Rick played," my father said. "He struck out four, and in the ninth inning hit a single up the middle. Robby what's-his-name stole third, then little Gary Havers looped a double into right to win it for Rick."

"I missed that one," I said.

"You missed a lot of them," Mom said.

Inside the yogurt shop the jukebox was blaring Bob Seger's "Old Time Rock & Roll." The yogurt flavors were listed on a brightly lit menu hanging over the counter. I quickly decided on peanut butter fudge. I looked over at my father. He was still scanning the options. His eyes moved from item to item, methodically considering the pros and cons of each of them. I turned to my mom. She'd already made up her mind. She was digging through her purse, probably checking to see if she had a cigarette to smoke after we'd eaten.

Her hair was almost as white as Dad's now. For a few years she had it dyed, but then stopped. It wasn't worth the effort she said. My father was taller than my mother by almost a foot. His back, broad and fleshy under his white, button-down, dress shirt, was ramrod straight. Proper posture, he'd told me during my early slumping years, was the trademark of a good soldier. As I looked at them, it was obvious to me that Mom had gained some girth. Not much, but enough to lower her center of gravity and make her look shorter than she was. She dressed in loose fitting clothes in an effort to hide the added pounds, but standing behind her the real story was there for all to see.

The teenage girl behind the counter handed my father their cups of yogurt. I stepped forward to pay for it. With dessert in hand, I followed my parents outside to one of the picnic tables.

There was no denying it. I came from those two bodies. They gave me my circuitry, the system through which I experienced my life. The nerves, metabolism, eyesight; the physical machinery that was my body, I inherited from them. I let a spoonful of peanut-butter fudge yogurt slowly melt in my mouth. Out on Route 19, an eighteen-wheeler rumbled past heading north. I had spent a long time, and traveled a lot of miles, trying to untangle myself from my parents. They raised me, imprinting me with their love, behavior, and neurosis; downloading it into me like a computer. After years of pushing into dark corners and psychologically tenuous places, I'd finally come to the realization that I wasn't only the product of my mother and father, there were greater forces at work. Human beings weren't simply biological organisms. We had evolved into creatures of extraordinary intellectual depth and emotional and spiritual complexity.

Out of the corner of my eye I saw my father shift his weight. He lifted the right cheek of his ass as the dull groan of a fart punctured the air. My mother rolled her eyes, and looked away. My father; who as a fullback had led the conference in rushing his senior year in high school, then fought in the Pacific during World War II, went on to graduate from Cornell University, and then to a highly successful career in advertising; chose, after this gaseous display, to raise his cup of yogurt, toast my mother with it, and giggle like an eight-year-old. As I said, we are creatures of enormous depth and complexity.

9

THE TRUTH WAS, I didn't really have a job waiting for me out west. I'd told my parents that so they wouldn't freak out. If I wanted to get back on the road to Pomona, I needed to make money. After filling out applications at a variety of garden shops and nurseries, I stopped to have lunch at the Eat'n Park on McKnight Road. As I was biting into an avocado and alfalfa sprout sandwich on wheat toast, I heard a familiar voice.

"McInnes!"

I turned around. Standing next to the cash register was my old friend Kirby Wynkowski. With his prodigious belly leading the way, he walked over to my table.

"You owe me twenty bucks, you jag-off," he said, shaking my hand. "I told you the Steelers wouldn't get to the playoffs last year." He sat down in the booth, and immediately grabbed the other half of my sandwich. He took a huge bite, chomped on it for a moment, grimaced in disgust, and then dropped the mangled remains back on my plate.

"Ugh, it's like eating air. How do you live on that kinda crap?"

I looked at his belly pressing against the edge of the table.

"Hey, hey, hey," he said. "You know this isn't from food." He rubbed his stomach, looking at it fondly, as one might gaze upon a small child or a floppy-eared puppy. "I've nurtured this baby with the finest hops the Iron City Brewing Company has to offer." He grinned and took a drink of my iced tea. "So avocado man, I've got to run into you at Eat'n Park? Why have you been in hiding?"

"Keeping a low profile. Hanging out with the folks."

"I forgive you. So what are you doing home? It's not Christmas."

"I'm looking for a job."

"Get-the-fuck-outta-here! You're gonna live in Pittsburgh?"

"At least for a while."

"That's great! I got season tickets for the Pirates! First base line! Man, this is perfect!"

"What's with their new center fielder?"

"He sucks. The guy couldn't catch a fart in a phone booth. Hey, do you want to work at the plant? I can get you something there?"

"What would I be doing?"

"Whatever. I'll figure something out." He slid out of the booth. "Be at my office at nine o'clock tomorrow morning."

"Kirb, I don't plan on sticking around too long."

"There's a surprise. Don't worry about it. The job is yours as long as you want it."

"Thanks. I appreciate it. Say hi to Jeannie and the kids for me."

"The kids . . ." Kirby shook his head. "What a pain in the ass Sam is lately. He's a hormone-crazed maniac. The other two think he's god. They do whatever he tells them. They're driving me nuts."

"The joys of being a parent, huh?"

"Better me than you, right?"

"I didn't say that."

"Yeah, yeah, sure. Listen, I gotta go. I'll see you in the morning. Wear a tie."

"What?"

"Just kidding."

Through the window, I watched him walk out to his Cadillac Seville. Before he even opened the car door he'd pulled out his cell phone and was talking to someone. He was always pushing for the next deal. When we were kids, he had a knack for trading to get the best baseball cards. At sixteen, he was driving a Mustang convertible he weaseled out of someone for practically nothing. After finishing college in three years, due to an independent study program he somehow managed to negotiate with the dean of the business school, he helped his father build, what was a small family dog food business, into Jerome Inc., a twenty-million dollar a year pet care conglomerate. They named it after Saint Jerome, who, upon pulling a thorn from a lion's paw, was rewarded with the grateful lion's lifelong fidelity; which actually sort of mirrored the friendship between Kirby and me. Although we'd already been friends for seven or eight years, after holding his head while he puked massive quantities of Boones Farm Strawberry Wine into the bath tub at Bobby Corsello's house, we hit a fusion point. After that, nothing stood between us. Twenty-seven years we'd known each other. Through Little League, proms, rollin'-and-smokin' 'em on drives to the Jersey shore, his marriage, the birth of his three kids, and gabbing long distance from all of my travels. Now, I was going to be working for him, the guy who vomited on my favorite Puma running shoes when we were fifteen years old. Strange, the circles we make.

My mother and father were outside on the back porch when I got home. My father was reading the newspaper, an empty highball glass next to his chair. My mother was at her portable workbench with the mallard, her newest duck. She'd taken up carving ducks years ago. There were over twenty of her hand painted creations nesting in various nooks and crannies throughout the house. Becky had a theory that Mom's woodcarving was her way of dealing with the legacy of perfection handed down by her mother. "Grandma was a great cook," Becky said. "She was an amazing seamstress, and she could dance beautifully. The ducks are Mom's chosen field of expertise."

"I got a job," I said as the screen door slammed behind me. "I'll be working at Jerome."

My father put down the newspaper. "You're thirty-five years old and you're employed at a dog food plant. Congratulations. I'm so proud of you."

My mother quickly rose to her feet. "What kind of job is it?" she said, attempting to smooth things over.

"Assistant dog bone supervisor?" my father said.

"Have another cocktail, Dad."

"Tommy—" My mother's hand tightened on my arm.

"Don't talk to me that way!" my father growled.

"Let's discuss this inside," my mother said, looking across the yard at Lud Blakely's house.

"If it's a problem, me being here," I said. "I'll leave."

"Go ahead run away," he said. "That's what you're good at."

I turned around and walked into the kitchen. He followed me.

"What do you have to show for your life?" he said. "Where's your career? Where's your family? Christ, you don't have a pot to piss in!"

I whirled around to face him. "What makes you so goddamn special that you think you can criticize everyone else? What have you done with your life? You helped sell diapers! Yippee! You act like that was god's gift to the human race?"

"I made a living! I supported this family!"

"And you were the perfect husband and father too, right?"

"Tommy!" my mother said sharply.

My father's face was crimson. He lifted his beefy right hand and pointed a finger at me.

"Don't point at me." I said. "It's not my fault that you were more interested in figuring out how to make a box of detergent talk to the camera than spending time with your wife and kids."

My father crossed his arms over his chest. "So you're blaming me for your sad, little existence?"

I raised my arms then dropped them to my sides. "No. I'm – Look, you do what you need to do, so do I. Leave it at that."

"At least what I did gave me a sense of purpose and a feeling of accomplishment. I had a career and raised a family. Where has all your roaming around contemplating your navel gotten you? Huh? Alone and back in my house, working at a dog food plant." He twirled his finger in the air.

I walked out of the kitchen and went upstairs.

In my bedroom, I immediately went to the window and crawled out on the roof. Staring up into the sea of blue immediately made me feel better. The first time I'd sought refuge out on the roof, I was seven years old. My father had criticized my mother's lamb chops. When Mom whipped his plate of food into the trash can and told him to fend for himself, Dad immediately began reminding her of all the outstanding meals her mother had prepared. Mom went into hysterics, and I climbed out on the roof. After three hours of intense ruminating on my parents mental and emotional deficiencies, Rick, finally discovering where I was, stuck his head out the window and proceeded to tell me that he'd found a way to stick a piece of gum under his tongue and blow bubbles out of his ass. Mind you, I was not a particularly stupid or gullible child. I did, however, worship the ground Rick walked on. I was not about to miss an opportunity to see my hero perform an act, which if successful, would have put to shame Kelvin Swaney's older brother. The summer before, Greg Swaney strung together six small marbles, swallowed them, and then invited twelve of us into his garage the next morning to watch him defecate onto a paper plate. Wearing the same yellow rubber gloves his mother used to wash the dishes, he pulled from his foul heap of excrement, the entire string of marbles still intact. Instantly, he became a neighborhood legend. After being forced to listen to Kelvin brag about this miraculous feat for over a year, when Rick proposed his bubble blowing demonstration, I was quickly lured from the sanctity of the roof. My parents were lying in wait. My father grabbed me, whacked me on the ass, and told me never to hide out there again. Rick stood on the other side of the room hanging his head. He'd violated a brotherly pact. He'd lowered himself to working undercover for the other side. He spent four dollars of his grass-trimming money on baseball cards and Mallo cups in an effort to regain my trust.

There I was, years later, back on the roof, pissed off and stewing about dear old Dad. It was pitiful. I was a grown man. I'd traveled. I'd had revelations about life and the existence of a multi-dimensional universe. Yet I couldn't have an adult relationship with my father.

I stretched my arms over my head. The heat from the shingles felt good on my shoulder blades. Next door, Lud's golden retriever Maxwell started barking. I thought about the other visits I'd had with my parents over the last fifteen years. It had always been the same thing. I'd come home, put on my best happy face, and leave after four or five days. I was pleased to have seen them, but I was definitely happy to be leaving. Still, I would make the effort to spend holidays with them. Invariably, as that time of year would approach, I'd begin cultivating elaborate fantasies of home: all of us sitting around talking, cups of steaming spiced cider, festive music playing on the stereo, my father building a fire in the fireplace, the pungent stench of his burned hair. But when I got there, it wasn't like that. Tensions would boil over. I wouldn't eat turkey, which was a break from tradition neither of my parents could tolerate. Becky would get pissy when my mother tried to dominate everything in the kitchen. Rick and my father would get drunk in the den and do their bonding ritual of listening to Frank Sinatra records which would make my mother crazy. It wasn't because Rick and Dad both loved Frank and she preferred Tony Bennett, that didn't bother her. It was the volume at which they chose to appreciate Frank. My father, having become well aware of this over the years, derived enormous pleasure from cranking up the stereo and singing, "I've Got You Under My Skin" in a loud, obnoxious voice.

I always wanted my parents to be more loving. I wanted to see my father hold my mother's hand when they walked in the mall. I wanted to see my mother touch him tenderly, to brush her fingers through his thinning white hair, over the bald spot, and have that be just fine. I wanted her to light candles at dinner on Saturday nights, and open a bottle of wine. That was the kind of relationship I wanted for myself. Looking back, I know that was one of the things that kept me going on my journey. I was trying to figure out how to have a kinder, gentler family. For all of my pushing and pulling into and out of relationships over the years, I never stopped hoping for that. My woman was out there somewhere, and along the way, I'd taken some hard knocks trying to find her.

10

MY ASS WAS NUMB when I arrived on my motorcycle in Taos, New Mexico. On top of that, imbedded in my neck, just to the right of my Adam's apple, were the mangled remains of a greenish-black beetle I'd hit traveling 55 miles an hour. Over the seven hundred incredibly beautiful miles from Austin, Texas to Taos, my little Honda 350 rattled my bones and had been blown all over the road by trucks on Interstate 10. When I finally laid my head down on the pillow in the Pueblo Motel, I was asleep before I could turn out the light.

The sky in Taos claimed a part of my soul and danced a jig on my head, all at the same time. It was so big and glorious and blue, that in its presence there was no escaping the truth that I was but a speck in the cosmic order of things. At the same time, the way it arched down, spreading itself low to the ground, azure blue from horizon to horizon, I felt as if I was in the middle of it, connected and vital to the boundless expanse.

It was into this outrageous blue sky that I was staring the next morning, when I stepped in front of the oncoming Toyota. Just before the loud screech of tires I heard someone say, "Hey!" The next thing I knew, I was laying on hot asphalt staring up at a long braid of black hair. It turned above me in tight clockwise circles. At the end of the braid was a small silver clasp in the shape of an eagle. I stared at the silver eagle for what seemed like a long time before the braid finally vanished.

From somewhere above, a male voice softly said, "Damn tourist. Gotta watch where you're going Bro."

Another voice, this one louder, said, "Hey, man, are you okay." I felt a hand on my shoulder.

The soft voice spoke again. "I didn't do anything. The guy walked right in front of me."

"We saw it happen, relax."

"Look at that, he pissed himself."

What seemed like moments later, I was lifted up. I could hear clothing brushing against people's skin. I listened to the wheels of the stretcher creak along the road and the metal against metal scrape as they slid me into the ambulance. The doors banged shut, and the siren began to wail. Just before I blacked out, I felt myself falling through space. I crashed through a darkened barrier and into an ocean of golden light. A moment later, I gently landed on a hillside of orchids. I looked around. Where were Dorothy and Toto? Then I remembered that it was a field of poppies they walked through with the Tin Man, the Scarecrow, and my favorite, the Cowardly Lion. What did the wicked witch say into her crystal ball, something about sleeping? So I did.

11

LABEL SUPERVISOR. THAT WAS my new job title. It was my responsibility to make sure the labels on the dog food cans were straight and properly adhered.

I hadn't been to the plant since we were kids. As Kirby gave me a tour, I could see that they upgraded the old place into a modern marvel of highly sanitized work stations, video game rooms for the employees, and a dining area which served gourmet food at peanut butter and jelly prices. At the center of the facility, overshadowing everything else was the processing plant or mix-o-rama as Kirby fondly referred to it. Dominating the room were three towering stainless stain vats looking like a trio of alien space ships in for a tune up. Burnished steel pipes and tubing leading into and out of the enormous vats snaked along the walls and ceiling. Suspended thirty feet above the floor in a control booth, high-speed computers hummed away like killer bees in a stinging frenzy. This was the Taj Mahal of dog food plants.

Such was the level of pride in the quality of their products, that prominently displayed throughout the facility were elegantly framed lithographs of all seven varieties of Jerome canned dog food: Liver Pate & Eggs, No Soy Vegetarian, Cluckston Delite, Beefy Beef

Tips, Pieces o' Pisces, Surf & Turf, and the original no-nonsense variety for dogs with a simple palate, Just Jerome. The artist producing the lithographs had obviously been influenced by the work of Andy Warhol, native son of the Pittsburgh area. Not unlike Andy's Campbell soup can, the lineup of Jerome dog food cans all had a factual yet whimsical style, effectively inspiring in the observer a breezy, familiar confidence.

"Jerome Inc. cares" Kirby said, as we walked back to his office. "We work hard to produce the finest, most nutritionally balanced dog food in the industry. Pets all over America rely on us for their health and well-being."

"This place is amazing," I said.

"You can work here as long as you want and leave when you're ready," Kirby said. He sealed the deal by taking me to lunch at the Duquesne Club. I ate an order of spots that melted in my mouth.

At ten thirty the next morning, while I was watching thousands of cans of No Soy Vegetarian rattle past, Aunt Helen fell and broke her hip. Terry had walked into the bathroom just as Aunt Helen was towel-drying her hair. It was an unfortunate collision of a deaf cat and a woman without her glasses. The paramedics said Aunt Helen cried all the way to the hospital. It was not the pain of the fracture that left her so distraught. She thought she had hurt Terry.

That evening, I smuggled the old codger into her hospital room. When she saw that Terry was healthy as ever, they stared at each other nose to nose like a couple of long lost pals. When Aunt Helen put him down, Terry curled up next to her on the bed.

My mother, who had already been at the hospital for hours, turned to me and said, "Tommy I really don't think it's a good idea for the cat to be in here. Why don't you—" She suddenly fell silent. I turned to Aunt Helen. As I suspected, she was giving Mom one of her classic stony looks. Although Mom had inherited this ability, and used it all her life, particularly on my father, she still had not found within herself the protective shield needed to save her when The Look was turned against her.

At this exact instant, with Aunt Helen armed and dangerous, my father walked into the room.

"I love the smell of antiseptic in the morning," he announced.

Aunt Helen stared at him for a full ten seconds. Her face was perfectly still. Without taking her eyes off of him, as if she didn't want to miss a moment of his reaction, she leaned to my mother and said, "How do you put up with him?"

My mother, still reeling from The Look, didn't react. My father, his back up armor undoubtedly placed on alert during the drive to the hospital, twisted his smile into a hawkish grin. His jaw jutted forward and he put his hands on his hips. Just then, Terry poked his head over the rumpled blanket, laid back his ears, and hissed loudly. My father reared back in surprise. Aunt Helen giggled, and Terry rewarded himself with a lick between the legs.

Mom, taking the moment to recover from Aunt Helen's Look, straightened the front of her skirt, nervously tapped her navy blue pumps on the floor, and then walked to the side of the bed. She looked down at Aunt Helen.

"Sweetie pie," she said. "The doctors have told me that it would be best if you moved into a nursing home after your surgery."

Aunt Helen didn't react. She continued rubbing Terry's belly.

"You're going need a lot of help with your rehabilitation." Mom said, forcing an optimistic smile. "And we want you up on your feet as soon as possible, right?"

Aunt Helen then did something that surprised me. She looked over at my father and said, "Richard, I want you to handle all the arrangements."

Shocked as I was at her asking him, his reaction surprised me even more.

"Absolutely, Helen," Dad said firmly. "I'd be happy to."

"I hear there's a decent place on Banksville Road," she said. "I don't remember the name of it, but Lois Erhart put her husband in there after he got too wacky for her to take care of. Lois told me they were very kind to him. The food was decent too."

"I'll look into it tomorrow," Dad said, as if it was something he did every day.

Aunt Helen nodded, patted her stomach, and then looked up at me. "How's the job, Tommy," she said, moving on to new business.

"Fine, Aunt Helen. The money is good."

"How is Kirby? I haven't seen him in ages."

"He's put on a lot of weight," Mom said.

"Drinks all that beer," my father said.

"He's a millionaire, he can drink what he wants," Aunt Helen said. She tried to scoot up in the bed but the pain in her hip was too much. Her eyes filled with tears, and she eased herself back down.

"Tomorrow morning I want my juice!" she commanded. "Who's going to take care of that?"

My mother reached down and held Aunt Helen's hand. "I'll be here bright and early with whatever you want, sweetie."

Aunt Helen's stiff upper lip began to quiver. Her narrow chest heaved deeply, and despite her obvious desire not to, she began to cry. Mom gently patted her frail, weathered hand and cried along with her.

My father hung his head, looked out the window, shifted his eyes back to the floor, and picked at his thumbnail. Seeing him squirm made me wonder if it was Aunt Helen's and Mom's display of emotions that bothered him, or if Aunt Helen's situation was an all too real glimpse into his own future of old age and declining health. I would have liked to ask him, but we didn't discuss things like that. As Mom and Aunt Helen continued to cry, Dad, with nowhere else to divert his attention, finally looked over at me. He shrugged his shoulders as if to say, "What can I do?" I shrugged back. We stood there for five minutes like a couple of shulubs until the nurse came in and raised holy hell about the cat.

12

WHEN I WOKE UP in the clinic after my collision with the Toyota, I was handed a medical bill far exceeding the money I was carrying. I could only afford to pay them half of my charges. They reluctantly accepted. As I signed over the travelers checks, I realized that the savings I'd managed to put together in Austin were now nearly gone.

Outside the sun was shining brightly. Shading my eyes with my hand, I searched the parking lot for someone who could give me a ride back to the motel. A Native American, with narrow hips and a broad barrel chest, pushed himself off the front fender of a car parked at the curb and walked over to me.

His face had the wear and tear of a person who spent, not only a lot of time in the sun, but had also taken a few punches over the years. His eyebrows were crisscrossed with scars. A short jagged one on his right cheekbone stood out against his brown skin. His straight black hair hung in a ponytail down his back.

"I'm Emerson Yazzie," he said quietly. "You owe me $126 to fix the dent your head made in the hood of my car." He pointed to the faded, piss-yellow Toyota Corolla sitting at the curb.

"You've got to be kidding," I said.

He handed me a piece of paper. It was an estimate for repairs from a place called Bart's Automotive. I handed it back to him and walked away.

"You stepped right in front of me," he said, hurrying after me. "Come on. Do the right thing."

I spotted a teenager getting into an orange Volkswagen. "Excuse me!" I called to him. "Can you give me a ride to the Pueblo Motel?" He waved me over.

Yazzie followed me to the car. He stood with his hands on his hips, watching me as the VW backed up. As we pulled out of the parking lot, I glanced back and saw him climbing into the battered Toyota.

Fifteen minutes later I was out in front of the motel reeling in a fit of nausea completely unrelated to my recent injury. I was staring at the now empty parking space where I left the Honda. Goggle-eyed and perplexed, I stood there waiting for it to miraculously reappear. Finally I gave up and walked toward my room to call the police. Slouching against the railing outside my door was a boy no older than sixteen. He was Native American with long hair and a bad complexion.

"Hey. You Tom McInnes?"

"Yeah. Why?"

A cocky grin spread across his face. "Want your motorcycle?"

The kid's car was a powder-blue Chevy Nova that had been painted generously and unevenly with a brush. As soon as I climbed in, he sped out of the parking lot as if he was making a getaway. Between his marginal driving skills, and the fact that the Nova had no rear springs or shocks and rode like a concrete block on wheels, my head was howling thirty seconds into our journey. Ten minutes later, roaring down a bumpy two-lane highway, I reached my pain threshold. As I opened my mouth to tell him to stop the car, my driver, who had obviously watched too many episodes of *Starsky and Hutch*, threw the Nova into a sharp left turn. With tires screeching, we slid across the blacktop toward a dirt road. We hit the berm and went airborne long enough for the first thirteen years of my life to flash before my eyes. When the car finally touched back down on terra firma, thankfully on all four wheels, the force of the impact propelled me out the seat. My already aching head clonked against the roof of the car sounding like a honey dew melon dropped on the kitchen floor. The kid laughed gleefully then stomped the accelerator, throwing me back in the seat. The Nova bounded down the dirt road, leaping ruts and potholes like some sort of mutant antelope on amphetamines.

Topping a sage covered rise, we careened down into a narrow valley. Across a lush green pasture was an adobe house surrounded by cottonwood trees. Out in front, parked next to the beat-to-shit yellow Toyota, was my motorcycle.

"This isn't funny." I said, as Emerson Yazzie walked out of the house holding my sparkplug wire. "I can have you arrested."

"Go ahead. You'll never see your bike again."

The threat of incarceration obviously having no impact on him, I tried a different tactic.

"Look, my head is killing me and I feel like crap. We both made mistakes in this accident so why don't we call it even?"

"You owe me, Bro."

"Your car is a piece of shit!" I blurted. "It's not even worth $126!"

"You're missing the point," he said, his voice maintaining the same low-key tone, "Your head did damage to my property. I need to be compensated."

The kid laughed. I felt my skin heating up. "What if I tell you that I don't have any money?"

"I'd say I just got myself a new motorcycle."

"This is extortion!"

The kid walked over to Yazzie. "I'm takin' off before the shootin' starts."

"Oh no," I said, "You're not leaving me here." With a flourish of bravado, I added, "I'm going for the cops, and that bike better be here when I get back."

I walked toward the Nova. Yazzie whistled. From around the corner of the house trotted a huge, wolf-like dog. Yazzie pointed to me. The dog immediately bared its teeth and started growling deep in its throat. I stopped walking. The dog slowly advanced on me.

Yazzie handed the kid some money. "Hey, thanks for your help, Albert."

Albert stuffed the bills in the front pocket of his greasy jeans. "Sure," he said. "Are you going to Window Rock for pow-wow?"

"Yeah. Gotta see my grandfather."

Flecks of white spittle formed in the corners of the dog's mouth. It was five feet away and the growling was getting louder as Albert got into the Nova. I turned toward the car. The dog lunged at me, its snarling muzzle stopping eight inches from my crotch.

"Stand still," Yazzie said calmly.

"Get your fuckin' dog away from me!" I said, trying sound more tough than scared.

Albert started the car. The dog leaned closer, as if it was just waiting for an excuse to snack on my genitalia. The Nova pulled out of the yard. The roar of the exhaust grew louder as the car picked up speed, and then gradually faded as it headed down the dirt road to the highway.

Yazzie whistled sharply. The dog immediately stopped growling. He trotted over to his master with his tongue lolling out. Yazzie petted the ugly brute and it rolled over on its back offering its belly to be rubbed. Yazzie looked up at me. "Good dog, huh?"

Emerson Yazzie was a Navajo. He grew up on the reservation in Arizona and made his living as a silversmith. Two years earlier, he and his girlfriend, Christine, a painter, moved into the adobe house in Taos. It was his cousin, Rachel, working at the motel, who told Yazzie the Honda was mine.

He told me all of this while we sat at his kitchen table haggling over my motorcycle. We were surrounded by Christine's vibrant primitive paintings. The bright colors she used: pinks and blues and purples, turned what were traditional domestic scenes in an 18th century Native American village into something magical.

While we argued back and forth about the motorcycle, I was acutely aware of the dog lying under the table. His lurking, silent presence, a deadly threat within inches of my lower torso, inhibited me from expressing myself with the emotional veracity that I was feeling. After a frustrating hour of restraining myself, I'd had it. The combination of the dog, my headache, and the increasingly obvious futility of further negotiations, prompted me to sign $125 worth of traveler's checks over to Yazzie. He cheerfully handed me my sparkplug wire and a cold beer from the refrigerator. I took the wire but refused the beer.

"Hey Bro, don't be that way," he said. "This was just business."

"Fuck you," I said, with one eye on the dog. "I don't drink with people who steal from me." I walked out the door.

"I didn't steal from you," he said, following close behind. "It was an accident and you were at fault."

I ignored him and bent down to put the sparkplug wire on the Honda. There was a new scratch on the gas tank.

"So it's alright for you to damage my property?" My voice was louder than I intended. The dog cocked his head, eyeing me like I was a scrap of tri-tip.

"Oh, man," Yazzie said, "hold on a minute." He hurried into the house. The dog sniffed at my ankle, growling softly.

"Get away from me!" I snapped.

The dog tensed and bared his teeth. I bared mine back. The dog immediately crawled under the wooden bench by the front door and flopped on his belly. I picked up my duffel bag and strapped it onto the gas tank.

"Hey, take this," Yazzie said, coming back out of the house. "It'll make up for the scratch."

He tossed me a necklace. I caught it by the leather cord. It was a silver pendent in the shape of an eagle.

"This looks like what you were wearing the other day when you hit me," I said.

"What are you talking about?"

"In the braid of your hair, I saw a silver eagle."

"I haven't braided my hair since I was ten years old."

I stared at the pendent in my hand. It looked exactly like the one I'd seen.

"Someone had long braided hair with a silver clasp on the end."

"It wasn't me."

"Maybe one of the paramedics."

"They were white guys. The only other person that got near you was the kid who works in the grocery store. He's got short, blond hair."

"But . . . I saw a braid . . . an eagle . . . just like this one. Are you bullshitting me?"

"No." Yazzie said, eyeing me cautiously.

An uneasy feeling pricked at the back of my neck. It was similar to what I felt the first time the table lifted up in Eldora Aguilar's kitchen. Things were not as they seemed.

Out of the corner of my eye I saw Yazzie reach into his pocket.

"Don't know why it's comin' to a white boy," he said, "but Eagle medicine is strong. I don't want to mess with it." He pulled out my traveler's checks and handed them to me.

By the time Christine got home from visiting an art gallery in Santa Fe, Emerson and I were flat on our backs in the middle of the pasture drunk on red wine. Having concluded that the eagle had come to offer me vision on my journey, Emerson insisted that we celebrate.

"It's a powerful sign when eagle comes," he said. *It was also a powerful sign,* I thought, *when a man who just extorted money chooses to give it back.*

"I don't have any idea what I'm doing," I said, "just fumbling along trying somehow to get to Pomona, California."

His eyes, glassy from the wine, shone like black onyx. "Don't worry," he said, "I'll help you understand your journey."

"How are you gonna do that?"

He handed me the bottle of wine, and pointed to a bluish-gray bulge of mountains far off in the distance.

"That's where you'll find it," he said.

The next morning, Christine laughed at us when we dragged ourselves into the kitchen hungover to beat the band. A big-boned redhead from an upper-middle-class suburb of St. Louis, Christine had wide hips and creamy, freckled skin. Four years earlier, she drove west with an actress friend who was moving to Los Angeles. In a trading post near Sedona, Arizona, Christine met Emerson. It was love at first sight. She unloaded her suitcase out of her friend's car and put it in the back seat of the same yellow Toyota that my head had dented. She and Emerson had been living together ever since. They just knew.

An odd couple, the well-bred woman from the Midwest, and the tough kid off the reservation, she admonished him for taking my motorcycle, and at the same time told me that if I had been paying attention to where I was going, none of this would have happened.

"The Great Spirit works in ways we can't begin to understand," Emerson said.

Christine punched him in the arm. "Oh, right! The Great Spirit told you to take his Honda and hold it for ransom?"

"Maybe," Emerson said, giving me a wink.

That afternoon, he explained to me about the vision quest. He was going to take me to a place in the mountains and leave me there for four days. I was supposed to fast, only drinking water from a nearby stream. On the fourth day, I would stay up for 24 hours praying and crying for a vision. If I had been respectful and deemed worthy, my Indian or spiritual name as well as a vision would come to me.

Now let me just say, I'm a guy who likes to eat. When I'm done with breakfast, I'm already thinking about what I'm going to have for lunch. Going four days without food sounded dangerous and painful. When I voiced my concern to Emerson, in as macho a way as I could manage, he looked at me and shrugged. "What's four days if it'll lead to a vision that may affect the rest of your life?"

"What if all I end up with is a shrunken belly?"

He scratched his chin and thought for a moment. "There's a message in that too."

The next morning, we loaded up Christine's Ford pickup with the supplies I would need. Emerson was lending me a backpack, sleeping bag, plastic ground cloth and a water filter. Their dog, Rocky, who was still not sure about me, jumped into the back of the truck and made himself comfortable.

Christine stood in the pasture waving to us as we drove down the dirt road, dust billowing up behind the truck like a dragon's tail. *Four days,* I thought to myself. Part of me wanted to say, no thank you, this is beyond what I am willing to do. But another part, the searcher, the unshaven lunatic on the Harley Davidson that I'd been dreaming about, the one willing to follow the signs no matter where they pointed, he was more than ready. I could feel him urging me on. Yes, yes, he seemed to say, this is really going to be something.

As the sage covered plains fell away and the road climbed up through a steep, rocky canyon, I thought of Lilly. I remembered her hands pressed against my belly as we roared through town on one of our late-night motorcycle rides. Her playfulness, her focus on what was real, and her willingness to teach me what she knew, all came rushing back. In enticing detail, I allowed my memory to roam over her body: the depth of her eyes, the soft indentation at the base of her throat, the swell of her breasts, and the aching curve of her hips. *I had left her, an amazing woman, and for what, the privilege of starving myself for four days alone on a mountain? How dumb was I?*

I immediately began backpedaling.

"You know Emerson," I said, "maybe it wasn't a vision I had. When I smacked my head I saw a flash of something, it doesn't have to mean anything."

He glanced over at me, and then shifted his eyes back to the road. "Don't be a pussy."

13

Rays of the setting sun glinted off the surface of the quiet pool. I knelt down and dipped a plastic Tupperware bowl into the water. Silvery ripples rolled away from my hand. I placed the bowl of water on a flat rock at the edge of the stream. Submerging the tube from the water filter in the bowl of water, I put the other end over the mouth of the plastic jug and began working the plunger. Filtering water had become my daily ritual, once in the morning and once at night. Five bowls to fill the jug.

My campsite was thirty yards away in the shade of a gnarled, wind twisted fir tree. The surrounding vegetation consisted of tufts of browned-out grass, several clusters of purple wildflowers and five or six battered old trees. It was a stark, barren plateau. On the west side was a vista overlooking a long, tree-lined valley.

I finished with my filtering duties and took a drink. The water was cool and sweet. Leaning back against a rock, I drank deeply from the jug.

The hunger pains had escalated from distracting and annoying to intensely painful. However, by the afternoon of the fourth day, I was remarkably comfortable and calm. The fearful chatter in my head ceased. My body stopped telling me that it was dying. In place of this desperate plea for sustenance came surrender. And in that surrender, I seemed to merge with the landscape. The light appeared brighter, the rocks deeper shades of brown and red.

The cool water sloshed in my empty stomach. I forced a loud belch. The sound moved away from me, out into the valley.

"If a man burps on a mountain in New Mexico," I said, my voice husky from days of silence, "can a dingo in Australia smell his breath?"

I laughed and kicked my feet in the steam. Water splashed up glistening in the sunlight. The droplets dangled from the hair on my bare legs. Since my second night on the mountain, I was naked. Strip off your clothes, the moon had said. Be naked and unafraid. Who was I to argue with the moon?

During my first day in the buff, I worried about someone seeing me and reporting me to the police. Soon I didn't care. I spent my days sitting in the dirt, scratching pictures onto sandstone slabs with my trusty pointed carving rock.

My first night on the mountain I was not so relaxed. Feeling vulnerable and alone, I climbed up on the car-sized, boulder lying across the stream. Sitting back on my haunches, listening for the movement of nocturnal animals, I seriously considered for the first time in my life where I stood in the food chain. Straining to hear the sound of any large predators coming my way, I felt the twitchy panic of the hunted. I saw in the darkness, the shadowy forms of bears and mountain lions stalking me across the ridge. My survival instinct immediately twitched on, and from that lizard part of my nervous system, shot surges of adrenaline. I frantically searched out escape routes and hiding places. I wasn't going to give up easily. They were going to have to earn their meal of my heart and liver. When I realized that what I spotted were large rocks, not bears or cougars, I chuckled nervously at my paranoia. Nevertheless, when I went to sleep that night, I said a silent prayer not to be awakened by a cold muzzle at my throat.

The stillness had also been difficult to get used to. With no family, friends, cars, television, music, or neighbors, all that was left was the mountain and me. It was a solitude that reverberated deeply, like a heartbeat. When I lay in my sleeping bag at night, I would dig my fingers into the dirt. Clinging to the earth like that, I felt an even greater connection to the rhythmic pulse that I had begun to feel a part of. Staring up into the immense canopy of stars, forcing myself to look between and beyond them, I sensed, in the black void of space, that same steady beat. It was everywhere.

A blur of movement caught my eye. My neighbor, a brown and black marmot, was on his lookout rock. He lived in a cluster of granite boulders seventy feet from my campsite. On my second day, in an attempt to get at the apples I was saving for my trip back down the mountain, he gnawed a hole in Emerson's backpack. After fending off his sneak attack, I put my precious fruit in a stuff sack and hung it from the tree. The next morning I found a hole gnawed in the nylon sack and a quarter-sized chunk eaten from one of my Granny Smiths. I was furious.

"These are my apples you little shits," I yelled at the rocks. I took the bag down and paced back and forth, debating what to do with it. Remembering a PBS documentary on wolves, I entombed the bag of apples in a pile of rocks and pissed around it in a circle, marking it as my territory.

"This is mine," I shouted, "stay away!" I jumped up and down for emphasis. I don't know if it was the toxic scent of my urine or the wild-man-of-the-mountain routine, but after that no critters got near my apples.

At Emerson's urging, I brought along three candles and a six-inch bundle of sage. I pulled them out of the backpack and set them on a rock. He told me on the final night, while I was to stay awake crying for a vision, I should create some kind of a ceremony. He also said that it would be best during my all-night vigil to sit within a protective circle. I had no idea what I was going to do exactly, but with the big night only hours away, I got busy.

Picking up melon sized rocks and hauling them back to the campsite proved to be a graphic reminder of how weak I'd become. Lean to begin with, over the last four days I'd shrunk to being down right skinny. Having to exert greater effort than I'd imagined, I gathered twelve rocks and arranged them in a wide circle around my sleeping bag. I positioned the candles in a triangle in the center. The sandstones I'd used for creating my primitive artwork were lined up on the north end of the circle.

In the middle of doing all of this, I thought of my parents. *What horrors would cross their minds seeing such a pagan display?* I lit the wand of sage and held it up to the sky.

"For Methodists and Baptists the world over." I laughed, waving the smoking sage above my head. Across the valley, the setting sun was disappearing into a notch in the mountains. Emerson told me that as the sun went down, I was to hold clearly in my mind the issue upon which I was seeking a vision. I sat down, crossed my legs Indian style, and holding the sage in my lap, closed my eyes.

Emptying my mind, I took three deep breaths and concentrated on one thought: *What was this journey leading me to?* In her lessons on meditation, Lilly taught me to focus on my breathing, following the breath in and following the breath out. Sage smoke wafted around me. My body relaxed. An ant crawled over my knee. I brought my focus back to the breath. I thought of getting lucky and receiving my vision right away. I brought my focus back to the breath. I wondered whose spirits might be circling around me. *Was Gram nearby?* I brought my focus back to the breath. I thought I heard Richard Harris singing "Camelot," and I thought of Dee Dee. I brought my focus back to the breath. I remembered my last night with Lilly, and I began to get an erection. I brought my focus back to the breath. I thought of a field of ice. It throbbed harder. I went back to the breath. Finally, I let go of trying to control it. *Wave proudly in the wind,* I silently commanded my willful appendage. I went back to the breath. Another thought flitted through my mind: *I am naked on a mountaintop, completely engulfed in sage smoke, sporting a raging hard-on. What would the neighbors say?* I couldn't help laughing. I opened my eyes. It was dark.

The night was long. The night was painful. The only way I could stay awake was to kneel. It was no wonder Emerson told me that I would be crying for a vision, it hurt to be on your knees that long. When the pain gradually faded, I discovered that the reason I didn't feel it anymore was because my legs were numb. I tried to massage the pins and needles sensation out of them, but then decided screw it, I'll suffer.

I spent hours looking into the sky. I stared into the flickering flames of the candles focusing and unfocusing my eyes. I poured melted wax on the ground and made weird designs. I recited, as if they were a mantra, three Buddhist sayings Lilly taught me: "Be lamps unto yourselves." "There is a path to the end of suffering. Tread it." "Do not go by reasoning nor by inferring, nor by argument; a true disciple must know for himself." I hummed songs to myself, focusing on Christmas hymns like, "Come All Ye Faithful" for the possible residual spiritual effect. While calling out to the Great Spirit to grant me a vision, I hopped and jumped around doing my best imitation of a Native American dance. No vision came to me.

After stubbing my big toe during a particularly frenzied moment of dancing, I sat down and moped. I had been deemed unworthy. I wasn't going to be granted a vision. In the morning I would have to hike back down the mountain and tell Emerson that I'd failed. Immediately upon considering this possibility I went back to my knees. Emerson's inspirational words, "Don't be a pussy," echoed in my head. I lowered my chin to my chest and forced myself to be still.

Pebbles dug into my kneecaps. I flowed in and out with my breath. After a while my obsession to have a vision faded. In its place came a desire to simply be respectful; not only of myself, but of the sacredness of the ritual. Once again, with strong intention, I offered up my question, "Where is my journey leading?"

Time ticked by. Still, I saw nothing. Drifting toward sleep, I caught myself and got refocused on my breathing. My back was tight. The muscles in my arms felt like cords of lead. Frustration crept back into my mind. I didn't want to fail. I was worthy. I was absolutely worthy. I began to rock back and forth, calling out for strength. My voice deepened and changed, becoming so full of longing that it surprised me. Guttural sounds began to come from my throat. I started thrashing my arms and pounding the earth with my fists. Wailing and howling like a primitive beast, I allowed the inarticulate within me to be expressed. Words didn't exist, time didn't matter; it was simply the expression of feelings, true unscreened emotion. It rose out of me louder and louder. My voice soared beyond where I thought it could go. Tears streamed down my face. From far away, I heard something. It moved closer, sounding like wind through the branches of a tree. *Singing Bow,* the lilting whisper said, *Singing Bow, Singing Bow, Singing Bow*. A searing flash of color shot across the darkness behind my closed eyelids. Like a rainbow on fire, another slashed. Something began to emerge: a pale blue sky, a row of trees, oranges dangling from branches, a narrow ladder, wooden crates overflowing with fruit. A low-pitched sound droned. The ground began to vibrate. The vision began to crack. Building louder and louder, the sound became a deafening roar. The picture suddenly shattered into a kaleidoscope of twirling, jagged pieces. My eyes flew open. Surprised to see the sky had brightened, I looked toward the valley. Emblazoned in the early morning rays of the sun was a flash of silver, a huge wing – the eagle! I threw myself to the ground, covered my ears, and loudly proclaimed my devotion to God, the Great Spirit, Buddha, Jesus, Mohammed, and anyone else who might be listening. A thunderous blast ripped the air above me. I looked up expecting to be seized by razor sharp talons and plucked from the earth like a helpless sparrow. Instead, I saw an F4 fighter jet streaking five hundred feet over my head. In an instant it was gone, howling over the ridge into the next valley, continuing its training run.

    I lay there, listening to the rumble of the jet fade in the distance. Then I laughed and kicked my legs in the air. It was over! I had done it! I'd received my spiritual name and had my vision! I had no idea what Singing Bow or the orange grove meant, but damn-it-all they were mine! I jumped to my feet and ran to the pile of rocks where my apples were hidden. Laughing deliriously, I tossed the rocks aside, a single ecstatic thought racing through my mind – *food, food, food!*

14

MY FATHER GRINNED AND held a two-quart sauce pan up to my face. "Look at this chili, Tommy," he said, taunting me. "Lots of beef for you." A swampy, primordial ooze of grease bubbled over the surface of the ground chuck and kidney beans.

"How can you eat that in this heat," I said.

"A little humidity doesn't curb my appetite," he said, proudly.

I cocked my head and tilted it toward his chest. "What's that sound I hear? I think it's your arteries slamming shut."

He laughed. "I'm healthy as an ox." He lifted a spoon full of chili to his mouth and ate it. Like a chemist finally getting his experiment right, he nodded and said, "Now *that's* a pot of chili."

Mom was out for her monthly dinner and gab session with the Northpoint Wood Carvers Association. Everyone brought their works-in-progress and offered each other tips and support. My mother had taken the new mallard she was working on.

"How's everything at the ole dog bone factory," Dad said, as he poured himself a glass of iced tea.

The muscles in the back of my neck tightened. "Dad, I read that the changes in Russia would have happened sooner if Reagan hadn't taken such a hard stand. All that stuff about him forcing them to their knees with our military buildup is BS. They were already there."

Dad picked up a serrated steak knife and sawed off a chunk of Italian bread. "Don't be so sensitive about the job, I'm just razzing you."

Peanut ran into the kitchen and skidded sideways across the floor.

"You oughta get that dog's nails trimmed," I said.

Peanut jumped against my father's leg begging for a hand out. "Go lay down," Dad growled.

Peanut slid into the cabinet next to the stove then skated meekly toward the back door and the firm ground of his cedar chip bed.

"He's not biting himself anymore," I said. "Another week or so and his skin should be healed up."

"I hope so. I'm sick of looking at his bloody ass while I eat my dinner."

"It's not the dog's fault."

"I know. Poor old thing. Eyes are going too. Have you noticed?"

"Yeah."

Later, when my father and I sat down to eat dinner on the back porch and began discussing Aunt Helen's two week tenure at Howland Rehabilitation and Nursing Center, I couldn't see a single lightning bug in the yard. On summer nights when I was a kid the backyard was alive with their blinking, yellow lights. I kept looking for them as we talked. We discussed Aunt Helen refusing to do physical therapy and her doctor's prognosis that she may never be strong enough to live on her own. When Dad brought up one of us gaining power of attorney over her affairs, I stopped looking into the yard altogether.

"If she gets senile or has a stroke," he said, "We won't have any control over her finances. The bills will keep coming in and if she's not capable of signing checks . . ." His voice trailed off.

"We can get a joint checking account," I suggested.

"That would help to a certain extent, but what about transferring money? What if she needs to cash in one of her CDs." He swiped at a mosquito that flew in between us. "I don't know how much she's got socked away but at four grand a month this nursing home is going to eat it up fast."

Peanut whined and scratched at the back door.

"I'll get him," I said.

As I walked Peanut to the cable that ran between the two pin oaks in the backyard, the dog pulled frantically rasping and lunging to get free.

"Just calm down," I said, trying not to trip over him.

"He's still strong," Dad called from the porch.

I hooked Peanut's collar to the leash on the cable. As soon as I let him go, he dashed madly back and forth along the run, yipping and barking.

"What are you barking at?" Dad said. "Crazy dog."

I looked into the sky. Hazy clouds obscured most of the stars.

"Your mother's thinking about buying nursing home insurance," Dad said.

"Really?"

"She doesn't want to lose the house if something happens to one of us."

I walked back to the porch. Dad was smoking a cigarette.

"Is it expensive?"

"Very. But it'll cover five years at one of those homes."

"Seems premature to me."

"That's what I said, but this thing with Helen has got her spooked."

"Aunt Helen is almost ninety-five years old."

"Your mother loves this house. She doesn't want to have to sell it to pay for nursing home bills."

He took a long drag on his cigarette. Who did he think he was kidding, I wondered? He was the one who loved the house. Mom wanted to sell it three years ago and buy a condo with a pool. He refused. He offered up the cliché that he was the man and this was his castle. Did he think I'd forgotten that?

"Goddamn insurance," he said, waving his cigarette in the air. "You're always betting against yourself."

"You're overweight and you smoke, I'd say in your case it's not a bad bet."

"I've got good genes," he snapped. He picked up his plate and went into the kitchen. He poured himself a cup of coffee and went into the den. Through the screen on the patio door, I could hear him humming. It was something he had done for as long as I could remember. Whenever a subject came up that he didn't want to discuss, he'd start humming Sinatra tunes. It drove my mother crazy.

I tried to figure out which song he was humming. After hearing the beginning of, "That's Life" and the middle section of, "All of Me," I realized that he was doing a medley. He only did medleys when he was really ticked off.

I stood up and walked to the edge of the porch. I looked out into the yard, searching for the reassuring glow of a lightning bug. I couldn't see any. I stepped off the porch and laid down in the yard. Blades of dry grass stabbed through my T-shirt. In the hazy sky I could only make out half of the Big Dipper. I took a deep breath and let it out slowly. A bat flitted between the stars and me. I watched its herky-jerky flight as it looped around tracking through the darkness, sonar beaconing the way.

Peanut whined and strained against the cable. He had done his business and wanted to go back inside. I got up and unleashed him. In the kitchen I gave him a doggy treat that he took over to his bed to eat in private. In the den, Dad was reading the newspaper.

"Article about that kid who blocked the tank in Tiananmen Square."

I sat down in the recliner next to the fireplace.

"Takes some big ones to make a stand like that," Dad said. "Goddamn Communists. Reagan had 'em on the run."

I grabbed the sports section. "It's like the '60s and early '70s all over again."

"I hope not."

"We could use some changes don't you think?"

"Change, yes. But all that protesting, fighting in the streets. Wasn't good for the country."

"Remember watching the reports from Vietnam on TV. It's like we were in the war. Bullets flying all over, guys screaming."

Dad stared off toward the fireplace. "Never watched much of that."

"Yeah, you used to walk out of the room. How come?"

"Better things to do." He lifted the paper and started reading again.

I shook my head. "See Dad, that's what I mean. I ask you about something and you shut me out."

He lowered the newspaper. "What? I'm reading the paper."

"Dad, come on."

"You've got more important things to worry about in your life." He went back to reading.

After a couple minutes of silence I tried again. "Who knows, Dad, by the time you're old enough to go in a nursing home, maybe I'll be able to foot the bill for you."

He lowered the paper and looked at me. He seemed surprised.

"It's a long way off," I said. "You've got a lot of good years ahead of you."

He swung his eyes away from me and sighed. "I hope so."

"Don't worry about it. It'll be okay."

He nodded. We sat there for a moment neither of us speaking. Then Dad folded the newspaper and set it on the coffee table.

"How about some big Frank," he said.

I stared at him, not sure I'd heard him correctly. I'd been listening to his Sinatra albums since the day I was born. But it was always from the kitchen or upstairs in my bedroom or with a group of people around. My father never invited me alone into the inner sanctum with Frank. This rite of passage was granted to Rick when he was a senior in high school. For twenty years now he'd been a man in my father's eyes. I was not.

"What do you think?" Dad asked.

"Yeah," I said, my voice softer than I intended. "That'd be great."

He got up and walked to the stereo. He looked over his records. "I'm going to start with, *Sinatra at the Sands*, okay?"

"Sure."

"It's with Count Basie."

Gently, and with a reverence I'd seen demonstrated only in his handling of the television remote control, Dad placed the album on the turntable. Picking up the red felt dust remover, he carefully ran it over the surface of the black vinyl. He lifted the needle and paused. The magnitude of the moment wasn't lost on either of us. The needle touched down. Scratchy hiss filled the room. A quick drum flurry erupted followed by cymbals and the deep voice of the announcer introducing the Count Basie orchestra. The horn section kicked in. Trumpets wailed. The announcer called Sinatra on stage. Frank offered up a quip then started singing "Come Fly With Me."

Dad sat down on the couch. His head began nodding to the beat. I leaned back, extending the leg rest out from the recliner. My toes tapped with the music. Peanut came into the den. He didn't run around or jump on anything. He seemed to acknowledge the sacred ritual that was taking place.

We grooved along with Frank for hours. We didn't talk much. At the end of a side, Dad would get up, flip the album over, and sit back down on the couch after giving me a look that said, *wait until you hear what's coming next.*

When my mother got home she knew better than to interrupt. She said hi, put the mallard on the coffee table, and went upstairs to watch television. We went through the entire Richard McInnes Frank Sinatra collection. When it was over and the last strains of "My Way" had lilted through the house, my father got up and turned off the stereo.

"Well, that's all there is," he said.

"That was great, Dad."

"Glad you liked it." He patted me on the shoulder and walked out of the room. I heard him start up the stairs. "Lock the back door when you come up," he called.

"I will."

I picked up his coffee cup and walked into the kitchen. Rinsing it out in the sink I thought, *so this is it, my father finally invited me into the club.* Frank's dulcet tones had worked their magic and now

Dad and I were deeply bonded. We'd talk more. We'd joke around like he and Rick. I really wanted to feel happy and relieved, but I didn't. A single thought circled in my mind: *Perhaps my father had extended himself to me, not out of affection, but out of fear.* Terrified of getting old and not being able to take care of himself, and wanting to ensure that I'd be there for him, he had purposefully ingratiated himself to me under the guise of love and acceptance. It was mean and manipulative, but it was also classic primate social behavior.

15

AFTER MY TRIUMPHANT RETURN from the vision quest, I was told by Emerson not to discuss it with anyone.

"What you experienced is now part of your personal power," he said. "To talk about it, to translate it into language, will desecrate its sacred meaning." He put his hand on my chest. "Own what you found," he said. "Walk with it, allow it to lead you."

Even though I knew I wasn't supposed to, I wanted to tell Lilly about my experience on the mountain. I wanted her to know that my journey to Pomona was moving forward. And I also wanted to convince her to come to Taos for a visit. When she answered the phone and I heard a male voice in the background, I immediately went on tilt.

"He's a friend," she said quietly.

"What kind of friend? It's eleven o'clock at night, what are you and this friend doing?"

"Casper, what did you want me to do?"

"I thought we had something special." I flinched as soon as I'd said it. It was such a chick thing to say.

"We did have something special,"

She sounded way too in control for my liking.

"Then," she said, "you decided to go off on your adventure."

"I had to go you know that."

"I understand, but you can't expect me to sit around waiting for you to drop back into my life."

"I thought maybe you'd come for a visit."

"Casper, I can't."

"Have you found another student to educate in the mysteries of love?"

"Actually I'm the student this time."

"Really," I said, unsure of how to respond, but positive that I didn't want to hear the details of her new man's expertise.

"He's traveled a lot," she said. "In India, he lived for a year with a secret society that teaches—"

"I miss you, Lilly," I said, cutting her off. "There's so much I want to tell you."

For a moment she didn't say anything. Then, her voice just above a whisper, she said, "I miss you too."

A long silence settled between us.

"This is fucked," I finally said.

"Life has taken us, hasn't it?"

"Yes."

I heard the male voice in the background.

"I'm so glad you called," she said. "I have to go. I'm sorry. Have a wonderful adventure. Love a lot." She hung up.

Even though I'd left her to get back on the road to Pomona, I'd been holding on to the idea that we would end up together. Pretty stupid but there it was. Her exodus from my life took the wind out of my sails. While moping and licking my wounds, I indulged my growing fascination with the Native American experience by reading *Black Elk Speaks*, Vine Deloria, Jr.'s *God is Red*, and *Bury My Heart at Wounded Knee* by Dee Brown. The prophetic vision at the center of *Black Elk Speaks* was something I absolutely related to. And the foundation of Native American spirituality, being directly connected to the natural world, also felt right to me. I pestered Emerson to tell me more. Aware of the eagle medicine he believed to be at work in my life, he did not deny my request. We drove to Canyon De Chelly, on the Navajo reservation in Arizona. At the White House Ruin, I was amazed by the ancient cliff dwellings, and at Pictograph Cave I saw hundreds of drawings of handprints, dogs, deer, spirals, flute players, lightning bolts, and rainbows covering the cave wall. The ceiling was painted with stars.

I found myself spending afternoons alone in the high desert, gazing into the distant horizon, listening, and looking for something that seemed just beyond my ability to see it. When Christine gave me a sketch of myself atop a galloping black stallion, it was as if I was seeing myself from a dream.

One morning I was talking on the telephone to my sister Becky. She was encouraging me to go home and visit our parents. She said that they would help me in any way that they could. I told her that I still needed time to come to terms with the things I was discovering about myself. Becky asked me what exactly that was. I told her about my connection with the Native American way. She laughed.

"Don't you remember," she said, "as a kid you always had to be the Indian. You would fight with Rick for that plastic bow and the arrows with the rubber tips. You would really go after him if he grabbed it first. I was always the buffalo you were hunting or the horse you were rounding up. We'd sit in a circle in the backyard, pretending to be around a campfire, and Mom would cook us those awful, dried out hamburgers."

"How do you remember that stuff?" I asked.

"I don't know. I just do. I didn't smoke as much pot as you and Rick."

"I vaguely remember the bow and arrows."

"You were the Indian back then, Tommy. You were always the Indian."

16

THERE WAS A MAN sitting in a chair at the foot of Aunt Helen's bed when I walked into her room at the nursing home. As soon as he saw me, he stood up. What little hair he had surrounding the pink dome of his head was snow white and neatly trimmed. He was holding a gift-wrapped package tied with a slender pink bow. I looked at Aunt Helen. She was asleep.

"Hi," he whispered.

His eyes moved quickly from me to Aunt Helen and back again. He walked over to me.

"I'm an acquaintance of Helen's." he said quietly. "Leo Hursen. It's a pleasure finally meeting you, Tom."

Aunt Helen coughed. He glanced over at her. "I'll see you again sometime," he said. "Please give this to Helen for me." He handed me the package and hurried out the door.

"See you later," I called after him.

"Tommy?" Aunt Helen said. Her voice sounded thin and weak.

I stepped toward the bed. "Yes, it's me."

She reached for the control pad and began to raise her bed up. I handed her the package.

"Your friend, Leo was here. He left this for you."

"Who?"

"Leo Hursen."

Aunt Helen's face went slack. She cleared her throat, choked up a wad of phlegm and spit it into a plastic cup. "Did you talk to him?" she asked, dabbing at the corner of her mouth with a tissue.

"We said hello. He already knew who I was. Have you been showing pictures and bragging about me again?"

"What else did he say?"

"Nothing. As soon as you started to wake up he left."

"I bet he did."

"What are you mad at him or something?"

"No. He's just a kooky old man." She shoved the gift onto the table next to her bed.

"Why don't you open it," I asked.

"I don't want to."

"Come on, I want to see what he brought you."

"I said, no!" Aunt Helen's face flared red. Her eyes narrowed. "I don't feel like talking today. Go home, Thomas."

"What's wrong?"

"Go on," she said, cutting me off. "Leave me alone."

"I—I'm sorry if I upset you."

"Well you did. So don't make it worse."

I leaned down to kiss her goodbye but she turned away.

"I'll call you tomorrow," I said. She grumbled and waved me out of the room.

As I made my way down the hall between several wheelchair-bound residents, I made a mental note to ask my mother what she knew about Leo Hursen.

• • •

MOM KICKED DIRT LOOSE from her work boots and took off her green and white striped gardening gloves. "Leo Hursen? Never heard of him."

She had just finished weeding the new vegetable garden I'd dug. I handed her the glass of iced tea I'd brought from the kitchen. She took a long drink.

"Thanks, I was dying." She held the cold glass up to her forehead. "He said he was a friend of hers?"

"An acquaintance."

"She's never mentioned his name to me."

We sat down on one of the railroad ties I'd used to box in the garden. The freshly turned earth smelled dank and musky. Digging the garden and planting had been invigorating. It brought back fond memories of my days in Scotland and once again reinforced my pleasure in working with soil and seeds.

"I wonder who he is," Mom said.

"She doesn't seem too eager to talk about him."

"Helen can be a pain in the ass sometimes, excuse my French. I'll get it out of her, don't you worry."

"Okay, whatever."

"What are you doing for the fourth? You're welcome to come to Nancy and Boyd's with us."

"Kirby is having a thing at his place."

One of the blue jays that had been squawking at us since we'd sat down, suddenly swooped over our heads and landed on the gutter above the back porch.

Mom tilted her head toward it. "Have you seen their dive bombing runs at Peanut?" she asked. "The dog's eyes are so bad he can't see them coming. He just ducks down on his belly while they zoom around him."

The screen door slammed and my father walked into the yard. "I'm going to the liquor store. I told Boyd that we'd bring wine for the picnic."

"You're not going out like that are you?" Mom snapped at him. "That shirt doesn't go with those pants."

Dad looked down at the green golf pants and the purple short sleeve shirt he was wearing.

"This is the shirt Becky gave me for Christmas last year."

Mom shook her head, raising her eyes to the sky as if to beseech the fashion police for divine intervention. Dad turned and walked back into the house.

"Mom, why do you treat him like that? You know he's color blind. He does the best he can."

"He doesn't even try. I label his clothes. I section off his closet. I've done all I can. My friends see him up at the club you know. My God, half the time he looks like a model for the Salvation Army."

"If you treated each other–"

"Don't start with me."

"But Mom—"

"You've screamed at me for years to stay out of your business, so you stay out of mine."

"You guys are my parents."

"And you're my child, but that doesn't mean you want to listen to my opinions."

"Mom, I'm just trying to—"

"Tommy, you're not married. You're too selfish to get married. And until you do you won't understand."

"I want you guys to be happy."

She groaned and rolled her eyes. "Oh come on. Get real. This isn't Ozzie and Harriet. It's life. I'm sorry if we can't be exactly the way you want us to be." She picked up her empty glass and stomped off toward the garage.

The blue jay on the gutter squawked at me.

"Oh, shut up," I muttered under my breath. I eased down on to the grass and closed my eyes. The sun baked in through my eyelids sending fiery red dots darting around in my vision. Marriage . . . For years now, I'd fantasized about the woman I wanted to fall in love with. But what would it really mean to say yes to someone? To say, "I will love you through it all." When her eyes fail and I have to cook the oatmeal every morning and scrub her dentures and buy her ten different medications so that her heart beats; her blood flows, and her stool is soft, will I still be able to say, "Darling, I adore you." Could I do that? And what if it's me with the problems? My grandfather was crippled with rheumatoid arthritis when he was in his fifties. What if it hit me? Could I put someone through that? What if I was to fall in love, get married, have children, create a wonderful life, the whole shebang – and then something happened? What if my wife fell in love with someone, else or I did? She could die; killed by a bus or cancer or hell anything could happen, you see it on TV all the time. Stuff happens to people. It was an unbearable proposition. Why risk the possibility of suffering such an emotional tragedy? This isn't Shakespeare, it's not Hamlet, it's my life. Why not make things easy by simply avoiding the hassle?

I used to see marriage as a means to attaining a steady supply of sex. I think a lot of young men do and maybe women too. But now I've seen too many people succumb to the attraction of the crotches. "Oh, we're good in bed together. You fill me up. You make me soooo hot. Let's be together forever." They cuddle and coo themselves to the altar never bothering to look beneath the surface of what's happening. Two years later someone is sleeping on the couch bitching about his or her lousy marriage.

"You just know." That's what friends have told me. "You meet the right person and – you just know." I met a woman years ago and I knew. I told my parents I would marry her. I'd never said that before in my life. I dated Melina for two years and she dumped me. She obviously didn't know. Afterward, when I could see things more clearly, and I finally stopped feeling sorry for myself, I realized that I wasn't in love with her. I just thought that I should be.

Love . . . it's such a nebulous thing. Poets try to write about it: a twinkle, a glow, the shimmering light of forever dancing in her eyes. I saw that glow in Melina's eyes. I was drawn to her. She ended up being a psycho bitch from hell that made my life absolutely miserable.

After spending countless hours attempting to comprehend the mechanics of what happens when two people fall in love, it was still unclear to me. Was it a frequency of energy; the electrical charge of one person combining with another person, somehow together forming a positive current? Were there chemical reactions that brought people together or pulled them apart? Or was it instead, our primate heritage which propelled human beings like an invisible force, not toward the vagueness of altruistic love, but rather with a keenly discerning eye directed at the more practical needs of survival and achieving a state of comfort?

Out of the corner of my eye, the blue jay dove straight at me like a feathered missile. It landed next to its mate on a low branch in the oak tree and immediately the two of them starting squawking at me. By spending most of the day bitching at the rest of the world, I wondered if they chose not to do it to each other. I hoped that was the case. Who could live with that racket twenty-four hours a day?

• • •

"Flip, flip, flip, that's all you do. Mr. Flipper that's who you are."

"Stay away from me."

"No. Give it here."

"Lots of good things on TV."

"Stop it! You're not allowed!"

"Did the Pirates win yesterday?"

"No more sports!"

"Shut up old woman!"

The man, tufts of gray hair sprouting from his nose and ears, tossed the remote control under the couch then widened his eyes and flashed a toothless, gummy grin. The heavyset woman in the wheelchair angrily stomped her pink-slippered foot on the carpet and bared her yellowed dentures at him. I backed out of the room into the hall making a mental note to warn Aunt Helen that the TV room was not a friendly place to visit.

I was thinking of ways to sneak up on the subject of Leo Hursen when I abruptly stopped in the middle of the hallway. Aunt Helen was walking toward me behind her wheelchair. It was the first time I'd seen her on her feet since before her fall. Not wanting to be told what to do and when to do it, she fought so aggressively with the physical therapy staff that they finally refused to work with her.

"Yes!" I said. "Way to go." I pumped my fist in the air.

She shrugged it off. "It's good to be up off my rear-end."

"I bet. You're doing great."

"Did you think that I was just sitting around in my room all day feeling sorry for myself?"

"No, I just figured—"

She cut me off. "One morning I woke up and thought to myself, 'Helen, why don't you walk over to the window.' So I grabbed the foot of my bed and I did it. Since then I've been working out every other day."

"I'm proud of you."

"Well, you should be, because I'm going home. This isn't any place for me. I want to get away from these old people."

"Good," I said. "I want you home too."

"How's Terry doing?"

"Mom saw him last night. She said he was looking good. Are you sure you don't want us to keep him at our place?"

"Heavens no. That dog would drive him crazy. He's too old for a change like that."

"Whatever you say."

"I'll be home soon. No sense upsetting him."

She stopped walking. I noticed her right arm was shaking.

"Are you getting tired?"

"No, I'm not," she said firmly. "I can make it."

Back in her room, she showed me the exercises she had been doing: leg raises while laying on her bed, sitting and standing from her wheelchair, walking back and forth from the door to the window, and knee bends using the support bars on either side of the toilet.

"Sometimes I cry when I'm done," she said. "But usually the pain doesn't last too long."

Reaching over to the nightstand, she removed the lid from the pink and blue ceramic half-moon my mother gave her to store her earrings. She held up the petrified wolf tooth that I gave her after her fall. I'd told her that the wolf was cunning and fierce. Drawing on its power would help her face her fear and allow her to get back on her feet.

"I hold it every night before I go to sleep," she said. "Seems to be doing the job." Tucking it into her palm, she leaned back in her wheelchair. "Some nights when I'm in bed I do a little growling. The Negro girls hear me and—"

"The nurses?"

"Yes. Most of them are Jamaican. Beautiful girls. They hear me growling. I know they think I'm daffy, but I don't care, it makes me feel strong."

I reached over to pat her on the arm. She brushed my hand away. "Don't feel sorry for me."

"I don't, I admire you. You're one of the toughest people I know."

"Well goody for that. Look where it got me. I'm stuck in here with all these, God bless them, old, crazy people."

"But you're getting better."

"That's right," she said, raising her fist, "me and the wolf."

17

THE HOUSE THAT HARRY Whitridge lived in was small. However it is my belief that any house Harry Whitridge lived in would seem small. Standing five-foot ten and weighing in at what had to be at least three hundred and sixty pounds, Harry was a large man, and a force of nature. His monstrous belly laughs were thunder, his walk, a rolling earthquake, his incessant belching and farting, difficult as it was to get used to, was like a tornado whirling around him.

When Christine and I first stepped into the house, and I heard Harry rumbling down the hall orifices ablaze, I didn't know what to think. Christine tried to prepare me, but when Harry emerged from the kitchen dressed in a paisley muumuu, there was no denying that I was in the presence of a unique individual. Harry eyed me with a jaunty tilt of his head.

"Oh, I see."

Not knowing what to make of that, I smiled and nodded; my usual gesture when at a loss for words. Harry led us into the living room. Unlike most homes in the Santa Fe and Taos area, it was not decorated in a western motif. Oriental rugs covered the floor and Chinese art hung on the walls.

As he squatted to sit on a delicate teak love seat, I braced myself for the sound of splintering wood. Instead, I heard a prodigious belch as Harry lowered himself onto the cushions. Like the velvety petals of a rose, the cushions gently folded around him. From his throne of pinched creases, Harry motioned for me to sit in the leather armchair directly across from him.

"Would you like me to leave," Christine asked.

Harry's voice boomed, "I think that will be unnecessary. Master Thomas is nervous enough without being left alone." Harry dipped his head and let loose a resounding belch. "Oh, yes, much better," he said, rubbing his stomach. "I think we're ready if you are."

I nodded and sat back in the chair. Christine gave me a supportive smile. Coming to Harry had been her idea. She wanted to help me get clear on my deepening connection with the Native American culture. As Harry closed his eyes and began to take deep breaths, I tried to remember what Christine told me. Harry was a trance channel. He allowed spiritual beings, primarily his guide Rodas, to enter his body and use it as a vehicle of communication. She also told me that he made a lot of weird sounds. A quiet belch burbled out of Harry to emphasize the point. As I watched him continue his breathing, the vast swells of his flesh began undulating. This odd rolling in his torso intensified until his entire body was quaking and shuddering. He suddenly made a choking, gasping sound and his eyes flew open and rolled back in his head. Thinking that he was having a heart attack, I jumped to my feet. I was about to slam him in the chest with my fist and attempt CPR when I noticed Christine frantically gesturing for me to sit down. I looked back at Harry. He had become very still.

"Blessings! Blessings!" a voice suddenly sang out. It came from Harry, but it sounded nothing like him. The voice was higher and had a faint accent.

"No cause for alarm. My good friend Harry is not dying," the voice said, reading my mind. "It's simply the dynamics of entry, you see."

"Hello, Rodas," Christine said. "I brought a friend."

"A pleasure to be in your energies divine Christine."

Christine blushed and said, "This is Tom McInnes."

Harry/Rodas turned to me. His face scrunched into a smile. "Well, it's about time, isn't it?"

Again, not knowing what to say, I smiled and nodded.

Harry/Rodas belched. "You may open your mouth," he said. "I know you can do it."

I nervously licked my lips. I was spooked. A moving table was one thing, but a direct one on one conversation with a temporarily embodied spiritual entity was something else.

"I—I'm pleased to meet you, Rodas," I said.

"And I, you." He hunched forward on the couch. Rodas seemed to want more mobility than Harry's bulk would permit. *Either Harry is an amazing actor,* I thought, *or this thing is real.*

"Your mother hasn't forgiven you for leaving," Harry/Rodas said, "and your father is still, shall we say, on the negative side of his own best intentions."

I stared at him, stunned by what he just said. His head tilted back and he straightened his shoulders.

"I'm real Thomas, just as real as you and Christine, minus a body of course. But that's why we have Harry, generous soul that he is."

"I believe you," I said. And I did. How else would he know such information about my parents and me?

"Tom has some questions about past lives," Christine said, keeping the session on track.

"Yes, it's time for this knowledge to be passed on." Harry/Rodas said, and he began to hum. It was more like making a tone, a low-pitched tone. After a moment he nodded his head, belched twice, and said, "Oh, interesting."

He proceeded to inform me that what was coming up for me was a life that I lived as a Mescalero Apache. It was a time when whites were beginning to reach out for control of native lands in the west. I had raided and taken many lives. He paused for a moment and clucked his tongue.

"Your father was one of the men you killed. You shot an arrow through his lungs. He died slowly, bleeding and gasping for breath."

He went on to mention other lives I lived: a highly skilled archer during medieval times and a confederate sniper during the Civil

War. In the war, my mother was the captain I'd served under. Rick and I had been brothers in Morocco, raiding other bands of nomads and raced camels together. I was the older brother in that lifetime. As an early settler in Utah, I led a pack train of mules on a steep, mountainous trail. Becky was my daughter. She was riding a mule that stopped and refused to go on. I pleaded and pulled on the reins but the animal refused to budge. Out of frustration, I smacked it on the rump with a stick, causing it to begin bucking and kicking. I watched, horror-stricken, as the panicked animal stumbled off the edge of the trail, hurling Becky to her death.

"These are the lives you've lived," Harry/Rodas said solemnly. "There have been many, many more, but I am most interested in the family connections. Fascinating isn't it?"

I didn't know what to think. Shooting my father with an arrow, sending my sister over a cliff, it was too much to get my head around. "Yes," I mumbled. "It's fascinating, and disturbing."

He chuckled. "I know, this information can be overwhelming, but these past lives are interwoven into your current relationships with these people. To better understand the complete energetic, psychic infrastructure will allow you to have greater compassion, both for yourself and for them."

I nodded, thinking of the arrow in my father's lungs. A loud belch brought my focus back to Rodas.

"As a Mescalero, you were afraid of death and the bodies of the dead. Tomorrow you must take a walk in the mountains. You'll find something there that will engage your spirit and allow you to move beyond your fear of death."

"Where in the mountains should I go?"

"You're a smart boy. You'll figure it out."

Christine stifled a laugh.

"Well, that's all I have time for. Harry's system can only handle my vibrations for short periods."

Christine placed her palms together, bowing her head reverently.

"Thank you for coming, Rodas."

"As always the pleasure to serve is mine. I have brought light and truth. It's now yours to carry however you choose."

Harry/Rodas nodded to both of us then began to make the low-pitched tone. Suddenly he stopped, leaned forward, and leveled his gaze directly at me. "One last thing, call your parents."

The following day, at Christine's urging, I hiked through the San Juan Mountains west of Taos. I wandered along trails, going in whatever direction seemed most interesting. I had no idea what I was looking for. I tried to imagine what my friend Kirby back in Pittsburgh would say if he knew I was following the instructions of Harry/Rodas. He'd never be able to stop laughing.

After five hours of wandering, I was ready to call it quits. I was halfway up a slope, and had just finished drinking from my water bottle, when I spotted a rock outcropping three hundred yards up the hill. I decided to use it as a lookout point. If I didn't see anything interesting from up there, I was going to start back.

It was a rigorous climb over jagged talus. By the time I reached the outcropping, sweat was pouring off of me. After drinking more water, I started out to the end of the rock overhang. Before I got there I saw a shallow hollow in the ground. I stepped closer. The depression was two feet across and lined with rocks. Broken sticks lay in the bottom. It looked similar to the picture of an eagle trap that I'd seen in a book on Navajo ceremonial life.

I knelt down and began searching through the debris lining the bottom of the trap. I found the wolf tooth wedged between two rocks. I didn't know if it was the thing that Harry/Rodas wanted me to find, but it was most likely from a dead animal. With the tooth in my hand, I sat down and gazed into the immense openness stretching across to the far mountain peak. *What a thrill,* I thought, *to have all this space.* There was plenty of room to fall and fly. If I were an eagle, I would have hung out there too.

• • •

WHEN I SPOKE TO my mother and father, the conversation went reasonably well. Mom was cheery and full of neighborhood news. She was quick to give me an update on the new duck, a Blue Wing Teal she was finishing, and she mentioned running into Dee Dee in the frozen food section of the Giant Eagle. She said that Dee Dee was looking as good as ever and wanted to know how I was doing.

My father, the calmness in his voice sounding strained to the point that I was certain he would eventually snap and lay into me, inquired into the soundness of both my finances and the Honda. Rick apparently told him that I bought a motorcycle. After confirming that I had money in the bank and a mechanically sound mode of transportation, I told them about Lilly, Christine and Emerson, and the fact that I let my hair grow long. I could sense Dad champing at the bit on that one. Long hair had always been one of his pet peeves. Surprising me, and I'm sure himself, he maintained his composure. His efforts toward peace prompted a desire in me to tell both of them about the past-life information Harry/Rodas gave me. I wanted to apologize for the arrow I shot through Dad's lungs, but I knew if I told them, they would freak out. They would think that I joined a cult or something.

As we were saying goodbye my father could restrain himself no longer.

"At some point, Tom," he said, "you're going to have to stop all this fooling around and get a steady job. Being part of the real world won't kill you."

The next day the reactor at Three Mile Island melted down.

I called to see if my parents were in danger of contamination.

"Don't worry," my father said. "Officials at the site have things under control."

"Don't believe everything you see on television or read in the newspaper."

"They have contingencies for situations like this," he said. "Stop being a paranoid radical."

"You stop sticking your head in the sand."

"Grow up."

"Wake up. Nuclear power plants are corporate America once again making huge short-term profits by ignoring enormous long-term risks. Dad, if you think I'm ever going to join ranks with the political and economic machine that foisted nuclear energy upon the innocent masses, you're crazy."

"Good luck, Tom," my father said. "I hope you find the utopia you're looking for."

We both hung up at the same time.

I couldn't stop thinking of the farmland in Pennsylvania that was now contaminated by radiation. Food sustained us. Without it we would cease to exist. Was cheap electric energy worth risking our ability to grow healthy food? Reminded of how uncertain the future was, staying in Taos, I decided, wasn't going to get me where I needed to be. It was time for a move.

Saying goodbye to Christine and Emerson was difficult. They were good friends and gracious hosts. Emerson had led me to receive my sacred name, Singing Bow, and also the vision of the orange grove. I didn't yet understand the significance of either of them, but I was optimistic that sooner or later clarity would find its way to me.

Rocky chased me as I drove away down the dirt road. He stopped at the top of the hill, barking and running in circles. I turned left at the highway and pointed the motorcycle north. The sky was bright and clear. I twisted the throttle. The little Honda pressed into the wind. The white lines on the blacktop flitted past blending into one long cord pulling me forward. I had a full tank of gas, two bananas, an orange, and a bag of pistachios. I was back on the road to Pomona.

18

Driving over to Kirby's house, I was reminded of the mainstays of the Fourth of July picnics I'd gone to while growing up: bratwurst on the grill, kegs of ice cold Iron City and Rolling Rock beer, and heaping mounds of German potato salad. If you were throwing a party you might have hamburgers and hot dogs, or boneless chicken breasts and red cabbage coleslaw. You could even get fancy with a couple kegs of beer brewed in Ohio or New York. But if you didn't also serve the main stays, when it came time to watch the fireworks, there wouldn't be many people left hanging around.

With his huge backyard decked out in red, white, and blue streamers and cardboard silhouettes of dead presidents, I could see that Kirby had all the standards and more. It was a feast far surpassing anything I'd seen in years. Picnic tables piled high with food bordered the perimeter of a square canvas tent. There was German chocolate cake, peanut butter fudge brownies, tubs of vanilla ice cream, and wicker baskets overflowing with M&M and oatmeal-raisin cookies. Along with the bratwurst sizzling on a twenty-foot barbecue, there were neatly arranged sections of salmon steaks, hamburgers, kabobs of lamb, and pork ribs dripping in barbecue sauce. Across from the five-piece band and wooden dance floor was the salad table. The centerpiece, surrounded by watermelon slices and strawberries the size of your fist, was a red, white, and blue Jello mold in the shape of the White House.

A rapid burst of firecrackers in the corner of the yard exploded. Kirby's three boys and several of their friends huddled together to light another batch. Kirby turned away from his conversation with Steve Petrovic, one of the line supervisors at the plant, and watched the boys light the string of firecrackers. When they moved a safe distance away, he turned back to Steve and continued talking. It gave me a grin to see Kirby behaving like a parent. I could still see him hauling his skinny seventeen-year-old body out the window of my father's Pontiac as I drove across the 7th Street Bridge. Laying up on the roof of the car, spread-eagle and stoned out of his mind, he kept screaming for me to go faster. I finally had to pull over two blocks from Allegheny General Hospital and drag him down. Now he was worried about his boys safely handling firecrackers.

Sam, Kirby's oldest, was born when I was living in New Mexico. Next was Jonathan. I was in Colorado when he came into the world. The youngest, Spencer, came on the scene when I was somewhere in Europe. While Kirby was building a great marriage with Jeannie, his college sweetheart, a successful business, a home, and a family; I was running around chasing visions and following signs. He was settled. I was adrift. As frequently occurred when I dwelled on the different paths we'd taken, I suffered an irritating sense of longing.

Janis Summervail was at the front of the beer line pouring an Iron City draft. I remembered her as tall and skinny with long blonde hair and a peace sign sewn on the ass of the bell bottoms she always wore to high school. Now she had short red hair and was carrying a few more pounds. The only continuity from my younger version of Janis was the small boy at her side. He wore a T-shirt with a large blue peace sign on the front.

"Tommy McInnes," Janis said, shifting her beer to her left hand and extending her right. "What's up with you?"

"Good to see you, Janis. Happy fourth."

"Yeah, thanks. You too."

"Who is this?"

"My son, Derrick."

"Hey, Derrick. Are you having fun?"

The boy's long lashes fluttered nervously. He hid his face behind Janis' thigh.

"Being shy, huh?"

"He gets like that," she said. "Don't you angel boy?" Derrick peeked out at me.

"You know who I just saw in the kitchen?" Janis said. She licked the foam from the edge of her beer cup. "Dee Dee Razinbach. God, she looks great."

"Dee Dee is here?"

"Oh, that's right, you guys were friends. She's in the kitchen talking with Jeannie."

"I'm going to—" I pointed to the house.

"Yeah, go ahead. I'll see you later."

"Nice meeting you, Derrick." I gave him the peace sign, and he giggled and ducked behind Janis.

Dee Dee and Jeannie were no longer in the kitchen. As I stepped back onto the brick patio, I thought of the last time I talked with Dee Dee. We'd written to each other in college, but the last time I actually saw her was ten years ago at Max's Allegheny Tavern. I was home for Christmas. She was with her fiancé, Matt who had just completed his MBA program. They were on their way to Portland, Maine, where he was starting a new job. Until I saw them together, I didn't realize that I'd been keeping a place in my heart open for her. And now I was about to see her again. It felt kind of weird.

"I've been looking for you," a voice whispered in my ear. I turned around, and there was Dee Dee. She threw her arms around my neck and gave me a hug. The experience of hugging a past lover and that of hugging an old friend, are distinctly different. The scent of coconut cream rinse in Dee Dee's hair, and the pressure of her hands on my back, triggered vivid memories of our bare skin, slippery with sweat, touching and moving together. I once again felt the roughness of the car's upholstery on my knees and heard Dee Dee's passionate cry, "Don't stop now or I'll kill you!"

"Mommy I have to go again," a small voice said. I looked down. A little girl was pulling on Dee Dee's white sun dress.

Dee Dee bent down and picked her up. The resemblance was uncanny.

"Jessie, this is Tom. We went to school together."

Jessie pushed a strand of curly blonde hair away from her face. "Hi," she said impatiently. "I have to poop."

Dee Dee stifled a laugh. "Honey, Mommy is the only person you need to tell, okay?" Jessie nodded and put her fingers in her mouth.

"I'll be right back," Dee Dee said. She reached over and squeezed my arm. "It's so good to see you."

As the afternoon turned into evening, we danced, ate, and got caught up on each other's lives. Jessie was Dee Dee's second child. Her first, Duncan, was visiting her husband's parents in Tampa. Duncan would be flying up to join Dee Dee in two weeks. They planned to spend the rest of the summer with Dee Dee's parents. Dee Dee and Matt had separated four months earlier. She didn't say why and I didn't ask.

"When Jeannie told me you were here it was weird," Dee Dee said. "It's been a long time."

I looked at Jessie who was falling asleep in Dee Dee's lap. "I know what you mean."

"I still can't believe you're not married."

"You and my mother."

"How are good old Dick and Merna?"

"Same shit, new decade," I said. Dee Dee looked down at Jessie.

"Sorry," I said.

"It's not like she's never heard the word. I just try to keep it to a minimum." She ran her hand over Jessie's golden locks.

"She's beautiful," I said.

"Thanks. And she's a smartie too."

Jeannie danced by leading a long line of parents and kids waving sparklers over their heads. Kirby grabbed me and pulled me to my feet. I waved to Dee Dee as we snaked our way toward the dance floor.

"See what you've been missing!" Kirby yelled above the music.

I could tell he was half in the bag. I jumped on his back and shouted, "You're a lucky man!"

"This is true!" he yelled, and piggybacked me across the lawn. A loud boom got everyone's attention as the sky to the west lit up. An oval of red twinkling lights rained down.

"The fireworks are starting!" Kirby yelled.

Jessie covered her ears as the public display from North Park was launched. She looked frightened through most of it, but when the finale started and they began blasting off everything they had, her eyes widened and a look of amazement spread across her dainty face. After the last rocket exploded in a giant circle of red, white, and blue, everyone in the backyard burst into applause. Jessie clapped her hands and called out, "Do it again!"

The party began to break up a short while later. Dee Dee's car was parked down the street in front of a wooded area. As she strapped Jessie into her seat, I leaned against the trunk of the car. The band up at the party started a new song. I couldn't quite make out what it was.

"She's already asleep," Dee Dee said. She slid up onto the trunk next to me.

"Great party, huh?" I said.

"Sure was. I can't believe how big Kirby's boys are."

"I know."

She put her hand on my thigh and she reached down to scratch her leg. "Mosquito got me," she said.

Her shapely, tan, calf contrasted nicely with the white fabric of her dress. She caught me looking and slipped the dress back down.

"I better get going," I said. I stood up quickly and stepped away from the car. "It was great seeing you, Dee."

"You too, Tommy."

"Should be a nice pool day tomorrow. Weather man said it might hit eighty-three."

"Yeah, I heard that," she said.

"My mother was telling me about a new water slide park. I guess they have – Oh God, blah, blah, blah." I looked at her and shrugged. "This is silly."

"What?"

"I'm nervous and I'm babbling."

"I know. I feel like I'm sixteen."

"What can I say? You look great. I was having flashbacks."

"I'm an old married lady now."

"Right. Mother of two."

"Hard to believe, isn't it?"

"You seem like a great mom."

"Thanks."

"So anyway, you guys are here for the summer, right?"

"Yep, me and the kids."

"Well, we'll get together and do some stuff. Go to Kennywood maybe."

"Duncan loves roller coasters."

"There you go."

I opened my arms and stepped to her. We hugged. It was a nice firm platonic hug. She gave me a friendly peck on the cheek. I gave her one in return. The next thing I knew, I was kissing her lips. She tensed, then made a growling sound and pulled me closer, crushing her breasts against my chest. As quickly as it began, it ended.

"Really good to see you again," Dee Dee said, straightening her dress and backing toward the driver's side of the car.

"I'll call you and, you know, we'll do something," I smiled a bit too broadly and bobbed my head like jack-in-the-box.

"Great! My best to your folks."

"Same here. Drive carefully!"

She started the car. The brake lights flashed and dimmed. I saw her eyes watching me in the rear view mirror. I couldn't tell if she was smiling.

19

THE MIGHTY HONDA DIDN'T make it very far. After leaving Taos, I was only an hour east of Durango, Colorado when the engine seized. With an ominous metallic sputter, my faithful steed gulped its final mixture of gasoline and air, belched a black cloud of exhaust vapors, and then soared off to a new showroom in Honda heaven. I reluctantly rolled the motorcycle into a ditch on the side of the road. More than a little apprehensive about hitch-hiking again, but with no other financially reasonable options, I took the license plate off the Honda, threw my duffel bag over my shoulder, and stuck out my thumb.

Two nights later I was stepping out of a Plymouth Fury in downtown Las Vegas. The driver, a pug-nosed car salesman from Salt Lake City, had come to town for an automobile convention. As he sped off in search of his hotel, I was left to gawk at the staggering dazzle of blinking neon. To go from the crunchy-granola serenity of Taos, to Las Vegas glitz, was an overwhelming sensory experience. I felt like I'd landed on another planet.

In search of inexpensive lodging, I walked four blocks off the strip to a cheesy motel called the Doo-Rite Inn. After killing two cockroaches and taking a quick shower, I changed my clothes and headed back to the casinos. I wanted to eat a cheap dinner and get to bed early. The map I bought before leaving Taos, showed that Las Vegas was five or six hours north of Los Angeles. With Pomona being only a short distance southeast of LA, I knew that I was getting close.

The Roman columns and colored lights outside of Caesar's Palace lured me through the doors like a fish to the hook. Inside, a roaring din of voices, music, and slot machines assaulted my ears. Polyester leisure suits dotted the crowd in splashes of eye-jarring color. Waitresses in cleavage revealing, mini-skirted togas twisted and turned through the crowd carrying trays jammed with cocktails and packs of cigarettes.

I went to a cashier and got five dollars' worth of quarters. If the Great Spirit was indeed leading me, perhaps financial abundance was meant to be a part of my path. With jackpots flashing in my mind, I walked to a row of slot machines and inserted a quarter. I paused with my hand on the lever.

"Seriously," I said, under my breath, "I promise to make big charitable donations."

I pulled the lever. I won nothing. I stuck in another quarter. Again I won nothing. I burned through the five dollars of quarters without winning a single thing. I dug through my pockets and pulled out my last lint-covered quarter. I dropped it in the slot and pulled the lever. The cylinders spun. Three lemons came to a stop. The lights on the machine rapidly flashed on and off. A rush of quarters jangled into the catch basin. Laughing at my good luck, I scooped up a handful of the coins, and looked around to share my celebration. The only person in my aisle of slot machines was a woman sitting ten feet away. She appeared to be in her early forties with sandy blond hair to her shoulders and a deep tan.

"I won." I said proudly.

"I see that," she said.

"I never gambled before."

"You're lucky."

"Yeah."

I began loading my quarters into a plastic bucket.

"I haven't won anything," she said. She deposited a quarter and pulled the lever. She didn't win.

"See," she said. She stood up and swung the strap of a brown, leather purse onto her shoulder. She was statuesque, five feet ten at least, with a lean, athletic figure.

"What brings you to Las Vegas," I said, enjoying my moment of victory over the odds.

"A conference," she said. "Boring, boring, boring. How about you?"

"I'm just passing through."

"Where are you going?"

"I'm on the way to Pomona, California."

"Oh. What's in Pomona?"

"Don't know exactly."

"Oooh. Sounds intriguing."

I laughed and thought, *if she only knew.*

"Tell me more," she said.

"It's a long story."

"Give me the Cliff Notes version."

"Someone told me to go. So I'm going."

"For your job?"

"Sort of."

"What do you do?"

"Seek truth."

She grinned. "Good work if you can get it."

"Not always easy."

"So who told you that Pomona, California was a good place to find truth?"

I hesitated then thought, *Why not, I'll never see this woman again.*

"A bird."

"What?"

"You heard me."

"A bird told you to go to Pomona, California?"

"That's right."

She looked at me strangely then asked, "Was it a blue heron?"

• • •

HER NAME WAS CARYN Trilling. She was married and lived in Boulder, Colorado. Over chocolate cake and cups of coffee, she told me about her career as a therapist. She worked with a group on Thursday nights who believed they had experienced encounters with beings from other dimensions. During the past six years, two people had openly talked about meeting energy forms resembling great blue herons.

"Really?" I said. "Just when I thought I was special."

"That's the same reaction a lot of people have at first. But feeling special can also lead to a sense of isolation."

"Yeah. Like you're a freak."

She thought for a moment then said, "Would you like to come to Colorado? You can work with the group. We have a network of friends all over the world dealing with this kind of phenomena."

"No thanks."

"You can stay with me and my husband. We have a guest cabin."

"Is this some kind of cult?"

"No. It's a support group. When this happens to someone there can be a great deal of confusion. People's lives get turned upside down."

"I got a sign. I'm just trying to see where it leads."

"I understand. But I think it's important you move forward on your journey in as grounded a manner as possible. This kind of thing can throw you for some serious emotional loops."

"It's nice of you to offer, but—"

"Do you think it was just a coincidence that we met?"

"I—I don't know."

"Come on. How many people in Las Vegas right now have had encounters with blue herons?"

"By the looks of some of them, I'd say quite a few."

She tried, but couldn't hold back a grin. "I'm not going to nag you into this. But if you're following signs this is definitely one of them."

"I don't know. I mean, I do have questions, but . . ."

"Like what?"

"I want to know about souls and other dimensions. I want to know what it feels like to be free of all this stuff that got piled on me. I want to feel who I really am underneath my bones."

"Are the answers to those questions in Pomona?"

"I don't know. I don't really know what's what anymore."

"My point exactly," she said.

Caryn saw the resignation come into my eyes. We left the next morning on the eight-twenty flight to Denver.

• • •

CARYN AND DON'S LOG cabin in Boulder, Colorado was nestled in a picturesque grove of aspens with a chimney made of river rock and a wide, inviting front porch.

When Don Trilling opened the front door, my first impression was that he looked like a forest ranger. Tall and broad shouldered, his bushy beard and rough outdoorsy appearance belied the fact that he was a CPA who ran his own accounting firm. He welcomed me into the house with a firm handshake.

"It's not Caryn's usual practice to bring stray men home from Las Vegas," he said, with a grin. She looped her arm through his and we moved into the living room. The vaulted ceiling gave the room a spacious, unrestrained feeling. Two brown leather couches and a recliner were positioned around a glass coffee table.

"Caryn told me that you're on your way to Pomona," Don said.

"That's right. But I seem to be moving in the wrong direction."

"Who knows," he said, "maybe it's exactly the right direction. If our friends can be of help, great, if not, we'll put you on a plane to Los Angeles. Fair enough?"

"Sure," I said.

Caryn walked me forty yards north of the house, through the grove of aspens, to their guest cabin. Smaller and older than the main house, the cabin was spotless. I could practically see myself in the shine of the wooden floors.

As I stashed the few clothes I'd brought with me into the dresser next to the brass double bed, Caryn told me that we would be going to a group meeting at four o'clock that afternoon. She invited me to settle in and relax for a few hours.

I found an old issue of Sports Illustrated in the book case and lay down on the bed. I opened the magazine, and there was a beer ad I immediately recognized. My father was the agency executive in charge of the campaign. Drink this beer and you'll get the pretty girl was the basic message. Do women really care what brand of beer a man drinks? "Image, image, image," my father would say, "It's all in the way things look." Rick bought into the high octane consumer culture my father helped create. He owned prestigious luxury cars, a big house in the right neighborhood, a membership at a super posh country club, and a garage full of manly toys. All of it purchased to satisfy what he perceived to be his God-given right to material and social happiness. He was also up to his tonsils in debt. But not me, I was seeking a deeper truth.

I rolled over onto my side and hugged a pillow to my chest. At four o'clock, I was going to be in a room full of people as wacky as I was. I wasn't looking forward to the experience.

• • •

THERE WERE TWELVE OF them in the room, twelve other people, plus Caryn, calmly sitting on chairs and couches patiently waiting for me to say something. I searched from face to face for the person in the group who was unquestionably a nut case. I wanted to feel superior to at least one person in the room. Unfortunately, other than Leslie, a cute brunette in her early twenties wearing a T-shirt with a purple space ship emblazoned across the front, everyone appeared to be perfectly normal.

"Why do you think this happened to you, Tom?" Caryn said. She smiled encouragingly from the back of the room. I saw Leslie nod her head. Candice, an older woman with dyed red hair, gave me a supportive thumbs up.

"Why?" I repeated.

"Yes, why you?"

I looked down at the tan carpeting. The meeting room and Caryn's adjoining office were both decorated in earthy shades of browns and greens. Mentally soothing and easy on the eye, they were probably strategically chosen to prevent the loonies from going berserk.

"I know it isn't easy to talk about," Caryn said. "But I think you'll find this to be quite a receptive group."

I looked up from the carpeting. I was disappointed no one had left the room. I glanced toward the door. Maybe if I ran fast enough.

Leslie shifted in her seat, and then stood up. "Tom, it's not like you're any different than us." She walked over to me. "If I'm up here with you, will that help you feel more comfortable?"

"No," I said sharply.

She raised her eyebrows in surprise. As she turned to go back to her seat, I grabbed her arm.

"Yeah, what the hell, the more the merrier."

She put her hands on my shoulders and turned me to face the group. She smelled good, like vanilla ice cream.

"Just talk," she whispered in my ear.

Before I could think about it, I let the words tumble out.

"Hi. My name is Tom McInnes. When I was seventeen I ate some mushrooms and had an encounter with a great blue heron. I don't know why it happened to me. It was weird and fascinating and scary. The blue heron told me I'd find my truth on the way to Pomona, California, so that's where I'm trying to go."

Much to my surprise, they all began clapping. Leslie put her arm around my shoulders and hugged me.

"It's a start," she said.

The group rose in a standing ovation. Looking out at Caryn and the rest of them clapping and whistling, two distinct thoughts flashed in my mind: *Thank you Great Spirit for bringing me to these nice people who understand what I've been going through,* and, *holy shit what am I doing with this bunch of nut cases.*

• • •

THEY LAID CRYSTALS ON me. They chanted over me. We hiked through the mountains. We danced naked under the full moon. I stared for hours into candle flames. I met people who adamantly claimed they'd been abducted by ETs from Zeta Reticuli in the constellation Reticulus. I heard stories about balls of light appearing in the sky, little fairies in the Olympic National Forest, silvery disks hovering over corn fields in Iowa, blue beams of light surrounding houses in the middle of the night, sex with aliens, hybrid babies, the appearance of glowing, heavenly angels, tall thin men, short gray men, beautiful beings from the Pleiades, stoic soldiers from Orion, the horror of anal probes, brain scans, needles inserted into eyes, ears, and noses, the mysterious appearance of scars, scoop marks and burns, the confusion of lost memories, and the ego bashing belief that we're all rats in a cage.

There were a lot of people out there, I learned, who suffered far stranger experiences than I. They left their spouses, jobs, sold their cars, houses, and basically became different individuals because of what they'd gone through. They endured considerable confusion and distress, but at the same time, they were invigorated by feelings of rejuvenation.

Finding out that I wasn't alone on my journey emboldened me to separate even further from who I had been. I grew a beard and started wearing sandals. Leslie pierced my ear and gave me a silver hoop to wear. I began working part-time at Don Trilling's accounting firm. I looked like the buccaneer file clerk.

I sought out the other two people who encountered blue herons. Gail Lovell, a secretary in her mid-forties, refused to talk about it. In the front yard of her modest ranch-style home, over the drone of her weed wacker, she told me that she'd blabbed about it for three years and had said all that she intended to say. She did, however, point out that her face never recovered from her encounter. A pinched nerve left her right eyebrow arched at an odd angle. It gave her face an oddly ironic look, sort of a jaunty, you-have-absolutely-no-idea expression.

Bud Endelman was a whole other story. A pot-bellied, red-nosed rancher with thinning gray hair and a cyst the size of a golf ball on the back of his neck, getting Bud to talk wasn't a problem.

"Jesus H. Christ," he said. "You should have seen that fuckin' thing." He tilted his head down. A brown stream of tobacco juice splattered in the dust inches from my boot. "Put the fear of God in me, I'll tell you that. Never been the same since." He looked toward his cattle grazing nearby. For a minute or so, he didn't say anything.

"Truth to tell," he finally said. "It was beautiful. That big sucker lit up my barn like it had a 220 watt spotlight up its ass."

"How long ago did it happen?"

"Six years."

"Do you mind telling me about it?"

"You a writer or something?"

"No."

"Hell, what do I care? Life don't bring you stuff like this often. Gotta talk about it or you might think you're goin' wacko. Know what I mean?"

"Yes, sir," I said, "I know exactly what you mean."

Over coffee and glazed donuts in his kitchen, Bud told me the details of his encounter. It happened at 4:30 in the afternoon on a Friday, two weeks after his wife Arlene died from lung cancer.

"I was in the barn fixing the fuel line on my tractor," Bud said. "The wrench slipped and I'd smacked the hell outta my knuckles." He wagged his finger at me. "Let me tell you, I was cussin' a blue streak. Arlene always told me to count to ten, but—" His eyes slipped off of me. With his voice full of tenderness he said, "She never much cared for my cursin'."

I looked down and peeled a chuck of sugary glaze off of my donut.

"Anyway," he said, his voice now stronger. "I'm waving my hand and hopping around, sorely ticked off for skinnin' my knuckles, when all of a sudden there's this poppin' sound. I turn around thinkin' my son Dylan come into the barn. It wasn't Dylan. It was that big blue fucker."

"Please don't be offended by my asking," I said, "but were you sober at the time?"

"Whataya mean was I sober? I hadn't had a drink since the night of Arlene's funeral."

"Okay. What happened next?"

"Well," he said. "It talked to me."

I leaned forward both elbows on the table. "What did it say?"

He shifted in his seat. "Why you asking me all these questions?"

"I saw one too, when I was seventeen."

"No shit?"

"I'm trying to figure out what it means."

Bud whooped. "Good luck! It's baffled the hell outta me."

"Tell me what it said to you."

"It was up in my head. Not like normal people talk."

"Telepathy?"

"Yeah, whatever, I guess that's right." He reached into a drawer below the telephone and began searching through a stack of papers.

"I wrote it down that night. I didn't want to forget. It's here somewhere."

Just then the telephone rang. He picked up the receiver from the cradle on the wall. "Yeah, hullo?" He continued looking through the papers as he talked. I watched his thick, calloused fingers move, trying to imagine him holding hands with his wife or caressing her cheek with those scarred, battered fingers. He plucked out a piece of lined tablet paper.

"Hold on a sec," he said into the telephone. He held the paper out to me. "Here it is." He went back to his conversation. I got up and walked over to the sink. The paper felt stiff, like it had dried out over the years. The message was neatly printed in the middle of the page.

> Let freedom ring. Boldly go to the furthest corners of your mind. There you will find me. Seek out the profound every day. See the forest through the trees, and always remember that you are not alone.

Like a jealous sibling I couldn't help thinking that his message was better than mine. It made a hell of a lot more sense than, "Don't let the rain hurt your head. Always wear a hat."

Bud said goodbye to whoever he was talking to and hung up the telephone. He gestured to the paper in my hand.

"Weird shit, huh?"

I nodded.

"Makes you wonder, don't it?"

"Yeah."

"You are not alone." His eyes playfully widened. "Oooooh, spooky, huh?" He picked up his empty coffee cup and put it in the sink. "Sometimes when I'm in the crapper I wonder who's watching me."

"I've thought the same thing."

"Crazy isn't it?"

I looked out the window above the sink. A squirrel was sitting on a picnic table in the middle of the backyard. It hopped down to the bench. I turned back to Bud.

"I really want to figure this out."

Bud shook his head. "It's a pisser that's for sure. When I told my son about it, he thought maybe an angel had come to visit me."

"An angel?"

"Yeah, you know, after Arlene passed on." He shrugged. "Who knows, maybe the whole thing was my imagination." He pulled on his down vest. "Well, enough gabbing. I've got chores to do."

20

FORTY-NINE PEOPLE IN the U.S. Embassy in Iran were taken hostage on November 4, 1979. In December, 40,000 Soviet troops invaded Afghanistan. On March 30, 1980, Salvadoran Archbishop Oscar Romero was assassinated while saying mass at a hospital chapel in San Salvador. On April 28th, eight American servicemen were killed in the desert during a botched attempt to rescue the hostages in Iran.

I tried to see the work of a divine presence in what was happening in the world, but it wasn't easy. Bad things were happening to good people. If there were angels out there, as Budd Endelman suggested, they had a peculiar way of showing themselves. Fueled by my desire to understand these dark days in human affairs, I stepped up my search to figure out what it was that Bud Endelman and I had seen.

Visions, I learned, were often experienced in meditative states. Alpha waves generated in the visual cortex of the brain, located at the rear of the head in the occipital lobes, were believed to contribute to the process. The visual cortex seemed to produce these alpha rhythms only when it was not distracted with input from the retina.

This went hand in hand with what I'd read about ancient Greece. An individual would enter into a torch-lit underground chamber and stare into the reflective surface of a bowl of liquid. Apparently, concentrating on the liquid made it easier for the visual cortex to ignore the stimulus coming from the eyes. The person meditating could then experience the rhythm of the alpha frequencies while still having his or her eyes open. By doing this, they were able to have visionary experiences.

What I wanted to know was, if the visual cortex wasn't interpreting signals from the eyes, where were the signals coming from? What were the alpha frequencies picking up and sending to the brain? Was it simply the fanciful notions of the imagination? Was it the subconscious trying to exact its will?

When I saw the blue heron I wasn't meditating. My eyes were open. The chemicals in the mushrooms had undoubtedly activated my visual cortex in a way so that I was able to see into this visionary world without the aid of meditation. When I was on the mountain in New Mexico doing my vision quest, it was possible that my fasting had somehow shifted my body chemistry, enabling me to have the orchard vision. But what explained Bud's experience? He was sober, wide-awake, and not suffering from food deprivation. Why had he been able to see the blue heron?

I thought about the clarity of the communication I experienced at Eldora's table. I wondered if the spirits of deceased humans dwelled in the same dimension as the blue heron or angelic beings. And what about the UFO experiences Caryn and Don Trilling's network of friends told me about? Was all of it originating from the same invisible world or was there a stratum of different realities?

During my studies with Lilly, I read that Hindus describe the world as Maya. Maya, seductive and tricky, presents the materiality of the world as being an independent reality, when in truth, according to Hindu belief, there are innumerable galaxies and multiple worlds.

If I wanted to figure out who I was beyond my physical form, I must escape the grasp of Maya. Once I had a comprehensive understanding of how to do that, then I would be able to travel beyond the material world, cruising out and exploring the many mansions within the Great Spirits house. If in my inter-dimensional travel I discovered that behind or under or surrounding the Maya there was a dimension where angels dwelled, then I had a couple questions for the one dressed in the blue heron costume.

On a humid afternoon in August while I was at work at Don's accounting firm, Leslie came by the office. Ever since that first day, when I stood in front of the group, we shared a unique bond. She helped me track down Bud Endelman, and had lent me books and magazine articles. Her frank, directness reminded me of Dee Dee.

"What are you doing in six weeks?" Leslie blurted as she walked in the file room.

"I don't know, what's going on?"

"I'm going to Peru," she said, bouncing up and down on her toes. "And I think you're supposed to go with me."

"Really?"

"This guy I know, Randy, he's been living there for two years. Yesterday I got a letter from him inviting me to come down. He knows of this place -- there've been like zillions of UFO sightings. He's actually seen ten different ships."

"Wow," I said. "That sounds interesting."

"So last night, after getting his letter and thinking, yeah I should go do this, I had a dream. It was a doozy. And you were in it."

"What happened?"

"I don't know what any of it means. It was freaky."

"Tell me."

She gripped the edge of a file cabinet with both hands. "Okay. In the dream this huge black jaguar came into my bed and lay down next to me."

"Yeah?"

"And I wasn't scared or anything. Then, and this is the woo-woo part, when I looked up, you were standing at the foot of my bed. Well, not standing, floating."

"Cool."

"You drifted over to the window. It was round with a – I think it was a red curtain. You pointed up at the stars, at the Big Dipper. A purple light popped into view way off in the distance – well, it was more blue really. Anyway, we watched it zigzag across the sky. You turned to me after a few minutes and said, 'Wouldn't you like to be able to fly like that?' Then I woke up." She bounced up and down on her toes. "So, do you want to go with me?"

Without knowing how I was going come up with the money, I found myself smiling and nodding my head. Extracting myself from the heavy-duty material culture of the United States might help me in my quest to shake free of the Maya. And encountering a UFO in the jungles of Peru could definitely be a cool experience. Hell, the aliens would be able explain about getting into other dimensions. They should know, right?

21

IT LOOKED AS IF Dee Dee's son Duncan retched up some sort of alien life form. I'd never seen anything that color come out of a human being. After projectile vomiting that horrible goo all over the two kids in front of him on the roller coaster, Duncan had the audacity to ask for more of the same purple candy that ignited the fuse of that startling mess. We were walking across the parking lot to my car, so with a pleading look, I urged Dee Dee to deny his request. The last thing I wanted to do was scrape purple puke off of my dashboard.

Up until the evacuation of Duncan's stomach, the day had been quite enjoyable. Kennywood was an amusement park that we had gone to many times as kids. We had as much fun on the rides as Duncan and Jessie.

However, walking through the park pushing a stroller was an entirely different experience. People looked at us as if we were a family. I felt an odd sense of pride that, yes, I could be the father of these children. I could have this lovely woman as my wife. Little did anyone know, I hadn't had a meaningful relationship in years, and all the possessions I owned fit in the back of my truck.

By the time we got back to Dee Dee's parents' house, both of the kids were sound asleep. Her folks left a note saying that they'd gone out for dinner and a movie. While Dee Dee put the kids to bed, I found two cold beers in the refrigerator and walked outside. I rolled my jeans up and sat with my legs dangling in the deep end of the kidney-shaped pool that her parents built when we were in seventh grade.

"Don't you look comfortable," she said, walking out onto the patio. Her hair was no longer in the braided ponytail she'd worn all day at the park. It was hanging loose to her shoulders. I twisted the cap off the other bottle of beer and handed it to her. She took it and clinked her bottle against mine.

"You did well today," she said, "for a single guy. I thought I might lose you when Duncan did his barf-a-thon, but you hung in there."

"That was some nasty stuff coming out of your child."

"That poor little girl in front him," Dee Dee said. "It was all through her hair."

Dee Dee sat down next to me on the edge of the pool, and as I watched her dip her shapely legs into the water, I considered my future. What if the reason I'd come back to Pittsburgh was to be with Dee Dee? What if our paths had crossed again for a purpose? We'd always gotten along. From what I could, see she was a terrific mother. She was definitely wife material. The only problem was she was someone else's wife.

"I still have the last letter you sent me," Dee Dee said. "I read it sometimes before I masturbate."

I blinked in surprise. Perhaps our future together was nearer than I thought.

"I'm assuming," I said, "that the letter wasn't about how poorly I'd done on my accounting mid-term."

She rubbed her wet hands over her tan, upper thighs. Rivulets of water coursed down between her legs.

"No," she said, "It was about how you wanted to rip my clothes off and do me from behind until I was screaming and shredding the sheets with my fingernails." She smiled sweetly. "Not exactly a gushy love poem, but it works for me."

Yes, I thought with giddy clarity, *I'd finally found my woman. The Great Spirit brought me home to be with Dee Dee.* She leaned against my shoulder and sighed.

"God, you used to turn me on."

Nothing is as strong an aphrodisiac to a man as hearing of his own sexual prowess. My blood began to pound. I put my arm around her. She started to hug me, but then abruptly stood up.

"So," she said, "how is it living with your parents?" Walking over to the patio table, she added, "Are you getting along with them?" She sat down and crossed her legs. Inside of me something squeezed shut.

"We're getting along okay." I pulled my legs out of the water and stood up. "I don't plan on living there a whole lot longer."

"No?" Dee Dee said. "Where are you going?"

It was out of my mouth before I could stop myself. "Back out west."

"What will you do out there?" she asked coolly.

"I don't know for sure."

"Then why go?"

"I have to."

"What do you mean you have to? I don't see anyone holding a gun to your head."

I walked out onto the diving board.

"Jesus, Tommy. When are you going to stop drifting?"

"I don't know, when it feels right not to." I bounced up and down, wondering if I could still do a one-and-a-half somersault.

"Well, I think it's time," she said.

I stopped bouncing. She was standing with her hands on her hips. She looked mildly irritated, but extraordinarily attractive.

"Dee, I'm not saying I want to *stay* out west."

"Is this still about that blue heron thing?"

I thought about trying a back flip.

With an incredulous tone in her voice that sounded remarkably like my father, she said, "Tommy, what are you doing with your life? You need to get a real job. Find a position with benefits and a pension plan, then buy a house, settle down with a good woman, have some children."

I whirled around and stalked off the diving board. I grabbed her roughly by the shoulders. She backed toward the pool trying to pull away. I tightened my grip.

"I don't know what I'm doing!" I said, my face inches from hers. "I just do it. I go where I feel I'm supposed to go. Whatever's been leading me in my life has brought me here. At first I didn't know why. Free rent was as good a guess as I could come up with. But then you show up, and I'm glad to see you and you look great and you feel great and I can't walk by the living room in my parents' house without thinking of you naked."

A smile tugged at the corners of her mouth.

"Wanna go for a swim?" I said quickly. It was a lame attempt to cover the vulnerability I was feeling.

"You can still see the scar on my lower back from the carpet burn I got that day," she said. She put her hand on my arm. "Come on, I'll get you a pair of Dad's trunks."

I let her go, but before I could follow her, she charged at me and shoved me in the pool. At the last second I grabbed her by the wrist. Together we hit the water with a loud splash.

We came up sputtering and laughing. Dee Dee immediately peeled off her wet T-shirt and threw it up onto the patio. I caught a glimpse of her still enormously impressive cleavage. While I tried to pull my shirt over my head, I allowed myself to embrace the distinct possibility that I may be minutes away from where I hadn't been in nearly two decades. Dee Dee must have been thinking the same thing because by the time I finally got my shirt off, her shorts, bra and panties were in a soggy pile on the patio.

I looked around. She was nowhere in sight. Then at the other end of the pool, she surfaced. Her hair was slicked back. She was half in light, half in shadow. She looked sleek and feral.

"The other night, after the party at Kirby's," she said, her voice husky and low, "when you kissed me, I nearly came on the spot."

Blue jeans are far from the easiest things to take off when they're wet. I felt like Houdini as I thrashed around underwater trying to separate myself from their octopus-like grip. All during the struggle I was imagining how it would be to make love with Dee Dee again. The thought of my mouth back on the same nipples that had driven me wild as a teenager and had also suckled her beautiful children, was oddly exciting to me. When I finally succeeded in stripping off my pants and dumping them onto the side of the pool, the primal man within me had emerged from his cave and was rampaging in my blood.

Dee Dee slid out of the shadows toward the center of the pool. Water glistened on her tan shoulders. I started toward her. When I was two feet away I held out my hand. She took it and floated effortlessly toward me. I leaned forward to kiss her. With a loud shriek, she shoved me away and began laughing hysterically. Thinking that maybe she was nervous, I grabbed her around the waist, and despite her struggling, pulled her to me. The touch of her naked body against mine was an amazing jolt. I tried to kiss her again but she broke free, thrashing through the water toward the other end of the pool. I figured it was a game she was playing and started after her. By now she was laughing so hard she was gagging. With considerable effort I finally pinned her into a corner. As I moved in to embrace her, she held up her hands, pleading for me to stop.

"I can't, I can't," she sputtered through her laughter.

"Come on, Dee. I want you bad."

This sent her into even greater hysterics.

"What," I said. "What's so funny?"

"Snot," she said. "There's snot hanging from your nose."

Lapsing into uncontrollable giggles, she pushed off the side of the pool and swam past me. By the time I'd wiped my nose and turned back around, she was up on the patio wrapping a towel around her body.

"I'm sorry," she said, barely restraining herself. "Really I—" With a loud snort she doubled over laughing wildly. Helpless to stop herself, she covered her mouth with her hand and ran into the house.

Alone in the shallow end of the pool, my body struggled to grasp what my brain already knew – the party was over. The chance of me getting any was slim to none and slim just left town. I struggled to make sense of it. How, after I had so graciously endured the public embarrassment and personal disgust of her son's power heave at Kennywood Park, was Dee Dee willing to allow a little nasal mucus come between us and a glorious carnal reunion?

I climbed out of the pool. Inside the house I could hear Dee Dee still laughing. I grabbed a towel draped over one of the chairs and began drying off. I learned years earlier, in my studies of primate behavior, that a male who was willing to accept and raise the offspring of another male was considered generous and outgoing. He was greatly appreciated by females. The studies unfortunately didn't list any data about males, who along with accepting the offspring of other males, also had snot running out of their noses. With no other reasonable way to explain Dee Dee's shunning of my advances, I fell back on the universal male rationale for aberrant female behavior: must be a chick thing.

22

AFTER NEGOTIATING A GENEROUS advance on my wages from Don Trilling, brushing up on my Spanish, and reading Fodor's travel guide of South America, Leslie and I flew on American Airlines out of Denver. We refueled in Miami and after a six-hour flight, landed on a smoggy, gray evening in Lima, Peru, "The City of Kings."

"What a shithole, huh?" Leslie's friend Randy said. He flicked the ash of his cigarette out the window and gave us a crooked-tooth grin.

We were driving north up the Pan-American Highway. Cool air blew through the open windows of his battered Mercedes sedan. Randy's brown, shoulder-length hair blew in chaotic swirls as he took a final drag on his cigarette. With a practiced flick of his ring-laden fingers, he shot the glowing butt out the window. He turned to Leslie in the front seat and rubbed his dark stubble of beard.

"Not exactly like home-sweet-home is it, amiga?"

Leslie nodded solemnly. The abject squalor of the sprawling shanty-towns we passed was heartbreaking: adobe brick buildings crumbling in decay, corrugated sheet metal shacks, children playing in ditches filled with murky water. We were definitely no longer in the shopping mall excess of America. This was a different world all together. I stared out the window, culture shocked and uneasy.

It began at the airport in Lima. We exited the plane expecting to see pan flute players and dancing Indians dressed in their native ponchos and colorful skirts and petticoats. Instead, we encountered Peruvian soldiers armed with machine guns. Our ethereal wow-look-at-the-cool-spaceship excitement plummeted to earth.

After making our way through the maze of passport checks and luggage searches, Leslie spotted Randy. At 6'3" he towered over the rest of the milling crowd. As soon as he saw Leslie his face lit up. Then he saw me.

"I thought your friend's name was Tammy," he said giving Leslie a hug. He eyed me in a macho, territorial way.

"Tommy," Leslie said. "Tommy McInnes."

"Hi Randy," I said, extending my hand.

"Hey, man," he said, and shook it. He stepped back and looked at the two of us. Perceiving no overt signs of romantic involvement, he seemed to relax.

On the way to the car, Randy explained to us that the political climate in Peru had recently destabilized. A rebel group called the Shining Path, a Marxist-Leninist-Maoist political party had recently ramped up its people's war. Their brutal tactics had caused the country's security to tighten everywhere.

"Where do you live," I called to Randy from the wind swept back seat of the Mercedes.

"Rimac," Randy said. "It's across the river from Centro."

"What's Centro?"

"Downtown Lima," he said. "We'll be there in a few minutes."

Lima was founded in 1535 by Francisco Pizarro after he and a small army of crazed conquistadors met with, and in a short span of time, slaughtered most of the hierarchy of the Incan Empire. For the next 300 years Lima was the capital of Spain's South American Empire.

With this gruesome slice of history fresh in my mind, thanks to Fodor's Travel Guide, I was not surprised to see two juicy tomatoes splattered against the chest of the equestrian bronze of Pizarro flanking the imposing Presidential Palace.

"The natives are restless," Randy said.

"Is it safe out here?" Leslie asked. She glanced nervously around the busy plaza.

Randy nodded, "Except for the pickpockets."

The sun just set leaving the sky streaked in ribbons of orange and pink. The plaza was a circus of beggars, businessmen, tourists, school children, and moped riders, all going in different directions.

"Anybody hungry," I asked.

"I could use a drink," Randy said.

"I need food too," Leslie said.

"Good," Randy said. "Enough with the sightseeing, it's time to party."

The three of us sat down to a delicious feast of spicy fish stew in the restaurant of the Gran Hotel Bolivar. Randy, his somewhat shabby appearance commanding stares from several patrons, kept ordering rounds of Pisco sours, a potent wine-brandy cocktail. It wasn't long before he was talking in the loud, brash manner that gives Americans abroad a bad reputation.

"Piiiiissscoooo makes you reeeally have to go," he said, in a Frito Bandito accent.

"So when can we see the spaceships," Leslie asked quietly. She leaned forward trying to engage Randy in conversation at a normal decibel level.

"Aaah, the mysteries of Lake Titicaca," Randy said. He turned to me. "I've see them."

"Leslie told me," I said. "When are we going to go?"

"Rush, rush, rush," he said, waving his hand limp-wristed through the air. "We'll leave Friday. Fly to Cusco, train to Puno."

"Can we take a bus instead of flying?" I said. "I'm on a tight budget."

"Too dangerous," Randy said. "I'll front you the money."

"I don't want to borrow any more money."

"You can pay me back later," he said, with a grin that was a little too slick and cocky. "It's not a big deal."

He spotted our waiter coming out of the kitchen and waved his arm. "La cuenta, por favor," he yelled across the dining room.

As we settled into the living room of Randy's dilapidated, one-bedroom adobe house that night, he emerged from the his bedroom in a pair of red silk boxers.

"How about some time with the big boy," he said brazenly to Leslie, gesturing toward his bedroom.

Leslie blinked in surprise. "You know," she said. "I'm really tired from traveling."

"You sure, babe?"

"Oh yeah."

"Maybe tomorrow?"

She shook her head. "Not going to happen, Big Boy. Sorry."

Randy looked stunned for a moment, then slinked off into the dark confines of his love den.

With whatever fantasy he'd concocted about Leslie now dashed, Randy became less boisterous and more brooding. Despite having to cope with his mood swings, Leslie and I were intent on enjoying ourselves.

Randy would meet up with us intermittently on our sightseeing adventures, but would disappear at odd hours to go to work. He told us that he worked for an exporter in the Miraflores district. I didn't believe him. What kind of export business was he doing at two-thirty in the morning?

During our three days of touring the city of Lima, I bought a small plastic bag of coca leaves and some ash from an elderly street vendor in the Plaza San Martin. Buying coca for personal use was legal in Peru. With a friendly smile, the old man showed me how to roll the dried leaves with a pinch of ash inside. I followed his instructions and tucked the wad into the side of my cheek like a chew of tobacco. Fueled by the mild stimulant, Leslie and I buzzed through our tours of the museums, gardens, and cafes of Lima.

After a pleasant visit to the Museo de Arte Nacional, we stopped for coffee at a cafe. Upon finishing her third double espresso, Leslie was vibrating in her seat.

"It's like layers, you know," she said. "Spanish influence on top of Incan, the conjurer over the indigenous people." She crossed her legs and then uncrossed them. "Cultures blend, languages merge. It's like soup. That's exactly what I think is going to happen or is already happening with the aliens. I think that they're merging with our species."

"What will the new human/alien species be like?"

She slid forward in her chair. "I was getting a colonic from Sherri Hydek last week and she told me that at some point we won't have to process food the way we do now."

"That'll put her out of business won't it?"

Leslie laughed and widened her eyes at me. "I'm talking down the road a few hundred years."

"I've never had a colonic," I said.

"Oh, God," she said, "they're soooo great. You wouldn't believe the nasty stuff that's inside of you."

I looked into her adorable face and wondered if by the intimate nature of our conversation we had moved to another level in our relationship. I started replaying the steamy jungle-love fantasy that occupied my mind all the way from Denver.

"I think Jesus was an alien," she said. "The wise men followed lights in the sky which were probably space ships. Jesus materialized those loaves of bread and the fish. Come on, that's multi-dimensional stuff. He was reaching through the doorways."

"What controls access to those doors?" I asked. "That's what I want to know?" I leaned forward. "Is it only through drugs or years of meditation or dying or being the Son of God that you can figure out how to get into that place?"

"I don't think we're supposed to know yet," Leslie said. "At least not everyone. Most of the world's population has been asleep for so long that if the real deal was shown to them it would cause too much turmoil. It would spoil the whole pot of soup. You know what I mean?"

I looked out at the rush of faces streaming past the cafe. There had to be someone out there who knew how to slip between the cracks and get beyond this reality. Someone must have figured it out.

. . .

SOUTH OF LIMA, ON the eastern side of the towering Andes, the city of Cusco has existed for nine hundred years. As well as being the ancient capital of the Incan Empire, at 11,000 feet above sea level, Cusco was also a city that challenged the cardio respiratory system of any visitor walking up a flight of stairs. Randy, who inexplicably upon landing in Cusco reverted to his cheery, belligerent self, told us that chewing coca leaves would help with the elevation.

After a short, adrenaline pumping cab ride from the airport, we got a single room for the three of us at a small, seemingly ancient hotel. The train from Cusco to Puno, which was located near Lake Titicaca, only ran a few times a week. While we waited to go south to Puno, we would take the tourist train three hours northwest to visit the ruins of Machu Pichu.

Our hotel room had a beamed ceiling and whitewashed walls three feet thick. The heavy wooden door was hung with giant iron hinges and instead of a doorknob there was a latch with a padlock. I suspected that later the two saggy double beds would ignite a heated negotiation.

After stowing our packs and enjoying a drink of bottled water, we stepped outside. All thirty of the rooms on both floors of the hotel opened into a sunny, brick-lined courtyard. A fountain, the tiled sides of its catch basin cracked and green with algae, was the centerpiece of the courtyard. Around it sat street vendors selling their beautiful alpaca blankets, scarves, gourds with intricately carved scenes of native life, lobe-stretching earrings made of old Spanish coins, silver bracelets, and hand-woven sandals.

After giving us directions to the ruins of Sacsayhuaman, Randy went off to meet with a business associate.

"He wanted you bad," I said, as we walked to the ruins. "It took him a while to get over it, but he seems okay now."

"I think Mr. Mood Swing might be into the Peruvian marching powder."

"He would have tried to get you high if he had it."

"Turn me into his coke slut?"

"Yeah."

"You're probably right. But believe me, I never gave him the idea that I was into him."

"I'm sure you didn't. But hey, you're a babe, men can't help themselves."

Leslie laughed and twirled her money pouch. "I'm more into women these days."

I laughed. "Yeah sure, women."

"No really." She smiled shyly. "You know."

I could see she wasn't joking. "Oh," I said, a dumb, dick-snapping-back-into-my-shorts look spreading across my face. "Oh," I said again, only snippier, attempting to cover the dumb, dick-snapping-back-into-my-shorts look.

"Come on don't be like that," she said. She put her arm around my waist. "I've considered jumping your bones."

I immediately perked up. "Does that mean we might, you know, have a shot at it someday?"

Leslie shook her head. "I don't think so. I'm just coming out. I need all the support I can get. Our friendship means too much to risk messing it up with sex."

"Okay, sure." I said, then added without much conviction, "I understand."

"Thanks, Tom," she said, giving me a squeeze. "I wanted to tell you."

Looking at the eighteen-hundred-foot long limestone wall that remained of the Sacsayhuaman fortress, I marveled at the engineering feat. How, I wondered, was a technologically primitive culture able to transport and perfectly fit together, without any mortar, stones of such enormous mass? It was mind-boggling to me. One of the giant monoliths, according to my travel guide, weighed 361 tons. The accepted theory, similar to the building of the great pyramids, was that hundreds of workers, pulling hemp ropes, rolled the stones into place on a roadway of logs. It didn't seem possible to me. Not even close. And the quarry was miles away.

"This is incredible," Leslie said.

"The rest of it was torn down after the Spanish took over," I said. "They used the stone to build their cathedrals."

"In three or four hundred years," Leslie said, "I wonder who'll be tearing down the Empire State Building and using it to build their –

whatever, transporter decks or garages for their moon scooters." She shook her head and started across the field.

We spent an hour walking along the wall sightseeing and people watching. A Japanese family was taking pictures of each other dwarfed by the immense rocks. I wondered what my parents would think of this place. When I told them that I was going to Peru they'd been disappointed. If I had the time and money to go to South America, why couldn't I go home and visit them more often? I'd tried to explain that it was an opportunity that I didn't want to miss. Our conversation concluded with my mother telling me in a clipped, curt tone, that she sincerely hoped that I would find whatever it was I was searching for. There was nothing I could say to comfort her. I was spiraling away from them. It probably scared them. It scared me too.

Leslie wandered off and was looking at the trinkets a vendor had for sale. I turned to the wall and pressed my palms against the coarse stone. Closing my eyes, I tried to imagine the power it would take to move so huge an object. Unable to get a clear understanding of that mystery, I switched thoughts and began to visualize Leslie naked in the arms of another woman. After a pleasant, although somewhat frustrating moment, I opened my eyes. With my hands still on the rock, I turned to the left and looked down the length of the wall. Thirty yards away was a slim, older man doing the same thing. His head was lowered and his legs were spread behind him. Suddenly, he turned and looked right at me.

"Tommy," Leslie shouted. "Look!"

I turned around. She was pointing at a huge bird soaring over the site. The wingspan must have been eight feet across.

"It looks like a condor!" I shouted. Other tourists looked and pointed their cameras skyward. I watched the condor majestically glide the length of the field. I had read that they were rare. Hunters and pesticides had taken their toll. As it circled back over the ruins, I heard someone singing.

The man I'd seen leaning against the wall now had his arms outstretched to the sky. He was chanting something in a language I didn't understand. He turned to me and moved his arms up and down. I didn't know what it meant. He did it again and nodded his head. This time I understood. He wanted me to join him. I raised my arms. He nodded, encouraging me. We both looked toward the condor. The great bird looped back over us. It caught a thermal and circled higher and higher until it was just a speck in the sky. Finally, it flew off toward the North.

"What are you doing," Leslie said. She was carrying a rolled-up tapestry.

I smiled sheepishly and lowered my arms.

"That old guy wanted me to do it." I gestured down the wall.

"What old guy?" Leslie asked.

He was gone.

After a lunch of boiled ears of corn with cheese, and potatoes in a spicy peanut sauce, we went back to the hotel to meet Randy. He was laying on one of the beds when we got there. Four paperback books were spread out on the other bed.

"Hey, you guys," he said. "How'd you like the ruins? Pretty cool, huh?"

"No, kidding," Leslie said. "How they put those stones together like that is, you know, out of this world, and I mean that literally."

"Benevolent alien construction workers?" Randy asked.

Leslie nodded, "That's my guess."

I grabbed a bottle of water off the nightstand. The cheese on the corn at lunch was incredibly salty.

"I bought you both some presents," Randy said, reaching over and picking up one of the books.

"This one is for you, Leslie." He handed her the book.

"The Essential Peru Traveler," Leslie said, reading the cover. "Thanks, Randy that was sweet of you." She opened it and flipped through the pages then stopped. "What's this?" She lifted out a piece of gold foil. It was in the shape of a human face.

"Oh, that's just something for a friend of mine back in the States," Randy said. "He'll get it from you when you get home to Boulder."

I leaned over and took a closer look at the gold foil. The eyes of the face were oriental looking. A delicate nose and small mouth gave the face a childlike quality.

"This is beautiful," I said. "Where'd you get it?"

"One of the guys who works for my boss."

"It must have cost a fortune," Leslie said.

"He cut me a deal. I bought a few other pieces."

Randy proceeded to show us six other gold and silver artifacts. All of them were small and fit easily between the pages of the books.

"Having you guys take them will save me a lot in postage," he said, carefully replacing a golden, double-headed serpent back into the last book. "I knew you guys would be cool about it." He reached over and patted me on the shoulder.

Something in that gesture felt wrong. It was as if he'd just sold me a used car that he knew needed a valve job. I watched him stack the books on the corner of the bed.

"Where did you get this stuff?" I asked. "Is it stolen?"

He turned to me with as perfect a poker face as I've ever seen and said, "No, we're cool."

Leslie picked up on my concern. "Then where did it come from?"

"I told you, people who work for my boss."

"Look Randy," I said, "this stuff doesn't just grow on trees. It looks Pre-Columbian."

"Yeah, it is."

"Then shouldn't it be in a museum somewhere?" Leslie said.

"If I wanted to sell it to a museum, I would."

"I don't think I want to do this," I said.

"Oh, fuck," Randy said. "Just stick the fuckin' books in your pack and forget about 'em. When you get home, my buddy'll call you and take them off your hands."

"What're we, your smugglers?"

"Hey, smart guy," he said, stepping toward me.

Leslie jumped between us. "Randy, come on, where did this stuff come from?"

He raised his arms and let them flop down to his sides. "I don't know, they find it. The shit's laying around in the dirt."

"No it's not," I said. "Pieces like these would have been buried in tombs with Incan royalty."

"Yeah, well there you have it," Randy said pushing his straggly mane of hair away from his face. "Another Hardy Boy mystery is solved."

Leslie stared at him trying to grasp what he'd just admitted. "You mean you got it from grave robbers?"

Randy shrugged. "A source is a source."

We both went for the books at the same time. Leslie whirled around and faced Randy.

"Get out of here right now," she said. "We're turning this over to the police."

Randy looked genuinely surprised. "Are you shittin' me?"

"This stuff belongs to the country of Peru," I said.

"So does coca paste but they don't mind selling that to the far corners of the earth. Lighten up, I got like four government officials helping me with this. It's no big deal. This is how they make extra money down here."

Anger shot-gunned through me, Watergate, Nixon, and the rest of that tribe of idiots were once again staring me in the face. I took a step toward Randy. "Listen asshole, how would you like someone digging up your grandmother and stealing her jewelry?"

"My aunt snagged it all before they dumped the old bird in the ground."

"Hit the road," I said.

He grinned, and I suddenly got a sick feeling in my gut.

"What do you think I'm gonna do, just walk away and leave you with two hundred grand worth of my property." He glanced at Leslie then back at me.

"Muy loco," he said.

He reached into his back pocket and pulled out a knife. With a flick of his wrist the shiny steel blade snapped open.

"Gimme my shit," he said.

Leslie glared at him, then handed him the book. I didn't. Randy stared at me as the room grew quiet.

"Tommy?" Leslie said.

My right hand clenched into a fist. The rage surging up in me was old and tired of sitting on its ass. I was sick of being lied to and manipulated so some bureaucrat could line his pockets and increase his power. I shifted my weight forward onto the balls of my feet.

"I will cut your belly wide open and hand you your spleen," Randy said calmly.

My fingers tightened around the book. My hand was shaking. I didn't know what I was going to do, but I wanted to do something.

"Give it to him, Tommy," Leslie said.

"No."

Randy waved the blade in front of my face. "Is it worth it?"

Leslie reached over and gently pried the book from my fingers.

"Don't worry," she said. "He'll get his eventually."

"Yeah, yeah, blah, blah, blah," Randy said snatching it out of her hand.

"You're bringing some bad karma down on yourself," Leslie said.

"Don't worry, the aliens will save me." Randy snickered and reached for his backpack. "Darlin', I've never seen a spaceship in my life. You're a fuckin' nut bag believing that crap."

He turned and walked to the door. "Oh, yeah," he said, "Don't bother stopping by if you come through Lima again. I don't live there anymore."

"Screw yourself," I said.

Randy puckered his lips and made a kissing sound then walked out.

• • •

Two hours after being at knifepoint, I was into my fourth Pisco sour and feeling no pain. Without Randy as our guide, Leslie wasn't sure what we should do. We tried discussing our options, but after a couple cocktails, we gave up. I took another drink, numbing myself even further from my feelings of helplessness. Leslie poked my arm.

"We need to get some food," she said.

I looked around to find a waiter. "Hey, that's the guy," I said.

"Who?"

"The condor guy."

Through the window of the bar, the old man was standing on the sidewalk talking to a boy who looked to be six or seven years old. I was up and out of my chair before I realized what I was doing.

"Hey," I heard Leslie say as I headed for the door.

Outside, I squinted into the bright afternoon sunshine. The old man and the boy turned and looked at me.

"Perdon," I said loudly. "Nosotros observer—" I said struggling to find the right words in Spanish. Bird, what was the word for bird. I flapped my arms. The boy laughed.

"The condor. Pajaro," I said.

The boy cawed like a crow. The old man nodded and smiled.

"It was beautiful," I said. "Hermoso."

"Si'," he said, "Beautiful."

His name was Miguel. He lived in Iquitos and he guided groups into the jungle. That was how he learned English. The young boy, Eduardo, was his grandson. Eduardo's mother worked as a maid in one of the new hotels.

"What were you doing at the ruins?" I asked, as we sat down in the restaurant.

His dark eyes fell on me. It felt like he was looking into me.

"I talk with the Grandmothers and Grandfathers. Espiritu," he said. "Condor was a sign from them. I sing thanks and wish good journey to condor."

"Once I received a sign from an eagle," I said.

He nodded and pursed his lips approvingly. "Good you sing with me," Miguel said. "Show grandmothers and grandfathers you respect them."

"We tried to stop a tomb robber," Leslie said. "Well, Tommy did, but the guy had a knife."

My suffering male ego roared back onto solid ground. Miguel's nearly gaunt face darkened into a scowl.

"That man is no good," Miguel said.

Leslie nodded. "He'll get his."

Eduardo growled. Miguel turned to him. They spoke rapidly in Spanish.

"Eduardo thinks the jaguar should catch this man."

"Me too," I said.

"A jaguar came to me in a dream," Leslie said. "That's one of the reasons we came down here."

Miguel studied her for a moment. Then he looked up at the slowly turning blades of the ceiling fan.

"Tomorrow go to Machu Picchu," he said.

"Oh good," Leslie said, "We wanted to do that."

"Sleep in ruins." he said.

"Are we allowed to?" I asked.

"No. Hide. Come out in the dark." He stood up. Eduardo slid out of his chair.

"Why do you want us to go to Machu Picchu?" I asked.

Miguel's face crinkled into a smile. "Bueno, bueno," he said. "Remember – greet the Grandmothers and Grandfathers when you get there."

23

THREE HOURS ON THE train, followed by a gear-grinding, zigzag bus ride two thousand feet up the mountain, and Leslie and I were standing at the gate to the ruins of Machu Picchu. We each took a moment, before entering, to close our eyes and greet the Grandmothers and Grandfathers in a silent prayer.

"Are you ready?" Leslie said.

"Yeah, sure," I lied.

We made our way along stone terraces past what appeared to be a series of baths. A group of Germans ahead of us kept stopping and taking pictures. We moved past them and into the main plaza of the ruins. The stonework was incredible. Without any mortar they fit perfectly one onto the next. There was science and a high level of craftsmanship in the structures.

During our lunch of trail mix and bananas I pondered how, since iron and steel hadn't been a part of the Incan culture, the builders so precisely cut the blocks of stone.

"Like I said before, aliens helped them," Leslie said. "They've been guiding us for a long time."

"If aliens helped the Incans build this amazing empire, why did they let Pizarro and his men march right in and destroy it?"

Leslie looked down at the raisin she was holding in her fingers.

"Why does something as ugly as a raisin taste so good?"

"Is this like a knock-knock joke?"

"No. A raisin tastes good because it's been left on the vine long enough to allow it to sweeten."

"What does that have to do with the Incans?"

"They'd had their days in the sun." She grinned. "They were ripe for the picking."

Plopping the raisin in her mouth, she rolled onto her stomach and pulled some postcards out of her pack. "I wonder when it will be our turn to be plucked from the vine," she said. "When will our civilization come crashing down?"

"There's a cheery thought," I said, laying back in the grass.

I stared up at the craggy, vertical walls of Huayna Picchu, sister peak of Machu Picchu, towering above us. Did the mighty fist of evolution also play a part in the birth and death of civilizations? Did nature weed out, through natural selection, the Mayans, Incans, and Anasazi? What about Spain and England? At one time they'd ruled most of the known world. Why were they no longer running the show? Was it strictly natural resources and politics that determined the shifts in global power?

Later, we hid on a brush-covered terrace below the east side of the ruins. Two thousand feet straight down the Urubamba River made a muddy horseshoe around the mountain. As we waited for the sun to go down, Leslie calmly watched several ravens circling below us. I tried to rest, but I was nervous and on edge. I wasn't sure why.

The moon was nearly full. It was bright enough to cast a shadow from the vertical stone column thrusting up out of The Hitching Post of the Sun. We stood before the massive carved rock listening for the sound of other visitors. All was quiet. I zipped my jacket to my throat. The air had turned cold.

"I'm digging this," Leslie said. She walked to the low wall facing out toward the valley. "Come over here," she said. "Let's sit for a minute and tune in, see if we can find out what the Grandmothers and Grandfathers want us to do while we're here."

"Okay," I said, not entirely certain that I wanted to know. We straddled the wall facing each other. Leslie closed her eyes and took a deep breath. She let it out slowly.

"Oh wow," she said, shrugging her shoulders and flexing her neck. "Is there a lot of energy here or what?"

I closed my eyes. Immediately, I saw a windowless room. Twelve feet long and six feet wide, it looked to be part of the ruins. In a flash it was gone. I opened my eyes.

Leslie was looking at me. "Did you get anything?"

I nodded. "I saw a room."

"Cool," she said. "I saw a window."

"I feel kinda weird."

She reached over and rubbed my solar plexus.

"Don't try to control what's going on. Relax and let it happen." She shot out her breath and inhaled deeply.

"Man, the energy here is really intense."

After five minutes of breathing and relaxing, I felt a little better. I remembered my time on the mountain in New Mexico during my vision quest: the darkness, the sound of the wind, the raw, chaotic energy of nature. It was a force that unsettled me, a power that left me feeling daunted and out of control.

Out of the corner of my left eye I suddenly saw a black object hurtling at my head. I ducked, practically throwing myself into Leslie's lap.

"It's okay," she said calmly.

I whirled around. A large bird banked and circled over the Hitching Post of the Sun. It looped around once, twice, and then flew toward the ruins.

"I would say that's a sign." Leslie announced.

"Fuckin' A," I stammered. "That bird almost gave me a heart attack."

She swung her leg over the wall and stood up. "Come on. Let's go see what's up."

Walking through the ruins at night was an entirely different kind of experience. The silvery half-light of the full moon draped everything in an effervescent aura, turning it into a glowing, primitive dreamscape. As we made our way through the narrow corridors of stone, I felt a distinct force leading me. Was it one of the Grandmothers?

Leslie stopped abruptly in front of me.

"There it is," she said. I moved up next to her. She was looking into a large, open room.

"The window over there, that's what I saw." She pointed to a single opening in the far wall of the roofless room. She walked into the room and turned slowly in a circle. "I like it here," she said. "I want to stay for a while and meditate."

"Okay," I said.

"Will you be alright?"

"Sure."

I stepped back into the corridor and continued walking. I'd gone no more than twenty feet or so when I saw the room. Small and cramped, it might have been an Incan woman's walk-in closet. I stepped inside. The walls were eight feet high. Above me I could see the moon. There was a two-foot high rectangle stone on the ground. I sat on it and leaned back. The stone wall still held some heat from the afternoon sun. I closed my eyes and tried to still my thoughts.

I had been led to the room, I was certain of that, but why and by whom? I sent out a silent thought to the Grandmothers and Grandfathers asking for protection. A moment later I saw the first snake. It startled me as it crawled across my interior vision. The angular markings on its skin undulated as it slithered past. I tried to clear my thoughts and get centered. That's when the world behind my eyelids exploded into a squirming mass of snakes. They covered the floor and walls of the room. They encircled my ankles and crawled across my lap. I began to panic. Breathing rapidly through my nose I tried to remain calm. The head of a huge boa dangled in front of me. Its tongue flicked in and out inches from my face.

This is a test of my courage, I told myself, struggling to remain seated. I reached into my pocket and pulled out the wolf tooth. *I am Singing Bow!* I shouted inwardly to myself. *I am on a quest for truth! This is a part of my path! This is my lesson! I am not afraid! I am not afraid!*

I heard a sound. My eyes flew open. I was momentarily relieved to see that the room wasn't actually crawling with snakes. A sudden movement to my left caused me to jump. Something landed on the top of the wall. It looked like a black shadow – the silhouette of a cat. The size of a lynx, it had a long thin tail with a bushy clump of fur on the end. The animal walked along the wall to my right. Its movements were feline but it didn't look like any cat I'd ever seen before. At the corner it stopped. Then it slowly turned and looked down at me.

Adrenaline surged through my body. The cat didn't move. I looked hard, trying to see the features of its face. There was nothing distinct there. Like a shadow, it was part of the darkness, but somehow separate from it. The cat leaned toward me. Its shoulders tensed. My last thread of control snapped and I jumped up and bolted out of the room. Slamming into a wall, I bounced off and ran down the corridor of stone.

"Hey!" I cried out, my voice thin and taut. I burst into the large room. Leslie was sitting cross-legged in the moonlight.

"Leslie!" I shouted. Her eyes snapped open.

"I saw this thing, this animal," I pointed in the direction of the small room.

"I see it," Leslie said calmly. I turned around. The cat was standing on top of the wall behind me. I held my breath. We stared at each other. It was as if I was looking into the darkened window of a house. There was something inside but I couldn't see it. The blackness was too intense. In a single, fluid motion it turned and began trotting along the top of the wall. Ten feet from the corner, directly in front of us, it vanished.

"Holy shit," I said. "Did you see that?"

"Wow," Leslie murmured. "It just – disappeared." She walked over and took my hand. "Are you okay?"

"I'm a little freaked."

"Me too."

"I saw a bunch of snakes. They were in my head . . . or somewhere."

Leslie looked up at the moon. "I was floating. In my meditation

I was inside this golden bubble and I was talking to the Grandmothers. They were all around me. They had dark, lined faces and long white hair. They were really beautiful."

"What did they say?"

"We talked about what it meant to be a woman, the power we have. Women are powerful." She sighed. "What a night," she said, her voice full of emotion. "God, I love this place."

• • •

THE STREETS OF CUSCO teemed with life. Fruit and clothing vendors yelling, cars, buses, donkeys, horns blaring, it was an assault on the senses after our surreal evening in Machu Picchu. We walked back to the hotel and checked into the same room we'd been in before. After dropping off our packs we went out to have lunch. Three blocks from the hotel I saw Miguel. He was looking in the window of a bakeshop.

"Que pasa, Miguel," I called as we crossed the street.

"Buenos dias," he said. "How was the journey?"

Leslie surprised him with a hug. "It was great."

He turned to me. "Did you see my cat?"

My mouth fell open.

"I sent him to—" Miguel paused, searching for the words. "To check on you."

"That thing scared the shit outta me!" I blurted.

Leslie laughed. Miguel eyed me carefully.

"Tell me," he said.

At a tiny cafe across the street, I told Miguel about the bird, the snakes, the cat disappearing, and how we spent the rest of the night huddled in our sleeping bags in the main temple. Miguel looked down at his empty espresso cup.

"Fear is not life," he said.

"It startled me," I said. "The bird too."

Leslie leaned to Miguel. "Are you like a shaman or something?"

He shrugged, but didn't say anything. He looked me in the eyes.

"You are afraid that you will die."

"No," I said. "See, I had this past life where I was a Mescalero Apache. Dead animals were bad stuff for me back then. So, I think that maybe this was like, you know, a test to see if I was over—"

Miguel held up his hand. "You are not dead now?"

"No."

"Are you certain?"

"What do you mean?"

"Death lives in the fear."

"What? I'm never supposed to be afraid? What about bears and cars in the street? Fear is an instinct. It's a way to protect yourself."

"Respect the power of the bear. Respect the power of the auto. No fear. Fear makes you dead."

Angry and defensive, I leaned back in my chair. During my time in Taos when I'd researched Native American history and traditions, I'd read about the power of shamans. They traveled between the worlds of spirit and the material plane. It was different than the communication of Eldora and her table or Harry Whitridge the trance channel. Shamans could actually shape-shift and create in the realm of spirit. I always thought that this ability was more mythical than factual, but that was before I saw the cat evaporate in front of my eyes. Miguel was the real thing. He was a man who knew the way in, a man who walked the razor's edge between realities. He was exactly who I'd been hoping to find. And I wanted him to respect me enough to share with me what he knew. I didn't want to be told that I was scared and that I was dead.

"Time to give up the past," he said quietly. "Snake came to tell you."

Leslie nodded. "I thought about that when he told me he saw snakes."

I gave her a look.

"I did," she said. "Shedding the skin, you know."

Miguel touched my arm. "Stop fighting."

"What am I fighting?"

"Fighting to stay alive. But way to live is – surrender to death."

"I don't want to die."

"Me either," Leslie said.

"Surrender to the circle – you are part of the circle. Circle is forever."

"How do I surrender?"

He thought for a minute. "Don't think of your body as only place where you live."

Leslie looked at me. "Cool," she said.

"Can you teach us?" I asked.

"I leave tomorrow for Iquitos. You both come."

"Okay," I said.

Leslie frowned. "What about Lake Titicaca? What about the space ships?"

Miguel shrugged. "Do what you want."

She thought for a minute. "Okay. I'll go with you."

"We leave tomorrow. Early." Miguel stood up and turned to go.

"Hey," I said, stopping him. "What was that thing anyway? It didn't look like any cat I'd ever seen before."

Miguel's dark eyes studied me. "No," he said. "That cat isn't from around here."

24

"They come out of the trees like shadows. I've seen them a couple times. They're beautiful but they certainly do leave their mark." Mom lifted the stem of one of the Beefsteak tomato plants. Half the leaves were chewed off.

"It would take a tall fence to keep them out," I said.

"I don't want to cage up my garden?" She plucked a leaf from one of the mangled plants.

"The squash and beans are coming in nicely," I said.

"You definitely have a green thumb," Mom said. "Now if you can just figure a way to keep the deer from eating everything."

"You could make Dad stand watch every night," I said.

She nodded. "He needs to do something with himself."

"Richard McInnes, garden security. It's a whole new career."

She laughed. "I don't think so. He might miss one of his TV shows." She waded into the garden and began pulling weeds.

I went over and picked up one of the watermelons and cradled it in my hands. Growing things still gave me a rush.

"Tommy," Mom said, "did you ever make love with a man?"

I nearly dropped the melon. "Mother, what would make you ask me that?"

"You're in your mid-thirties, you've never married; you don't bring girlfriends home for the holidays. And your pals, those girls—"

"Leslie and Tara?"

"Yes. They're lesbians."

"So that means I'm gay?"

"No. Not necessarily, but it makes me wonder."

"I'm not gay."

"Are you sure? When you were little you loved the soundtrack to *South Pacific.*"

"Oh, come on."

"You did."

"Mother!"

"I just want you to know that if you are—"

"I'm not!"

"Honey, don't get upset. I'm trying to create an atmosphere of acceptance."

"Mom, I was with Melina for two years."

"And she was enough to drive anyone to swear off women."

"Need I remind you that you saw me naked with Dee Dee when I was seventeen?"

"A lot of boys date girls and then – something happens."

"Where is this coming from? Did *Reader's Digest* do an article about parents and gay children?"

Her face immediately clouded over. "No, it wasn't in *Reader's Digest*. That's your father's magazine."

"Where then?"

"I worry about you. I want you to be happy."

"I'm happy and I'm straight, anything else?"

"Then find a nice girl and settle down."

"And end up like you and Dad?" The words were out of my mouth before I could stop them. Mom's eyes flared.

"Your father and I have done pretty darn well."

"I know you have," I said, trying to soften the blow.

"You have no idea, Tommy. All of this, whatever you call it, self-exploration that you've done, just imagine another person putting up with that. That's what a marriage is."

"It takes a lot of work I'm sure."

"Don't patronize me," she said sharply.

"Mom," I said quickly, trying to change the subject, "Dee Dee is back in town. I saw her at Kirby's—"

"Your father and I have gone through a lot with you – roaming around all over the place. Don't you think we worried when you were in the jungle? You sent us a postcard of a giant snake for God sakes. The only thing I could think about for the next week was that snake swallowing you. It hasn't been easy on us."

"I know, Mom. I was trying to figure stuff out."

"And you're still trying. When will it stop? Honestly Tommy, a man of your age. You're awfully self-absorbed. You do see that don't you?"

"Truth doesn't come without self-examination."

"Who said that?"

"I did."

"Oh, boy."

She looked down at the zucchini at her feet. "It's amazing to me," she said, "how a simple act like sexual intercourse can create the very complex process of raising a child. It's out of balance. A person can't drive a car without passing a test. Seems to me that if screwing—"

"Screwing, Mom?"

"You know what I mean. If it was more difficult to do maybe people would think twice before having children."

"Are you saying you wish you hadn't had any of us?"

"I love you all, but from time to time the thought has crossed my mind. You three have been a handful."

"Maybe if Dad would have helped you more."

"Your father's done fine. And just because he isn't able to express his feelings doesn't mean he hasn't got them."

"I know that."

"Do you?"

She gave me a long stern look then turned away. "He was a very different man when we first met. He was wild."

"Dad, wild?"

"You bet."

"That's hard to believe."

She looked toward the house. "He used to get drunk and come over to my parents' house late at night. We'd whisper through my window." She shook her head and laughed. "The things he would say to me. He was so sweet. One night during the winter when your father had been drinking beer, he threw up on my parents' porch railing. It froze there along with one of the gloves I'd given him for Christmas. The next morning my mother saw it. Boy, she let him have it like nobody's business."

"I've never heard Dad talk about that stuff."

She paused, a faraway look coming into her eyes. "Your father was never the same after the war." She forced a smile and looked down at the dead leaves and weeds in her hand. In the silence it suddenly dawned on me that outside of being my parents, I knew very little about the two people who had brought me into the world. They had been parents; mother, father, protector, nurturer, and tormentor. They had been the ones to rebel against. They had been my persecutors and jail keepers. Hearing about my father as a younger man made me understand that even before I had been around to torture them, they had suffered. They had lived and been taken down and built up by their experiences.

Mom pulled a pack of Salems out of her shirt pocket. She slid one out and put it to her lips. Out came the lighter, two clicks, a flame, and a deep inhalation. I wondered how many times she had done that series of movements: cigarette, lighter, inhale, cigarette, lighter inhale. She looked at me as if reading my mind.

"I don't want to hear it," she said. She blew a cloud of smoke skyward. "Once when your Dad was a teenager he stuck his brother in the rear end with an ice pick."

"You're kidding?" I said, "Uncle Lou?"

"Lou had been giving him a hard time all day. Finally your Dad had enough of it."

"So he stuck him in the ass with an ice pick?"

"Lou could be very annoying at times."

"Wow."

What a revelation, Mr. Discipline, Mr. Control, lashing out in an act of violence against his older brother.

"They called Lou, The Agitator," Mom said. She took a deep drag on her cigarette. On the smoky exhale, she added, "He picked on everyone mercilessly."

"How far did the ice pick go in?"

"Good heavens, I don't know."

"Did it bleed a lot?"

"You'll have to ask your father."

"Domestic violence at Grandma Vera's, that's pretty crazy."

"She and your grandfather never talked about it. I found out from Lou's first wife, Ruthie."

"Ruthie?"

"You never met her, she died before you were born. Cancer. Nice gal. Not the brightest bulb in the circuit, but very sweet."

Inside the house the phone started ringing. Mom frowned.

"He won't get it. He'll just sit there in front of the TV."

"That's why you have the answering machine," I said.

She sighed. "That's what he says." The ringing stopped. We started walking toward the house.

"Mom, I've always wanted to know, what's the story with that Japanese cup?"

"Don't touch it," she said. "He'll know if you do, believe me." She shook her head at what must have been a less than pleasant memory.

"But why is he so freaky about it?"

"I don't know, Tommy. Since we've been married I asked him twice, and it wasn't pretty. It's from the war, that's all I know." She nervously rubbed her hands together. "So how is Dee Dee these days?"

"Really good." I said, noticing how uncomfortable the topic of the cup had made her. "She's separated from her husband."

Mom's eyes widened. "Uh oh."

"It was weird to see her. She looked great."

"Behave yourself, Thomas. She's probably extremely vulnerable."

The back door opened. My father stepped onto the porch.

"Merna, telephone."

"Oh my God," Mom said, under her breath, "It's a miracle."

Dad held the screen door for her as she went in the house. He gestured for me to follow. "Kojack's on in a few minutes," he said.

"I'll be right in."

He stepped back inside.

"Hey, Dad?"

"Yes."

"Can we talk later?"

He hesitated. "About what?"

"Your time in the war. Stuff like that."

He looked at me as if I'd asked about a purple hippo sunbathing in a lounge chair on the roof.

"Why would you want to hear about that?"

"Because – I'm interested."

He shifted from one foot to the other. "Kojack is on."

"We can do it later."

"Well," he said, and then didn't say anything else.

I shrugged, "Some other time."

"Sure," he said, closing the door before I could ask when.

25

Surrounded by an emerald green expanse of tropical rain forest, Iquitos was a city in the middle of nowhere. One of the farthest inland ports in the world, it teemed with exotic characters. In my mind drug smugglers and expatriate embezzlers slouched around every corner.

Our AeroPeru flight to Iquitos left me feeling queasy. The bumpy two hour bus ride out of the city didn't do much to settle my churning stomach. Leslie, on the other hand, oohed and aahed out the window, asking Miguel a hundred different questions.

I leaned my head back on the seat hoping that what I was feeling was only an upset stomach and not a nasty dose of microbes doing the La Bamba in my intestines. I didn't bother to consider the obvious. I was scared. Miguel was leading us into the unknown, and my stomach was tied in knots because I didn't know what was going to happen. Who or what was I going to discover lurking beyond my fear?

Miguel's house was in a picturesque clearing along a slow-moving tributary. A dense wall of trees, hanging vines, and ferns surrounded the small two bedroom bamboo house. The air was alive with the screech of birds and the constant drone of insects. Inside the house, reed mats covered the bamboo floor and elaborately carved walking staffs and gourd rattles hung from hooks on the walls.

Miguel decided that it would be best to eat an early dinner. He wanted to get up at dawn and take us into the jungle. So, as the sun set and the roar of insects grew louder, we dined on rice and sweet potatoes.

"I want to understand how life works," I said to Miguel.

"Life doesn't work," he said. "It just is."

"Yeah," I said, "but how?"

He mulled this over. "Because," he finally said, "the world is not afraid to die."

"What's with this death thing?"

Miguel raised his hand. "No more talk," he said. "Tomorrow we talk."

As I lay in the dark, listening to the symphony of jungle sounds, I was seized by a moment of panic. Tomorrow Miguel would take us into the jungle, into a place where Leslie and I would be completely out of our element. We wouldn't know where we were or how to survive. We would be at his mercy. How could we be sure that he wouldn't sell us to a primitive Indian tribe who still ran naked through the forest and hunted with blowguns? Across the room, I heard Leslie roll over.

"Stop it, Tom," she said. "I can feel you worrying all the way over here. It's going to be fine."

"How do you know?"

"I'm a woman, I know these things."

"I hope you're right."

"Go to sleep."

"Will you come over here and comfort me?"

"Shut up."

By eight the next morning we were deep into the rain forest. Thorns and branches along the narrow trail tugged at my clothing. Miguel seemed to move effortlessly through the dense foliage. His body was like water, flowing under, around, and over whatever was in his path. His pace was steady and his mood was light. In between pointing out different species of birds and various plants he used in his healing work, he played cheerful riffs on an old harmonica. There was such a buoyant, positive quality to Miguel, that my concerns for our safety gradually diminished. After four miles of rigorous hiking we came to a small clearing.

"My camp," Miguel announced.

On the left side of the clearing was a bamboo lean-to. In front of the lean-to was a circle of charred rocks and a dozen clay pots.

"Sit," Miguel said, pointing to a log on the opposite side of the fire circle. He leaned the battered rifle he was carrying against the wall of the hut. He turned to us.

"Time to talk."

He asked us why we came to Peru. Leslie explained her attraction to the stars and her ideas about beings from other dimensions. I told him about the blue heron and my journey to Pomona. He asked me about my experience with the eagle. He listened intently, seeming to weigh each response for its merit and truthfulness.

"I want to understand who I am on a soul level," I said, "and how this world interacts with other dimensions."

"If you are strong," he said, "the vine will teach you."

"What vine," I asked.

He explained to us that he used the camp to brew ayahuasca, a concoction he used in his work as a healer. He called it the "vision vine," made by boiling together the mashed pulp of a vine and the leaves of a small shrub. He showed us samples of each. After slow cooking and straining off the pulp, the liquid that remained was cooled. This clear, greenish drink caused the potent visions.

"I've heard of that," Leslie said. "It's supposed to be wild stuff."

Miguel shrugged and poked his walking staff in the ground. "It is a teacher," he said. "Just like your mushroom was a teacher."

I honestly wasn't sure if I was ready for another mind-bending hallucinogenic experience. One episode had been enough. I mean, come on.

"What do we have to do?" Leslie asked eagerly. "How soon can we take the vision vine?"

Miguel frowned. "Not to hurry. You must be ready."

Over the next ten days, while sorting through my apprehension over facing whatever awaited me in the ayahuasca nether worlds, Leslie and I endured a rigorous dietary and cleansing regime. Miguel ordered us to eat only roasted yucca, mashed bananas and boiled sweet potatoes. Every other day he would give us awful tasting herbal drinks. The most noxious smelling was a ferocious laxative. Leslie, with her preoccupation with colon cleanliness, quite enjoyed that one. I spent those afternoons in the forest cramped up in the fetal position. Another one of Miguel's elixirs caused explosive projectile vomiting. The last, and my favorite, made us break out in drenching sweats.

For ten days we purged through every pore and orifice of our bodies. When we weren't off in the forest releasing our bodily toxins, we soaked for hours in the stream. At night, Miguel talked to us about his use of ayahuasca. It led him through the forest to healing plants and helped him to see the illness in his patients. He had been introduced to it by an Indian friend of his father's. At seventeen he learned the ways of the shaman.

"It showed me you," he said, pointing to both of us. "One month ago in a vision I saw you at Sacsayhuaman."

"How did you know for sure we were the ones?" I asked.

Miguel nodded his head. "I knew."

The last day we fasted. As much bitching as we had done during the process, by the tenth day Leslie and I felt incredible. Our skin glowed and our eyes were bright and clear. We were energized and exhilarated. Late in the afternoon, led by Miguel and his harmonica, we started hiking into the rain forest. We carried hammocks and a sack of fruit. In a small clay pot secured in his pack, Miguel carried the ayahuasca.

We arrived at the camp just before sunset. The droning cicada hiss serenaded us as we busied ourselves hanging our hammocks and storing packs in the lean-to. As Miguel set about building a small fire, he began to chant. His lilting voice filled the clearing. Twigs were soon crackling in the fire. Miguel filled his pipe, intricately carved with two soaring condors, with jungle tobacco and lit it. He walked over to Leslie and began blowing pungent smoke around her head and shoulders. He turned to me and did the same thing. He took four more puffs on his pipe blowing smoke in each of the four directions.

"It is time," Miguel said. He picked up the clay pot and poured the ayahuasca into three small gourd cups. He handed one to me and another to Leslie.

"I will guide you," he said.

Leslie sniffed at the cup, and then lifted it to her lips.

I offered up a prayer, beseeching the powers that be to protect us and prevent us from becoming human vegetables. I held the wolf tooth in my left hand and raised my cup.

"Le'chayim," I said. "To life." I downed the bland, dark-green liquid.

"It tastes better than wheatgrass," Leslie quipped.

Miguel motioned us to be quiet. He began chanting and playing his harmonica. A while later, a faint buzzing started in my ears. It grew louder, merging with his playing and chanting. The higher the pitch of the harmonica, the louder the buzzing became. It built in intensity until finally there was a pop and my body clenched in a violent spasm. A brilliant blue flash was followed by a barrage of swirling colors and geometrical images. A cat screeched. I turned to look. The animal I'd seen at Machu Picchu was standing there.

Blue light sparkled from its eyes. It took a step toward me, faded then became a huge black jaguar. It leaned up on me, placing its massive front paws on my shoulders. Its iridescent blue eyes shone inches from my face. Opening its jaws, the cat stretched its neck forward and engulfed my entire head in its mouth.

Fight or flight instincts ignited throughout my body. The jaws began to close. Miguel's voice was suddenly inside my head. It was exactly like the telepathy I'd experienced with the blue heron.

"Death is the way to life," he said, his voice calm and soothing. "When you no longer fear death, your life is your own."

I took a deep breath and relaxed. With that, the giant cat clamped its jaws shut. Colors squeezed to black. I felt myself split from my body. Tumbling through an intense darkness, a profound exhilaration infused my senses. It was as if I was falling through the ether and the ether was falling through me.

A pinpoint of white light appeared far off in the distance. I moved toward it. The light grew. The colors changed. Orange tracers shot past me. An image of my mother floated up. She was alone at the kitchen sink drying the cup I used as a baby. An image of my father reading the newspaper flashed past followed by rapid snapshots of Rick and Becky in their caps and gowns from high school graduation.

The light, full of sound and spinning energy, enveloped me. I whirled like a dervish in this exquisite tornado, absorbing and being absorbed by it. A shrill whistle sounded. I immediately found myself back in the clearing.

From the corner of my eye, I saw an eagle diving through the air. It landed at my feet, talons digging into the damp earth. Turning my head toward the trees, I followed its gaze. A small gray bird was perched on a flowering bush. The bird was singing. I stared at it, not believing what I was seeing. The sound was visible, emerging from the bird's throat in purple swirls.

Miguel's voice beckoned. "Follow me." The jaguar appeared next to me. Together we walked out of the clearing and into the jungle.

Shimmering bluish auras emanated from the plants and trees. The cat stopped next to a dew soaked bush. I moved closer. I traced the unusual pattern of veins in the leaves. My perspective spun and blurred. A gentle pulse of electricity hummed. Granules of light pushed past me. It took a moment to realize what had happened. I was *in* the bush. Photosynthesis was happening in and around me. Energies of the sun and the earth powered through me. I sluiced through the complex system of branch, stem and leaf. *Connected, connected, connected,* I heard over and over in my head. Bursting upward I was released into the air like a molecule of oxygen.

I floated through the dense tangle of trees; up, up, up until all the Amazon was beneath me, then higher, above South America, above the earth, into the stars and beyond. I wasn't anyone's son or brother or a citizen of any country. I wasn't an ape or a lizard or a human being. I was a particle of energy in the universe. I was nothing and I was everything. I was connected to it all.

• • •

I AWOKE THE NEXT morning in my hammock. As soon as I opened my eyes, Leslie's shrieked.

"That was soooo cooool!"

Miguel was looking at me from beside the fire circle. He watched as I sat up and rubbed my face.

Leslie bounced around in her hammock. "Tom, did you dig that or what?"

I stood up feeling wobbly and disoriented.

"You died well," Miguel said. "You both did."

"It's all connected," Leslie said. "This world and that."

I was too overwhelmed to say anything. All I could do was nod my head.

I was still dazed by our experience a week later. Over and over in my head I replayed our night in the jungle. I tried to remember how the shift between this world and that had taken place, but I kept coming back to the moment when I was inside of the plant; the surge of light and sound, the weighty sensation of the plant fibers balanced by a heady drone of high frequency energy. I couldn't stop thinking about it.

Leslie wasn't at all introspective. She was expansive. She wanted to go adventuring. She hiked with Miguel. She took photographs. She begged me to go on an Amazon River tour. I declined, so she went by herself. On the boat she met a woman from Holland. They fell in love.

Tara was a stocky blonde with creamy pale skin and a wide friendly face. After spending a week together, they decided to go to the States. Leslie would meet Tara in Iquitos, and together they would fly to Lima and then on to Denver.

"Take it slow," I told Leslie, as I strained to get the zipper on her backpack closed. "And trust your instincts."

"Call me as soon as you get back to Boulder," she said.

I stood up and gave her a hug.

"This has been a kick-ass trip," she said in my ear. She turned to Miguel. "Thank you for everything."

Miguel held out one of his carved gourd rattles. "You are on your way," he said, giving the rattle a shake then handing it to Leslie. She immediately burst into tears and embraced him. "Thank you, thank you so much."

I spent the next four months working with Miguel. I helped him around the house and ran errands for him. My favorite chore was assisting him on his expeditions into the forest to gather medicinal plants. The smells and textures of the plants and the earth, and the sounds of the jungle quieted me. It was a feeling both remarkably familiar and oddly strange.

We hiked to Miguel's camp and ingested ayahuasca on two more occasions. The first night was equally as rewarding as the experience I'd had with Leslie. I once again felt a profound connection to the plant life that appeared. Images of trees, roots, bark, and flowers rushed though me. I tried to spot the blue heron in this collage of natural wonders but it never showed up.

My last journey into the ayahuasca ether was awful. All night I saw weird, contorted images of bloody battles and the bodies of soldiers hacked to pieces. The next morning, I was depressed and felt like crap. When we got back to Miguel's house the first thing I heard on the radio was that John Lennon had been murdered in New York City.

"Why do we keep killing each other?" I asked Miguel.

"Birth and death – part of sacred wheel of life," he said.

His response was not comforting. John deserved better.

On my last night in Peru, Miguel presented me with a walking staff. He had been working on it at night after I'd gone to sleep. On the top of the staff, carved in magnificent detail, was the head of a jaguar.

"To remind you what you learned," he said. "Jaguar will protect you."

I returned the favor by giving Miguel my Olympus camera and the silver eagle pendent Emerson Yazzie had given me. We spent our final night together drinking beer and telling stories out on his back porch. It was a great end to an even greater five months.

26

WHEN I ARRIVED BACK in Colorado, I was immediately aware of the impact Ronald Reagan was having on the country. After going through the recession and the ongoing drama and feelings of helplessness surrounding the Iranian hostage crisis, all my friends were suddenly upbeat and enthusiastic about the future.

I started back to work for Don Trilling's accounting firm. It was dull and tedious but we'd made a deal. Every week a quarter of my paycheck would be deducted to pay back the money he lent me to go to South America.

I visited the blissfully happy couple, Leslie and Tara, at their rented one bedroom bungalow. Their new love pad was decked out in Garden-of-Eden-meets-Abdul-the-tent-maker decor. Every room was choked with ferns and potted palms. The walls were draped with tapestries, and overstuffed pillows covered the floor.

I put out the word through Caryn Trilling's network of friends that I was gathering information on ayahuasca and other medicinal plants.

Ten days after returning from Peru I got a telephone call.

"Is this McInnes?" a voice shouted.

"Yes," I said.

"Roger Herrick here!"

"Why are you yelling?"

"Am I yelling!?"

"Yes."

"Oh!" His voice dropped a few decibels. "I didn't realize. That better?"

"A little."

"Sorry about that. Just got out of the tub. Like to drag the stereo speakers in there while having a soak. You oughta try it. Get that volume blasting good and loud. You can feel the sound waves right there in the water with you. Really gives your internal organs a high frequency massage. Gotta be careful of your musical selection though. One time I made the mistake of listening to Wagner's, "Entrance Of The Gods Into Valhalla." When that fantastic timpani crescendo at the beginning boomed, felt like the bass end was gonna tear my prostate loose. Now I stick with piano concertos. They're mellower, easier on the body. So I hear you're trying to find out about Banisteriopsis caapi."

"What?"

"Ayahuasca; yage, vision vine. What do you want to know?"

"I'm interested in how medicinal plants work in the body."

"Wow, where do you want me to start? No, no, wait a minute. Ring me back. This should be on your nickel."

I called him back and we talked for two hours. Roger told me he'd been a professor of molecular and cell biology at Berkeley. During a self-administered experiment with a powerful psychedelic, called DMT, Roger encountered what he perceived as a "gloriously gorgeous divine presence." A week later he left the hallowed halls of academia and committed himself to the study and preservation of psychotropic plants from around the world.

"I'm a loose cannon in the scientific community," he said. "But that's what frontier crashing is all about, right? To put your brain cells on the line and boldly go where the lab rats fear to tread." He laughed in a high-pitched, squeaky voice that sounded manic and a little crazed. I wondered if in his campaign to crash the boundaries of reality he'd sacrificed too much gray matter.

"So," he asked. "Have you taken ayahuasca?"

"Yeah, I just got back from six months in the jungle."

He grunted his approval. "Did you dig the telepathy?"

"Yeah! You've done it too?"

"I've done it all, mate. I'm a professional."

"Cool."

"Okay," he said, "so serotonin is a chemical that regulates and balances the flow of information through your brain. It locks you in to perceiving a "normal" reality. Psychoactive drugs like ayahuasca stimulate your levels of serotonin. The increased level bumps the system and confuses it to the extent that you lose attachment to your body and "normal" reality. It gives you a Pass Go card that permits you to transcend into realities beyond."

"Is there actually a transcending that happens," I asked. "Or does the drug just make you think that's what's happening?"

"I've got twenty-five people in a study I've been doing on the effects of synthesized DMT. Not one of them has ever complained that what they're seeing is a mere hallucination. The vividness and specificity is quite convincing. Over half of the members in my group have consistently popped into similar dimensions."

"You mean they've seen the same stuff?"

"Exactly."

"Like what?"

"Different things. Bugs."

"What do you mean, bugs?"

"I've seen them too. They look like a chrome-plated praying mantis."

"What about birds?" I asked. "Anyone ever see a great blue heron?"

"Sorry, mate, can't help you with that one. Would you like to try some DMT?"

"I don't think so."

"Okay. Let me know if you change your mind."

"I won't change my mind."

"Don't blame you a bit. Those bugs are freaky."

• • •

When I merged with the plant and zoomed through space, I felt the cellular mind-thumping joy of being absolutely free and at the same time ecstatically connected to everything. If the awareness, or spirit, or soul that had taken that journey was truly a part of me, why couldn't I have access to that kind of freedom and connectedness all of the time? I shouldn't need drugs. Human beings were not meant to be walking around drugged up. So what was holding me back?

Three days later, something Lilly told me popped into my mind. She'd said that the Buddha believed man's existence was inevitably linked with sorrow. The Buddha taught that the cause of dukkha, life's suffering, was tanha, selfish craving. To extinguish the fires of this craving was to find peace. In that instant, I realized that my striving to get to Pomona and my searching for the blue heron and the truth of who I was and what I was supposed to do in this world was tanha. It was a brass ring dangling over my head. The constant strain of trying to grasp it was poisoning me. I decided that it had to be cut off like a gangrenous limb and flung into the forgiving arms of the Great Spirit. By relinquishing my intense desire to understand, and then supplicating myself to the power of emptiness, true understanding, I hoped, would come to me.

The Buddha taught that freedom from craving could be achieved by following his Eight-fold Path: right knowledge, right aspirations, right speech, right behavior, right livelihood, right effort, right mindfulness, and right concentration. The practice by which this unification of the self could be attained was meditation.

I began meditating for two hours every day. I'd wake up at four o'clock in the morning, drink a cup of herbal tea, and then go sit on my blue and white striped meditation cushion from four-thirty to six-thirty. It was difficult and uncomfortable at first, but gradually I was able to go deeper.

On a snowy morning in February, after only meditating for a short time, I saw the broccoli. Balanced on two equally crispy-looking stalks of celery, the broccoli floated up before me on the screen of my inner awareness. I didn't know what to make of it. I simply watched and waited for something to happen. For six days, every time I sat down to meditate, the broccoli would appear. On the seventh day, after it floated before me for a full three minutes, the celery stalks slowly tilted up. The broccoli slid down, and like a diver going into the deep end, it flipped off the ends of the celery and tumbled through the air. As it fell in slow motion, turning end over end, the surface of the broccoli puckered and the blue-green clusters drooped and began to melt. The thick stalk collapsed and dripped. Finally the entire thing dissolved. Beneath where it had been, was a tall glass of broccoli juice.

• • •

"A juice bar?" Leslie said skeptically.

"Yeah. Organic juices."

She snatched two bagels out of the toaster and dropped them on a plate.

"We can have different kinds," I said. "Vegetable, fruit – we can mix and match them – create our own elixirs." I slapped the kitchen counter with the palm of my hand. "It's gonna be great!"

Tara laughed and flipped over a piece of French toast that was on the griddle. "It's good," she said. "People like juice. The college kids will go for it."

"I don't know," Leslie said. "I think they're too busy drinking beer to want fresh mango juice."

"Then we mix something up and pitch it as a hangover remedy. Wake up juice, hangover juice, menstrual cramp juice. It's all in how you sell it." The salesman pitch startled me. I sounded like I was channeling my father.

"How much would something like that cost?" Tara asked.

"I don't know. I've done some preliminary budgeting but I'm still trying to convince a wholesale produce guy to sell to me."

Leslie shook her head as she sliced a cantaloupe into thirds.

"Where are you going to get the money, Tom?"

"I'm hoping that Don can help us get a loan. He deals with bankers all the time. He's bound to know someone who can front us the cash."

Leslie looked doubtful. She handed me the plate of cantaloupe.

"I'm not talking store front," I said, reaching over and putting the plate in the center of the table. "I'm thinking like a cart we can wheel into the Crossroads Mall."

"I don't know," Leslie said.

"Tara can't work anywhere without a green card," I said. "This is the perfect way to get cash into her hands."

"Okay," Leslie said. "If you can put the money together, I'll do it."

"*We'll* do it," Tara said.

I cut my hair, shaved my beard, took out my earrings, and riding on the tidal wave of optimism generated by the release of the Iran hostages, I was able to borrow five thousand dollars from a savings and loan. After three days debating over a catchy name, the TLT Juice Company was born.

The permits were relatively simple to obtain. Finding the right supplier was tricky. As a small operation, if we wanted to make any money, we would have to buy our produce at the cheapest possible price. With that in mind, I convinced Leslie and Tara to go with me to meet the wholesale produce supplier. When the two of them, coifed and dolled up like a couple of eager, heterosexual, business women, walked into Frank Martini's office, I practically had to lift poor Frank's jaw off the desk. Clearly not in the habit of negotiating with beautiful women, at least not for fruits and vegetables, he was so tongue-tied that I quoted him the prices that I wanted to pay. He just kept staring at Leslie and saying, "Yeah, sure, sounds good."

I bought a cart from a florist out by Palo Park for two hundred bucks. The blenders and used cash register we found in a restaurant supply store. We customized the cart and decorated it with fake palm fronds and bamboo, and for good luck I hung the walking staff Miguel had given me above the cash register.

After a month of experimenting with juice mixes, we finally printed our menus. It was a sunny, June Saturday morning when we loaded all our equipment onto a U-Haul trailer, and trucked it over to the Crossroads Mall. It was 8 a.m. when we set up the cart. By 4 p.m. we'd sold every drop of juice we had. TLT Juice Company was off to a blazing start.

My father was pleased. "Owning your own business will teach you everything you'll ever need to know. It'll challenge you, Tom. Be ready." Mom carved a miniature mallard to go on the cart. Tara named the duck, Lucy. She became our mascot.

Leslie and Tara ran the cart during the week. In the evenings, I helped them prep, and on the weekends, I'd work the cart by myself. It was a heady time. We quickly became the popular hot spot for high school kids and retirees as well as the students from the University of Colorado. To help keep people around for a second sale, I got the mall management to chip in on ten round, cafe tables. On any given day we'd have a retired couple leisurely drinking Mango Rippers, while at the next table, a coed was slurping down a Tara's Big Bad Carrot.

Six months after returning from Peru, I made my final payment to Don Trilling for the money he'd lent me. Five months after that, I paid off the loan I'd taken out to start up the business. Debt free and with business booming, I started working less hours for Don, and began working afternoons with Tara and Leslie. We considered starting up another cart. We scouted locations and brain stormed about who we might hire to work for us.

I felt as if I'd finally found my peace. By letting go of my need to search for the blue heron, and surrendering to meditation and the Eight-fold Path, I had created an environment of acceptance that enabled the juice bar idea to come to the surface. I was contributing in a positive way to my community. I was providing a super healthy product. I was making good money, and my parents were proud of my efforts. I was going to be the juice king of Boulder, Colorado.

A week later, all of it came to an end.

I had just finished serving one of our specialties, Garden in a Glass, to Roxy, a high school student. As I was putting her money in the cash register, I heard a voice call out.

"Hey, Leslie!"

I looked up. When I spotted the shaggy mane of hair and the crooked tooth grin, I turned to Tara and said, "Oh shit."

"Hola, amiga!" said Randy, the grave-robbing smuggler. He swaggered over to the cart, and without hesitating, swept Leslie into a passionate hug.

"Get your hands off of me," she said, pushing him away.

"Whoa there darlin'," he said. "Are you still pissy about what happened in Cusco?"

I stepped around the corner of the cart. "Get outta here, Randy."

"Just a little welcome home hug, amigo. Don't be jealous."

Tara moved over next to Leslie. Leslie reached down and held her hand. Randy cocked his head.

"My, my, my!" he said. "What's this? Maybe she's the jealous one?"

Tara glared at him. Randy flicked his tongue at her and turned to Leslie.

"How 'bout a three way?"

I stepped in front of him. "Hit the road!"

He looked over my shoulder at the girls. "Lesbo love! Who would have guessed?" He puckered his lips at Leslie and made an obnoxious kissing sound.

"Shut your mouth!" I commanded in my toughest Buddhist voice.

Randy put his hand on my chest and gave me a shove. The next thing I knew my right fist made contact with his jaw. The stunned look on his face was priceless. His knees buckled and he staggered back. Tara and Leslie ran behind the cart. Randy reacted to their movement like a bull in the ring crazed with the scent of its own blood. He charged at me. We crashed back against the cart. Wood splintered, Leslie screamed, and with a queer groan the entire cart toppled over.

As the cash register, blenders, and Lucy the duck smashed to the pavement, all thoughts of the Eight-fold Path and the interconnectedness of the Universe went out the window. The only thing I wanted to connect was my fist to Randy's face. We went at it kicking and punching. I flashed on Randy pulling his knife in Peru, so before that could happen again, I got my hands on the walking staff.

"The jaguar will protect you," Miguel said. With a fierce blood lust howling in my ears, I swung the staff at Randy like I was going for the upper deck. The jaguar head caught him square in the ribs. As he went down in a heap, I dove on top of him, knowing that somewhere in the Peruvian jungle Miguel was smiling. In the chaos of spilled juice and Plexiglas shards, my right hand found a stalk of broccoli. I was beating Randy in the face with it when the security guards finally pulled me off of him.

Randy had two broken ribs. The bad news was that the cart was totaled. The worst news was that in the process of investigating the fight the police discovered that Tara was working without a green card. Despite our pleas, they called the INS. When the INS said they would deport Tara, Leslie went into hyper-mode. She emptied her house and moved all of her belongings into storage. She gave me her key and a note for her landlord explaining her hasty departure. The next morning she was on the plane to Amsterdam with Tara.

In one day I had gone from being the juice king of Boulder to having a busted up cart and no partners. I was out three grand to Randy for his busted ribs and I'd been forced to listen to my father harangue me over the phone about appropriate methods of dealing with the public.

My attempt at living the Eight Fold Path failed miserably. Burying the head of the jaguar in Randy's ribcage had shown me that I was far from being a highly evolved human. When he shoved me in the chest, my life wasn't threatened. I could have called security or simply walked away. But I didn't. I punched him, and not out of a primal fight or flight reaction, but because I wanted to protect – what, my pride, my manhood, Leslie and Tara's right to love whomever they wanted? But what was so important about any of it that I would risk the possibility of killing another human being?

Where did that hair-trigger reaction come from? Was it because of my life as a Mescalero Apache? Or perhaps it was from the other lifetimes Harry/Rodas told me about? I thought of my grandfather fighting in WWI, my father in WWII, and all my childhood dreams of battles and shooting and escaping. Was I genetically predisposed to be a warrior? Or was it simply human nature?

Selling off the juice company equipment was depressing, but I needed the cash. With no other plans coming together, I decided to get back on the road to Pomona. The day I finally got rid of the last of our stuff, I got a phone call from Amsterdam. Leslie was talking a mile a minute.

"We met this guy in a pastry shop yesterday," she blurted. "He's like a genius. Tommy, you gotta talk to him. Daniel told us, that's his name Daniel, he's into all this stuff: UFOs, other dimensions, the true nature of man, the whole deal."

"Slow down, slow down," I said. "Who is he? What are his credentials?"

"He's a computer guy. He's installing some big, new network at the Amsterdam Hilton. He's kinda shy and geeky in a cool sorta way."

"Look, Les, I was planning on heading for Pomona in a couple days—"

"Get your ass on a plane!"

"Are you serious?"

"Yeah! You gotta meet this guy."

"You better be right."

"I am."

I was walking through the jam-packed Denver airport eight days later. A spring snowstorm had brought in skiers from all over the country. I stopped at a gift shop to buy a magazine for my flight. As I put my wallet back in my pocket and turned to leave the store, my old girlfriend Lilly walked past. It was as if someone had stuck a Taser in my armpit. My muscles went slack and I sagged against the counter.

She was with a tall, Scandinavian-looking man. Both of them were elegantly dressed. The cost of their overcoats alone would have kept me in rice cakes and tempeh for years. Feeling like I was in a demented stalker film, I followed them as they walked arm in arm down the concourse. By their body language I tried to figure out which of them was the teacher. I couldn't tell for sure, but Lilly certainly looked happy. I didn't feel happy. I felt like an empty sack looking for something to fill me up. After they boarded a United flight to San Francisco, I watched the plane for twenty minutes. When it finally taxied down the runway and out of sight, I sat there trying to guess which of the departing planes Lilly was aboard. I watched fifteen jets lift into the air. When I finally walked away, I found that I had missed my flight.

The next departure for Amsterdam wasn't scheduled until early the following morning. There was no point in going all the way back to Boulder, so amidst other stranded travelers I found a spot on the floor and tried to make myself comfortable.

Blocking out the sounds and voices swirling around me, Lilly's sweet face flashed through my mind. What a fool, I thought, remembering our nights in bed and morning motorcycle rides into the hills. Then I thought of Dee Dee, and our passionate summer after graduation. Would I ever find a woman like either of them; someone strong, and sexy, and funny, and able to see me for who I was, not some idealized version of a man, but me, in all my crazy weirdness. Was that too much to ask?

27

STEAM CROWDED AGAINST ME like damp cotton. I leaned back against the tile wall. Working the line at the Jerome plant was hard on my body. I let out a breath and tried to ease the tightness in my shoulders. The hissing valve in the corner of the steam room abruptly stopped. Silence filtered through the mist.

I had a date with Dee Dee and I wasn't sure what I wanted to happen. Maybe I was afraid of being rejected again. It's not easy having a woman laugh in your face when you're naked and coming on to her. There was no denying that she still did it for me. But was it a meaningful relationship kind of attraction or just a sex thing? Over the years I'd worked hard to heighten my level of discernment in that area. It's a confusing dance. Love and lust are like identical twin sisters who keep exchanging clothes. It's hard to figure out who's who.

I thought of our visit to Kennywood Park with the kids. As we made our way through the throngs of people, I felt protective and concerned for Duncan and Jessie's safety. Watching out for them made me feel like a dad. It seemed natural and sort of familiar. Of course, five hours with them was very different than every day for the rest of their lives. But, if I was willing to be a father to them, and I think I was, how could what was happening between Dee Dee and me simply be a humpy, testosterone thing? No, it had to be something deeper.

From out of the dark recesses of my mind charged the familiar image of the unshaven rider on the Harley Sportster. "Are you fucking nuts!" he screamed as he whooshed past. He pulled a screeching U-turn, popped a wheelie then careened to a stop. "What about Pomona," he shouted, clenching a Clint Eastwood stogie between his teeth. "You have an obligation to yourself! A purpose!"

I buried my head in my hands. I'd been wrestling with him for so long that I knew the dialogue by heart. I knew he'd give me a disgusted look, flick his cigar butt at me, and call me a weenie-boy. Then he'd crank on the throttle, drop the clutch and peel out in a haze of blue exhaust smoke and burned rubber. He'd tear down the road morphing into Jesus, Buddha, a Native American warrior, the orange grove vision, and last but not least, my mother and father. As you can imagine, it was a bit unsettling.

After eating a tasty dinner of angel hair pasta with pesto, Caesar salad, and a somewhat oaky but still enjoyable chardonnay, Dee Dee and I drove to North Park. We circled the lake, reminiscing about the countless times we'd been there as teenagers: beer parties, family picnics, groping with dates in the back seats of our parents' cars. I drove past the county swimming pool toward the glaring lights of the baseball field. We pulled into the parking lot and saw that a Little League game was being played. I found a spot along the third base line and parked the truck. As soon as I'd turned off the ignition, Dee Dee released her seat belt and leaned against my shoulder.

"My son loves the Pirates," she said.

"What does he think of the new center fielder?"

"Is that the guy who keeps dropping balls?"

"Yeah."

"Duncan calls him the Oops Man."

I laughed and turned my attention to the game. Over the right field fence I could see the scoreboard. It was six to five in the eighth inning. From the sound of it, the team at bat was losing. Standing at the plate was a husky boy with short blonde hair. His teammates were on their feet in the dugout yelling for him to get a hit.

"I'm sorry about the other night," Dee Dee said. "I just couldn't stop laughing."

I wasn't sure how to respond. I didn't want to let her know how much her reaction had bothered me. But I also didn't want to seem like it was okay either. I slipped my arm around her and gave her shoulders a squeeze. When the right words fail to present themselves always go for a hug. It creates intimacy while giving you time to think of what you really want to say. Unfortunately for me the stalling tactic failed. My mind was blank.

The kid at the plate swung at a low pitch and missed. His teammates raised the volume of their encouragement. I looked at the scoreboard. There was one out.

"Were you angry with me?" Dee Dee asked. She turned and looked at me.

I knew that to admit I was angry would escalate the discussion to a place I didn't want it to go. Instead, I tapped my thumb on the steering wheel and mumbled, "I wasn't angry. I just felt kinda stupid." As soon as I'd said it, I felt even more stupid.

The batter at the plate swung at a fastball down the middle. He missed. Two outs. The boys on his team began rooting on the next batter. A tall, lanky kid stepped up to the plate

Dee Dee sat back. "Nerves, I think," she said quietly. "We're both on edge about what's happening."

I leaned down and whispered in Dee Dee's ear, "I'm just trying to figure out what's right. Ya know?"

Dee Dee smiled. "You're a thinker. That's what I've always liked about you. You have so much to offer."

"Thanks Dee."

"And you know, I was thinking, if you'd talk to your father, he could probably help you get a good job. He knows a lot of people."

"I did that when I was living in New York. I was miserable."

She snuggled against me. "But now it will be different."

"Oh," I said, in as noncommittal a tone as possible.

The boy at the plate fouled off a high pitch. Hang in there kid, I silently encouraged him.

"I was driving through Fox Chapel yesterday," Dee Dee said, "and I saw the most beautiful house for sale. It sits in a grove of oak trees on, oooh, must be at least an acre and a half. Got the number of the realtor."

"Fox Chapel is a great area," I said, again avoiding any hint of disagreement or consent.

The pitcher threw a fastball. The boy at the plate never got the bat off his shoulder – Two strikes, two outs.

Dee Dee reached over and slowly ran her hand over my stomach. "Don't you think we make a great couple?" She rubbed her hand up and down my thigh. A wave of heat rolled through me. She kept stroking. My head involuntarily leaned back against the headrest.

"Our kids are going to be beautiful," Dee Dee said dreamily.

"Uh huh," I mumbled, my brain beginning to shut down as blood headed southward.

There was a sharp metallic sound. A roar erupted from the field. I looked up as the ball skittered between the shortstop and the third baseman. Run boy, run like the wind, I called in my heart to the lanky kid at the plate. He threw down his aluminum bat, and with long limbs flailing, ran toward first base. The boy in left field was pudgy and slow. When he finally got to the ball he acted like he was bobbling it. The lanky kid at first base took the bait and started for second. The chubby kid quickly scooped the ball up and fired it on a clothesline to the second baseman. My boy was tagged out five feet from second base.

Dee Dee's hand inched over to the freshly formed bulge in my jeans.

"Ooooh my," she said, her voice a low purr. "What have we here?"

The Braille Trail was built in 1976 with money raised in car washes, bake sales, and raffles. It was where the visually impaired could come and enjoy a nature experience. A soft rubber guide wire ran along the right-hand side of the path leading into the woods. The trail looped in a lazy circuitous route back to the gravel lot into which I had just parked my truck. I quickly extinguished the headlights and looked around. There were no other cars.

"Mother nature's calling," Dee Dee said, a sexy twinkle in her voice.

The dull crunch of leaves beneath our feet was the only sound as we made our way through the moonlit woods. Two hundred yards down the trail, Dee Dee and I approached the first wooden bridge, a rustic log walkway covering the stagnant waters of a creek. Dee Dee stopped next to the wooden bench in front of the bridge. Twirling around, she searched the woods for an unwanted audience.

"Dee," I said, but before I could go on, she grabbed me by the arm, unzipped my fly, and had me in her mouth faster than you could say Audubon Society. She pressed something into my hand. I held it up. It was a lubricated condom.

Dee Dee pushed away from me. "Hurry up and put that thing on," she said, her voice smoky with passion. In a flash I had my jeans and boxers down around my ankles. Rolling the condom into place, I sat on the bench and watched with great delight as Dee Dee did a strip tease in the silvery moonlight. Like a wood nymph gone wild, her eyes shone with a predatory desire that both excited and challenged me. She was down to her blue lace panties and bra when I felt the first burning sensation. I didn't pay any attention. I was mesmerized. Dee Dee eased out of her underwear like a snake shedding its skin. The years had sculpted her body into a voluptuous masterpiece. No longer girlish and narrow, her hips now followed the dangerous curves of a woman. Her breasts, having endured the burden of nursing and the laws of gravity, hung lower but with a fullness that absolutely turned me on.

A sharp twinge of pain flared between my legs as Dee Dee cupped her breasts in her hands and gave me a sexy smile. The fiery ache intensified as she took two sensuous steps toward me.

"Teach me that Chinese lovemaking stuff, Tommy," she said, her voice a low whisper, "Lets wake up all the animals in the forest."

A blistering burning in my crotch yanked me to my feet. Yelping like a dog just clipped in the hindquarters by a fast-moving Buick, I frantically began tearing at the condom. Dee Dee, thinking that this was part of the Taoist lovemaking ritual that I'd briefly mentioned to her, answered my high-pitched yelp with one of her own. She too began pawing at her crotch.

"Is this right?" she asked excitedly, "Baby, am I doing it right?"

Ripping off the toxic condom, I began hopping up and down with my pants around ankles, my belt buckle clanking with every frenzied leap.

"Oww, oww, oww," I cried, fanning my burning penis with my hand. Dee Dee echoed my cries as she hopped up next to me, her breasts heaving to and fro.

"Oh man this is good," she said, mimicking my fanning, "Really, primal."

"It's burning," I cried. "My dick's on fire."

"Well, so am I baby," she said, grabbing my ass and pulling me to her. "Put it in me."

A screech of pain tore from my throat. Dee Dee tilted her head back and howled like a wolf. I broke free from her, hopping madly toward the creek. Stumbling and tripping over my pants, I lunged forward and landed face first in the scummy water. Frantically splashing handfuls of that green, slimy liquid onto my crotch, I tried desperately to douse my inflamed appendage. It didn't do any good. The spermicidal lubricant in the condom had found its way into me, and like General Sherman on his march to the sea, was burning everything in its path. As it blazed up my urethra, I fell back on the bank of the creek moaning in agony. Dee Dee looked down at me from the bridge.

"That water's gross," she said, wrinkling her nose in disgust. "Do I really have to do that?"

It was the first serious allergic reaction I'd ever had in my life. Hay fever sufferers consider your selves lucky.

• • •

WHEN I TOLD KIRBY what happened on the Braille Trail, he laughed so hard I thought I'd have to call the paramedics. His face turned bright red and he was gasping and coughing loud enough to cause

Nancy, his secretary, to come into the office twice to make sure he was okay. When he finally stopped laughing and a normal shade of pink returned to his chubby cheeks, Kirby told me that if I married Dee Dee, he'd give me an executive position at Jerome, a company car, an expense account, and season tickets to the Steeler games. He'd teach me the entire business from the ground up: sales, distribution, manufacturing, advertising, and management.

"We'd almost be like partners," he said, a broad smile lighting up his face. He winked at me. "Tommy, it's finally your chance to have a career."

I leaned back in the brown leather armchair. Kirby leaned forward over his desk.

"And," he said, "I can make you an excellent deal on a lot I own out in Cranberry Township. It's an acre and a half with a creek running through the back corner. The kids will love it." He rapped his knuckles on the desk and gave me a self-satisfied grin. He knew he'd sunk the hook deep.

"I don't know what to say, Kirb. It's a generous offer and—" He cut me off with a wave of his hand.

"You don't have to give me an answer yet. Think about it. But personally, I'd think you'd be a dope to let Dee Dee get away. The sight of her ass still knocks me out."

That night I went to bed and, like a weird scene out of a science fiction movie, my mind began sprouting a crop of highly disturbing questions. Shooting up from the dark, fear-laden patches of loamy gray matter I'd been tenaciously avoiding for years, the tangle of questions roamed over a multitude of subjects: marital fidelity, crib death syndrome, interest rates, thirty year mortgages, birth defects, medical insurance, orthodontists, property taxes, dental coverage, optometrists, mutual funds, quieter sex with kids in the house, homeowners insurance, calculus homework, ballet classes, drum sets, first menstruation, drivers licenses, car insurance, drinking, drugs, teenage pregnancy, college tuition, retirement plans, social security, writing a will, grandchildren, and divorce.

In my mind, beneath the zing and whoop of this cacophony of future concerns, thumping like the recognizable base line from a popular song, was the distant, yet distinctive rumble of a certain Harley Davidson. Its innervating auditory reminder was more than equaled on an olfactory level by the familiar stench of a cheap cigar.

As sleep eased up on me, all the noise and disturbance in my mind finally began to disappear. I drifted, like a fat tuna in the gulf-stream, toward the delightful peace of sleep. Just as I was about to go through the portal into the adventures of the dreamtime, I heard footsteps – boot steps to be exact. A dingy room came into focus. The boots got louder. I looked around the room. The walls were dusty and bare. Behind me was a wooden door. On it, painted in red, was a small elephant. I stared at it, trying to figure out what it meant. The elephant on the door began to dissolve and drip to the floor. Running like melted wax, it gathered into a small puddle in front of the door. Outside the room, the boots stopped. The puddle of red color immediately reformed. Looking like a slug that had just done the backstroke through a gallon of crimson paint, it crawled laboriously back up the door. As I watched, it painstakingly re-formed itself, inch by inch, into the picture of the orange grove. The details were exactly as I'd seen them during my vision quest.

The door jiggled. The knob turned. Slowly it began to open. One inch, two inches, a foot – with a dramatic final bang the door swung all the way open. Guess who? Cigar smoke was already filling the room. My lone wolf, the perennial bachelor/mystery man, clomped into the room in his motorcycle boots. He stopped in the middle of the room and stared in my direction. I could see myself reflected in his highly polished mirror sunglasses. I looked much smaller than I did in real life.

"Don't be afraid," he said, with uncharacteristic tenderness. "You're almost there." He reached up and removed his sunglasses.

I had never seen his eyes before. During all the years I'd been hounded by his lunacy, the mirror shades had always been a mask separating us from eye to eye contact. As I looked into the dark, round pools beneath his shaggy mop of hair, a familiar tingling and buzzing started in my head. My leather clad friend grinned. He reached up and casually removed the cigar from the corner of his mouth. Then, like a gigantic roman candle, he erupted into a fiery mass of sparks. I covered my eyes as heat and light blasted into my face. I heard a sound that made me think of a raven that flew by just over my head in the desert outside of Santa Fe. The rustling sound came again. I took my hands away from my eyes.

The blue heron was standing before me.

28

THE NEXT MORNING ALL I could think about was what the blue heron said to me. "Don't be afraid, you're almost there." Almost where, I wondered? Don't be afraid of what? The only thing I could come up with was that I was almost to Pomona. That's what it had always been badgering me to do – get to Pomona. Apparently my journey west was near at hand. Dee Dee, of course, had a different theory.

"Grow up!" she said, glaring at me across her parents' kitchen counter. A squeal of laughter came up the stairs from the basement where the kids were playing videos.

"Just because you've had an occasional odd dream, traveled around a bit, and seen some weird stuff doesn't mean you have to act like a child for the rest of your life."

"Dee," I said. She cut me off before I could go any further.

"It was a frigging hallucination, Tommy. You were seventeen years old and you were stoned on mushrooms. You act like God stuck his face through the clouds and pointed his finger at you."

"I'm trying to follow my path."

"Your what?"

"The path I set out to travel in this lifetime."

"Don't give me that mumbo jumbo," she said. "We both know the path you want. It ends right here." She grabbed her crotch and flashed me a sexy grin. A portion of my brain turned to mush. She came over and put her arms around my neck.

"Baby," she said. "I don't want you to go out west. Whatever is in Pomona isn't going to make you happy. I'll make you happy. Me and the kids, we'll be a family." She kissed me. Her lips tasted like watermelon.

"I'll tell you what," she said, resting her head on my shoulder. "I think we need to do some sort of, I don't know, exorcism to get rid of this blue bird thing."

"Dee Dee, this is an important trip for me to make."

She put her hands on her hips. "How are we supposed to have a relationship if you go running off every time some figment of your imagination tells you to?"

"It's not in my imagination. You know that."

"No, I don't."

"Come on, Dee."

"You are sooooo weird. What am I doing with you?"

We stared at each other for a painfully long moment. Questions of our compatibility rose up in my mind. Could I be with someone who didn't respect my outlook on life? Was my outlook worthy of respect? Was I insane? Was she insane for wanting an insane man in her life?

"Okay, okay, I got an idea," she said, breaking the stare down. "This whole thing started that day at your parents' house, right?"

"Yeah."

"What if we re-enacted it? What if we did the same stuff we did that day?"

"Make love in the living room?"

"Why not? It would bring us full circle. Maybe it would break the hold this thing has on you, and we'd have closure."

"I don't know if I want closure."

Dee Dee scowled. "Do you want me? If you do, I'm not going to sit around waiting for you to crisscross the damn country looking for God-knows-what."

"You're not even divorced yet."

"That doesn't mean anything. If we're going to be together, we should be together. Now what's it going to be, me, or some fantasy out in Pomona?"

Ultimatums have always been a surefire way to motivate me. I don't like being told that I can't do something. So, without truly considering the outcome of the decision, and reacting from a twitchy, king-of-the-mountain mentality, I heard myself agree to Dee Dee's idea of re-enacting the moment when I first laid eyes on the blue heron.

Two days later, my parents told me that on Saturday morning they'd be going to Greensburg for a couple hours to visit one of my mother's college sorority sisters. I immediately called Dee Dee and gave her the news. She said she'd have her parents watch the kids. We made a date for Saturday morning at ten-thirty.

Neither one of us had any idea where to get psilocybin mushrooms, so Dee Dee suggested shots of Tequila. At eleven-fifteen in morning, under the watchful, yet cataract impaired gaze of Peanut, Dee Dee and I downed our sixth shot of Herradura.

"Okay big boy," Dee Dee said, unbuttoning her jeans. "Time to make the feathers fly." She grabbed me by the hand and together we walked into the pristine white of the living room. I spread an old beach towel on the floor to protect us from carpet burns.

"All right," I said, "are you ready?"

Dee Dee blew me a kiss.

I turned and walked out of the room. In the den, I dug out the old *Camelot* album and put it on the turntable. I paused before lowering the needle. Was this really smart, I asked myself, staring at the spinning record.

"I'm waiting," Dee Dee called from the living room.

Screw it, I thought. Dopey as it seemed, if following through with this bizarre enactment would allow me to settle down and have a normal family life, then it was worth a shot. I put needle to vinyl and headed for the living room.

Dee Dee was naked and on her back. "Do you know what I was just thinking?" she said. "If you ever, you know, die, I'm gonna have you cremated. And then I'll stuff your ashes in a dildo, and that way you can still do me. Cool idea, huh?"

In my Tequila-infused state, my heart swelled with joy at finally finding a woman who cared that much for me.

Dee Dee lifted her hips off of the floor and began undulating her pelvis.

"Wasn't I doing something like this?"

"Yeah," I said, appreciating her attention to detail.

Dee Dee grinned. "My ass was a lot smaller back then."

In the den, the *Camelot* album began to skip. Dee Dee shook her head. "Forget about it. Drop those drawers, mister."

I slid out of my jeans and pulled off my black tee shirt.

"Oooh, yes, take it off, take it off!" Dee Dee yelled.

I lay down next to her on the beach towel. Even as I reached to touch her, thrilled as I was to be naked and finally lying beside her, I still wasn't certain that I wanted my mysterious dance with the blue heron to be over. It had led me most of my adult life. The one time when I broke away from it while living in New York City, my life immediately spiraled into a dark and lonely place. Why would I want to do that to myself again?

"Gimme that thing," Dee Dee said reaching for me. "Make it big baby, come on make it big. Let's get that weirdo bird out of our lives once and for all."

We kissed. She squeezed. We kissed. She stroked. She stroked. She stroked. With a whoop and a growl the Cro-Magnon man stormed out of his cave and shouted "Yee haw!" In that instant, all of my concern for the blue heron was offered up and sacrificed to the humpy, horned Gods of lust. I reached for the condom in the pocket of my jeans. Dee Dee sat up.

"Did you hear that?" she said.

Half expecting to see my fine, feathered friend, I quickly looked around the room. It was empty.

"What?" I said.

"I heard something."

We both listened for a moment. The only thing I could hear was the *Camelot* album skipping in the den.

"I must be losing it," Dee Dee said. She looked down at my waning erection.

"Oops," I said.

She slid down and took matters into her own hands, and mouth. I laid back, surrendering to the pleasure. A second later the front door flew open.

"Surprise!" my mother's cheerful voice rang out. "Guess who is – OH MY GOD!"

My mother, father, and Becky were standing in the entryway. The profound look of horror on my mother's face indicated that seeing me naked as a teenager had been considerably less offensive than the present sight of my less firm, except for one exception, nearly thirty-six-year-old anatomy. My father took one look at us, started humming "You Make Me Feel So Young," and backed out the front door. Becky grinned.

"God Dee Dee, you look great. And you've had two kids."

Dee Dee and I grabbed our clothes and ran into the kitchen. As we hurried to get dressed, I couldn't help thinking that other than the Beatles, Roberto Clemente, and my seventh grade art teacher Miss Sherwin, nostalgia was definitely not what it was cracked up to be.

Oddly enough, my parents seemed to be more embarrassed than angry about what happened. At least that's the way they acted.

"You two need your private time together just like any other couple," Mom said. Then with a slight edge in her voice added, "But don't you think you should wait until she's divorced? And please, why the living room? What's with the two of you and our living room?"

I didn't dare explain the ritual we were enacting, so I told her that Dee Dee liked being surrounded by all the white.

"Really?" Mom said. "She leaves her eyes open?"

My father's only comment came later that afternoon. As I walked into the kitchen, he was stirring a pot of split pea soup. He continued stirring for a minute, and then with thin-lipped restraint, no doubt dictated by my mother's desire to keep the peace, he said, "Dee Dee certainly has maintained her figure over the years." I agreed with him, and that was all that was said, at least from my parents.

"So Tommy," Becky said, "is this relationship with Dee Dee going somewhere beyond the floor of the living room?"

I looked up from where I was trimming the arborvitae on the side of the porch. Stretched out on a lounge chair in her red, two-piece bathing suit with a towel wrapped turban style around her head, Becky looked like the Mata Hari at Daytona Beach.

"She's great. I like her a lot."

"Uh oh. Here it comes. The infamous, She's nice, but . . ."

I put the hedge clippers down and walked over to her. "We're just really different."

"I hope so. If she was like you, I'd be calling social services and having her kids removed from the house."

"Very funny," I said. "She doesn't get me."

"Who does? Face the facts Tommy you're a wacko. Your pursuit of your soul or the Great Spirit or whatever it is that you've been trying to find all these years is hopeless. Spirituality is a pair of dark glasses we put on to avoid facing the truth. All human behavior is ultimately predicated by genetic self-interest."

"Chuck Darwin speaks," I said. I sat down in the grass next to her and crossed my legs Indian style.

"You feel attracted to Dee Dee, right?" Becky asked.

"Yeah, sure."

"So you take her to dinner, you give her flowers, whisper sweet things to her, take her kids to Kennywood, play with them in the pool, etc., etc., right?"

"Yeah."

"You express behavior that we as a culture have accepted as being indicative of love. But what's causing you to behave that way? Is it love? If that's true what's creating the feelings of love? Is it something that Dee Dee brings out in you? Is it a mystical, magical aura? Wrong! I'll tell you what it is, and it's not easy to accept because if you do then you're forced to face the monstrous self-delusion we live in. What sends you and Dee Dee swooning into each other's arms isn't some Hallmark-card-Valentine's-Day-gushy-love thing.

It's your genes, howling like a band of hungry monkeys, demanding to be passed into future generations."

"So we're just machines at the mercy of our genetic quest?"

"You got it." Becky sat up and pushed her bangs off of her sweaty forehead. "We've cloaked ourselves with philosophies and theologies that attempt to take the edge off the brutal truth. But the reality is – kindness, sympathy, compassion, love, trust, nurturing our children, all of it comes from a drive to replicate our genes into a continuing reality."

"Okay Galapagos girl," I said. "If that's true, if nature formed us through the gauntlet of survival of the fittest, what's behind nature? What's the force that programmed our genes to be as ruthless as you say they are?"

"There is no programmer," Becky said, her voice pinching in frustration. "There's no master plan, no wizard behind the curtain. It's all happening through evolution."

"I don't buy that. Human beings are highly complex, amazing creatures. How could we have possibly turned out this way simply by chance?"

Becky dabbed at the suntan lotion pooled in her bellybutton. "So you still think there's some guiding force out there pulling the cosmic strings?"

"Out there, in there, I don't know exactly how it works."

"I don't know either, Tommy. But your compulsion to give your life's direction over to experiences that you had in a drug induced state is, to me, frightfully naive."

"That brings up another point—"

"Spare me."

"No, really. If we're creatures of the evolutionary process, why would there even be an inclination to communicate with God or whatever – spirit. How would a belief in an abstract concept like God contribute to our ancestors feeding themselves or reproducing?"

Becky threw up her hands. "Are you like this with Dee Dee?"

"Sometimes."

"She must think you're a nut."

"That's part of our problem."

"Sounds like you two need couples therapy."

"Right. That's just what I need."

Hell, I didn't know what I needed. Between trying to figure out how I felt about Dee Dee, marriage, buying Kirby's property, and becoming an executive at Jerome, Inc., I didn't know which end was up. And what did it mean that our ritual to break my blue heron connection had gone unconsummated? There was a part of me that was relieved that we hadn't actually done it. Was it a sign that Dee Dee and I shouldn't be together? Or was I just looking for an excuse to get out of town and avoid facing responsibilities? Was working at Jerome Inc., and settling down with Dee Dee and her kids, the truth I had been seeking all these years?

29

It was a damp, gray afternoon when I met Daniel Toberni in the red-light district of Amsterdam. He was gazing intently into the display window of a brothel at a pale, middle-aged prostitute sprawled on a shabby love seat. Dressed in red lace panties and a black bra, the combined heft of her breasts looked to be equal to Daniel's entire body weight. Five foot two at best, he was skinny as a rail.

"She'd hurt you," Tara said.

"Smothered in love," he said. He had a slight southern accent. A stubble of beard showed through his olive-toned skin.

"This is our friend, Tom McInnes," Leslie said.

"Yes," Daniel said.

"Good to meet you," I said, as we shook hands.

"Your friends have told me about you."

"All the evil stuff," Leslie said.

"Where can we talk?" I asked, eager to hear what Daniel had to say.

We left the neon glare, sex supermarket atmosphere of the red-light district and headed west packed into Tara's black Citroen. Chugging through the snarling traffic around Dam Square, she zigzagged along canals and crossed over bridges. She took us past the house where Anne Frank and her family attempted to hide from the Nazi's during World War II. Tara told us that her own mother grew up eight blocks away and suffered terribly during the war.

"That's why the Dutch have so much compassion for the choices that other people make in their lives," she said. "Hey!" She pounded the horn. "Move it!" She hesitated a moment then wheeled the car around a stalled delivery truck. "After what our country went through during World War II, we don't like to be told what to do. We try to give people freedom to live as they choose." She downshifted and, with tires squealing, made a sharp right turn.

With the precision of a diamond cutter, she parallel parked the car in a spot half as big as I thought she needed. We walked two blocks past crowded shops and several restaurants to a cafe called The Bulldog. The psychedelic paint job outside should have been a hint. As soon as we stepped inside, the smell hit me.

"I believe there's some dope smoking going on in here," I said.

Leslie giggled. Daniel raised his eyebrows and sniffed the air. A pungent cloud of cannabis smoke hung over the eclectic gathering of customers jammed into the cafe. Leather-jacketed biker types sat across from clean-cut, obviously stoned, college students. Over the sound system, Van Morrison's song, "Into the Mystic," was playing.

"Another example of Dutch tolerance of individual rights?" I asked.

"You got it," Tara said.

We squeezed around a table near the door. Leslie ordered hot tea and a brownie. When I ordered the same thing, Tara leaned to me and whispered, "It's a hash brownie. Is that what you want?"

"Wow," I said. "No, I'll just have tea."

I was relieved to see Daniel order regular coffee. When our drinks and food arrived, Leslie and Tara didn't waste any time. They laughed and fed each other pieces of their hash brownies. Two pony-tailed guys at the next table couldn't take their eyes off of them.

I leaned across the table to Daniel. "So what did you say to Leslie? She was determined to get me over here to meet you."

Daniel dabbed at a ring of coffee with his napkin. "Are you sure you want to know?"

"Yeah," I said. "Absolutely."

"Okay," he said. He slid his chair around the corner of the table and sat next to me. "I think it's about evolution."

I leaned closer to hear over the music.

"I think the human species is moving toward a shift of some kind."

"Go on," I said.

"Just as there were jumps along the way from Homo Erectus to Homo Sapiens, there's also going to be a leap from Homo Sapiens to the next stage of human development."

"Oh, yeah?" I said.

"Yes. We're moving up the evolutionary ladder."

"What about UFOs? How do they fit into the process?"

Daniel thought for a moment. "I think they're here to remind us that we're not only of this planet. We're connected to the whole universe."

"I don't know about that," I said. "I've got friends who have told me horror stories about people getting abducted and experimented on. They'll tell you that UFOs are more than visual aids."

Daniel frowned. "I didn't say that. I think they're acting as an environmental stimulus. They're here to push us. The psychological and emotional threat of UFOs will force us to accept the reality of life beyond this planet and this dimension. Coming to terms with this will propel our consciousness into a higher place."

"What higher place?"

"Acceptance of our own universality," Daniel said.

"Okay," I said. "And how is accepting our universality going to change us as a species?"

Daniel leaned closer. "By accepting it we will be claiming our birthright, our freedom to be multidimensional beings."

"Oh, I know about dimensions," I said. "But don't tell me that all I have to do is accept that I'm some universal being and bingo I'm through the door. There's more to it than that."

He smiled. "I believe that people who are open, people with the right kind of adaptive nervous systems are going to be the ones to initiate the shift. They'll be the Adams and Eves of our future."

"You mean the lab rats."

Daniel shook his head. "No. I don't think it's an experiment. There isn't a mad scientist behind a curtain trying to create some kind of monster. This is the natural order. Humans are evolving to another plane of experience. Just as there were Cro-Magnons roaming around at the same time as the less creative Neanderthals, there will be human beings among us with abilities far outreaching what is presently held to be normal."

"What kind of abilities?"

Daniel shrugged. "Forty bits a second, that's what humans are consciously able to perceive, forty bits."

"And what does that mean?"

"The human eye," Daniel said, "sends at least ten million bits to the brain every second. The skin sends a million bits a second, the ear one hundred thousand, our sense of smell another hundred thousand, and taste buds contribute maybe another thousand bits. Do the math. That's around eleven million bits a second coming into our senses from the world. But what do you consciously experience? Forty bits a second. What are you doing with the rest of that input?"

"What's a bit," I asked.

"Come on, stay with me on this."

"I don't know what we do with the rest."

"Exactly, and that my friend, is the direction I believe the species is heading – access to a wider bandwidth of consciousness." He nodded thoughtfully. "It's going to create dramatic shifts in human behavior."

"I hope that's true. But didn't Jesus and Buddha offer themselves to the world as examples of what an evolved human being could be? We're still doing horrible things to each other."

Daniel gave me a long steady look. "Organized religion has been both a component of and a hindrance to the growth of consciousness. Faith will survive the transition, but the rest shall pass."

He reached into his pocket and pulled out a tin of mints. He took one and slid the tin across the table toward me.

"Would you like one?"

I picked up a mint and popped it in my mouth.

"Daniel," I said, tasting the sugary peppermint, "how can you be sure that this isn't a big propaganda scheme being fed into your mind by an invading army of aliens in a giant mother ship hovering over Mt. Shasta."

He laughed and leaned back in his chair. "To consciously accept the shift that's coming, human beings will have to deal with those kinds of fears. But remember," he said. "Submitting to a higher power is not the same as being destroyed by it."

"Whoa, wait a minute," I said. "There's a fine line there. You can't know the truth until you actually commit yourself, and then it's too late to change your mind."

His intense blue eyes locked onto mine. "Submission of human judgment to the divine mystery is about faith. You have to listen and follow the signs."

"Hey, I listened to a great blue heron when I was stoned on mushrooms. Believe me, I know how to follow signs."

Daniel smiled and glanced across the cafe. "I know it isn't always a pleasant experience, but integrating into the truth of who you are is important."

"Yeah, yeah, integration. Screw it. Right now I'd just like to get laid."

Daniel laughed. The skin around his eyes crinkled into crow's feet. "Who knows, Tom, maybe you're one of the pioneers."

I snorted. "Yeah, right! Always wondered why I was leading such a wacky life. Participating in the evolution of the human species was never one of the theories I came up with."

Daniel smiled. "You should go to places where the energy is high. It'll be good for you." He shrugged his shoulders and grinned. "Who knows, maybe you'll even get laid."

He pushed his chair back from the table, pulled out several crisp dollar bills, and dropped them on the table.

"Take it easy, Tom." He went over to Leslie and Tara and gave each of them a hug.

"See ya'll," he said, and walked out of the cafe.

• • •

DANIEL TOBERNI'S THEORIES DISTURBED me. As much as I wanted to disregard them as fantasy, most of what he said made sense. His statements about the capacity of human consciousness and the UFO influence on our development were of particular interest to me. It brought to mind a slew of questions. The next morning, I went in search of answers.

At the front desk of the Hilton Hotel a woman with pewter-colored hair and a gold name tag identifying her as Ava, smiled at me.

"Can I help you," she said with an English accent.

"Daniel Toberni's room, please."

She tapped a series of keys on a keyboard. She studied the screen then looked up at me.

"I'm sorry sir," she said. "We don't have a guest by that name?"

"Oh. Did he check out this morning?"

She punched several more keys. "No sir. He never checked in. We haven't had a guest by that name all week."

"Are you sure? I was told he was staying here. He's installing your new computer network."

She raised her chin and sighted down her nose at me. "One moment please."

At another computer terminal she conferred with a tall, balding man in a gray, double-breasted suit. The man glanced over and gave me a curt smile. With Ava trailing behind, he walked over to me.

"Good morning, sir," he said. "I'm William Reid the manager of the hotel. You were asking about our computer network?"

"Yes," I said. "A friend of mine is working on it. I wanted to speak to him if I could."

"Sir, there is no computer installation going on in this hotel. Our system was overhauled last summer."

I stared at him. "But . . ."

"Sir, perhaps your friend is working at a different hotel."

Ava was kind enough to check with several other hotels. Not one of them had a guest by the name of Daniel Toberni, and none of them were in the middle of a computer installation.

With Tara and Leslie's help I called every hotel, rental cottage, Bed and Breakfast, and canal house in Amsterdam. No one I spoke to recognized Daniel's name or a description of him. Leslie went to the pastry shop where she and Tara first met Daniel. The women behind the counter didn't remember him.

I wandered the streets of Amsterdam searching everywhere for Daniel Toberni. I even took a shuttle to the airport to question airline employees. No one had seen him. Finally, after yet another fruitless day of searching, I'd had enough. A block away from the smoky confines of The Bulldog, I slumped into the booth of a cafe. I was halfway through a cucumber and tomato sandwich and my second Heineken when a middle-aged couple came in and sat at the table next to mine. The woman's long blond hair was pulled back in a ponytail and the man was wearing small, round, John Lennon sunglasses.

"TaNeisha told me that it's extraordinary," the woman said. "She said the energy was really high."

I put down my pint of beer and looked over at the couple.

"The Druids used to worship there long before the church was ever built," she said. "Apparently it's always been a kind of sacred place."

"We have to be in Monte Carlo by Friday," the man said.

"I know. But she told me on Thursday mornings they move the chairs to clean the floor. That's when she was able to walk the labyrinth."

"Did you mail those postcards?"

"Yes. Doesn't it sound intriguing?"

"My cousin went there in '72 or '73," the man said. "He told me Chartres was just another old church. He didn't see what all the fuss was about."

"Dean is an idiot," she said. "TaNeisha said that walking the labyrinth was an amazing experience. She said that—" The man cut her off.

"I know, I know," he said. "The energy is high."

He leaned to her and said something but I couldn't hear it. Daniel Toberni's final instructions were echoing in my head: "Go to places where the energy is high."

30

THANKFULLY, WITH THE FAMILY gossiping about Rick and the divorce situation brewing in Atlanta, for most of Becky's visit I was able to avoid facing the specter of my own convoluted future.

My father informed us that Rick's soon to be ex-wife Denise had hired the best divorce lawyer in the city. Denise was planning to squeeze Rick for every dime she could get. Becky seemed to think that it was a fair turn of play.

"He's my brother and I love him," she said, "but he's a pig. Leaving his wife for a bimbo younger woman – it's gross, he's a bad cliché."

My father of course immediately stormed to Rick's defense. He went after Denise like a rabid badger. He criticized her childrearing abilities, her permed hairstyle, the amount of eyeliner she wore, and her excessive spending habits. My mother, the great rememberer, chimed in like the holy elephant of social decorum. She listed, as if reading from a written page, every single etiquette infraction Denise fumbled through in the twelve years she and Rick were together.

As I listened to this scathing indictment of Denise, who at one time both my parents lovingly referred to as their daughter, all I could think of was, why do I want to get married? If you tough it out and stay together for forty years you end up like my parents, picking and sniping at each other. If like Rick, ten years go by and you refuse to ignore the deep undercurrents of dissatisfaction in your marriage, splitting up is a nightmare. You get accused of being a letch and your soon-to-be ex-wife gets viciously slammed for using the wrong fork at a Thanksgiving dinner nine years earlier. It's a lose/lose situation.

Again, I was forced to consider whether mating for life was a natural instinct of the human species or, if instead, it was a paradigm that we or God or blue herons or alien rulers from a galaxy far, far away had inflicted upon us strictly out of the need for social and genetic order. Of course life would be a chaotic mess if everyone was free from moral, legal or religious restraint to simply go about copulating at will with whomever they desired. The genetic mutations alone would send us scuttling into hermit caves. But is 50 years of marriage to the same person going a bit too far? How can you grow and change as an individual if you're focused on making a partnership stay together? Something has to give. Either you stop evolving or the marriage goes tits-up in a gush of tears and nasty accusations.

My father, not a big proponent of individual change and growth, had, after two days of slamming his soon to be ex-daughter-in-law, these final words on the subject: "If Rick wants to trade her in and have himself another, why shouldn't he? He's got the money. Let him do what he wants." I thought Becky was going to throw her plate of scrambled eggs at him. Aunt Helen, whom we'd rescued from the nursing home for this champagne Sunday Brunch in the fern infested atrium at the Sheraton Hotel, looked up at my father and said, "You putz."

Nearly spilling the orange juice he was pouring into my glass, our pimple-faced waiter, brazenly sporting a painful-looking hickey on his neck, snickered back a laugh and hurried toward the kitchen. Once there, he would undoubtedly warn the rest of the staff about the family fracas at his table of five.

My father set his fork down and glared daggers across the table at Aunt Helen. Not wavering a bit, she pouted out her wrinkled lower lip and glared right back at him. My mother, ever on the alert for potentially embarrassing public displays of family unrest, raised her mimosa in a toast.

"Here's to you kids," she said. "It's nice having you home."

My father, breaking away from his stare down with Aunt Helen, tipped his head toward us and said, "Even if we can't have a peaceful meal together."

Aunt Helen's fork clattered against her plate.

"Don't blame it on me," she said. "What do you expect me to do when I hear as idiotic a thing as you just said about Ricky? Lordy be, talk about stupid."

"All right you two," my mother said. She looked around to see if any of the other Sunday brunchers had heard.

"Honestly," Aunt Helen said. "What are you some kind of cave man?"

"That's right," I heard Becky say under her breath.

"Trade her in?" Aunt Helen continued. "What is she a Chrysler? She's the mother of your grandchildren for heaven's sake."

"That's enough," my father said.

"The boy's run wild since day one and you've condoned it. If you were any kind of a father, instead of making excuses for Ricky, you'd get on the phone and talk some sense into him."

My heart swelled with pride for my dear old Auntie. She was a warrior.

"I'm not a cave man," my father said, trying to maintain his head-of-the-household-king-of-his-castle dignity. "I just think that if Rick wants to get a divorce he should get one"

"This melon is delicious," my mother said, her voice straining to remain calm. "I think you should have some Helen."

Fully aware that my mother was asking her to put a muzzle on it, but equally intent on finishing her argument, Aunt Helen picked up her spoon and stuck it into her bowl of Cream of Wheat. Her lips continued moving, so I knew that she wasn't finished with Dad. Her verbal attack had simply been reassigned to covert status. As she raised a spoonful of the gelatinous mush to her lips, a single word punctuated the tension at the table.

"Dipshit!"

This sent looks zinging between everyone; Becky smirking at me, my mother attempting to placate my father, my father shaking his head at Aunt Helen, and the waiter trying not to laugh as he refilled my father's coffee cup.

Ah yes, another pleasant Sunday morning with the family.

After our sumptuous dining experience, Becky and I drove Aunt Helen back to the nursing home. As we cruised down Route 19 Becky leaned forward between the front seats of my Blazer.

"Aunt Helen," she said. "Are you going to tell us about your boyfriend, Mr. Hursen?"

"Mind your own business," Aunt Helen snapped.

Becky took another approach. "I think it would be really fun if the four of us could do something this afternoon before I catch my plane."

"Yeah," I said. "Maybe listen to some jazz down at the Balcony."

"Does Leo like music?" Becky said, turning on her sweetest, most manipulative charm.

"I'm gonna smack the both of you if you don't stop with this business right now." Aunt Helen swung her hand at Becky's head. Becky ducked back into her seat.

"What's the big deal about Leo Hursen?" I said.

Aunt Helen turned away and stared out the window. We drove in silence the rest of the way to the Howland Nursing Center.

• • •

MONDAY MORNING I WOKE up with a dream hovering at the edge of my consciousness. I was standing on the rim of a cliff. It looked like the Grand Canyon. The air was really dry and hot. I was alone, but I seemed to be waiting for someone. Hearing footsteps in the dirt, I turned around. Dee Dee and her husband Matt were standing there. Matt had on a long white robe and a headband. Printed in orange day-glow on the front of the headband was E = mgh.

I was trying to figure out what that formula meant when Matt shoved me off the edge of the cliff. I tumbled head over heels in a free fall. A hundred feet above the boulder-strewn ground, I eased to a stop, hovering on a cushion of warm air. I looked up into a blue sky wispy with clouds, thankful that I'd stopped falling. From my right came an odd huffing sound. I turned to see what it was. Thirty feet away on a rock ledge, a brown marmot began furiously barking at me. In a flash of fur he darted straight up the face of the cliff. That's when I saw it. Drawn on the rock in faded, but distinct black letters were the words, Let Her Go. I stared at it wondering what it meant. Then it hit me, but I didn't want to believe it.

Later that day, during our mid-morning break at work, I was standing in the cafeteria eating a banana and a cup of yogurt. Kirby and Steve Petrovic walked over with Styrofoam cups of steaming coffee.

"You catch any of the game last night?" Kirby asked.

"Nah," I said.

"That idiot centerfielder dropped another one," Steve said.

"How can they keep playing him?" I asked.

Kirby snorted. "Because he's fast as a greyhound."

"He looks like he's out there bird watching or something," Steve said. "Always looking up. What the fuck is he looking at? Guy's a total jag-off."

"He'll pull it together," Kirby said. "He's hitting well."

Steve grunted. "They oughta trade him." He put his hand on my shoulder. "Sometimes the best thing to do is just let 'er go. You know what I mean?"

I stared at him. "What did you say?"

He thumped me on the back. "Let her go. I think it would be best for everyone."

I took a step back. "Why did you say that?"

"The guy is hurting the team."

"You said her."

"Did I? Huh."

I shook my head. "Oh man. This is too weird."

They both stared at me. "What's up?" Kirby asked.

"Nothing," I mumbled. "I'll see you guys later."

Let her go. I spent the rest of the day thinking about Dee Dee. She was sexy and fun and we had a long history together. But something was missing and, no matter how hard I tried to ignore it, it was still there. Dee Dee didn't look at the world the way I had come to see it. Compromise is important in making relationships work, but martyring myself to make her happy wasn't the right thing to do. I'd learned that in my relationship with Melina. Ouch.

That night, I picked Dee Dee up after work. She was wearing white sandals and a cotton summer dress. Her hair was rich with the scent of tropical islands.

As we drove along Ingomar Road toward North Park, I told her that I had something I wanted to talk to her about. The warm smile on her face told me that she'd made an incorrect assumption about what I was planning to say.

I parked across from the Boat House and we strolled over to the swings. While Dee Dee got herself swinging back and forth, I stared out at the lake trying to gather my thoughts and my courage.

"I bring the kids out here," she said. "Jessie loves to go really high."

"Dee Dee," I said. "I don't think this thing between us is going to work."

There was a long, I repeat, long, tense pause as the chains on the swing creaked and groaned.

"You're such a coward," Dee Dee finally said. "You don't want to get hurt so you never let anyone get close enough to you."

"I love you."

"I know."

"But we're not meant to be."

She jammed her sandals into the dirt bringing the swing to a sudden stop. "How do you know that?"

"We see things differently."

"That's what makes a marriage great. You bring your opinions, I bring mine."

"But you want me to have the same opinions as you."

"If I'm right, I'm right!"

"Every time we've tried to make love something has kept it from happening. You don't have to be a genius to see the signs."

"You and your signs!"

"Come on Dee, we don't belong together."

"Then why are we so attracted to each other?"

"It's our genes howling for expression."

"I've got two kids! My genes have already expressed themselves."

"I don't know."

"That's for sure."

"Maybe it's – a test."

"A test?"

"Yeah, to see if this is as much as we want."

"What are you talking about?"

"You don't appreciate what I've done in my life. You think I've just been playing around."

"That's why we're together, so I can help you get back on track."

"My point exactly – I *am* on track. Lately I'd begun to doubt it. I thought maybe it was time to be more like everyone else."

"Heaven forbid."

"Listen to me. After Melina, I didn't think I'd ever meet anyone I'd want to settle down with. I really didn't. But when I saw you, I thought, wow, Dee Dee and me. It made so much sense."

"And it still does."

"No – it doesn't. Be honest, you could give a shit about all my questions about spirituality and other dimensions. You don't care about that. You just want me to be with you and that's it."

"What's so terrible about that? You should be grateful. You're not exactly a normal guy."

"This is who I am. This is the world I live in."

"Well, maybe there's no woman out there who can meet your earth-mother-holy priestess standards. You ever think about that? You've been looking for, whatever it is, for a long time."

"Yeah I know. And I'm sorry but this isn't it."

Dee Dee shook her head. "Did your pal the blue heron tell you to give me the boot? Is that what this is all about?"

"No. But I did have a dream."

"You're doing this because of a dream!"

"It got me thinking, that's all."

"Take me home! You're a lunatic! You live in a fantasy world. You probably don't take a pee without checking your guides or bugs or birds or whoever the hell it was you think was using me to test you."

"Dee let's not end it like this."

"Fuck you! You can't control my feelings like you control your own. I want to rip your dick off, shred it and feed it to the fish. And if that's not exactly what you want to hear right now, if that's a little too much emotion – tough titties!"

In Islam, the Shahadah is the Muslim confession of faith. During daily prayers and especially in moments of turmoil and crisis when life rears up and staggers their faith, Muslims are quick to speak the words: "There is no god but God." As Dee Dee stomped back to the truck, I found myself muttering, "There is no god but God, there is no god but God, there is no god but God." By the time I sat down behind the wheel, the doubt and insecurity which had descended upon me like a hungry vulture, had faded into a distant corner of my heart. Filling the hole torn by Dee Dee's departing affection and companionship was the somewhat gratifying awareness that I was now free to take the next step on my journey.

31

THE SOARING PROFILE OF Chartres dominated the horizon. Its pointed gothic towers jabbed into the clear blue sky like a bully's finger, poking and challenging. "Look at us," the cathedral's spires seemed to cry out, "Aren't we extraordinary? Aren't we beautiful?" Yes, was the answer poised on my lips.

Standing in the empty parking lot, my breath escaping in icy plumes, I was dwarfed by the massive, stone church. Built over the course of twenty-six years, from 1194 to 1220, the construction of Chartres was funded by monarchs from all over Europe. This fact, at least according to the book I'd picked up in Amsterdam, created the rumor that the geometrical and astronomical alignment of Chartres' walls, floors, arched ceilings and stained glass windows made the cathedral something more than just a structure. Could it be, the author proposed, a book of stone containing the mystery traditions brought back by the Knights Templar from the Crusades in the Middle East?

I stamped my feet on the pavement to warm them. The first mystery I needed to solve was how I was going to get inside. Just before the sun came up, I watched a group of five women, who I thought might be the cleaning crew, walk up to the front doors and enter the church. If one of them spoke English I would be in luck. If not, I would have to fall back on hand gestures and pantomime.

When I gave it a firm tug, the heavy door swung open. I stepped inside and quietly pulled the door closed behind me. Allowing my eyes to adjust to the dim light, I saw no movement or heard anything. I took a quiet breath, afraid of disturbing the amazing vibe that was in the air. Battered and exulted by the dreams, prayers, confessions, and grief purged from thousands of people's hearts, the stillness in the church seemed to have a palpable strength to it. It felt capable and enduring. Forgiveness, deceit, joy, lust, hatred, greed, doubt and despair all convened within the massive stone walls to create a sound, or lack of sound, which reverberated in me simultaneously as both a sob and a raucous shout.

I moved forward into the cathedral. Morning light inched its way into the gray interior. The wooden folding chairs were still in place. The cleaning crew, or the women I'd thought were the cleaning crew, were nowhere in sight. I walked further into the cathedral searching along the floor for signs of the labyrinth.

In the middle of the wooden folding chairs I found it. Dark pavement lines circled between two massive stone pillars. I quietly began moving the chairs out of the way. As I revealed the spiraling design hidden beneath the chairs, I saw that it was much larger than I thought it would be. When I'd managed to clear all the chairs away, I stepped off the distance. The labyrinth was over forty feet in diameter with painted spikes jutted outward from the perimeter of the circle and curving walkways folding toward a six-petaled pattern in the center.

Standing at the point of entry, I felt like a rat about to enter a maze. I had no idea what this thing was going to do to me. I'd read in the book I'd bought in Amsterdam that, La Lieue, The League, as the labyrinth was called, had been used as a penance path. In lieu of a pilgrimage to Jerusalem, Christians could serve their needs for atonement by walking the pathway of the labyrinth.

A loud bang from the front of the church made me jump. I waited, expecting the cleaning crew to show themselves. Nothing moved. I looked down at my feet. I had stepped into the labyrinth.

Atonement . . . I thought of punching Randy in the face and of my desire to find out why. I unbuttoned my jacket, took a deep breath, and slowly began to walk forward.

Nothing happened. I let my stride lengthen as I curved and looped and wound my way along the labyrinth. Somewhere inside my mid-section I began to feel a fuzzy tingling. It was similar to what I experienced on Eldora's table. It felt as if static electricity was traveling through me. And like some sort of rotor, the feeling would slightly intensify the faster I went. I jogged the last twenty feet and entered the six-petaled center feeling buoyant and energized. Everything was sharply in focus: the gray stone of the walls, the light streaming down from the stained-glass windows, and the intricate grain of the wood in the folding chairs. I stood there, my body humming with vitality. Then, the tingling energy slowly began to fade. I tried jumping up and down and jogging in place, but it didn't work. I watched helplessly as the world around me once again became dense and heavy.

A door slammed. From up near the altar I heard footsteps. I ducked behind a pillar. Voices speaking in French echoed in the cathedral. Dizzy and disoriented, I headed for the door. When I looked back, three women were standing where I'd cleared the chairs away. I quickly pulled open the door and ran outside.

I somehow made my way to the station and boarded a train traveling west. Without any conscious idea of where I was going, I gazed blankly, lost in a strange internal fog, at the passing French countryside. I didn't talk with anyone and I didn't eat anything. I simply stared out the window. When the train stopped near the city of Verdun, I got off.

During World War I, from February 21, 1916 to mid-December 1916, 542,000 French soldiers and 434,000 German soldiers died in the fighting around Verdun. Ten months of fighting and nearly a million dead men. I quickly got back on the train and headed east.

That night, staring out the window into undefined darkness, bloody battle scenes raged in my mind: soldiers falling and crying out, bone-jarring explosions, gore-lined trenches, and the stench of rotting corpses. It was a vivid reenactment of my haunting childhood dreams. Was this really my life, I wondered. Is this bloody horror truly my past?

Falling asleep shortly after changing trains, I woke up just as we were pulling into a station. I stepped down from the train, rubbing my eyes in the bright sunlight. I was in the town of La Havre in Normandy, France.

I sat on the beach where 5,000 British and Americans soldiers died on the first day of the D-Day invasion. As the waves rolled in, I struggled not to see German machine guns strafing all those young men and bleeding the ocean red, but I couldn't stop the shadowy, surreal images. Locked in my head, they played over and over, a gruesome testament to the horrors of that day.

Where, I wondered with numbing dread, would my penance path lead next?

I crossed the English Channel on a blustery, white-capped sea. The ferry heaved and pitched, leaving me sick as a dog. Upon landing in England, I immediately got on a bus. The first place it stopped was Hastings.

On October 14th 1066, six thousand Normans and the same number of English fought the Battle of Hastings with swords, axes, shields, lances, and bows and arrows. The Normans used knights on horseback, and the English, on foot, formed shield-walls with their troops. The Normans eventually battered them down and marched to London, putting an end to the old Anglo-Saxon kingdom in England. I walked through the pleasant fields hearing the birds and feeling the breath of the wind on my face, while at the same time witnessing more brutal killing, more blood, and more dead men falling at my feet.

Two hours later I was on a bus heading toward West Penwith.

On the tiny peninsula on the southwestern tip of England, I roamed over the wet, windy, Cornish countryside like a mad, lost monk. I found stone circles and crawled in subterranean chambers,

I slept in fields and barns, I spent long hours walking in silence trying to come to terms with what I had found on my gory penance path.

Lying in a pasture one night, staring up at the big dipper, I thought of the potent stillness I'd experienced at Chartres. It wasn't other people's years of sorrow and grief that I now felt, it was my own. The battles, the slaughtered soldiers . . . it sickened me. Was this truly the legacy of my soul? Was this what I was under my bones, a killer of men? If it was real, and it certainly felt that way, what other horrors awaited me?

On a blustery afternoon, while sitting in the dark confines of a stone dolmen, I found myself daydreaming of pagan rituals. Early humans had undoubtedly come to this bleak, wind-whipped place and attempted to pierce the mysteries of the earth and the stars. I wondered if they had come to terms with their place in the universe. Had they been able to find a sense of peace while staring into the boundless uncertainty of a new day? I thought of my ancestors who, generations before, roamed the highlands of Scotland. Theirs had been a life of battling over land and scraping out a brutal existence. What had their dreams of the future been?

I breathed deeply, taking in the dusky smell permeating the stone chamber. In all likelihood, somewhere beneath my denim-clad posterior were the rotting bones of Neolithic men and women, human beings with steely courage and the fortitude to face overwhelming adversity on a daily basis. Without access to the scientific data we have today, they hadn't been able to fully comprehend their environment on an intellectual level. Their mental process had to have been a more visceral, cognitive one; a way of thinking based, not on what they knew as fact, but on what they perceived as truth. So, if their survival depended on a heightened intuitive awareness rather than an intellectual, fact-sorting process, then what had we lost over thousands of years of evolution by moving away from our intuition into the more rational, logical orientation of our brains? Had we somehow buried our most acute sensibilities? Were we now in denial of our strongest survival tool? If that was the case, what were we as a species listening to? What was leading us? What were we depending on to get us through the complex energetic shifts that were coming? Was rational, linear thinking enough?

I leaned my head back against the giant stone slab that was the east wall of the dolmen. After a moment, the bombardment of thoughts and images began to taper off. I closed my eyes. A few minutes later, I stretched out on my left side and tucked my arm under my head. I tried not to fall asleep, but after a few minutes I slipped into a hazy, half-slumber.

I don't know how long I was lying there before the image began to appear. In my mind, through a jumble of gray and black flashes, I saw a blaze of orange flame. For a quick second, I thought I was going to see the orange grove, but then beyond the flame I saw bearded, dirt-smeared faces. Men were dancing around a roaring bonfire. I could see their bare knees poking out from under their skirts. Hold on a minute, I thought, men wearing skirts?

A man appeared inside the flames. As he stepped out of the bonfire in my direction, I saw that he was playing bagpipes. I immediately felt a surge of pride. Those weren't skirts, they were kilts! The men were Scottish highlanders!

Two days later, I boarded a train heading north to Edinburgh, Scotland.

32

Even though deep in their hearts, or perhaps not so deep, my parents were thrilled that I was finally leaving, my decision to stop seeing Dee Dee and head west, still threw them for a loop. At their age, change didn't come without a lot of grumbling. My mother wouldn't talk to me. My father shook his head and muttered, "What else is new?" Kirby was ticked off because I was walking away from what he regarded as a great future with his company. Aunt Helen was the only one who encouraged me.

"Thomas," she said. "To follow a dream isn't easy. I don't claim to understand why, but if your dream is to go to Pomona then go. It shouldn't matter what anyone else says. Just remember to send me a postcard."

I made plans to leave town the following week. I gave my parents a thousand dollars from the money I'd saved. They didn't want to take it, but I insisted. I hoped this would somewhat mitigate the mental and emotional torment I'd put them through.

Wanting to leave things on a positive note, I tried to talk to Dee Dee several times. She never returned my calls. When I heard through Kirby that her husband was trying to patch things up, I stopped calling.

Four days before I was to leave, Aunt Helen lost her balance and fell in her room. This time it was her other hip that broke. The pain and disappointment of again losing her mobility was compounded by a negative report from her doctors. After recovering from the fracture, they said that her leg strength and balance would be far too tenuous to risk ever living on her own. She would have to remain in the nursing home.

Two days after Aunt Helen was given the bad news, I smuggled Terry in to the nursing home to see her. Aunt Helen was lying in bed with full makeup on and her hair done to perfection. She smiled when I walked in, her eyes bright and clear. I was surprised. Mom told me that Aunt Helen cried and fought with her the day before.

"Welcome to my new house," she said with a sarcastic edge. I shut the door and unzipped my gym bag. Terry poked his head out.

"Hello there mister," Aunt Helen said to him.

I put him on the edge of her bed. As if knowing the source of her pain, he immediately curled up against Aunt Helen's hip.

"He loves coming to see you," I said.

"This is his last visit."

"What do you mean?"

"Mrs. Culver across the alley is going to take him. She's been very good with him since I've been stuck in here. Her cat, Morris, and Terry are old friends."

"But why? Mom could—"

"Thomas," Aunt Helen said, cutting me off. "I have some things I want to discuss."

"Okay."

"I have a favor to ask you."

"Whatever you want."

"Being interred in a nursing home isn't exactly the way I'd hoped to spend my remaining years. Fate has played a cruel trick on your auntie and she doesn't like it one bit."

She rubbed Terry under his chin. His purring got louder.

"But," she continued, "I have choices, and I've considered all of them. This isn't going to be easy. So I've decided that you're the one to help me."

Horrible images immediately flashed through my mind: Aunt Helen taking an assortment of pills from my shaking hand, me jamming a pillow over her face, the two of us struggling to inject a syringe of God-knows-what into her skinny arm. I shook my head.

"Aunt Helen, I can't do what you're going to ask me."

"Yes, you can."

"No, I can't."

"Thomas—"

"I'm not going to help you die."

"Oh for heaven's sake, don't be so dramatic. If I wanted to kill myself I wouldn't need you to help me."

"Oh. Okay. Well, then what can I do for you?"

"I want you to sell my house and my stocks, and auction off all of my furniture. Then I want you to set up an estate or some kind of fund that will pay the bills for this home that fate has cast me into. I have no intention of being a financial burden to my family or the Medicare system."

She raised her bony finger and shook it at me.

"And if you think for one minute I'm going to let your mother and father deal with this on their own, you can forget it. I know you want to leave for California, but I'm asking you to delay your trip a couple weeks, or however long it will take to get everything into place. I need you here, Tommy."

"Aunt Helen," I said, my throat tight with emotion. "I won't leave you. I promise."

"You better not," she said. "Now, let's get busy. There's some paper and pens in the drawer there. I want to make a list of things the family should keep."

• • •

SEAL UP AUNT HELEN'S house and it would be a perfect time capsule of life in America over the last 100 years: A rocking chair and two maple chest-of-drawers from the late 1800s, a dozen oil paintings from the 1920s, photographs of Aunt Helen sitting in a horse drawn buggy, a Model T Ford, a 1957 Chevy Bel Air, and a color 8x10 with my mother watching the Space Shuttle land. There were silver and china from the turn of the century, hand-stitched linens, cut crystal vases, and a CD player. In the kitchen drawer below her high-tech, industrial-strength juicer was a hand mixer that had to be seventy years old. Her dining room table was vintage 1930s, while in the corner of her bedroom she had a brown, leather Lazyboy that could massage your back three different ways.

"Look at this," Mom said. She pulled a quilt from the bottom of the cedar chest at the foot of Aunt Helen's bed. "This was my grandmother's."

On the edge of the faded blue border, hand-stitched in yellow thread, was the date: 1885. Mom laid the quilt out on the bed. The center section, a checkerboard of pale yellow and white, was in a little better condition than the border.

"Did she make it," I asked.

"She sure did."

"That's a lot of work."

"Oh, if you think Aunt Helen is tough, you should have seen your Great Grandmother." Mom sat on the edge of the bed and smoothed out the creases in the quilt. "She used to get us with her knuckle. She'd dig it into our backs. Oh, I hated coming up here to visit her. She was nearly blind the last three years of her life but she still scared me to death."

"Your mother wasn't like that. Not that I remember anyway."

"No, she was very kind. She got away from her mother when she was sixteen. 'A mill doesn't turn on water that is past,' that's what she'd say when we'd ask about her debutante days. It was always moving on to the next thing with her."

"She went down to Alabama, right? Montgomery."

"No. I grew up in Montgomery. She went to Birmingham first. She only went down for the summer. Her second cousin Francis lived there. But once mother experienced the gracious ways of southern living, she refused to go back home. Great Grandma let her stay. Mother went to boarding school in Birmingham and turned into a southern belle."

"When did she move back here?"

"Not until after your Dad and I got married. When he got out of the service and took a job here in Pittsburgh, that's when she moved back. She didn't want to miss out on you kids growing up."

"Remember that carrot cake she used to make. God was that good."

My mother ran her fingers along the yellow and white border of the quilt. When she finally spoke, her voice was quiet.

"Sometimes I really miss her."

Over the course of six nights, Mom and I rummaged through the attic, the basement and all of the bedroom and hallway closets in Aunt Helen's house. With the help of mom's stories, it became more than simply a quest to compile a list of Aunt Helen's worldly possessions. It was a long overdue introduction to Mom's side of the family.

The oak desk in the corner of the den had belonged to Uncle Bert, my Grandmother's older brother. He was a burly, thick-wristed stonemason. He helped build Heinz Chapel in Oakland and once played tackle on a semi-pro football team. Mom told me that when he died, he weighed 360 pounds and it took six men to pick him up and squeeze him into his coffin.

In the upstairs hallway there was a landscape painting that had been done by Grandmother's other brother, Henry. Henry had been in the infantry during World War I. While waiting for orders to march through a cow pasture in northern France, Henry was crouched behind a tree enjoying a chocolate bar when he got shot in the head. He miraculously, survived. Unfortunately, the damage to his brain completely wiped out his memory. He had to spend months relearning everything about himself and his family. The one thing he did remember was the cow pasture. He completed over a hundred oil paintings of it during his lifetime.

We found a blue ribbon that my mother's sister, Evelyn won in a baking contest when she was in high school. It was stuck in a first edition of, *The Sun Also Rises*. We found the book underneath a dusty box of old golf shoes in the attic. We got a chuckle out of the ribbon. Aunt Evelyn burned down one house and scorched the kitchen in another because of grease fires in her oven.

From Aunt Helen's list we pulled aside items that she wanted us to keep. "It's for you kids," my mother said, teary-eyed. I watched as she carefully wrapped cups and saucers for Becky and stacked them in a cardboard box.

"When I get home," she said. "I'm going to inventory the whole house. I'll get things appraised so if something happens to me you kids won't throw anything valuable away."

"Mom," I said. "If you quit smoking you're going to be around for a long time."

She flipped me the finger. "I don't want to hear it." She sat down on the couch and rubbed her eyes. "This is harder than I thought it was going to be."

"Go home, Mom. I'll stay up and finish this."

"Do you mind?"

"Not at all."

"Aunt Helen's got the papers giving me power of attorney. She's going to sign them tomorrow."

"Good."

Mom stood up and stretched her back. "I'm glad you decided to stay, Tommy. I couldn't have done all this on my own."

"Dad would have helped you."

"Like I said, I couldn't have done this on my own."

I walked her to the front door. She picked up her purse and car keys off the table in the entryway.

"Tom, your father's glad you stayed too."

"Sure he is."

"You think it's easy being a parent? When you kids were little, I used to lock myself in the bathroom just to have some privacy. I'd paint my toenails and listen to your brother breathing on the other side of the door." She laughed. "One morning after you and Rick had been exceptionally wild, I packed the two of you up to visit my mother. I walked out to the car and got in the back seat. I sat there for three or four minutes until I remembered that I was the adult and I was the one who had to drive."

After Mom left, I went back to work. I was pulling a box out of the closet in the spare bedroom when I found Leo Hursen's gift to

Aunt Helen. It was still in the box, but it was unwrapped. Inside was a 5x7 black leather photograph album. I sat on the edge of the bed and opened it. On the first page was Leo's address and phone number. That was followed by a series of pictures of Leo with two women who looked to be in their mid to late thirties along with five children ranging from an infant to what looked to be about a nine years old. Daughters, I wondered, grandchildren? I turned the pages. Leo Hursen beamed proudly from what looked to be a recent photo taken at Disney World with the same children surrounding him. On the last page there was a black and white snapshot of a much younger Leo holding hands with a dark haired woman. She had a daisy behind her ear, and Leo wore a fedora.

When confronted by my mother, Aunt Helen said that Leo Hursen had been one of her students. I looked at the photo album. They must have been pretty close, I thought, for him to give her pictures of his family, and in a nice leather album. I looked at the clock on the nightstand. It was just past ten. I reached for the phone.

We met at the White Castle restaurant in town. Leo was sitting with a cup of coffee when I came in. I ordered a glass of orange juice and a side of fries.

"Aunt Helen is going to stay in the nursing home," I told him. "She's selling the house."

His lips tensed into a thin line. "I was afraid of that."

"Leo, you obviously care about Helen."

"Yes."

"You were one of her students at Pitt, right?"

He stared back at me.

"That's what she told my mother," I said.

"I see."

"Is it true?"

He stood up. "I have to go."

"Hold on a second, Leo."

"This is Helen's business. If you want answers you'll have to get them from her." He walked toward the door.

I followed him. "I've tried to get her to talk about you, but she won't."

At the door he turned to me. "It's not my place."

"She's tough," I said. "If she says she isn't going to talk about something – You couldn't pry it out of her if you wanted to."

"Yes, I'm aware of that."

"Look," I said. "I saw the photo album you gave her. I don't know what it means, you seem like a nice man, but I can't have you hanging around her if she's going to get upset."

"Believe me, I don't want to cause her any trouble."

"Okay, but – Why does she get so ticked off when I mention your name?"

Leo studied his brown penny loafers. "This isn't how I wanted it to happen," he said. He suddenly seemed frail and unsteady. I led him back to the booth and we sat down.

"Last year," he said, "I was watching one of the talk shows and there was a group of people trying to find their birth parents. I'm adopted, and I figured that by now my parents were dead and I wouldn't be invading their privacy, so I decided to find out who they were."

I let out a long breath. "Wow. I never knew Aunt Helen had any children."

"She didn't."

"I thought you were—"

"She's my aunt."

"Oh. But, wait a minute. How can that be? Aunt Helen and Grandma were the only girls in the family."

"Yes, they were."

I stared at him as the realization sank in. "No."

"Yes."

"Get-outta-here! My Grandmother was your mother?"

He nodded.

"Really?"

Leo sighed. "Really."

33

JUST WHEN I THOUGHT I was getting clear on the family genealogy, in walks Grandma's illegitimate son. Talk about shaking the family tree. As I sat there listening to the details of how Leo found us, all I could think about was how difficult it must have been for him. I knew what it was like to live with a mystery. They percolate and steam in the back of your mind. They can mess with your focus and your ability to connect in personal relationships. Leo had suffered long enough. He deserved to be embraced by all of us.

Leo told me that his parents adopted him in Alabama. Grandma's summer vacation in the south suddenly took on new meaning. He told me his adopted father worked for a tool and die company. He was transferred to Cincinnati when Leo was six years old. Leo grew up there and won a scholastic scholarship to Carnegie Tech in Pittsburgh. He stayed in Pittsburgh after graduation, married, and raised two daughters. Romy was in Lansing, Michigan and Janice lived in the suburbs of Seattle. After his wife Sylvia died two years ago, Leo was on his own.

Seeing the TV show led Leo to an agency that then led him to my grandmother and Leo's father, an eighteen-year-old boy named Seth Kercher. Seth died in San Pedro, California in 1947 when the car he was driving collided with a truck. Seth never married and he had no other children. His only sibling, a brother, died in 1975. Leo couldn't locate any other relatives.

"I've kept my distance out of respect for your mother and grandmother," Leo said. "But I would like to help care for Helen. She needs all the friends she can get now."

"Yes, she does."

"Your mother doesn't have to know who I am."

"I'll talk to her. I can make it work."

Leo smiled shyly. "That would be great. Hey, your mom looks a little like me don't you think?"

"You guys have the same small eyes."

"So you think it might be okay to meet her?"

"I'll make it happen."

"That would be wonderful. That would be really wonderful."

I spent the night at Aunt Helen's. I lay in bed for a long time thinking of the convoluted trails my family and I had wandered. Nothing was as you thought it should be.

Sometime around 3 a.m., I sat bolt upright in bed. The session at Eldora's table was crystal clear in my mind. *My secret*, grandma had tapped out. *Tell her when the time is right.* I laughed out loud in the dark. "Gram," I said. "You were talking about Leo weren't you? Did you help make this happen?"

Sunlight streamed through the kitchen window the following morning when Mom and I sat down at the table with cups of coffee. I still hadn't figured out how I was going to break the news to her. I turned to a spot on the floor where sunlight gathered like a puddle of shimmering bronze. I looked into it, hoping to find the appropriate words, but I saw nothing.

"Mom, when you and Aunt Evelyn were growing up down south, did you ever wish you had a brother?"

"It wasn't so much that I wished I had a brother. I just wanted a different sister. Evelyn was kind of a ditz."

"A brother would have been good though, don't you think?"

"I don't know. After seeing what Becky had to put up with from you and Rick, I don't know if I missed out on anything. How much did you get done last night?"

"All of it."

"Great. Now we have to—"

"I want you to promise me something."

"What?"

"Promise me that you won't freak out."

"Oh my God! Did you break that crystal vase? I'm going to smack you!"

"No, the vase is fine. Guess who I talked to last night?"

"Who?"

"Leo Hursen."

"Oh. What did he want? Did you get any gossip about Helen?"

"Yes, as a matter of fact, I did."

"Well, come on, tell me."

With no idea of how to soften the blow, I shot from the hip and hoped for the best.

"Mom, Leo says he's your half-brother."

Her face didn't change expression. "What?"

"Grandma had him just after she turned seventeen – in Alabama. That's probably why she went down there."

Mom's eyes widened. "Were you drinking last night?"

"No."

"Then what in God's name are you babbling about?"

"According to him he's your half-brother."

"Don't be ridiculous."

"That's why Helen is so weird about him. She doesn't want the family secret to get out."

"There's no family secret."

"How do you know for sure?"

"Oh come on!"

"I think we should ask her about it."

"This is the silliest thing I've ever heard."

"I'll ask her."

"Fine. Go ahead."

The lobby of the Howland Nursing Center was crowded with wizened men and women hunched over in wheelchairs muttering and staring blankly at the walls. I wondered what secrets they held in their hearts. Secrets they'd never discussed with anyone. What confusion had they left behind because of those mysteries?

Aunt Helen greeted us at her door in her wheelchair. It was her first day out of bed since the second fall. She wanted to go for a spin around the "highway" as she had begun to refer to the hallways in the nursing home. I pushed her wheelchair while Mom walked behind us. Mom didn't seem too anxious to initiate the subject, so I jumped in.

"Aunt Helen," I said. "I talked with Leo Hursen last night. He hopes you're feeling better."

"Good for him."

"He told me about Grandma."

Her shoulders stiffened. I stopped pushing and came around to look at her.

"He told me that she was his mother."

Mom chimed in, "Isn't that the silliest thing you've ever heard?"

Aunt Helen scowled at me. "Do you believe everything people tell you, Thomas?"

"Is Mr. Hursen mentally ill?" Mom asked.

"Grandma would want you to tell the truth," I said. Then added, "I'm positive she would."

"You don't know what you're talking about," Aunt Helen snapped.

"Leo deserves to know his family."

Aunt Helen reached over and punched me in the stomach. It was a good, hard shot.

"Sometimes," she said, "you're more your father's son than I'd like to admit."

Mom knelt down next to the wheelchair. Aunt Helen's lack of an immediate denial had Mom nervous. "It's not true," she said, her voice shaky. "Right, Helen?"

Aunt Helen turned away from both of us and looked down the hall.

"Tell her," I said.

Aunt Helen slapped her palm on the arm of the wheelchair. She turned to my mother. "Merna, every family's got their skeletons. Unfortunately ours is still alive and kicking."

Mom's face blanched. Aunt Helen sighed. "Your mother got pregnant when she was sixteen."

"Oh my God." Mom sat on her butt in the middle of the hallway.

"She was sent down south to have the baby." Aunt Helen said. "Mother and father bullied her into giving it up. They made us all promise never to talk about it. We missed her terribly, but that was the way it was handled. They did what was best for the family."

"He wants to meet you, Mom."

"Oh my God."

"He's a really nice guy."

"Oh my God."

With my mother in a state of shock, we walked back to Aunt Helen's room. I filled them in on the details of Leo and his family and Seth. This seemed to calm Mom down. When I mentioned that she and Leo had the same eyes, a wistful smile parted her lips.

"A brother," she said. "Wait until Evelyn hears about this."

That night at the dinner table, my father could not restrain himself. After years of being under the demanding rule of grandma and then Aunt Helen, he wasn't about to let this news pass without comment.

"Knocked up at sixteen, huh? So the old gal was wild in her day."

"Don't start," Mom warned him.

"The southern belle had a bun in the oven before she was out of high school. Must have been a big scandal back then?"

"You can be such an ass, Richard."

"Well it's true. Your family must have told some tall tales to keep that story under wraps."

"Dad, cut it out."

His eyes shifted to me. "You didn't have to put up with years of that woman's holier-than-thou attitude. She was a ball buster. God bless her, she was good to you kids, but boy she could lay into a guy when she wanted to."

He sawed off a chunk of his strip steak and stabbed it with his fork. "And I don't mean just me," he continued. "She had your grandfather on a short leash too. Poor old Irv, huddled on the back porch, staring into the yard with that shell-shocked look in his eyes."

"That's because he was drunk," Mom said. "He drank to cover the pain of his arthritis."

"He was a whipped man," Dad said. "Irv couldn't say boo without The Great South Wind howling down on him."

Mom slammed her knife down. "If you could stop criticizing my dead parents for a minute, I'd like to discuss what we should do about this."

My father's face immediately softened. "I don't know," he said. "What do you want to do?"

Mom shook her head. "If I accept this man into our family then the memory of my mother will be – people will think poorly of her."

"But if you don't," I said, "Leo will never have a chance to—" She cut me off.

"I know, I know. Still, my family has been in this city for a long time and I've got to consider the ramifications."

"A mill doesn't turn on water that is past," I said, quoting her mother.

Mom shot me her watered down version of The Look.

"What about what you want?" I said, fighting through her hard stare. "Don't you think it's a good thing to do? Your mother didn't have a choice. You have a choice."

The look on her face was one of pained, pinched restraint. Still held in the grip of her family's past, it was as if they were all at the table conspiring to keep their secret locked away.

"I think we should have him over for a cookout," I said. "Dad, don't you think that would be a good idea?"

My father looked blankly at me.

"It would give you an excuse to buy that smoker you've been talking about."

"Oh," he said. "I could do that."

"We'll have some ribs and corn," I said. "And veggie burgers."

"I'll buy a case of beer," Dad said.

"Dad and I will take care of everything. You can just sit back and relax. And when Leo's here, you can call Aunt Evelyn and she can talk to him on the phone."

Dad winked at me and looked back at her. "What do you say wifey?"

Mom slowly nodded her head. "Okay. We'll have him over. But I want Helen here. I need her support."

My father's cheerful expression folded in on itself. "Inviting her is a good way to ruin the party."

"I'll ask her to behave herself."

"I don't want to hear a single comment from her."

"I'll tell her."

"Good."

"We'll do it next Saturday."

"Sunday would be better. Two o'clock?"

"How about four?"

"All right then."

And that's how the deal was negotiated to bring Leo Hursen into our family.

• • •

WHEN I CALLED LEO and told him that I wanted to talk, he invited me out to his house in Fox Chapel. On the drive down Route 8, I thought of how strange it must have been for Leo to never know where he was from or who his real parents were. It must have always been nagging at him from some corner of his mind, and believe me I knew how that felt.

A couple miles later, after turning left onto a secondary road, I was thinking how much Grandma must be enjoying this turn of events. Her first born, her only son finally reunited with his sisters. It was amazing how it all happened, the way our lives intersected – Suddenly a dog shot out in front of my car. I yanked the wheel hard to the left, just missing the hindquarters of the collie. Tires screeching, the Blazer spun 180 degrees across a lane of traffic ending up in a cloud of dust facing a vacant building. I stared wild-eyed at the stained front awning – Cully's Collectibles. A realtor's sign was in the front window. I let out a breath and unclenched my hands from the steering wheel. My heart was still pounding like a Keith Moon drum solo as I slowly drove out of the lot.

I pulled in Leo's driveway and checked the address to make sure I was at the right place. The house looked as if it had come off the cover of *Architectural Digest*. It was a colonial three story with dark blue shutters and a lookout perch in the center of the roof. An American flag fluttered from a pole in the middle of the sprawling front lawn. As I parked in front of the three car garage, Leo came around the corner of the house.

"Tom," he called. "Come on in."

After pouring glasses of iced tea, Leo led me out of the kitchen and through a set of French doors to the patio. Atop a low stone wall, five clay urns were bursting with red geraniums. Beyond the wall was a vast expanse of rolling lawn. And I do mean vast. It looked like a par five fairway at Oakmont Country Club.

"Who cuts the grass?"

Leo chuckled. "There used to be six acres of woods out there."

"Makes me want to pull out a nine iron and take a swing."

"I used to do that from time to time, but the golf balls wreaked havoc on the lawn mower blade."

"Do you have something against trees?"

"No. I just like an unobstructed view."

"I guess so. It sure is pretty."

"Thank you."

Leo took a sip of his iced tea. I had to admire his patience. He wasn't pressing me for information.

"Leo, I talked with my mother."

"Yes."

"She wants you to come over to the house next Sunday for a cookout."

His face curved into a wide smile. The man was all teeth.

"Wonderful," he said. "That's wonderful."

"Four o'clock, okay?"

"Wonderful."

"Do you like ribs?"

"Wonderful."

We sat on his patio and talked. He showed me pictures of his daughters and five grandchildren. I told him about Becky and Rick. He wanted to know all about my mom and Aunt Evelyn, but most of all he wanted to know about his mother.

"Her parents sent her to Alabama," I told him. "Aunt Helen said that Grandma was forced to give you up."

"She was just a girl."

"Her mother was a tough lady."

Leo stared into his glass of iced tea. "I wonder what she thought when they took me away."

I tried to lighten the subject. "She baked a great carrot cake. We used to beg her to make it."

Leo nodded, but I could tell he was still thinking about their last moment together. He slipped off his glasses and rubbed his eyes.

"What about Seth," I asked.

"Other than the accident when he was killed, I've not been able to find much information on him."

"That's too bad."

"I'll keep looking. Right now I'm happy to have found Helen and your mother."

"It's amazing to me that you waited this long."

"I never thought about it much. I figured that it was meant to be. My adopted parents were good people. It was only after my wife died that I started thinking about all of this."

"Didn't it bother you?"

Leo looked out at the lawn. "My adopted parents gave me a great life, but you're right, I never quite felt like I belonged."

"Yeah," I said. "I know what you mean."

He picked up his glass of tea and toasted me. "Thanks Tom," he said, "for helping to bring home the lost sheep of the family." Leo sipped his ice tea then asked, "What is it that you do, Tom?"

"Seek truth."

He laughed.

"I make money doing other things," I said. "Bartending, farming, I ran a juice company for a while."

"Have you ever thought about settling down?"

"I've tried, but it never seems to work for me. Life seems to want to keep me moving." I turned and looked out at the lawn. Twenty yards away a robin was poking in the ground.

"I did it in sections," Leo said. "When we moved here in '59, the trees came up to that little rise over there. I wanted the girls to have more room to play. I cleared back thirty feet the first year."

"Must have been a lot of work."

"Oh, it was. It was thick back there. One day I was running the brush hog and I accidentally ran over a rabbit's nest. For years after that, there was a one-eared rabbit running around the place. With that lone ear sticking up he looked like a shark coming at you through the tall grass." Leo chuckled to himself. "The girls always watched out for him."

"Do you get to see your daughters much?"

"They've got their own families. It's hard to load up kids and strollers and get on a plane." He turned and gazed out at the lawn. "They say my grandson Travis looks more and more like me as he gets older. He's a good boy. He sends me crayon drawings."

We sat for a moment, neither of us speaking. I watched a jet streak across the sky leaving a ghostly vapor trail in its path.

"It's nice to have all this open space," I said.

He nodded. "I appreciate an unobstructed view."

34

AFTER MY VISIT WITH Leo I drove over to Kirby's house to tell him the news. I was stepping out of my truck when Kirby walked out the front door followed by Dee Dee.

"Uh oh," Kirby said.

Without missing a beat Dee Dee said, "Buddha Boy has come."

"What are you guys up to," I said, keeping my cool.

"Meeting Jeannie and the kids," Kirby said, "over at the mall."

"Oh," I said.

An awkward silence fell over the three of us. I didn't know what to say so I stared at the light fixture next to the front door. Finally Kirby broke the deadlock.

"The Pirates traded that centerfielder today."

"Oh yeah? Who picked him up?"

"The Yankees."

"I hope he plays better in New York."

"He couldn't do any worse."

Silence descended once again. Kirby, always alert to making the smart move, reached around and patted his rear pocket.

"Darn," he said. "I forgot my wallet. I'll be right back."

He hurried to the front door. Dee Dee and I shuffled our feet and stared holes in the concrete driveway. After a minute of praying for his hasty return, it became clear that Kirby wasn't going to rescue me. He was probably peeking through the curtains watching me squirm.

"Dee," I said, trying to take control, "I'm sorry about, you know, what happened with us. I didn't want you to get hurt."

"Don't flatter yourself. We're adults. We knew it was a long shot."

"Yeah, but I'm sorry you're mad at me."

"I'm not pissed anymore. Not really. I still think you're a nut case, but I'm over what happened."

"I heard you and Matt are trying to work things out."

"I got over that too. After you dumped me I thought that maybe I should go back to him. The kids, the house, the years we've had together, all that stuff. But then I remembered what living with him was like. He's a wimp. I've put up with his whiny crap for too long. It's just not worth it. You woke me up, Tommy. You showed me how to look at a situation, I mean really look at it, and then have the balls to say no, this isn't what I want."

"What are you gonna do?"

"We're leaving Saturday to go back home. My girlfriend has a four bedroom house that we can share with her for a while."

"You should keep your house."

"The hell with it. He loves the house. He can have it. I just want the money."

"Are you sure?"

"Yep. It's going to be okay." She gave me a sly grin. "And there's this guy who works at the real estate office across from Duncan's karate school. We met one day in the parking lot. He was nice as can be, and cute too. He flirted with me, right there next to his Mercedes. As soon as we get settled in I'm going to ask him out to dinner."

"Good for you."

"Tommy, you make me crazy. I have a soft spot for you and we both know where it is. But you're right. It's not meant to be."

I gave her a hug. She whispered in my ear, "We never actually ended up doing it. Strange, huh?"

"Yeah."

"Good luck with whatever you're looking for, you psycho."

"Thanks, Dee. Good luck with the real estate guy."

The front door opened. Kirby, seeing that the coast was now clear, emerged from the house smiling.

"I found my wallet. You all set, Dee Dee?"

"Yeah, let's go. See ya, Tommy."

I waved as they backed down the driveway. Dee Dee held up her hand. As I watched them pull away, it took me a moment to realize that her middle finger was the only digit on display.

• • •

TRUE TO HIS WORD, my father spent the following week preparing for the cookout with Leo. He bought the smoker, a case of Rolling Rock beer, two dozen ears of yellow corn, green beans, fresh carrot and celery juice for Aunt Helen, and he mixed up a huge batch of his potato salad with French dressing. I wasn't sure if his enthusiasm was out of consideration for my mother's vulnerable emotional state or from a gleeful sense of vindication that his mother-in-law, who had foisted her strong opinions upon him for years, had been caught in the humbling glare of scandal.

Mom spent most of the week down in the basement working on her mallard. She didn't say much to anyone, which was unusual for her. When I'd get home from work, she'd come up from the basement, eat the meal that Dad prepared, and then walk right back downstairs. She made no further arrangements for the sale of Aunt Helen's belongings.

I was surprised to see how sweet Dad was to her. After dinner, he'd bring her a cup of coffee with a couple of her favorite chocolate chip cookies. Thursday night, when we went grocery shopping at the Giant Eagle, he debated for ten minutes about which paper towels to buy.

"Tom," he said, holding a roll in each hand. "Your mother likes ducks. She likes the towels with the blue ducks. But the only ducks here are red. Now, should I get the blue swirl pattern or the red ducks?"

After getting her hair done on Saturday afternoon, my mother came home with a one-pound bag of peanut M&M's. She knows that my father loves them, but she didn't say a word. She just put the bag in the back of the cupboard. When Dad discovered it, he got all excited. He thought he found an old stash he'd forgotten about. Mom never said anything. She simply smiled and went back downstairs to work on the mallard.

Upon becoming aware of these random acts of kindness between my parents, something inside of me began to shift. Perhaps my harsh judgment of their standoffish behavior had been prompted by my own limited vision of what love really was. Perhaps I had bought into the greeting card, Movie of the Week idea of romance. Giving affection didn't have to mean overt physical displays. Chips Ahoy cookies and peanut M&M's were just as effective.

Sunday morning before the cookout, I found myself watching their every move. I wanted to better understand their dance. It was ingenious. Their behavior was orchestrated in such a way that they were frequently in close proximity to each other but never quite touching. Even when the chair across from my father was empty, my mother always sat next to him at the kitchen table. He buttered her toast and handed her the slices. When he served cups of coffee, she put sugar in hers and poured milk in his. He made sure she got the arts section of the *Post Gazette,* and she made sure she gave him the section with the crossword puzzle.

Not the heat of a tango or the wild abandon of the jitterbug, their dance had the steady, intricate rhythm of a waltz. It was their way of being together, and I had never noticed it before.

After I picked up Helen from the nursing home and brought her to the house, Mom and I got her settled into her wheelchair in the kitchen. She was in her Sunday best: pearls, hair coiffed, her favorite red dress, and the ivory brooch she'd brought back from India in 1964. Mom had suggested, commanded really, that I go by Aunt Helen's house and pick up these items and drop them off at the nursing home. She hoped that if Helen were happy she would stick to her promise to keep off Dad's back during the cookout. I had a hard time believing it would turn out that way. Brooch or no brooch, the two of them playing nice-nice for an entire evening was like asking Jack Lambert to play middle linebacker in a pink tutu. It just wasn't going to happen.

I went outside to put placemats on the picnic table and found my father was showing off the new smoker to Lud Blakely.

"It's a nice one," Lud said, carefully examining it.

My father grinned and assumed the cocky, loose-hipped stance of a man who'd just been handed his bragging rights.

"But," Lud said, the smug edge of a challenge in his voice. "Mine has a digital temperature gauge and they threw in a monogrammed hot pad." He rocked up on the balls of his feet, feeling good about his comeback.

Dad immediately scrambled for a response. Their neighborly competition had been going on for thirty years. To lose one battle was to risk losing the entire war. Dad rapped his knuckles against the steel lid of the smoker.

"I paid ninety-six fifty for it. Good price, don't you think?"

Lud squinted intently at the smoker. He clenched his jaws and gritted his teeth. A vein on his forehead began to bulge. Unable to muster another worthy comeback, he let out a low whistle. In their rules of one-up-man-ship my father's great bargain had apparently outscored Lud's digital temperature gauge and monogrammed hot pad. Shaking his head, Lud conceded the victory with a hearty clap on my father's back. He whistled for his dog Maxwell, who was busy appreciating the aromatic wonders of Peanut's rear end. Lud and Maxwell walked across the side yard to Lud's house.

My father spent the next thirty minutes reveling in his victory. He turned up the volume on the stereo and blasted Sinatra's, *Ring-A-Ding Ding!* album. I was certain this would get a rise out of Aunt Helen, but she held her tongue.

I just finished mixing the iced tea when the doorbell chimed. Aunt Helen and Mom stopped talking. They looked at each other for a moment. Mom stood up.

"I'll get it," she said.

I followed her out of the kitchen. She paused to straighten her skirt in front of the entryway mirror. She pushed back her shoulders then opened the door. Leo, with two bouquets of white roses in his arms, was standing there looking nervous.

"Hello, Mrs. McInnes."

"Please come in, Mr. Hursen."

Leo stepped into the house. He held out one of the bouquets. "These are for you."

Mom took the roses from him. "They're beautiful," she said. She lifted one of the buds to her nose. "Mummm. Thank you so much."

"You're welcome. Thank you for having me over."

"Hey, Leo," I said.

"Tom, I brought these for you and your father." He pulled out two cigars and handed them to me. "They're Cubans. A friend of mine brought them in from Italy."

"Thanks. We'll fire 'em up after dinner."

I heard the creak of Aunt Helen's wheelchair as she came around the corner.

"Helen," my mother said. "You know Mr. Hursen."

"Hello Helen," Leo said. "I brought these for you."

Leo stepped past my mother. He laid the roses on Aunt Helen's lap. She looked down at them and then up to Leo.

"There's not much to say is there?"

"Thank you, would be nice," Mom said firmly.

Aunt Helen shook her head. "No, I mean what I've put Mr. Hursen through. I should have said something when he first came to me."

Leo patted her arm. "What happened in the past doesn't matter. I'm glad to be here now."

The screen door to the porch slammed. "Is he here," my father's voice boomed. He walked in behind Aunt Helen's wheelchair. "Leo, hi," my father said. "I'm Richard McInnes. Welcome to the family."

• • •

AFTER AN HOUR OF polite chitchat, Mom and Leo fell into a groove. Soon they were interacting like long lost friends. Over dinner, Mom told him stories about her mother and father, Henry, Uncle Burt, and Aunt Evelyn. And in what I considered extremely poor taste, she also shared several highly embarrassing anecdotes from my childhood. Leo was enthralled.

When Leo was getting ready to leave, Mom disappeared downstairs. She returned carrying her new mallard. It had a red ribbon around its neck.

"I want you to have this," she said to Leo. "I made it myself."

Leo took it gingerly in his hands. He looked up at us and then down to the mallard. He touched the bill that Mom labored so hard to get right. His eyes filled with tears.

"I have to let the dog out," Dad said. He hurried out of the room. Mom gave Leo a hug.

"Thank you," Leo managed to say.

He kissed Aunt Helen goodbye then shook hands with me.

"Okay," Leo said, "I want you all to come to my house, weekend after next, for another cookout."

"We'll be there," Mom said.

"Take it easy, Leo," my father called from the kitchen.

"Thank you, Richard. I like that smoker."

After he'd left, and I'd returned Aunt Helen to the nursing home, I went out on the back porch. Mom was sitting in one of the redwood chairs smoking a cigarette. Her feet were propped up on the picnic table bench. She looked more relaxed than I'd seen her in years.

"Good party," I said.

The cigarette glowed red as she inhaled. "He's a sweet man," she said.

"He really seemed to appreciate the mallard."

"Yes, he did."

"Aunt Helen couldn't stop talking about him on the way back to the nursing home. I think it was hard on her keeping that secret all these years."

"I'm just sorry it took us this long to find each other."

She reached over to the redwood table and put out her cigarette in a clamshell ashtray. "Tommy, do you know what Leo told me?"

"What's that?"

"He said he wanted to help out with Aunt Helen. He suggested that we move her back into her house and get a private nurse."

"That kinda thing is pretty pricey isn't it?"

"He said he'd help pay for it."

"Wow, that's cool. What did you tell him?"

"I said I'd talk it over with your father and Helen."

"Can you guys afford it?"

"I've got some PNC stock that mother left me."

"Dad has all those Disney shares."

"I don't want to ask your Dad to sell any stock. He's planned for us to have that in our golden years. Leo and I can do it." She paused and smiled. "My brother, Leo."

That night I lay on the "hippie pad" futon in my bedroom. With everything now in order with my family, I was free to get back on the road and finish my quest to Pomona. The blue heron/motorcycle man said that I was close. Once again I felt the old thrill of hitting the road.

Over at Lud's house, Maxwell started barking. His bark became frenzied as if he had something cornered. Lud yelled twice, and then all was quiet.

35

AT THE NATIONAL LIBRARY of Scotland, I found a book on Scottish Clans. With their badge of holly and a tartan of blue, green, and a bit of yellow, I read that the McInneses were the original inhabitants of Morvern and Ardnamurchan. Early in the 13th century the clan received a vicious ass-whupping by Alexander II during the conquest of Argyll. Some of the McInnes clan split off to serve as Constables of the Castle of Kinlochaline, while others became hereditary bowmen to the chiefs of the MacKinnons on the Isle of Skye.

My session with Harry/Rodas flashed in my mind. He said that I'd been an archer during medieval times. I crossed the room to an atlas laying open on a waist high wooden stand. On the furthest western tip of the mainland of Scotland, I found Ardnamurchan. From the town of Salen, the isolated peninsula ran seventeen miles out into the Atlantic. To the southeast, across Loch Sunart, was the diamond shaped peninsula of Morvern. Up the coast, jutting into the North Channel, was the Isle of Skye.

• • •

A FALCON SKIMMED LOW across the cold waters of Loch Aline. From forty feet up on the battlements of Kinlochaline Castle, I watched the falcon tilt its wings and gracefully bank southward. With lazy wing flaps it headed toward the bottle-neck mouth of the loch two miles away. Down the length of the loch I could see all the way across the sound to a gray hump of mountains on the Island of Mull. Clan McInnes had chosen well. The views from the square keep were exceptional.

I spent an hour prowling through the low corridors and narrow, winding staircases in the castle. Staring into the fireplace high on the parapet projected over the front door, I saw, as if from a dream, the smoke blackened pots of bubbling oil that were heated there. I saw myself pouring the boiling contents down upon the men of the MacDonald clan as they'd attempted to batter down the door in 1645. Burning flesh, screaming men, swords slashing, severed limbs, pumping arteries, blood and grime and smoke – all of it echoing in my mind, distant, but somehow real.

Enough, I thought. I don't want to see anymore. The penance path has done its job. Why drown me in blood?

I left Morvern and headed north. It had taken me a couple of days to get used to driving on the left side. I'd had a few angry fists waved at me and horns blared, but after a hair-raising near-collision east of Fort William, I had no more lapses in concentration. At Salen, instead of traveling further west into Ardnamurchan, I chose to continue up the coast to the Isle of Skye.

It took 30 minutes on the ferry to cross from Mallaig to Armadale on the Isle of Skye. Rain began to pelt the windshield as I drove off the ferry. Heading north, I passed through the town of Knock, then onto flat, green fields, before entering the long, straggling village of Broadford. Once through town, I turned onto A881 and headed south onto the Strathaird peninsula. According to what I'd read at the library, Strathaird had once been home to the MacKinnon clan.

After going south for a while, the hilly road began to curve westward. Through the now misting rain I glimpsed the craggy peaks of the Black Cuillin range. Halfway down the peninsula, I felt light-headed and pulled off the road.

The sun was shouldering its way between rain clouds as I stepped out of the car. Light danced in the freshly washed air and the trunks of the birch trees seemed to glow. I took a few deep breaths to try and clear my head. The cool air was pungent with the smell of wet earth and the sea. I walked around the front of the car to the side of the road. Thirty yards away, across scrub grass and rocks covered with a greenish haze of bracken, there was a crumbling stone wall. Beyond it through the birch trees I saw more ruins. I left the car and walked through the sopping grass to the wall. It was five feet high and twenty feet long. It was made of flat slabs of stone stacked one on top of the other. Moss and lichens sprouted from the cracks and fissures. Who had built it, I wondered, and how long ago? Pushing through rhododendrons on the other side of the wall, I made my way further into the site.

The air was eerily still as I moved among the crumbling walls and weed-covered piles of stone. The squishing of my shoes in the boggy ground was the only sound as I started across the clearing. After five or six steps a prickly chill shot down my spine. I immediately had the feeling that something or someone was directly behind me.

I slowly turned around. The clearing was empty. The odd feeling didn't go away. Cautiously, I moved to my left. In an odd swooping slow motion, the trees and stone walls tilted then blurred out of focus. I closed my eyes to better get my equilibrium. Instantly the air erupted into a maelstrom of battle sounds: horses galloping, the clang of swords, men shouting. I sensed a long bow in my hands and a quiver of arrows on my hip. Quickly, and with a familiar, practiced motion, I notched an arrow. The muscles in my forearms tensed as I drew it back. A man leapt on top of a wall in front of me. I shifted my shoulders, my arms steadied, and with a breath, I released the arrow. The *thoooong* of the bowstring resonated deeply, familiar as my own heartbeat. The arrow struck true, driving the man back over the wall. I notched another arrow and let it fly; more arrows, more bodies falling. The blood lust of battle pounded in every cell as around me men were dying and bleeding and screaming and rallying each other to keep up the fight.

From my left came a blur of motion. I turned to see a man running at me with his sword drawn. I let loose an arrow, striking him in the chest, but he kept coming. He swung back his sword. I dropped my bow, pulled a dagger, and dodged to my left. He missed with his sword, and I lunged at him, driving my dagger deep into his side. He grabbed me by the shoulders and we went to the ground. He reached for his knife and I drove my dagger in again. His eyes blinked as if in surprise. He opened his mouth, and a gush of blood splattered my face. His eyes softened, a gasp escaped from his throat, but his arms didn't release me. He clung to me, forcing me to listen to his last wheezing breath. Looking into his dead, staring eyes, I felt a horrible flood of pity and sadness. In a panic, I thrashed my way out of the man's grasp and jumped to my feet. I began kicking his body and stomping his face with the heel of my boot. I didn't want to feel that kind of tenderness and remorse, so I punished his corpse, mutilating his face beyond recognition.

I don't know how long I was in this altered reality. When I came out of it, I was lying on my back in the wet grass. I sat up and looked around. The sun was lower in the sky and the temperature had dropped. I hugged my damp jacket to my body.

"Ciamar a tha thu," a voice called out.

A bearded old man was standing by one of the toppled walls. He was wearing a floppy rain hat and a stained yellow slicker. My first impression was that he looked like the guy on the box of Gorton's Frozen Fish Sticks.

He took a drag on a hand-rolled cigarette and exhaled the smoke. I got to my feet.

"What did you – I didn't understand," I said to him.

He tipped his head toward me. "You alright then?"

"Yeah," I said. "I'm okay."

"Peculiar place for a sleep"

His lilting brogue made it hard to understand what he'd said. I walked toward him as if putting us in closer proximity would help.

"What used to be here?" I asked.

"This here?"

I nodded.

He watched me carefully as I approached. Above the white swirl of his beard was a bulbous nose and alert dark eyes. The butt of the hand-rolled cigarette burned close to his lips.

"Walls of a castle," he said. The cigarette bobbed up and down as he spoke.

"Who did it belong to?"

"The MacKinnons."

"Wow," I said.

"That your machine?" he asked, pointing across the field toward the rental car.

"Yes," I said only half paying attention to him. I was still reeling from the battle I'd just experienced. Was it evidence of what Daniel Toberni was talking about? Had I just experienced an increase in the bandwidth of my consciousness?

The old man started walking toward the road.

"Come on now then," he called over his shoulder. "I'll be needin' you an' your machine."

He directed me a mile down the road. We turned right onto what looked to be nothing more than a muddy cow path. My rental car splashed through a shallow creek, and nearly got stuck in a ditch, before skidding between two grassy knolls and out into his pasture.

The deep, green waters of Loch Scavaig lay before us. Above, the peaks of the Cuillins looked on hard-edged and flinty. A hundred yards down the gently rolling slope was a low, thatched-roof stone cottage. Two smaller outbuildings, also made of stone and thatch, stood off to the north side of the house.

"Drive on down," he said, impatiently.

With a long rope and a rusty chain, we used the rental car to drag fourteen loads of driftwood up from the beach. By the time we stacked the last of it next to the cottage, the sun had set.

"Tatties and neeps is what I'm cookin'," the old man said. He turned and walked away. I took this to be an invitation and followed him into the cottage.

Inside it was snug and warm. The rooms possessed a functional austerity that reflected the old man's gruff personality. The sparse decor also told me that there probably hadn't been a woman living there in quite some time. In front of a fire burning hot with bricks of peat, he served up potatoes and rutabagas, the tatties and neeps he'd promised. When I passed on a leg of mutton he didn't say a word. We ate in silence. Afterward, he poured us cups of thick black tea.

He told me his name was Ewen MacKinnon, and he was a crofter. His father, grandfather, and great grandfather had lived and died in the cottage and worked the same parcel of land.

"I'm a McInnes," I said. "My people used to be bowmen for your people."

He licked the edge of a cigarette paper and twisted it expertly around a sprinkling of tobacco.

"Knew one once," he said. He flicked a match against the stone hearth and lit the cigarette. "Andrew McInnes. Daffy sort, he was. Always hanging about dreaming of places he'd never get to. One spring morning – it was the day after the MacLeod girl had her baby boy – Donald Ferguson run over Andrew with a lorry of peat. Didn't hear any more tall tales out of Andy after that."

"Was he badly hurt?"

"Dead. Squashed like a bug."

MacKinnon retired to his bedroom without as much as a word to me. He simply pointed to the rumpled day bed in the corner, threw some peat on the fire, and walked out of the room. From his bedroom, I heard him drop something and curse under his breath. A few moments later all was quiet.

I took off my mud-splashed clothes and got into the bed. I lay there, wide awake, pinned beneath heavy wool blankets. I wasn't sure if the high voltage energy running through me was from the caffeine in the tea or from witnessing the battle.

My stomach churned at the memory: desperate fingers grasping my arms, the man's breath and blood on my face, my sharp dagger jamming hard between his ribs, and his final, straggled gasp. Not the impersonal kind of killing done with a bow and arrow, or a rifle, or a cannon, but face to face, hot blood running through my fingers. I curled into the fetal position feeling like I wanted to puke. Gripped in the arms of the man that I stabbed, the horrible truth of killing a human being was revealed to me: It was dehumanizing. It robbed me of my soul, leaving me with a moral pain that was beyond healing. I clutched the blanket to my throat as tears ran down the sides of my face. Who was I now that I had faced this bloody past? What awaited me on the other side of my greatest sin?

• • •

"Good mornin' to you, McInnes," Ewen MacKinnon said, jolting me awake, "The sun is up, why aren't you?"

I was out of bed and dressed in three minutes. After a breakfast of toast and eggs, we went to work, boy did we ever. We cut peat for ten hours. I worked like I hadn't done in years. I did it out of pride. I didn't want the old man to think I was a slacker and daydreamer like Andrew McInnes. I intended to raise the reputation of my clan in Ewen MacKinnon's eyes.

It was all I could do to keep up with him. He was at least forty years my senior but with the strength of a teenager. When we were done, and I had washed the oily grime from my face and hands, MacKinnon took a bottle of scotch and two glasses from the cupboard.

"You worked like a crofter today, lad," he said. He poured scotch into the two tumblers. "Uisge beatha," he said and handed one of the glasses to me. "Water of life." He gestured for me to drink. The scotch whiskey burned the peat dust out of my throat and dulled the ache in my back. We sat down to a supper of salt herring and boiled potatoes. I don't know if it was the whiskey that loosened his tongue, or that by the amount of work I'd done MacKinnon had deemed me worthy of conversation, but the man started talking and didn't stop until past midnight.

"Most of the others moved to the mainland to work in factories and merchant ships, and the fish farms," MacKinnon said.

"But not you?"

He turned to the glow of peat in the fireplace. "Dirt on my hands, sun on my neck, seeing the field green with what I put in the ground – make a man proud." MacKinnon brought his eyes back to me. "You might want to give it a try."

After several more whiskies he told me about the storm of '51 that tore his roof off and left him with a broken right arm. Six months after the storm, a bus crash on the mainland took his young wife.

The bottle was empty when we finally called it a night. I hadn't drunk that much booze since my freshman year at Penn State when, upon hearing the news that President Ford had pardoned Nixon, Duane and I wrapped ourselves around a couple of fifths of Southern Comfort and cranked up the volume on, *Exile On Main Street.*

I drove away from MacKinnon's croft five days later. I went up the slope and out the cow path to the road. In the town of Broadford I called the rental car company. I told them that I wouldn't need the car anymore and that they could pick it up in the lot next to the BP station. I hitched a ride back down A881 with a young couple on their way to Elgol to pick up their niece.

I worked Ewen MacKinnon's croft for the next four months. I tilled the rocky soil, planted and fertilized, milked his cow, chased his sheep, stacked bricks of peat, repaired the thatch on his roof, and rebuilt the sidewall of his storage shed. I got dirt under my fingernails, stray seeds in my pockets, and a new lease on life.

"Not bad for a McInnes," MacKinnon said. "You'll be a crofter yet."

I agreed. I had found that working the land was something that mattered to me. Growing things gave me purpose and intention. It challenged me and made me think and struggle to problem solve. And I seemed to be pretty good at it.

On a sunny day in the beginning of October, I was walking on the beach just below the cottage. I was thinking about a letter I'd recently received from Leslie and Tara. They joked about the look on my face when I'd swung my walking staff into Randy's rib cage. They said that I looked like a blood thirsty warrior in battle.

I bent down and picked up a piece of driftwood. It was six feet long and slender with nubs and thin branches sticking out of it. As I was examining it, the screech of a herring gull caused me to look up. Out over the water, two gulls were fighting over a fish. As I watched them dive and peck at each other, I sat down on a rock and pulled out my Swiss army knife. The aerial combat went on for quite some time. One gull would be forced to drop the fish, and then the other would swoop down and snatch it, only to be dive-bombed by the first gull. The whole cycle would then start all over again.

While watching the gulls I was vaguely aware of the knife in my hands and my absentminded whittling. After a while I looked down. I had trimmed away all the twigs and nubs along the length of wood, notched the ends and carved a platform for an arrow to rest on. I had created a bow. I stared at the thing, mystified as to how or why I had done it. I ran my fingers over the smooth wood. What was my subconscious or my jiva, as Hindus refer to the soul, trying to tell me?

I held the bow and sighted down the shaft of an imaginary arrow. How many times had I carried a weapon like this in past lives, five, ten, a hundred times? I thought of my father dying a tortured death with one of my arrows piercing his lungs. I thought of the man I killed with my dagger. And then there was Hastings, Normandy and Verdun. I'd killed too many men.

Out on the loch, a sailboat skimmed through the water. Who was in it, I wondered? Someone I killed in another lifetime coming to have their revenge? The boat cut through the waves, dipping and plunging into the green sea, the watery womb from which life had come.

I stood up and took off my clothes.

Like the seed I read about in the Kabbalah, I could not grow to perfection as long as I maintained my original form. I needed to put an end to Singing Bow the medieval archer, the renegade Apache, the killer of men. I needed to cleanse myself of the violent, warring nature that had lashed out at Randy back in Colorado. I wanted to be shattered like the seed and reborn into a greater form. I wanted to be a man who farmed the land and contributed to the well-being of others. Instead of reaping death and destruction, I wanted to harvest life.

With the bow clenched tightly in my fist, I dove into the waters of Loch Scavaig. The second my body hit the icy water, I knew that I had made a terrible mistake. I didn't even have a chance to gasp. My chest muscles constricted like steel bands and my lungs refused to expand. Doing a bad imitation of the carp I used to feed in North

Park Lake, my mouth opened and closed as I made strangled, sucking sounds. Clinging to the bow as if it were a life preserver, I felt the current pulling me out toward the North Channel.

I realized that unless I did something and did it quickly, I stood a good chance of not only ridding myself of my warring nature, but all of my natures. I kept reminding myself that I was a strong swimmer. I'd won first place ribbons at the neighborhood pool when I was a child. I tried to do the breaststroke but my muscles seemed incapable of recollecting my childhood glories. My face dipped under water as I struggled to tread water.

Dumb way to die, I thought. After everything I'd been through, drowning was a silly way for it to end. I clung desperately to the bow as the frigid water drained my body of strength. Several panicky minutes later, the last of my energy gave out. With a final look of longing at Ewen MacKinnon's cottage up on the hill, I quietly slipped beneath the waves.

The sun's rays filtered down through the silent green world I had entered. At least it was quiet, I thought. At least I wouldn't be dying in the din of battle. With my breath running out, I decided to finish what I'd dove into the water to do in the first place. I held the bow out in front of me. No more warring, I called silently into the swirling green sea. No more killing over land or possessions or women or precious metals or oil or borders. No more death on my hands. In my next lifetime, and in all lifetimes to come, I would be a man of peace.

I let the bow slip from my hand. I watched it drift away. Turning my face toward the fading light from the surface, I thought of what Miguel told me about becoming part of the circle. *Come Great Spirit*, I thought. *I am ready now.*

Imagine my incredible surprise when I felt an arm wrap around my chest. Oh wow, I thought, Great Spirit certainly has a firm grip. I was propelled upward. The next thing I knew, I was laying on the deck of the sailboat looking into the face of a beautiful woman. Her clear brown eyes, olive skin, and full, red lips were gorgeously framed by a tangle of dark, wet hair. She gently touched my cheek. I knew then that relinquishing my warring nature had not gone unnoticed. I had made it into heaven.

"What the hell were you doing?" the beautiful woman asked. She seemed miffed. Do people in heaven get miffed?

"I saw you take off your clothes and jump in. Were you trying to kill yourself or something?"

The lips were so close and I so happy. I was either alive or in heaven, either way, it was a joyous occasion. I reached up and kissed those luscious, warm lips. Then everything went dark.

36

Melina Mazza was a sculptress and a recreational scuba diver. After sightseeing with her for a few days, and sharing several romantic nights, I was ga-ga in love. Not since my relationship with Lilly had I experienced such passion.

"Tommy," she said, after a particularly rigorous evening of lovemaking. "Why don't you come to New York with me? You make me feel," and she really did say this, "like a woman in a romance novel."

I looked into those beautiful passion-glazed eyes – and I knew. At the moment of releasing my dark past, she had come like some sort of angel and saved me. Why in the face of such a miracle would I be cautious? Let passion rule the day!

On the afternoon of my departure, Ewen MacKinnon poured a glass of Scotch whiskey for himself then he poured one for me.

"You're a fine crofter, McInnes," he said. Then with a wink added, "Other 'n that swim in the loch, you did your people proud."

He sipped his whiskey then lowered the glass and looked intently at me.

"You came a long way to get here," he said.

I nodded.

"New York City . . ." he said.

"Yeah."

His fatherly gaze bore down on me.

"What?" I asked.

"Are you certain about all this?"

I averted my eyes and stared at the glass in my hand.

"She's beautiful," I said. "Don't you think?"

"That she is. A pretty lass."

"Yeah," I said.

Outside a car horn honked.

Ewen gave me one last look. "Well, okay then."

I walked outside and climbed into Melina's rented Land Cruiser. I leaned over and gave her a kiss. The accompanying surge of lust successfully washed aside any feelings of doubt that had reared up in my conversation with MacKinnon. I turned back to the cottage. He was standing at the door.

"Beannachd leat, McInnes," he said.

• • •

MELINA'S LOFT IN SOHO was half sculpting studio, half living space. Fourteen foot windows flooded the place with light, and the fully equipped stainless steel kitchen looked like it belonged in a high-end restaurant. Our first night in New York we had Chinese food delivered. With candles flickering and Chet Baker's trumpet crooning, we slow danced on her rooftop deck. It felt like I had found my corner of heaven.

Melina's talent and accomplishments as an artist blew me away. I wanted her to respect me in the same way, so a week after arriving in New York, I got a short haircut, bought several suits and ties, and with the help of a friend of my father's got a job at Klein/Wallace Advertising.

"Why would you cut your hair?" Melina said, her eyes flashing.

"I needed a job."

"You didn't ask me about any of this."

"Advertising is where my contacts are."

"Baby, I told you I can take care of things."

"I appreciate you saying that, but—"

"I loved your hair. It was sexy."

"I'm going to work hard and help create a great life for us."

"But I loved grabbing your hair. You know I loved that."

"I love you." I said, pinning her against the wall and kissing her.

• • •

WORKING AT THE ADVERTISING agency was part torture and part, well, more torture. Office politics, giant egos, and a passive-aggressive boss who was armed with more mind-games than an individual should be allowed to possess, made going to work every day a highly traumatic event. But even while suffering through that minefield, I found myself generally upbeat and optimistic. I was providing for myself and my woman. Together we were forging a relationship that, although not perfect, felt like it was going somewhere – sort of.

One night after work I walked into Melina's studio. Still in her pajamas, she was slumped on the leather sofa.

"You okay?"

She didn't answer. For a second I thought she was reading something in her lap that I couldn't see.

"Hey, you want to go out for sushi," I said. "I'm starving."

She looked up at me through a mass of dark curls, and I swear to God she snarled.

"The good corporate soldier has returned," she said. She pushed the hair out of her face and leaned back on the couch. "That fucking suit – You remind me of my father."

"Whoa," I said.

"Did you kiss some good ass today?"

"Hey, I don't know what happened, but don't be pissed at me."

"Oh, of course not, you never do anything wrong."

"What does that mean?"

She dug her fingers into her mane of hair and growled, "You suck!"

"What's your problem?"

She was up off the couch and in my face. "My problem! I don't like your fucking job or your stupid-ass short haircut or the fact that you don't hold me like you used to."

"What are you talking about? I can't keep my hands off of you."

"That's 'cause you want sex. You don't do it because you care about me. You're too busy sucking up to that boss of yours." She jabbed her finger in my chest. "Are you fucking her?"

"Baby, what is going on? Why are you saying this stuff?"

"You are aren't you?"

"No!"

"You bastard!"

"I'm not sleeping with her or anyone else! I'm crazy about you!"

"You're just fuckin' crazy, period!"

I tried to put my arms around her. She shoved me away.

"What's your deal!" I shot back. "Why are you being so crazy?"

"Now I'm a bitch!"

"What? I didn't say that."

"Fuck you, Tommy!" She shoved me toward the door. "Get out! Get the fuck out of here!"

I discovered that Melina, the Italian diva of the SoHo art scene, lived out the shattering seed theory on a daily basis. She believed that her best work only came when she was in grip of an emotional upheaval. And why go looking for it out on the streets when she had me handy. If she felt uninspired, "pasty" as she called it, she'd pick a fight with me. We'd go bonkers on each other for a while, and then, with her creative juices jump-started by yours truly, she'd burst forth from her "pasty" seed pod and spend the next two weeks working eighteen hours a day.

I compounded the problem by throwing myself into my work at the advertising firm. I put in sixty-hour weeks obsessing all the while about my meager salary as assistant to one of the copywriters. When it became clear that making more money was going to be a long climb, I doubled up and got a part-time job in the evenings doing telemarketing for the opera.

All of this effort, I convinced myself, was to provide us with a strong financial future so Melina wouldn't have to obsess over her art. We could start having fun together. It didn't work, not even close. She resented me for being part of the corporate advertising world, and I resented her for resenting me. I was a mess. My friends saw the toll it was taking on me.

"It's not like you think you're a god or anything like that?"

"What do you mean?" I asked.

Across the break-room table, Colleen, a sophomore at NYU and one of my fellow telemarketers at the opera, lifted her steaming cup of tea and blew on it.

"There are so many guys," she said. "They think they're – I don't even know what – some kinda gift from God or something – like you should feel honored to go out with them." She shrugged. "You're not like that at all. You're down to earth."

"Until she gets me all twisted in some insane argument."

"Tom, you have to accept that Melina is who she is."

"I can't. That means having to accept that my life is always going to be like this."

"Or . . ."

"Yeah, yeah, move out. I know. But if she could just . . ." my voice trailed off.

"My mother says 'people don't change, they just become more so.'"

"Oh Lord."

"Do you really want to live your life riding that roller coaster?"

"No. Not really. Right?"

Colleen rolled her eyes. "If you get your own apartment that will give you guys some space. Maybe that will be enough to wake her up to see what a crazy bitch she's been." Colleen dramatically clapped her hand over her mouth. "Sorry, did I say that out loud."

I couldn't help but smile. Colleen was a refreshing breeze blowing over the simmering pile of crap that had become my life.

"But I love her," I said. "She's the one."

"I know, I know, you told me," Colleen said. "The woman dove into icy, unknown waters to save your life. You guys are meant to be together. You're going to get married, have magically gifted children who live extraordinary lives and create great changes in the world."

"Yeah," I said meekly, still clinging to my dream.

"Good luck with that, Tom."

Luck was not enough. When my relationship with Melina finally tanked for good, it wasn't because I came to my senses and decided to leave her. That would have been too smart, too mature on my part. It ended, and as far as I'm concerned it was the lowest blow any reasonably intelligent man could suffer, because she left me for the cut abs and vacuous smile of a twenty-one-year-old underwear model named, Kip.

With my five cardboard boxes of belongings on the sidewalk in front of Melina's building, I breathed in the chilly, faintly urine-scented night air along Spring Street. Not since I was in college had I felt so lost. There was a wide gulf inside of me. I was on one shore, tired and bitter, and my old self, the searcher, was standing far away in a place that I could barely remember. How had it come to this? Perhaps I was right when I saw the billowing sails of her boat crossing the loch on that fateful day. Maybe Melina was someone I killed in a past lifetime. Maybe she was yet another victim of one of my arrows. If that were true, then she deliberately went to the trouble of resurrecting me from my watery grave for the purpose of watching me suffer through a mental and emotional crucifixion.

Payback's a bitch.

I moved into a one-bedroom apartment a block up Fifth Avenue from Washington Square Park. After several weeks of sulking and feeling sorry for myself, I began to go out with friends.

"Ask not what the universe can do for you," Colleen said, "ask what you can do for the universe." She popped a cherry tomato in her mouth and grinned. It wasn't the first time she had me over for dinner. Colleen was doing her best to lift me out of my post-Melina funk.

"A dance studio and summer workshops for kids," she said, "that's what I'm going to contribute after I graduate."

I toasted her with my glass of red wine. "If I can help in any way let me know."

"Thanks Tom, I appreciate that. I'm focusing on autism. It can be difficult, but really rewarding."

"Sort of like dealing with Jack."

A chunk of tomato flew out of her mouth and I laughed along with her. Colleen began bobbing her head and flaring her nostrils as she launched into her impersonation of Jack Stamper, one of our elderly volunteers at the opera and a hard core Yankees fan.

"Don Mattingly is a pure hitter," she said in Jack's creaky, Bronx saturated voice. "Doubles, the man hits doubles. I like ball players that hit doubles." As she was flexing her neck and poking her tongue in her cheek in perfect imitation of Jack, out of no-where Daniel Toberni's final words of advice boomed through my mind. "You should go to places where the energy is high. It'll be good for you. Who knows maybe you'll even get laid."

"Maybe you'll even get laid?" I said out loud.

Colleen's eyebrows rose in surprise. Still using Jack's geriatric voice she said, "Sorry kid, I ain't a switch hitter."

Oh no, I thought. Oh no. Were Melina and I supposed to have just been a sex thing? I held my head in my hands. Had I tried to force what was meant to have been a brief, passionate affair into something more? Was I so caught up in the thrill of having released the past that I completely missed what was really going on between the two of us? Dumb ass, I thought. Be more careful about asking for what you want and remembering what you asked for.

It was at this moment of profound self-loathing that the really big turd I'd unloaded in my life decided to reveal itself. It hit me like a fast ball in the chest.

I sold myself out.

On Ewen MacKinnon's croft I'd been inspired and fascinated working the land and raising crops. It felt more real than anything I'd ever done before, and I was good at it. Then Melina kissed me and I ran away from what made me happy as fast as my lust would carry me. What an idiot!

Colleen, still doing her impersonation of Jack, reached over and whacked me on top of my head. "Come on, come on, kid, shake it off."

• • •

I IMMEDIATELY CUT BACK my hours at the advertising agency. I prowled around the neighborhood gardens until I found a woman who was willing to share her plot with me. It was November, but I didn't care. I happily crouched amongst the dried cornhusks and empty tomato stakes, describing to Colleen the garden I would plant in the spring. Having my hands on a piece of earth lifted my spirits considerably. And with thoughts of Melina behind me, I was finally moving forward in my life.

Saturday afternoon, with snow flurries gusting through the frosty air, I was standing at the corner of 4th and Broadway. I'd just come out of Tower Records where I'd bought Miles Davis', *Kind of Blue*. Waiting for the light to change, I was surprised to find myself thinking about Pomona. During my time with Melina, my quest for Pomona would flare up, but I never gave it any focus. I never told her about the blue heron or the orange grove vision out of fear she'd think I was crazy. Standing in the wind freezing my butt off, I indulged in the idea of heading west and finally putting the Pomona thing to rest. The sunshine would do me good.

"Hey, Tom!"

I turned around. Colleen was jogging up Broadway. Under her green New York Jets stocking cap, her nose and cheeks were bright red.

"You're more dedicated than me," I said.

"New Year's resolution," she gasped, panting as she ran in place. "Gotta lose ten pounds by March."

"Going to the beach for spring break?"

She nodded. "Don't want to look like Shamu the whale girl."

"You look great."

"Lie all you want, I love it."

At that moment the light changed. With a quick wave, Colleen shot past me into the crosswalk. Out of the corner of my eye came a blur of yellow, a loud thump, and Colleen was flying through the air. Brakes screeched. A cab fishtailed to a stop. Colleen landed on her back in the middle of 4th Street, her heading slamming hard on the pavement.

Time, sound, and movement shifted into low gear. I was running into the street. I was screaming something that I couldn't understand. Faces turned. Cars stopped. My knees hit the pavement next to Colleen.

Her left leg was twisted back and her thigh bone was sticking through a rip in her sweatpants. Blood streamed from her nose and ears. Her hat was gone and her eyes were closed.

"Don't move her!" a woman yelled from somewhere far away and above me. A siren began blaring a few blocks away.

My hands wanted to be busy. They wanted to pick Colleen up off the cold pavement and cradle her in my arms, but I didn't do it. I was afraid of hurting her. I grabbed her hand and leaned down to her ear.

"Colleen," I whispered, "I'm here with you."

I squeezed her hand. I wanted her to be able to make that trip at spring break. I wanted us to have dinner together and drink wine and laugh. I kept talking to her and squeezing her hand until the paramedics arrived.

It didn't do any good. She was dead before they got her to the hospital.

• • •

MY FAITH DIED ALONG with Colleen that day. What happened to her was senseless and it served no one. For her to be snuffed out by a cabby running a red light was unforgivable. Why hadn't I died when Emerson Yazzie hit me with his Toyota? Why Colleen and not me?

I stopped meditating. I gave up going to the garden. I quit looking for signs. If I got a flash of intuition, I shoved it aside and forgot it. I let go of my quest for Pomona.

Two weeks after the accident I quit my jobs at the advertising agency and the opera. I began bartending. I figured I was already staying out half the night I might as well get paid to do it.

In the late hours and smoky darkness I became a nameless face ready to draw a beer or mix a drink. I heard about people's crappy jobs and ex-wives, their teenage girlfriends and married boyfriends.

I was nobody to them and they were nobody to me. I liked it that way. I didn't want to let anyone inside. I was there to watch the show, not be in it; the pushed up cleavage, the come-on lines, the bleary-eyed drunks trying to get laid, get home, find someone to understand them, or better yet, love them. The night crawlers weren't worrying about Karma or spiritual quests or evolution. They were too busy chawing on the bones of life. They didn't worry about why a terrific, young woman was killed in the middle of 4th Street because a cab driver was in a hurry. They weren't compelled to try and understand what kind of God allowed that to happen. They wanted to pretend that they were watched over and that someone would be there to catch them if they fell. Chaos isn't a comforting blanket to wrap around yourself when you go to bed at night. A martini maybe, a soft warm body certainly, but not chaos, and definitely not the concept of a God that allows nineteen-year-old girls to be run over by cabs.

I began reading end-of-the-millennium-doomsday theories about polar ice caps melting and catastrophic movements of the earth's crust. I came across a book that told of ancient civilizations that supposedly left us clues as to when these dramatic earth changes would occur. The dates would be revealed from the mathematical and astronomical configuration of the Sphinx or Great Pyramids.

I didn't know whether to believe it or not. What I did get out of it was that the earth had its own agenda, and it had nothing to do with the evolution of human beings. It was about constant change and survival. And if, in the midst of its geological humping and bumping, we humans somehow managed to make it through, then yea for us. If we didn't make it, if we somehow became extinct like the dinosaurs, it didn't matter. The planet would be fine on its own, probably better.

I bought a book of photographs on all the space flights. I spent hours soaking in the bathtub staring at the pictures. Looking back from the moon, the little blue/green orb of the earth wasn't very significant. In the infinite expanse of black empty space it looked vulnerable and exposed.

I wondered if God would protect us from falling asteroids. Could the memory or writings of Jesus or Buddha or any other spiritual leader save us from a huge meteorite smashing into the planet and vaporizing all of us back into the carbon molecules from whence we came? It seemed monstrously doubtful to me. So what was the point of worshipping something that didn't have the ability to protect you when you needed it most? Or was the gigantic asteroid that hit the Yucatan peninsula 65 million years ago an act of God? Was that His or Her way of killing off two-thirds of the life forms on the planet and starting fresh?

Without a benevolent connection with the planet and feeling that there wasn't a fair, kind-hearted divine presence watching over me, I drifted deeper into the dark corners of myself and away from other people.

I was surprised how fast the years slipped by. The scramble for big dollars on Wall Street hit a fever pitch, Reagan was re-elected, the space shuttle Challenger exploded, and family farming went through its worst depression in 50 years.

While all of this was going on, I was absolutely alone in the middle of Manhattan with millions of people crowded around me. The separation I'd created between myself and the rest of the world was both a comfort and the source of a deep, unrelenting ache. I didn't know how to fix it, so I continued on.

I was Tom, the bartender. That's who I'd become.

37

On an unseasonably warm day in March, things changed. I walked from my apartment on the east side to my job at Chumley's in the west village. Halfway through my shift, a dapper older man with a neatly tapered white mustache came in and sat at the end of the bar. He shot the cuffs of his tweed jacket and ordered a bottle of Grolsch beer and a bag of sour cream and onion potato chips. After I served him, we got a rush of people into the restaurant. Every once in a while, as I was making drinks, I would catch him watching me. When things finally slowed down a little, he grinned and gave me a thumbs-up.

"Not too bad," he said, his voice strong and clear. He sounded younger than he looked. "I tended bar myself," he said. "Long time ago."

"Oh yeah?"

"Always liked talking to people. Amazing the things they tell you."

"You got that right."

"And you have to listen between the lines. What they don't say is as important as what they do say."

He sipped his beer while I mixed a gin and tonic for a woman at the other end of the bar. When I finished he waved me over.

"Don't let yourself think that it doesn't matter," he said, "what you say to people. Bartenders have a responsibility to offer the best advice they can. It's part of the bartender's oath." He raised his glass. "I will pour no beer nor whiskey nor wine until my patrons have peace of mind."

I laughed. "That's a good one."

"Yes, it is."

"Peace of mind? Does anybody have that these days?"

"You don't?"

I shrugged.

"Come on," he said. "Somewhere along the way you had it."

"I guess."

"When?"

The sun coming up over MacKinnon's croft flashed through my mind: the smell of fresh turned earth, the sweet taste of a carrot straight out of the ground.

He picked up his glass of beer and finished it. Reaching into his jacket pocket he pulled out a tin of mints and popped one in his mouth.

"Would you like one?" He slid the tin across the bar.

"Thanks," I said, picking a mint out.

He put the tin back in his jacket pocket and stood up. He flicked down seven, crisp one dollar bills, glanced at the gin and tonic woman then brought his gaze back to me.

"See ya'll," he said, and walked to the door.

As I watched him go, I was struck with the vague feeling that I'd seen him walk out the door once before. I popped the mint into my mouth and turned to put his money in the cash register. The taste of peppermint instantly brought back the memory.

"Holy shit!"

"Excuse me," said the gin and tonic woman.

"Watch the register!" I called to one of the waitresses. I ducked under the bar and ran out the door. I sprinted around the block three times but the old man was gone.

When I came back inside, the woman sitting at the bar gave me a curious look.

"Daniel Toberni," I said to her and ducked under the bar.

I paced back and forth like a caged animal. The gin and tonic woman watched me, unsure of what was going to happen next. It was so bizarre I couldn't get my head around it. Daniel offered me the same kind of mints in Amsterdam. He'd flicked down fresh new bills in the same way. And when he walked out of the Bulldog Café he'd looked at us and said, "See ya'll."

Was it a weird coincidence, some sort of cosmic joke? And if it *was* Daniel, what was he some kind of angel, a spirit guide, an alien?

That night I had a dream. I was wearing swim trunks and sunglasses and I was on a crowded beach somewhere in the tropics. A shapely woman in a white bikini was strolling down the beach. She was with two lean, hard-muscled men. Her dark hair was blowing in the warm breeze. Suntan oil glistened on her taut body. Just as she was about to walk past, she turned toward me. With a flick of her wrist, she flipped her hair away from her face and gave me a wink. It was Colleen.

I didn't push the dream away and forget about it. For the first time since Colleen's death, I allowed myself to remember. I saw her head slamming to the pavement. I remembered holding her hand and urging her to stay with me. I heard the sirens and the smell of the cherry bubble gum that the paramedic was chewing. I felt the emptiness that folded in on me when I found out she was dead. I remembered the angry questions that I asked myself: Why had she died? Who made that decision? Why hadn't I pulled her back and saved her?

I was watching TV two nights later when the realization hit me. Accepting the inevitability of my own death was one thing, I had done that in Peru when the jaguar chomped down on my head, but accepting the death of someone else, someone I cared about, that was an entirely different matter. The loss was too painful. I wasn't able to see things clearly.

Bud Endelman's message from the blue heron shot up like a flare from my long-term memory: *Always remember that you are not alone*. And the rest of it opened before me like a dream. My belief that I was watched over and guided was severely challenged when Colleen died. And once again, just as I had done in Scotland with Melina, I threw away what mattered most to me. It was easier to be angry and fearful than it was to have faith. Personal truth, I was learning, was difficult to hold on to.

· · ·

I WENT BACK TO the gardens. March in New York isn't the best time of year to sink your fingers into the ground, but I did what I could to get ready. When I wasn't sketching out diagrams of how to most efficiently use the corner plot that I'd wrangled from the cousin of a waitress I knew, I was prowling around buying seeds and trying to figure out what I wanted to plant. I also built fencing and put in a narrow brick footpath.

One evening in April, after laying the last of the bricks, I decided to meditate. I wanted to commune with the garden deities to see if they might be inclined to grant me a prosperous harvest. I was deep into an exceptionally peaceful place when I received a vicious kick in the back. I rolled onto my right side and stumbled to my feet. Something smashed me on the left side of my face, sending stars splintering through my head. I staggered, almost fell then was grabbed by the front of my coat and shoved backward. I hit the ground on my ass, and as I tried to clear my vision something hard and cold pressed against my cheek. The unmistakable smell of gun metal hit me. I shifted my eyes to the right and saw the barrel of a large revolver. The face of the man holding the gun was equally hard and cold. He scowled at me through a mop of limp hair and a week's worth of whiskers.

"Wallet," he snapped.

"I left it at home."

"Too bad," he said, and thumbed back the hammer on the gun.

I felt no panic. There was no desperate need to lash out at him, or to try and kill him to save myself. Instead, I looked at the hostile smirk on his face and I wondered what was behind it. What fearful darkness had he endured in this or other lives to put that gun in his hand?

"You know what," I said calmly. "You need a shave and a haircut. I have seventeen dollars in my pocket. Take it, and go get yourself all gussied up."

He looked absolutely astonished, then he burst out laughing.

"Gussied up," he said. "You're one nutty fuck. Costs me thirty bucks for a shampoo and trim where I go." He laughed again. "You got balls, I'll give you that." The gun lowered and he held out his hand. "Okay. Give me the money."

I dug the wad of bills from my pocket and handed it to him. He grinned and muttered, "Gussied up." Then he slapped me on the back as if we'd just shared a beer.

"Hey," I said, stopping him at the edge of my plot. "Shouldn't you be doing something better with your life than robbing people?"

He glared at me over his shoulder. "Shouldn't you be doin' somethin' better than dreamin' of tomatoes in April?"

The next day I emptied my savings account and bought a used Chevy Blazer from a soap opera actor in Jersey City. I packed my belongings and drove over the George Washington Bridge headed for Pittsburgh.

38

When we moved Aunt Helen from the nursing home back into her house, the first thing she wanted was to see was Terry. I brought the deaf, old, bugger over from Mrs. Culver's house and he jumped up onto Aunt Helen's lap and immediately curled into a ball and fell sound asleep. Aunt Helen couldn't have been happier. The next item on her list of priorities was to make sure that Crystal, her new caregiver, was well informed on how to operate the juice machine.

With Dad at home with an upset stomach, he thought he ate bad mushrooms in the turkey tetrazzini he'd made, Leo and Mom helped me move Aunt Helen's bedroom furnishings from upstairs down into the den. Under Aunt Helen's direction we did our best to create a comfortable new room for her on the first floor.

That evening, my mother had her meeting with the Northpoint Woodcarvers Association leaving Dad and me on our own for dinner. While he was in the kitchen making spaghetti sauce, I was up in my bedroom packing my stuff to leave for California. I had just finished when I heard a loud crash downstairs.

"Dad," I called.

No answer.

"What are you throwing around down there?"

No answer.

I walked to the top of the stairs. "Dad?"

Peanut's long nails were clicking on the kitchen floor. Thinking the dog had dragged the pan of ground meat off the counter, I rushed down the stairs.

I found my father sprawled on the floor in front of the stove. Meat sauce was splashed on the lower portion of the cabinets and on the floor. Peanut was licking the cuff of Dad's khakis.

One look at my father's ashen face told me that he was dead. All the air went out of me. I got down on my knees next to his body. My mind began downloading hundreds of options of what I should say or do, but nothing seemed to make sense. I didn't want to be angry that he was dead. I'd learned that lesson with Colleen. And I didn't want this final moment to be filled with gloom. I took a deep breath and closed my eyes. Sadness flooded through me and I was momentarily distracted by what we had not had together as father and son. Then I remembered that this moment wasn't about me, it was about honoring his transition to another place. I silently began to pray. I prayed for his spirit to have safe passage. I encouraged him to soar to his highest truth and not to worry about the family or me. I prayed that whatever had kept him closed off in this lifetime, be lovingly revealed to him. I apologized again for the arrow through his lungs and the horrible death I'd caused him. I cried out to him in my heart, telling him that I loved him and that I appreciated him bringing me into this world. I called upon Shiva the Destroyer, the Hindu deity who resolves all finite forms back into the everything from which they had come, to lead my father on his journey. I placed my palms together, bowed my head, and spoke to the spirit of my father.

"Dad," I said, my voice clear and strong, "go on your journey with peace and love."

I opened my eyes. Much to my surprise, so did my father.

"Tommy," he rasped, "There's peach pie for dessert."

· · ·

THE EMERGENCY ROOM NURSE told him that based on preliminary blood tests they thought he'd had a heart attack. With the half-smile of his crisis face firmly in place, he politely thanked her then went back to reading a Popular Mechanics magazine. I could tell that what she'd told him hadn't registered. Five minutes later, the emergency room doctor told him that they were pretty sure he'd had a heart attack. Again, my father deflected it with a blank smile and a courteous thank you. After they moved him up to the sixth floor Cardiac Care Unit, one of the nurses explained to him that enzymes present in his blood indicated that he'd had a heart attack. I expected him to start humming a Sinatra tune. When he didn't, I realized that he must finally be getting the message.

Dr. Noonan, a cardiologist, came into the room. He was too tall and looked much too young to be a real doctor. I was tempted to ask for proof of his credentials but thought better of it. He peered down at my father through wire-rim glasses.

"Mr. McInnes, it wasn't indigestion you had a few days ago. It was a heart attack. The fibrillation you experienced this evening was a result of the damage you suffered in the earlier attack. The bump on the back of your head is from hitting something when you fell, the kitchen counter or the floor."

Monitors bleeped softly. Dad blinked twice and didn't say anything. Dr. Noonan glanced down at the clipboard in his hands.

"Were you involved in any kind of strenuous activity tonight?"

"I was cooking," Dad said. He grinned and bobbed his eyebrows up and down. "I do get kind of excited about my spaghetti sauce."

The doctor didn't crack a smile. "We'll have the results of more tests in the morning. Get some rest."

Dr. Noonan slightly ducked his head as he went out the door. Dad put his magazine down.

"Well," he said. "I guess I had a heart attack."

"I'd say so."

"It wasn't the mushrooms after all."

"No, it wasn't."

"I wonder where that fella played basketball. He's a big boy. Not much of a sense of humor. Hey, you wanna watch TV?"

As he reached for the control pad by his side, I saw that his hand was trembling. I leaned over and patted him on the arm. Before I could pull my hand away he grabbed it. I expected him to let go, but he didn't. He held my hand while he watched the evening news on the television. It was awkward holding hands with my father. I didn't know if I was supposed to be the comforting son and tell him that everything would be all right or if I should get tough with him and tell him to quit smoking and lose some weight. A few minutes later he turned to me.

"Tom, if anything happens," he said stiffly, "I want you to take care of your mother. I want her to have everything she needs." A sad, forlorn expression crossed his face. For a moment I thought he was going to cry.

"Oh, geez," he said. "I have to take a leak." He pushed back the blanket on the bed.

"You're not allowed to get up," I said.

"I have to go."

"You're supposed to use this." I handed him the plastic bottle that was hanging on the rail of the bed.

"I'm not going to piss in a bottle."

"What are you going to do unplug all this equipment?"

He grumbled and took the bottle. I pulled the curtain closed around his bed and walked across the room and looked up at the TV in the corner. Tom Brokaw was talking about the AIDS crisis. I could hear Dad behind the curtain struggling to get into position to use the bottle.

"Do you want me to get the nurse?"

"I got it, I got it."

There was a long pause.

"Dad?"

"Shit. Now I can't go."

There was another long pause. Suddenly the volume on the TV went up. A moment later he muttered, "Damn," as he urinated into the bottle. A couple seconds later the volume on the TV went back down.

"Tom," he said weakly. "Take this for me."

When I opened the curtain he was laying on his side. With one hand he was using a magazine to try and cover the wet spot that was spreading on the sheet. In the other hand he was holding the plastic bottle of urine.

"Take it," he commanded me.

The tone of his voice stopped me cold. Two distinct reactions welled up in me. The child, remembering all too well the sting of his belt and the nasty taste of Ivory soap, straightened up, stood a little taller, and thought to himself: Finally I have power over you old man. I'm the one in control. At the same time, the adult that I'd grown into looked down and saw, in the middle of that piss-drenched sheet, the man who gave me life, the man who did the best he knew how in trying to raise me and help me survive. Who was I, the man or the boy?

I took the bottle from him.

Emptying his urine into the toilet, I grabbed a towel and when I went back to his bed I laid it over the wet spot.

"I'm glad you're here, Tom," Dad said, as I helped him lean back and get comfortable. "It means a lot to me."

Without a thought to what he'd done in the past or to what his ancient primate survival instincts were propelling him to do now, I tucked the blanket around him and said, "I'm glad I could be here with you Dad."

He smiled at me then reached for the TV control pad.

Later that night, when I was finally able to reach my mother at home, the first thing she said was, "What the heck happened in the kitchen? There's spaghetti sauce everywhere! Can't you guys be left alone without destroying the house?"

"Dad had a heart attack. I'm at the hospital with him."

There was a long silence. She cleared her throat.

"Did he bring any decent pajamas?" Her voice tried to stay strong. "I hope he didn't take those holey green ones."

Thirty minutes later she was at the hospital with an overnight bag of toiletries and half a bag of peanut M&M's.

"Sorry about the mess in the kitchen," Dad said as soon as she walked in his room.

"It's not a problem," she said. "I cleaned it up."

Mom busied herself straightening the sheets on his bed.

"How was your meeting?" Dad said.

Mom told him about the various projects people in the wood-carving association were working on. They bantered back and forth about what her new project should be. Dad encouraged her to break out of her duck mode. Mom wanted to do one more.

"Joy Benedict showed me a picture of a Northern Shoveler. It has a beautiful long bill – be a good challenge."

"Are you sure," Dad said. "You've done a lot of ducks."

"I love ducks."

"I know, and you do a great job with them. I'm just saying . . ."

I was amazed. While around them the machines monitoring my father's damaged, unstable heart clicked and hummed, all the two of them could talk about were ducks.

"I'm going to go call Rick and Becky," I said.

"Don't make a big deal out of it," Dad said. "I'm fine."

"When I got home," Mom said. "Peanut was in his bed with his little belly all swollen."

"What a waste of ground chuck," Dad said.

"You dropped it."

"I had a heart attack."

"It wasn't a heart attack tonight. It was a fibrillation."

"Whatever."

"You want an M&M?"

"Yeah, sure."

"Are you allowed?"

"Probably not, but one or two won't kill me."

She handed the bag to him. He dug out a few M&M's and popped them into his mouth. With a contented sigh he settled back onto his pillow.

How nice, I thought, to be that comforted by a couple pieces of candy. Then I noticed Mom's hand resting on his chest.

• • •

Mom and Dad told Rick and Becky not to come home. Mom wanted them to save their money and come at Thanksgiving.

"We'll have a big feast," she said to Rick over the telephone. "And I want everyone here. You clear it with Denise so you can bring the boys. It'll give you guys a chance to meet, Leo."

Becky informed Mom that she had a new boyfriend, Anthony. She said it was serious and she wanted Mom and Dad to meet him. Mom said, "Bring him. The more the merrier."

With Dad's cholesterol at 340 and the lower portion of his heart irreparably damaged, I hoped he would make it to November.

"Quit smoking, get more exercise, change your diet, and you'll be on your way to being healthy," Doctor Noonan told him.

"I'm a carnivore, Doc," Dad said. "I need my meat!"

"Chicken and fish," Dr. Noonan commanded from his lofty height. "And try eating tofu. It's a great source of protein."

"You're kidding!"

"Do I look like a kidder, Mr. McInnes?"

"That stuff is awful. Tastes like Styrofoam."

Dr. Noonan put down the chart he was holding. He folded his long arms across his chest and stared at Dad. At over six-foot-six he was an imposing presence.

"This minor heart attack was a wake-up call, Mr. McInnes. If you don't change the way you've been living, you might not be so lucky next time." He picked up the chart and walked out of the room. He was young, but he knew how to make a point.

• • •

After three days in the cardiac care unit, Dad was transferred to a regular room on the sixth floor. I was dropping off magazines and some mail when I ran into Leo Hursen. He and Dad were just saying goodbye so I rode down in the elevator with Leo.

"Your father is looking pretty good," Leo said. "Does that mean you'll be heading west soon?"

"I think so. I'll probably wait another week and then take off."

The elevator door opened and we started across the lobby.

"Are you doing anything right now?" Leo asked.

"No," I said. "What's up?"

"You want to go for a ride?"

On the way down McKnight Road Leo explained to me that he had gone to the Carnegie Library and searched through old City Directories. He found an address where his father, Seth was listed as a boarder in a house.

The small, brick, two-story was in a quiet neighborhood on the south side of Bloomfield. Leo pulled his Lincoln Town Car up to the curb and parked. We got out and stood on the sidewalk.

"I wonder which room was his," Leo said, looking at the house.

"I'll see if anyone is home. Maybe they'll let us in."

"No, no, no. I couldn't do that," Leo said, backing away.

"Come on. All we can do is ask."

I walked up on the porch and knocked on the door. When I looked back, Leo was still next to the car.

"Yes," a female voice said. I turned to the door.

Through the screen her eyes shone back at me with, I don't know what, but they made me smile. Spilling down from where it was gathered on the top of her head, strands of brown hair framed her open, friendly face.

"Hi," I said.

"Hello," she said. "How can I help you?"

I could no longer remember why I was there. My face heated up.

"Who is it, Kate?" a voice called from inside the house.

An elderly woman in a pink cardigan sweater shuffled up to the door. She peered at me through thick, black-framed glasses. "Don't know him," she said under her breath to Kate. "Hurry up and close the door."

"Granny—" Kate said.

"I'm Tom," I said quickly, finally remembering my purpose. "The man over by the car is Leo Hursen. His father lived here a long time ago. Leo wanted to see the house."

"Ha!" the old woman said. "What's his father's name?"

"Seth Kercher."

"Seth," she said quietly. She stepped around Kate and looked past me at Leo.

"You Seth's boy?" she called to him.

Leo brightened. "Yes, Ma'am." He took three strides toward the porch steps. "Did you know him?"

"Nope," she said. "Never heard of him." She tugged on Kate's elbow. "Time for a cookie."

Leo went droopy, like he'd taken an uppercut to the solar plexus. Kate turned to her grandmother.

"Okay, Granny," she said gently. "Go in the kitchen. I'll be right there." The old woman tottered off into the house.

"I'm sorry," Kate said to Leo. "She's not quite with it today." Kate pushed the door open and gestured for us to come inside.

Our tour of the house went by in a blur of movement and muted sounds. The only thing I could keep in focus was Kate: the smooth skin rising over her cheekbones, her open-eyed ingenuousness, the way she held Leo's elbow when he went down the stairs, the way her jeans hugged her shapely posterior when she went up the stairs, and the loving tone in her voice when we came upon her Grandmother standing in the middle of the kitchen with her dress hiked up to her armpits.

"They don't want to see your new girdle," Kate said warmly as she helped her Grandmother lower the dress. "You're such a show off, Granny."

Kate offered us apples and pears that she recently picked. Standing in the kitchen watching her eat the fruit, I couldn't stop myself from thinking about holding hands with her – just holding hands. How weird was that?

Leo was beaming by the time we were back at the front door. So was I, but for different reasons. While Leo gushed his thanks to Kate, I was busy talking myself into and out of, and then back into asking her to dinner. I'm leaving town, I sniped at myself. But I feel a connection with her. Pomona is waiting. I want to hold her. Back and forth it went. I half-expected to hear the throaty-roar of the Harley Davidson and the motorcycle man/blue heron bellowing at me to not be a weenie-boy. "Pomona!" he would shout. "Forget the chick. You got places to go!" Then off he would roar, tires squealing and do his morphing thing. I shushed the frenzied debate in my head and strained inwardly to listen. Not a rasping manifold to be heard. Not a whiff of cigar smoke anywhere. Hummm, I thought, what does *that* mean?

"It's meant a great deal to me," Leo said, still wringing Kate's hand. "Thank you again."

"You're welcome, Mr. Hursen. I'm just glad I was here. As you could tell, Granny isn't too friendly with people she doesn't know."

Nodding in agreement, Leo finally let go of her hand. He backed across the porch then turned and walked down the front steps. Kate's eyes swung over to mine.

"Well," she said.

"Well," I said back.

She smiled. She had a great smile.

"It was nice," I said. "What you did."

"He seems like a sweet man."

"Yeah, he is."

"You seem sweet too," she said, "for helping him. And Granny doesn't show her girdle to just anyone you know."

Being that close to her and looking into her eyes was extremely awkward, and at the same time, wonderfully sublime. It was like eating a bowl of your favorite ice cream while standing naked in front of a complete stranger.

Down on the sidewalk, Leo shuffled his feet. Finally, I managed to open my mouth.

"Can we talk later?"

"I'd like that," she said.

39

KATE WORKED AS AN administrator at Sewickley Academy. She lived a mile from the school in a three bedroom town house decorated with an eclectic assortment of furniture found at garage and estate sales.

"Give me a musty old attic or garage crammed with junk and I'm a happy girl," Kate said, as we walked to the Italian restaurant she'd suggested for dinner. "You never know what mystery is hiding inside the next steamer trunk or spider web encrusted hat box in the rafters."

I ordered pasta primavera and she had the capellini with tomato and basil sauce. I was instantly impressed. Most women won't order long pasta on a first date. Fusilli, yes, Penne and lasagna certainly, but the dangly stuff requiring constant noodle management was usually passed over until at least the fourth or fifth date.

I watched her twirl the noodles around her fork. She wasn't afraid to take a healthy amount. No dainty, be-careful-not-to-look-like-a-hog-at-the-trough concerns for her. She ate like a woman who loved food and wasn't afraid to show it.

Kate told me about her mother emigrating to the U.S. from France, and her father's brief minor league baseball career. Her sister and two younger brothers also lived in Pittsburgh. They gathered for dinner every other Sunday at their parents' house in Mount Lebanon.

I told her about my family, including how Leo fit in.

"That's so wild," she said. "If you hadn't done that, if you hadn't cared enough to convince your mother to meet him, that would have been, I mean, he never would have had the opportunity to be part of your family." Kate cocked her head, eyeing me intently. "See," she said. "I knew you were a sweet guy."

"I had to help him."

"No you didn't," Kate said. "You could have stuck your head in the sand or let your mother or your Aunt steam roll over you."

"I know what it's like to live with a mystery."

She leaned forward. "Really? What's your mystery?"

I looked down in the tangle of pasta on my plate. Wow, I thought, do I really hit her with the blue heron on the first date? Instead, I shot her a grin. "I'll save that for another time. What do you say, interested?"

She smiled. "Maybe."

After dinner we walked back to her place. We sat down with cups of tea in her living room.

"Oh. I forgot," Kate said. "I have peaches. Mmmm, they're so good." She went to the kitchen and returned in a few minutes with a plate of peach slices.

"These are the best!" She grabbed a slice and held it out to me. I leaned toward her and opened my mouth. It was the sweetest peach I'd ever tasted.

"Good, huh?" Kate said.

"Oh my God. May I?"

"Help yourself." She leaned back on the couch. "I love fruit. I must have had orchards in a past life."

I looked at her. "You believe in past lives?"

"Sure. It's kind of silly to think that this is it. 'Worn-out garments are shed by the body, worn-out bodies are shed by the dweller.'"

I grinned. "You're familiar with the Bhagavad-Gita?"

"A bit. I haven't read it all or anything, but it makes sense."

"Yes, it does."

"What do you think you did in your past lives?"

"A mill doesn't turn on water that is past."

"What's that from?"

"My Grandmother."

Kate took a sip of tea. "Does that mean you don't want to talk about your past lives?"

I laughed and looked down at the plate of peaches. I could feel Kate's eyes on me.

"That's okay," she said, "another mystery to learn about later."

I glanced up at her. She was looking at me with a directness and warmth that surprised me.

"Date three?" she asked.

Something uncoiled inside of me. It was as if I finally let go of a bar from which I'd been dangling for a long, long time. The relief was intense and inescapable.

"I was a soldier," I said. "I killed a lot of people."

For a long second or two Kate didn't say anything. Then she reached over and put her hand on mine. "A mill doesn't turn on water that is past."

• • •

I WASN'T SURE WHAT I was feeling. I had never experienced this sort of thing with Dee Dee or Melina or even Lilly. It was as if I'd jumped into a cool, refreshing lake, only to discover that I couldn't swim. The water felt amazing, but the mounting panic was hard to ignore. I tried to breathe and keep myself centered and open, but whenever I thought about Kate it all went goofy.

Kirby gave me his box seat tickets to the Pirates game against the Cubs. Kate hadn't been to a baseball game in years. She really got into singing, "Take Me Out To the Ballgame." When she caught me watching her, she grinned and sang even louder. So I did too. People turned and looked at us, and then they all started singing louder. It spread across our entire section along the first base line. By the end of the song, Kate was standing on her seat waving her arms like a conductor directing a chorus. When they flashed a shot of us up on the jumbo screen she grabbed my arm.

"Oh my God," she said, in an exhilarated gush. "I love baseball!"

This woman was rocking my world.

After the Pirates won 8–6, we went across the bridge to Point State Park. The afternoon sun danced in silvery flashes through the fountain's spray. We found a bench and sat down. Out beyond the roaring fountain, boats cruised the choppy confluence of the three rivers.

"When I was little," Kate said, "my friend's family had a boat and her father took Carrie and me on camping trips. One time we were going through a lock on the Allegheny River at the same time as this huge barge. Our boat was maybe seventeen feet long and this barge was massive. I was pretty certain that we were going to get crushed. Carrie's father looked into both of our scared faces and said, 'This is it girls. Bend over and kiss your asses goodbye.' Then he started laughing. So did we, and I wasn't scared anymore."

Kate turned and looked at me. It was as if she knew exactly what I'd been feeling. That made me smile. She smiled back at me. Then she started to laugh. I did too. A second later we were both out of control with laughter. In that giddy, fearless moment we shared our first kiss. It was sublime.

When the kiss ended, Kate said, "Just now, when we were kissing, and by the way that was the best kiss of my entire life, I saw a bird flying. I don't know what kind it was, but it was big and sort of blue. Does that mean anything to you?"

I was stunned. "Yes."

"I thought so."

"A blue heron," I said, my mind trying to grasp what she just told me. "It's part of the mystery I want to explain to you."

"Cool."

"How did you – I mean—"

"Sometimes I see things," Kate said.

"Wow. Me too."

"Really?"

I nodded. "Dreams and stuff."

"Yeah," Kate said. "My family thinks I'm odd."

"Mine too."

"Your family thinks I'm odd?"

"No. They think I'm a little tweaked."

"Well, I certainly hope so."

She hugged me and once again those big feelings welled in my chest. That's when I told her about the blue heron and Pomona.

"Whoa," Kate said excitedly. "That is the coolest thing I've ever heard. What did you do after Maggie said she was going to California?"

"I kept heading west with her. She eventually abandoned me in Biloxi, Mississippi."

"So what happened when you finally got to Pomona?"

"I haven't gotten there yet."

"Seriously? Why not?"

"That's a good question."

"Man," she said. "You're full of mysteries. I love that."

Delicious kiss number two happened at this point. Is there a feeling beyond sublime? Whatever it is, I had it.

By the time I got home my chest was fluttery and I was spacey and distracted. I felt detached from myself while at the same time intensely aware of everything about Kate. It reminded me of the simultaneous sensations of ecstatic freedom and absolute connection that I'd felt while traversing the dimensions on ayahuasca.

At breakfast the next morning, I blurted this list of disturbing symptoms to my mother. She listened calmly and then said, "I think someone shot you with an arrow."

"What?" I said, alarmed that I had suffered some sort of psychic retaliation from another of my past victims.

"Honey," she said. "Cupid has finally gotten to you. You're in love."

Wow, I thought. I'm in love. That's incredible. Then I remembered I was leaving for Pomona.

Leslie answered the phone on the first ring. As soon as she heard my voice she said, "I was just thinking about you. What's going on?"

I told her about meeting Kate. The first thing Leslie said was,

"Oh." Then she said, "Wow." Then she yelled, "Tara! Pick up the other phone! Tom's in love!"

I told them all about Kate, what I was feeling, and my dilemma of whether or not to go to Pomona.

"She sounds amazing. Why would you leave her?" Leslie said. And from the other phone Tara said, "Don't screw this up."

After I got off the telephone with them, I headed to the hospital to visit my father. I figured, after a dose of his stoic pragmatism, any romantic notions coo-cooing in my heart would be jettisoned back into the cold, glomming light of reality.

I found him sitting on the side of his bed, staring blankly out the window.

"Hi, Dad," I said. "How are you feeling?"

He didn't say anything. I walked around the bed. He continued staring out the window. The vacant look on his face reminded me of the way grandpa Irv used to stare off.

"Dad?"

He blinked. When he spoke, his voice was flat and distant. "You can keep yourself from thinking about it when you're young. Job, family, plenty of distractions – but eventually they come out from where you've hidden them." He lowered his head into his hands.

"Dad, what's wrong."

"I didn't sleep at all."

"Do you want me to get a nurse?"

He shook his head.

I sat down next to him on the edge of the bed. "What is it? What's going on?"

He got up and walked over to the window. His shoulders clenched and his hands balled into fists. After a long moment of struggling to control his emotions he cleared his throat.

"Go on home. I'll talk to you later."

I went to the door and closed it. I walked over and stood next to him. "Dad, does this have to do with the war?"

"It doesn't matter," he said sharply. "Go home. Get me the book of crossword puzzles that Becky gave me last year for my birthday."

"You can talk to me," I said.

He shook his head.

"Hey," I said, looking him in the eyes. "Somewhere, sometime, we all have blood on our hands."

A flicker of surprise flashed in his eyes, then a low groan came out of him and he sagged against me.

"Will I have to face them when I die?" He broke down sobbing. I held him, feeling tears in my own eyes. After a few minutes, Dad lifted his head from my shoulder.

"He was drinking a cup of tea," Dad said, through his tears.

"Yeah?"

He wiped his eyes with the sleeve of his robe. "Man oh man." He went over to the nightstand and grabbed a tissue. He blew his nose. We both sat on the bed. For a couple of minutes neither of us said anything. Then Dad let out a long sigh.

"It was on Tulagi," he said quietly. "The Japs were holed up in caves all over the island. None of them would surrender so we had to root them out." He wiped his eyes with a tissue. "We went down into this ravine and they had us in a crossfire. Guys were getting machine-gunned all around me. I slid down an embankment and rolled in front of a cave. Bullets were hitting everywhere so I crawled inside."

Tears welled up in his eyes and he lowered his head. "It was filled with dead bodies. The smell was—" He stared at the floor not speaking. Finally, he cleared his throat and raised his head. "Something moved in the back of the cave. A Jap was sitting there drinking tea." Dad shook his head. "In the middle of all those bodies he was having a cup of tea."

"What happened?"

"We looked at each other for a second or two. Neither of us moved. Then I shot at him and he shot at me, but we both missed. I dove behind the bodies and he ran at me with a sword. I blocked it with my rifle but he kicked the rifle out of my hands. I caught hold of his ankle and we went rolling over bodies. He was a little guy but real strong. I got him in the chest with my knife. Had to do it three times to get him to stop fighting. Then I threw up."

I put my arm around his shoulders.

"I can still see his face," Dad said, "and smell that cave. Twenty-six bodies we found in there and not a single round of ammunition. The bullet he fired at me was his last. That's why he came at me with the sword."

"The cup in your office – that was his?"

He nodded. "I sawed apart a canteen and stuffed it with old rags. I carried that cup in there for the rest of the war."

"Why?"

He looked down at his hands. "Drinking tea was civilized. What we were doing wasn't. It reminded me that I was still human."

"I'm sorry you went through that, Dad."

"You have no idea." Again his eyes filled with tears. "I'd just turned nineteen."

Another moment of silence passed. Then he groaned as if in pain.

"I've never talked about this before," he said.

"It was time."

He grunted and looked at me. "You always were good at this kind of thing."

"What do you mean?"

He stood up and reached for a tissue. "When you were a little boy tying your shoes confused the hell out of you, but understanding the big stuff was never a problem." He blew his nose and tossed the tissue in the wastebasket. "Remember what happened when – what was that kid's name? The Reese boy?"

"Todd."

"Right. I think you were five when he died."

"He had some kind of cancer."

"Bone cancer."

"Yeah."

"When I sat you down to explain what happened to him, you looked at me as if you could see right through me. You already knew. Somehow you understood."

He looked out the window. "That happened a bunch of times when you were a kid," he said. "You with that know-it-all look in your eye. You never needed me to help you with the big things."

Neither of us said anything for a long moment. Then I turned to him and asked, "Did Rick need you for stuff like that?"

"Oh, sure. Ricky was always confused, about everything. I don't know where he would be without me."

"Yeah," I said. "You guys have always been really close."

Dad looked at me. His eyes fixed on a spot somewhere between me and the end of his nose. He seemed surprised at what he saw. He started to say something then stopped. He looked down in his lap.

"It's okay," I said.

"Jesus Christ!" he snapped. "What do you want from me?" He got up and walked to the window. "You were my boy. I wanted you to look up to me. Your brother, bless his heart, isn't a deep thinker. He always looked at me like I was the cat's pajamas."

Dad tugged at the plastic hospital bracelet on his wrist. Down the hall a buzzer went off.

"Dad," I said. "Tell me something. How did you know that you were in love with Mom?"

He looked puzzled for a moment then he glanced up at the ceiling. Lost in his thoughts for a second or two, his gaze finally shifted back to me.

"The first time I saw your mother she was walking down the sidewalk in a white blouse and a navy blue skirt. Her hair was pulled back in a ponytail and she was laughing." He shook his head. "She was something else."

"You knew right then?"

"Oh, no. I knew that I wanted to meet her. You know me, Tom I have to think things through. No, I didn't know I was in love with her until three months after we were dating."

"How? What happened?"

Dad reached up and scratched the side of his head. "It was strange. We were sitting in my Ford at a traffic light. It was pouring rain. Your mother was talking, telling me a story about something or other, and I found myself watching her hands. I couldn't take my eyes off of them. When she finished her story, she reached over and put her hand on my arm. And that's when I knew."

"But why? Why right then?"

"I don't know. I just knew."

"Man," I said. I looked out the window at the parking lot.

"Don't worry about it," Dad said. "It'll be okay."

I sighed. "It's not easy this stuff."

"I know."

We stood there and watched a blue van back into a parking space.

40

"Edgar Winter, 'Free Ride,'" Kate said.

I shook my head in amazement. "How do you know that?"

"That was one of my brother's favorites," she said. "He played it all the time."

I tuned the radio to another oldies station. The song that was playing was vaguely familiar but I couldn't—

"'Life is Carnival,' The Band," Kate said. "Robbie Robertson – very cool."

"You're amazing."

"Thanks for noticing," Kate said, playfully. She picked up one of the apples we just bought and held it under her nose. Her eyes closed as she inhaled. Her face flushed and her lips slightly parted as if the scent of the apple was pure oxygen. I nearly drove off the road watching her.

Back at her place, Kate suggested that we make a vegetable stir-fry for dinner. She pulled out a cutting board and we got to work.

"Both of my grandparents were vegetarians too," Kate said. "You know Granny, the one you met at the house. They had a farm. I used to love going to visit them."

"A farm?"

"Yeah, it was my Grandfather's family – a bunch of generations."

"Where?"

"South of York, Pennsylvania." She put down the paring knife. "I'll be right back."

She returned with a photo album containing snapshots of the farm. The white clapboard farmhouse and steep-roofed barn were quaint reminders of simpler times, life at a slower pace.

"It's beautiful country," I said.

"Look," Kate said. She pointed to a black and white photograph. "This is me at seventeen." In the photo, she was wearing a light-colored sun dress and was standing in a vegetable garden with her arms outstretched to heavily-laden tomato plants. With cabbage, watermelons, and squash abundant at her feet, Kate looked like the goddess of the garden.

"Everyone says I look like Granny in that shot."

I peered at the photo trying to see in Kate's angelic smile the withered face of the woman who flashed me her girdle. I couldn't see the resemblance.

"Does your family still have the farm," I asked.

"My uncle Everett sold it nine years ago. Broke my heart to see it go."

"Yeah, I bet."

"Lots of fond memories," she said. Her fingers brushed over a photo of a lanky, raw-boned man. "I think Gramps is still around. I feel him sometimes. Do you know what I mean?"

"Yes," I said, "I know what you mean." I took her hand and held it. "What do you think he'd like to say to you?"

Kate dropped her chin, scrunched her face up, and in a deep gravelly voice said, "Don't forget to water the garden." She laughed and added, "He was always looking out for his cabbage."

"A man must tend his garden."

"Yes, he must," she said. "And please think of my lips as your garden," she puckered them playfully. I leaned over and kissed her. "Hummmm," she said, "Hey there Mr. Green Thumb."

"That's right."

She leaned her head on my shoulder. "I've thought about farming for a living," she said. "Carry on the family tradition."

"Really? Me too. For the longest time."

We looked at each other.

"Seriously?" Kate said.

"Yeah. I worked on a farm in Scotland. It was great."

"Very cool."

"So how can we make it happen?"

Kate's eyebrows lifted in surprise. Mine must have done the same thing because I was shocked by the words that had come out of my mouth.

Kate sat up straighter on the couch. "Well, it's not exactly farming, but I've been thinking – What we really need around here is a place that sells organic vegetables."

"A produce market?"

"Exactly."

"Huh."

"It could fly," Kate said.

"Yeah, I think you're right."

We looked into each other's eyes seeking confirmation that we were really talking, not just bullshitting around. Part of me wanted to run as fast as I could in the opposite direction. The other half of me was absolutely certain that it was perfect.

"This is crazy," Kate said.

"Tell me about it."

"I've never met anyone like you," she said. "Who wants to be a farmer these days?"

"Just us crazy people who see things."

I put my arms around her and held her. It felt – right. So very, wonderfully right. Tears came into my eyes. My God, I thought. I really am in love.

That night as I was falling asleep, Cully's Collectibles, the store I'd seen after almost running over the collie, flashed through my mind.

• • •

"THOMAS, YOU'VE GOT A sparkle in your eye," Aunt Helen said, as I sat down at her kitchen table.

"Yeah," I said. "But . . ."

"If your heart has found a mate get out of your own way." She took off her glasses and rubbed the two red indentations on the sides of her nose.

"I know, I know," I said.

She put her glasses back on, and leaning forward in her wheelchair said, "Love isn't for the faint of heart. It's for the bold and the daring."

"The bold and the daring? Isn't that a soap opera?"

Aunt Helen took a swing at me. I ducked out of the way.

"Don't mess with me kid," she said.

"So what was it like when you met John?"

"Oh," she said. "John."

Her husband was dead for over four decades but as soon as she said his name her eyes lit up. She suddenly looked 50 years younger.

"He was a wonderful man," she said warmly. She reached over and patted my arm. "Thomas if you're in love with Kate do something about it."

"What about Pomona?"

"Oh for God's sake, I'm sick of hearing about it! If you're going to go, go!"

"What should I tell her?"

"That's up to you."

She fished around in the pocket of her sweater.

"Here," she said, pulling something out. "Maybe this will help you."

In the wrinkled palm of her hand was the wolf tooth.

"It got me through a lot," she said. "You need it now."

• • •

I SET UP AN appointment for Saturday to see the Cully's Collectibles building. Kate agreed to meet me at the store and we'd have lunch afterward.

I sat in my bedroom on Friday night staring at my packed duffel bag. It was stained and torn, the handle ripped off long ago. For fifteen years I'd hauled it around. Now, once again, I was taking it back on the road.

I really don't know if it was chemical reactions, bands of spiraling energy, my genes howling for expression, or all those things wrapped up in one delicious sensation, but my feelings for Kate, her feelings for me, all of it took me to places inside of myself that I couldn't get to on my own. I didn't want to leave her. But I had to finish what I'd started.

• • •

I DROVE INTO THE wide gravel parking lot that arced in a semi-circle around the store. The brick two story building was old but looked to be in good condition.

Kate was standing by the front door in a pair of jeans and a bulky red sweater. Her long brown hair was pulled back in a ponytail. All I could think was – what kind of a dumb-ass would leave a woman like that. I clutched the wolf tooth in my hand for a final surge of courage then got out of the truck.

"The realtor had to meet another client," Kate said. "She gave me the key." She kissed me lightly on the lips. I kissed her back not so lightly.

"Mummm," she said. "Good morning."

"Can we talk for a minute before we go in?"

"Sure."

"I have to tell you something."

"What?"

"Kate, I'm going away for a while."

She smirked at me and laughed.

"What's so funny?" I asked.

"I don't know. It sounded like a line from a movie. 'Kate, I'm going away for a while.' Like you're being sent to prison or something."

"I'm going to Pomona."

"Oh," she said. Then she grabbed me by the arms and gave me a shake. "Why are you so serious?"

"I don't want to go."

"Then don't."

"I have to finish this blue heron thing."

She turned and looked up at the building. I wondered if I'd pushed her weirdness barometer too far.

"I read a quote by someone once," she said. "How did it go? Oh yeah. 'We are not called to success but to obedience to our visions.'" She put her hand on my arm. "If that's where you need to be, then go. You have to."

That's when I knew. In that moment, I knew that I wanted to be with Kate for the rest of my life. She had extended freedom to me and showed me that her love was not just about what I had to give to her; it included who I was and what I needed for myself. It also made it even harder to leave.

"I don't want to go."

"I know."

Before I could stop myself, the words flew out of my mouth. "You're the one."

Without hesitating and with a certainty that pinged like sonar deep inside of me, Kate said, "You bet your ass I'm the one."

We held each other so tightly I don't think we were breathing.

"Come on," she said, not hiding the tears in her eyes. "Let's check this place out."

The realtor informed me that the store had been out of business for three years. It stood empty while the heirs of the owner litigated the estate. In the three months it was on the market only one other person had taken a look at it.

"This'll come off, no problem," Kate said. She pulled away a piece of crumbling plaster. "I like the bare brick walls underneath."

"It's got potential," I said, looking up at the eighteen-foot ceilings. The crown molding was still in good shape. In the back, a wooden staircase led to the second floor.

"I'm going upstairs," I said.

At the top of the stairs I stopped and glanced out a window that was partially blocked by a stack of dusty plastic crates. The window looked out on a rear parking area. I leaned my forehead against the glass.

I would miss Kate terribly when I was gone. But, I reminded myself, faith in the journey was faith in the journey. The willingness to sacrifice was sometimes necessary. I looked to my right. At the end of the hallway was a door.

The brass knob turned easily and I pushed it open. Dim light slanted through half-closed Venetian blinds. A large oak desk was against the far wall. In the corner, next to the window, was a black file cabinet. Stacks of dusty boxes leaned against the left wall.

I walked to the file cabinet. Sitting on top was a tarnished silver tie clip in the shape of an elephant. I moved around behind the desk and pulled open the center drawer. In it were pens and pencils and three packs of wooden matches. I closed the drawer and wandered over to the other side of the room. Behind the stack of boxes was a corner of dark-stained wood jutting out.

I pulled on wood but it didn't budge. I shoved a couple boxes out of the way. This time it slid out easily. One look and I sank to my knees. For a long moment I just stared at it. Then I reached out and touched it to prove that it was actually there. It was a painting of the orange grove. The trees, the crates, the ladder on the ground; all of it was exactly as I had seen on my vision quest. At the bottom of the frame was a small dust-smeared plaque. I rubbed my thumb across the metal surface and leaned forward to read it. Etched in a neat flowing script were the words:

Pomona, California – 1932.

"Holy shit!" I jumped to my feet. "Kate! Kate! Come up here!"

41

WITH THE HELP OF a friend of Leo's at Mellon Bank, Kate and I bought the building the following week. Our lives immediately got crazy busy with a series of frantic dashes between meetings with the architect, and running around choosing counter tops, shelves, paint, flooring, and cooling units.

From my old contacts with the juice company, I was able to round up the names of organic farmers in New York, Vermont, Massachusetts, and California. Kate and I slipped away on long weekends to see their operations. We wanted to have a hands-on, personal relationship with our suppliers. The name we chose for the market was, Pomona Farms.

Kate got it in her head that she wanted to have the remodeling in the main part of the store completed in time for our families and friends to celebrate Thanksgiving. She said it was the perfect way to start our new business. I appreciated her sentiments but I tried to talk her out of it. Planning and preparing for a big gathering was the last thing we needed to worry about. She agreed, so she sent notes to everyone suggesting specific dishes they could bring. We would provide the turkeys, and everyone else would take care of the rest.

Five days before Thanksgiving, I was installing light fixtures at the market. Mom was at the mall shopping, and Dad was home alone. Sometime around eight o'clock in the evening, on his way to put Peanut on the leash in the backyard, Dad got tangled up with the dog and accidentally stepped on Peanut's paw. Peanut whipped around and bit him. Dad immediately let go of the dog's collar and grabbed his bleeding hand. Then, afraid of incurring Mom's wrath for letting the dog run away, he made a desperate lunge for Peanut's hindquarters. This time Peanut, confused by his clouded vision, bit Dad on the ring finger on his right hand. When the dog wouldn't let go, Dad had to pry the mangy little beast's teeth open to pull out his mangled finger. After carefully cleaning up the blood that he'd dripped on the kitchen floor, Dad left a note for Mom: Be home soon.

Ignored in the emergency room for over three hours, Dad passed out and smacked his head on the desk of the nurse's station. This finally seemed to get their attention. When he came to and told them that he'd recently had a heart attack, they called Dr. Noonan who immediately admitted him to the hospital.

That night Dad was in bed reading when one of the nurses ran into his room.

"Mr. McInnes, are you alright!"

Dad looked at her calmly and said, "Of course I'm alright."

"Your heart," she said. "I was at the nursing station – your heart stopped for four seconds."

Three days later, under a local anesthetic, Dad had a pacemaker implanted in his chest.

• • •

ON THANKSGIVING AFTERNOON THE smell of paint, lumber, turkey, and my mother's pumpkin pies filled Pomona Farms. My parents came early to help us get everything ready.

"He's still working out the flights and all that," Mom said, as she and Kate arranged her wooden ducks into centerpieces. "But, we talked about going to Bermuda thirty years ago, now we're finally doing it. I'm so excited."

"I've never been on a cruise," Kate said.

"Eating," my mother said. "It's all about eating."

"Smith just ran one in for Dallas!" My father announced from where he was opening bottles of wine and setting up the bar.

"Steelers gotta watch that guy," I said.

"Damn right they do," he said, his eyes glued to the TV. "They have to get this season back on track."

I looked around the store. Over the past few months I'd learned a lot while helping tear down, rebuild, and rewire most of the interior. I'd stood toe to toe with a brick mason and made him rip apart a half-finished wall because it wasn't done right. Kate wisely baked him chocolate chip cookies the next day to make amends. We were a good team.

Another couple weeks of wood trim work, a bit of decorating, and Pomona Farms would be ready for its grand opening. My eyes settled on the painting of the orange grove hanging in its place of honor over the front door. It really was a miracle.

An hour later our guests began arriving.

"Touch it, go ahead," Dad said to Kate's nieces, Page and Beth. He tapped on the pacemaker just under the skin. "This hard round thing is like a magic credit card my heart borrows from when it needs to."

"Really," Page said, touching it, "neat."

"I wanna feel it too," Beth said.

"You're our bionic grampa," Rick's boys, Ian and Collin said.

Dad laughed. "You got that right. Don't make me go invisible 'cause I'll do it. I will. I've got powers." He tickled the boys and hustled them off to introduce them to Kate's parents.

Rick sidled up next to me. "Kate is hot," he said, "Well done. But a vegetable market? It's so '70s. Where are your Birkenstocks?"

"Rick," I said, ignoring his sarcasm, "I'm happy you and the boys are here."

"Yeah man, wouldn't miss it. So Uncle Leo, huh?"

"Yep."

"Seems like a good guy."

"He is."

"Mom's all happy about having a brother."

"Aunt Evelyn still doesn't think it's true."

"Our family just gets weirder and weirder. Hey, there's Kirby."

Kirby, Jeannie and the boys were walking through the front door.

"I'm getting' a beer," Rick said and headed for the bar.

"Lookin' good," Kirby said as we shook hands. Jeannie hugged me and whispered. "I'm so friggin' happy for you."

"Jeannie," Kate called. "Bring the boys over to meet my nieces."

As they walked away, Kirby leaned to me and said, "How were you able to do it?"

"I told you, Leo's buddy at the bank really—"

"No, not that. After you dumped Dee Dee, I gave up all hope of you settling down. How could you commit so quickly with Kate?"

I looked him in the eye. "I just knew."

Later, as everyone sat down for dinner, I gave silent thanks to all the people along my journey who helped me find my way home. I was grateful for their love, support, and kicking my ass when I needed it.

"Great Spirit," Aunt Helen prayed from the head of the table. "Thank you for bringing us all safely together. Thank you for leading Leo to us, and Kate and her lovely family. Thank you for Rick and Ian and Collin being here. Thank you for Becky and Anthony coming into town. We are blessed to have—"

"Please don't forget," Mom said, interrupting her, "to give thanks for the member of the family who is no longer with us."

Startled looks shot around the table. I thought Mom was referring to Rick's ex-wife, Denise.

"Please hold Peanut in your thoughts," Mom said, her voice filling with emotion. "If Peanut hadn't bitten Richard and sent him to the hospital, we may not have known about his irregular heartbeat until it was too late. Peanut is a hero," Mom said proudly. "We should give thanks for his final act of loyalty."

My father's jaws clenched. He had a less poetic version of the dog-bite incident. After he'd been chomped, Mom reluctantly, and I repeat, reluctantly, agreed that the dog's cataract-clouded eyes may cause Peanut to get confused and bite someone else. After a heated discussion, including a detailed recitation by my mother of all the great deeds Peanut accomplished in his eleven years of life, they agreed to put the dog to sleep.

Dad opened his mouth to share his rebuttal of Peanut's status as a hero. Aunt Helen, anticipating his reaction, unleashed The Look. Dad didn't have a chance.

Some things change, some don't.

But other than that minor skirmish, the turkey was moist, the mashed potatoes lump free, and everyone seemed to get along fine.

After dinner I stepped outside to the rear parking lot. A cool wind blew and I turned up the collar on my sport coat and shoved my hands into the pockets. Above me the stars burned like a billion fiery pinpoints. Through the back door I heard Becky's new boyfriend, Anthony start playing his guitar. A hairy, somewhat bland New Englander, he didn't exactly fit the image of the guy I thought Becky would end up with. But he was a large, powerfully built man, and along with these positive genetic attributes, his orthodontic practice was extremely successful. I was happy for them both.

Rick's voice, sounding slightly drunk, rose above the twang of the guitar. "Play some big Frank!"

Earlier in the evening Kate and I pulled out the preliminary artwork my father helped us create for our advertising campaign. We were using the black & white photo of Kate in her grandparents' garden. In the bottom corner of all our ads would be a tiny drawing of a great blue heron. As I was showing Kirby and Jeannie the sketches, Kirby said, "Did you hear on the news yesterday about that guy? The center fielder the Pirates traded to the Yankees?"

"No," I said. "What about him?"

"He's living in Manhattan now, right. He heads downtown to the village with his girlfriend to go to some jazz club. They get out of a cab, walk two blocks, the guy hears something, looks up, sees a baby that's fallen out of a window eight stories up, and the guy catches this kid. Saves her life. He couldn't catch his own ass with two hands when he was in Pittsburgh. He goes to New York and now he's catching falling babies. That amazing or what?"

I grinned and turned to Kate. "Sometimes people end up exactly where they're supposed to be."

Behind the store, I bounced up and down on my toes trying to stay warm. I had set out for Pomona in search of answers. I came back not only with answers but also more questions. I didn't know where the blue heron or Daniel Toberni or the old man with the white mustache had come from. I didn't know why some people died and others lived. I didn't know if the signs I chose to follow were really signs or simply coincidences that I'd turned into signs. I didn't know if the guiding force that seemed to be at work in my life was my soul or God or the Great Spirit or Buddha or Allah or Shiva or Jesus or a cosmic super-being from a distant universe. What I did know, and had come to have faith in, was that beyond my sense of touch and my ability to see, beyond the snarling clamor of genetics and survival of the fittest, reality warped and curved. The past and present overlapped and tucked into the future. From within one of these folds in the fabric of the universe something had reached out and led me on an amazing pilgrimage.

I was standing in a new world. I had somehow slipped through a doorway and entered into a different reality. I was nose to nose with a future of mortgage payments, insurance policies, business meetings, investment planning, and the pitter-patter of little feet. Mind-smacked as I was by this dramatic shift, I was also exhilarated. I had successfully transitioned from one reality into another, and I had done it without the use of ayahuasca or mushrooms. I don't think this was exactly what Daniel Toberni was talking about, but I was feeling very much like a multi-dimensional being.

I hunched my shoulders against the cool night air. In the maze of starlight I found the Big Dipper. I raised my finger and traced its outline. What possibilities awaited me, I wondered? Now that I'd finished my quest for Pomona, would my adventuring life be over?

The back door pushed open.

"Tom?"

"Over here, Kate. Looking at the stars."

She walked over and I wrapped my arms around her.

"Your Dad wants you and Rick to sing, "Fly Me to the Moon" with him."

"Get the camera ready," I said. "This will be a first."

She hugged me.

"I love you," I said and kissed her. Her arms went around my neck.

"Mysteries inside of mysteries," Kate whispered. She tilted her head back and looked up into the sky. I wondered which of the constellations called to her. Which one of them was her touchstone?

"There it is," she said, and with one arm still around my neck, pointed into the boisterous gleam of the Milky Way. One look into that teeming wonder of stars – I knew our adventures were far from over.

Acknowledgments

With much gratitude I thank Sandy Farrier for designing this terrific book cover, Erika Stokes for her impeccable layout design, Sam Kimball for his logo artistry, Patricia Van Eman, Robin and Nat Bernstein, Fontaine and Andre Dubus III, Mark Fudoli, Lynn Nelson, Marc Clopton, Beau L'Amour, Betsy Rapoport, Tracey Cohen, Jami Seta Richards, Bill Dow, Rebecca Shemwell, Steve Barnes, John Kabashinski, and Sara Quay for their insightful editorial feedback and rousing encouragement along the way.

About the Author

Charles Van Eman is also the author of the novel, *The Weight of Loss*. He has worked as an actor, director, screenwriter, teacher, and researcher. He currently lives north of Boston.

Visit his website – charlesvaneman.com

Made in the USA
Charleston, SC
16 November 2013